MW01245673

CROSSROADS OF
AWAKENING
MEMORY

Copyright © 2024 by M.D. House. All rights reserved.

No part of this book may be reproduced, stored, or transmitted in
any form without the express written permission of the author.

Cover art and interior design by Lance Buckley
Editing services by Julie Frederick

Books by M.D. House:

The Barabbas Trilogy
I Was Called Barabbas
Pillars of Barabbas
The Barabbas Legacy
Sophia: Daughter of Barabbas (Spin-off #1)

The Patriot Star series (Science Fiction)
Patriot Star
Kindred Star
(with more coming)

The Servant of Helaman
(sequel coming 2024)

Amulek: Revenant

CROSSROADS of AWAKENING MEMORY

THE END TIMES CONVERGENCE

BOOK ONE

M.D. HOUSE

Continent Of Rega

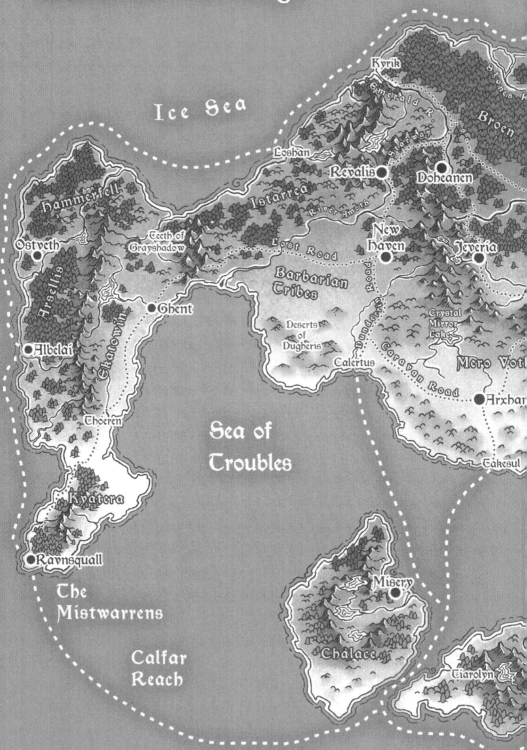

Ice Sea

Kyrik

Emerald R.

Broen

Loshan

Hammerfell

Revalis

Doheanen

Istarica

Starway

River Anorb

Teeth of
Grayshadow

New
Haven

Jeveria

Ostveth

Lost Road

Barbarian
Tribes

Arsellis

Crystal
Mirror
Lakes

Chatowin

Ghent

Deserts
of
Dugheris

Mero Voth

Albelai

Caravan Road

Calertus

Arxhar

Thoeren

Sea of
Troubles

Takesul

Kyatera

Ravnsquall

Misery

The
Mistwarrens

Chalace

Calfar
Reach

Ciarolyn

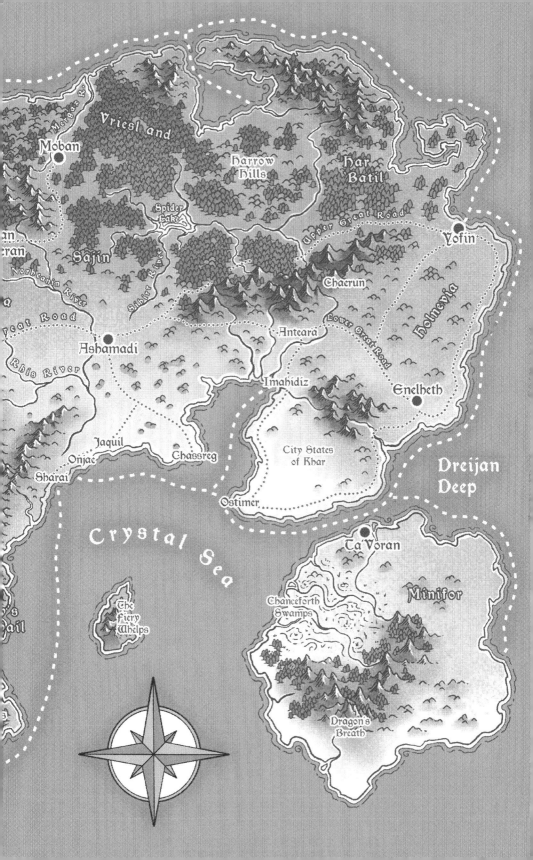

INTRODUCTION

I've wanted to write a good fantasy novel for a long time, especially since I enjoy reading the genre so much. After starting with some science fiction (the Patriot Star series) and a surprising number of historical fiction novels, the time has finally come.

I'm glad to have had great help, as I wanted to make this book special and get it as close to "right" as possible. This manuscript went through at least ten drafts, three of them guided by my fantastic editor in England, Julie Frederick.

Apparently, I challenged Lance Buckley with the cover, as he told me he had to step away several times to let the concepts percolate. As you can see, the end result was well worth the wait. Blew me away. Again.

Crossroads is Book 1 of a planned epic fantasy series called *The End Times Convergence*. I won't say too much about what's coming next, so as not to spoil anything for you, but I can guarantee surprises and some new perspectives on traditional outlooks.

Despite all the hard work—or perhaps because of it—I thoroughly enjoyed writing this book and love how it turned out. Enjoy!

M.D. House
April 2024

Council Guard trainee Rain Barynd's late nights with Tashiel under the not-so-watchful eye of her uncle had finally caught up to him. His grand dreams were finished if he didn't win this bout. He knew it. If there really was a god, as most people in New Haven professed to believe, that vaunted being may as well have branded his forehead with failure, then sent a blunt notice to his hard-working parents and soon-to-be-lost girlfriend.

Strangely, Tashiel's uncle approved of Rain's pursuit of both his niece and a position in the Guard. In fact, Patron Herrick's position on the Lower Council might be the *only* reason her parents tolerated him. He still wasn't sure why the man liked him, especially given the lower social status of his rural family, but that thought wavered in a distant haze as he struggled through the late morning's exercise with practice swords.

The sun had turned the stone-walled training yard into a shimmering furnace, and his strength evaporated at an alarming pace. His feet stumbled on the dusty, hard-packed ground as if his boots were shod with lead instead of leather. His right shoulder—his primary sword shoulder—throbbed in protest at the continuing contest. How could he be this tired? Most of the thirty-seven other trainees paired off for sparring seemed fine, and none of them kept all the curfews, either. His opponent, the wiry, smarmy-faced

Garrett, also appeared relatively fresh, even though they'd been at it for what seemed like an hour.

He parried a thrust from Garrett, air escaping his lungs in a rush as he sought to reposition and drive his opponent back with a pommel punch. He missed, but it was largely intended as a feint anyway, and he succeeded in making Garrett wary of his next move. He sucked in more air as they circled each other, Garrett goading him with his usual sneering chuckle. Rain struggled to ignore it.

Though the Guard played a largely ceremonial role in this idyllic corner of the continent of Rega, its members occasionally rotated to the distant border forts manned primarily by New Haven's northern neighbors the Istarreans, keeping watch over the nomadic barbarian tribes to the west. Hence the professed need for combat training, overseen by Master-at-Arms Ileom Mystrevan, a war hero from the east as cantankerous as a wounded bear on his best days.

With a determined grunt, Rain lunged at Garrett while swinging in a heavy arc. The thick wooden practice swords met with a thunderous clack that echoed off the smoky gray walls of the inner keep. The imposing stone rising above them in ever-lightening courses reflected the sun's angry glare from dozens of elegant ivory towers. Rain's opponent stumbled a bit with his parry, so he swung again, harder and lower. Garrett blocked and kicked at the same time, and Rain struggled to save his balance as he reacted. Ileom's training had taught him it was generally foolish to be so aggressive, but he would win this fight soon or not at all. And he *must* win.

"Hold!" Master Ileom surveyed the scene with a dark eye from a ten-foot-high wooden platform, his usual disdainful glare falling sharply on all the recruits, but particularly Rain. Was it his form? Or could the fabled battle master tell he was fatigued and distracted—two cardinal sins for a man on Ileom's Council Guard? It didn't help that Rain had arrived for the morning's session a few minutes late and wearing last year's breeches, which threatened to rip wide at every extreme movement. Frost it, why couldn't he have at least worn proper pants!

He took a step back, dropping both his eyes and the point of his practice sword—really just a sheaved bundle of shaped sticks. He burned with shame, more so because part of him was grateful it had ended. He should have won! It was all he could do to control the trembling in his limbs, to keep his breath from coming too fast as sweat soaked into his leather armor and steel-braced helm.

The darkly foreboding silence lengthened, and then Ileom roared again, his mighty storm unleashing on Rain. "What kind of slack-jawed maneuver was that, *child*?" The term *boy* was bad enough; *child* was far worse. "Overextending yourself so your opponent could break your knees or smash your skull? Have I taught you *nothing*?" He gagged as if he might choke on his rage, his graying black hair seeming to give off steam.

Rain almost flinched. In typical fashion, Master Ileom made it sound like his personal honor had been affronted by the ineptitude of his students. But he was bathed in holy flames today. He had fought in many battles, a rarity for any resident of New Haven, natural born or not. Rain and the other trainees often had to listen to how little Ileom thought of the fighting ability of native New Haveners—known as Sarenites for their religion. The hulking, near-mythical warrior had expressed some rare optimism in Rain before, but that fairy tale had apparently been shattered.

Rain avoided eye contact and said nothing. What *could* he say? His face caught fire, the heat of the sun now magnified by the displeasure of his teacher, the man he practically worshipped, whose war stories from across most of Rega he could recite by heart. Rain prided himself on being the hardest working of all the trainees, and he'd volunteered for the harsh tutoring of Ileom's Council Guard. Most young men just wanted to be in Saren's Legion—a joke!—with the rich ones given the officer posts.

"Well?" Master Ileom's bellow demanded an answer.

Rain raised his eyes from the ground to meet those of his idol, throat dry as a bucket of dust. He noted the jagged scar under Ileom's left eye pulsing with a red glow, his face a bevy of thunderclouds. His powerful hands strangled the wobbly railing of the platform. Clouds ... water ...

CROSSROADS OF AWAKENING MEMORY

Rain feared his dry mouth couldn't form intelligible sound. "It was a poor maneuver, sir." The words came out as a rasp. He swallowed air and lifted his chin. "I thought I could win with my quickness and athleticism, but I didn't think it through. My mind failed my body."

"And you disconnected the two, which I would expect from a first-year recruit, not from you." That hurt, worse than the anger.

Ileom shifted his gaze to Rain's opponent. "Garrett, that was commendable work. You stood up to a physically stronger and more skilled—well, *allegedly* more skilled—opponent and held your ground. You have some potential, boy."

Rain glanced at Garrett and wanted to spit, though he couldn't have gathered enough moisture for that. Ileom had *complimented* the obnoxious twit? Garrett's falsely modest smile did nothing but accentuate the haughty look he cast at Rain.

"Just make sure you don't waste it," added Ileom, "as I know you are wont to do."

Garrett's smile faded at the warning, which made Rain want to grin despite the continuing shame of his clumsy debacle. Even given an obvious disdain for hard work, Garrett had an inside track of becoming a Council Guard Third Rank before turning sixteen. The bar was set lower, of course, for the sons of nobles and priests, despite Ileom's occasional grumblings to the Council of Eight, who apparently cared little about the technical details and preferred to please the upper crust of society. Some of those elites believed linking their progeny to the famed battle master enhanced future commercial prospects. The barbarians, the Council argued, were too weak and disorganized to ever pose a threat, anyway.

Rain, on the other hand, had to toil for every scrap of progress toward the full measure of a Council Guard under a bona fide soldier like Master Ileom. It didn't seem fair. Having turned fifteen six months ago, he didn't have much time left to beat out Garrett. His harder life out on the farms had made him stronger, and he was bigger than most boys, in thickness as well as height, but if he couldn't develop the mental acuity to go with strength and natural talent, that would avail him little.

Master Ileom's face appeared to freeze for a moment in his consternation, eyes searching a far distant place, and then he announced a sudden end to sword practice for the morning. Rain shuffled on numb feet to return his bundle of sheaves to its place in an open barrel in one corner of the yard before lining up with the rest of the trainees. It was all he could do not to study the others and gauge their judgment of him. He could guess what they were thinking. He really *had* lost to Garrett, who was a milksop. Some of the other trainees—out of jealousy, he was certain—had recently taken to calling Rain 'unsuited' for the Guard, often where Ileom could overhear, and even once in the presence of Tashiel. Fury soon added to the heat of embarrassment, and his fists clenched. Oh, how he would like to hit somebody, especially phony, smug-faced Garrett ... but he couldn't get himself kicked out—he *wouldn't* let them push him to that. Familiar fears of failure fanned his humiliation with fiery wings, making him question once again if a poor kid like him, born from nothing, could succeed in becoming an actual member of the Council Guard, whether the position was largely ceremonial or not.

Ileom descended the well-worn stairs of the platform and barked an order for the trainees to fall in behind. He led them through the short, arched tunnel passing further into the keep, his pace slowed by the pronounced but curiously inconsistent limp he had acquired as a young mercenary serving one of the eastern warrior kingdoms. He had never said which one, and the rumors were far more numerous than the countries, all of which made Rain's blood tingle. Well, they usually did. Not today.

He trudged along in his place, his only consolation that the next scheduled session of the day was horse training—his favorite activity behind dinner, rest, and any time he got to see Tashiel. Thinking of her made him feel worse. Someday she would leave him; how could she not? If he wasn't promoted to the Guard soon—even just Third Rank—she would need to find someone better and avoid embarrassing her parents further. What in the holy stars was he to do? He was *not* a farmer.

Across the expansive, stone-flagged Inner Courtyard of the Holy Keep of the Four Stars, graced by fancy stalls offering the best merchandise west of the Miracle Mountains, they marched in something approaching well-ordered unison in two lines. To distract himself, Rain studied the nobility wandering among the stalls, considering this or that showy trinket while maintaining an ever-vigilant eye toward other elites who might take notice. He despised them for the most part, though Tashiel and her family were fast moving up the social ladder. One day he wanted to buy Tashiel some of the fine goods always for sale in the Inner Courtyard. He also longed to present her to the Holy Priest of God's Favor and the Council of Eight in the innermost Blessed Courtyard, with its marble statues, lush gardens, and wide stone benches for discussing philosophy and the grand issues of the world. If the Holy Priest agreed to marry them, Rain would believe in miracles. He might even offer an actual, heartfelt prayer of thanks to the mysterious 'Father God' and his 'Witnesses,' who his parents swore were real. His favorite Witnesses were those of Fire and Beasts—but only because their stories were the most interesting to him. Each season also had a Witness, as did Earth, Light, Water, Storms, Stars, Birds, the Moons, and a few others he didn't remember. Did Air have a Witness?

After passing through another short tunnel, they crossed the Yard of Petitioning, where those with grievances or requests lined up to seek audience with the Holy Priest or other High Priests among the Council of Eight. The trainees then traversed a longer passageway to enter the north stables, where the scent of straw and manure lay thick on the air. It was a good smell, a natural, invigorating aroma.

A horse's scream arrested his daydreaming … a chilling cry that made him reach instinctively for a sword that wasn't there. Ileom called a halt. All eyes went to the master, who turned to face his students.

"Nothing but a lame mount being put down," he said gruffly. "And rather poorly." He spat to the side before continuing. "Now get your tack and prepare your mounts before I get grumpy and sell the lot of you to a sheep trader." He limped toward a stool, grumbling what sounded like threats under his breath. A groom was already preparing Ileom's horse, so he would have plenty of time to lament his trainees until everyone was ready. Rain and the others broke formation and hustled into the large, well-appointed tack room to collect saddles and bridles, blankets and quirts.

The tack room was massive, the equipment organized among three distinct areas, with half-walls marking the boundaries. Various sizes and shapes of hooks and rings sprouted from the stout wooden walls and broad posts throughout. The area for the nobility, who rented slots in the capacious stables for their finest horses, was the largest and nearest the door. The next served the middling or rising class, those on their way up who might reach the noble class through industriousness or connections—generally connections. Tashiel's parents had a spot there. They owned two horses in the stables, though Rain had recently discovered they were borrowing money to maintain them, a fact Tashiel didn't seem to be aware of.

The last, smallest by far and farthest from the doorway, was left for the few people of the working or 'shy' class who could afford to stable a horse in the city … and for Guard trainees. The Council Guard itself, along with Saren's Legion, occupied the smaller stables on the south side of the keep.

Rain was reaching for a worn leather bridle when something small and hard struck him in the back of the head. He spun more out of surprise than anger, then blinked as the other trainees shifted to open a wider path between him and the hurler of the object. It was Garrett, as he could have predicted, bouncing another small rock in his hand and grinning. He was flanked by his friend and protector, a mountain of a kid named Jervin, who made Rain and almost every other man in New Haven—excepting Master Ileom—look puny and insignificant.

"What's wrong, Rain?" Garrett sneered from twenty feet away, and before Rain could respond he hurled the second rock—right at his face, in front of everyone. Rain dodged, and it glanced off the wood behind him to clatter along the floor. Rain's heart pounded, his blood burning. He was suddenly afraid. It was two on one, and this wasn't a training scenario. Real malice faced him, and nobody would help him, except maybe Brem—no, that wasn't likely. He glanced to where Master Ileom normally sat on that stout stool as the trainees gathered their tack, but he wasn't there. Of course. Privy break, probably. Rain forced himself to unclench his fists while staring back at Garrett, grasping for what to say or do.

"What? No profound words?" Garrett took two steps closer, followed by Jervin, who appeared more than ready to use his muscles and fat fists for destructive purposes.

"Quit throwing rocks at me," Rain warned in a voice that sounded too small and timid.

"Or what? Did your 'girlfriend' teach you a magic trick? It better be a powerful one, 'cause that's all you've got."

"We're supposed to be getting our tack." Rain turned back toward the wall to retrieve the bridle, shame washing over him. This wasn't the first time another trainee had tried to pick on him or provoke him—he was both a peasant and a big target. It also wasn't the first time he had been afraid of actual confrontation, for various reasons. How did he ever expect to be a Council Guardsman that a hero like Ileom could be proud of if he was such a coward when it came to a *real* fight? And which scared him more—being blamed and punished for an 'incident' based on his lower social ranking, or actually losing such a fight? In this case, Jervin tilted the scales massively against his prospect of winning, so he'd probably get beaten up *and* officially reprimanded, further dashing his dreams. Nobody would help him, not even Brem, who sometimes acted like his friend. Rain's confused, tired mind had no hope of finding an acceptable way out.

"Don't turn your back on me when I'm talking to you," growled Garrett, and Rain felt a minor tremor as the boys approached. Rain spun again, bridle in hand, and had just planted his feet and raised his fists for the expected onslaught when a bellow from the far doorway made everyone freeze.

"What the blazes is going on here!" Thank the stars Master Ileom had appeared. "Have you lame-brained fools forgotten how to pick out your tack? Am I your *mother* now, too? Get moving! We've had a change of plans. We'll carry weapons—bows and swords—and I haven't got all day to babysit a squawking gaggle of weak-minded young chickens."

The next instant brought a frenzy of activity to the trainees' small area of the tack room. Garrett looked as if he'd been spooked by a long-dead ancestor, while Jervin, despite his great bulk and his father's influence in the tiny nation's sham of a military, took on the semblance of a young boy caught stealing a pie from the neighbor's house. Rain would have laughed out loud if he hadn't dreaded Ileom's wrath as well. As it was, he hustled like the rest.

Rain was the first ready to mount. In the mad confusion, he had been able to select Sun Tamer, a lively young mare of perfect proportions with a magnificent coat of black silk, new to the stables from the warmer southern climes of Mero Vothas. He patted her neck before stepping up and swinging into the saddle, then sat fingering the reins in the formation area just outside the great stable doors, re-living the latest ugly scene in his mind. Why hadn't he said or done something different? In his imagination, he always said the right things. Brave, clever, and decisive. Why couldn't he do that in real life? If Sun Tamer decided to throw him today and he broke his neck, it wouldn't be a disaster for New Haven's Council Guard. And he was double the fool for *that* defeatist thought!

Despite his brooding, he sat Sun Tamer with a straight back as Ileom finally led the troop along the broad arcade ringing the Keep. They would turn east to pass under the Storm Tower, one of two octagonal fortifications rising majestically on east and west—the other being the ill-named Sea Tower, which had no view of any significant body of water. Storm and Sea protected the Sun Tower in the center, where the Holy Priest and the Council of Eight held High Communion to interpret directions from God for the city and the small nation it governed. Nobody had ever been able to adequately explain to him how that worked.

The arcade's arabesque ceiling prevented him from clearly seeing the central tower and its two forts, along with the soaring filaments of footbridges connecting them. He had been to the top of the first rising of the Sun Tower, which provided an impressive enough view by itself, but only a select few were allowed to ascend the second rising—nobles, mainly, and occasionally a superfluous lookout. The third and fourth risings were reserved for the leaders of the Church and those they specifically invited.

Thick, oaken doors lay open at the base of the Storm Tower to let them enter the long, broad passage leading to the ever-raised portcullis in the outer wall. Most of the horses were accustomed to this dim crossing nearly bereft of torches, but Sun Tamer pranced and skittered several times. Rain sensed she was more impatient than frightened, but he still stroked her neck with one leather-gloved hand while keeping a tight hold on the reins with the other. Soon they were outside, bathed in the blazing noonday sun of late summer. At one time, many decades ago, they would have crossed a moat and then descended into the city proper, but the Sarenites had determined that moats were both unsightly and difficult to maintain, and they didn't need one.

Rain took a deep breath of the clean, warm air, for a moment forgetting his recent disgrace. Raising his eyes beyond the well-ordered streets and structures of New Haven City, he surveyed the broad plain ascending in gentle courses from the majesty of the Fortress of the Four Stars and its Holy Keep, pride of the pilgrims, home of the True Keepers of the ancient covenant. Small farms, separated from each other by rocks and hedges, extended well into the first foothills of the towering Miracle Mountains just visible many miles eastward. Far to the north, the land became beautiful rolling hills leading to Revalis, capital of Istarrea, while to the south it seemed Rain could see forever, on into the vast deserts of Dugheris, though he knew that broken, mostly barren hills interrupted the landscape beyond his vision.

New Haven, the land and the city of the anciently persecuted but now wealthy and respected Sarenites, seemed well situated. Though a small realm, it boasted powerful friends: Istarrea to the north, with its rich, productive farmland and the great northern trading route; and Mero Vothas to the south, in the flatlands past the edge of the desert wastes, with its innumerable herds of cattle, its fearsome light cavalry, and the relative protection of its geography. Neither the Five Kingdoms nor the so-called warrior kingdoms farther east had any interest in tiny New Haven, partly because it would be difficult to move an army through the mountains, partly because of New Haven's allies, but mostly because of New Haven's reputation as a neutral trading broker that also boasted incredibly skilled artisans and armorers. The rich mines and smelters on the western side of the Miracles, from which New Haven obtained most of its metals under a complex agreement with the autonomous and doughty dwarves, were a tempting target but for the fact one would have to fight the dwarves to get at them. Few aspiring conquerors had ever been that stupid—the exceptions not living long.

By rote, the trainees formed two columns of nineteen once everyone was outside the main portcullis. As they walked their horses down the broad avenue, Master Ileom began to inspect the troop. He was taller than Rain, taller than most Sarenites, and only the creases at the corners of his eyes and the streaks of gray in his close-cropped black hair gave away his age. Two parallel scars under his left ear—not a result of battle—marked him a veteran in the east, aside from his facial scar and the limp. His armor was plain, if well made, nothing like most of the fabulously crafted and wonderfully expensive armors coming from the best smiths in the city. Ileom could afford any of those others, Rain had heard—something about a reward for saving a prince of Har'Batil more than twenty years ago—but he often denounced them as frivolous. He had spent some serious coin on his mount, though, a powerful, fully trained bay warhorse he had reportedly purchased from a breeder on the eastern coast of distant Holnevia just before arriving in New Haven three years ago. Rain could only dream of owning such a perfect animal.

After a brief perusal of his charges, Ileom nodded, though it was hard to tell if he was angry or just disgusted. Probably both. His horse whickered and shook its head as he called a brief halt, as if joining him in his disapproval of the trainees. Ileom absently patted its neck as he barked, "We aren't heading for the parade grounds to run escort formations. We're going on a long patrol today. Another change." Heads turned and reins shifted. Saren's Legion was responsible for patrols beyond the city—not the Council Guard, and especially not its trainees. Further, rarely did those soldiers travel in groups larger than ten. Even highwaymen posed no threat to New Haven and its lucrative trading activities, owing to the highly competent guards hired to protect the caravans, including former Istarrean soldiers and even dwarves. It had been so for long, peaceful decades.

This was clearly another mental training ploy from Ileom, to see how they would react. "Due south we will ride after passing the outer limits of the city, and you will execute the patrol formations as I call them out, with quickness and precision. There have been reports of bandits near Jerel's Altar. No lagging or daydreaming." He looked at Rain, the jagged scar under his left eye puckering as he squinted. Rain blinked, then looked down, pretending an issue with Sun Tamer, but she stood still as a statue, as if she knew exactly what was happening. Rain reviewed the various patrol formations they had learned, calculating his present place in the lines—head of the third quarter—and where that would put him in each configuration. There could be no more missteps today, though they hadn't practiced these much. By tradition, the Council Guard didn't use cavalry formations at all. At least not until Ileom arrived.

After a few uncomfortable seconds, Ileom whirled his mount. "Double spear file, hie!" He led the way without glancing back as the trainees assumed their formation in something resembling professional fashion and spurred their mounts to a trot. From the middle of the group on the left side, Rain tried to appear observant while bouncing lightly in his saddle. Two years ago, he would have dreaded a long ride like this, but Tashiel adored horses, constantly begging him to go riding with her ever since they met, which was shortly after his family had moved to the foothill farms from the drier western plains. Now he rode every chance he could get, and he fancied himself somewhat skilled.

From the small rise on which the Keep reigned, the land remained generally flat until a mile or so past the eastern gates of the city; then it began to rise slowly as it aimed for the Miracles. Until a few years ago, Tashiel's family had lived in a small but thriving village called Wundering hidden in a fold of the first foothills. Rain's family lived about ten miles north and east of New Haven, well into the foothills, in an artisan town called Mari's Mask, though they were farmers. They had no intention of ever moving to the city, even if the opportunity magically arose.

The troop passed through the city and its eastern gates, Ileom keeping the same pace and formation, then turned south onto the Ring Road to skirt the city. Just before the road started curving back toward the north, Ileom found a narrow path angling southwest. Rain hadn't ever taken it, even on his many rides with Tashiel, but assumed it must cut over to the broad Dunderrin Road, or Dunroad, which plied its north–south course a few miles west of the city. That major artery linked Istarrea with Mero Vothas and the southern ports along the eastern shores of the Sea of Troubles.

Half an hour later they indeed reached the Dunroad, its fine gravel packed hard and smooth by the traffic of trade. Ileom still hadn't uttered a word, hadn't changed their formation, hadn't hardly looked left or right, just alternated their pace between walking and trotting. He guided the troop onto the road, apparently lost in thought, taking it south where it ran straight as an arrow for five miles or more.

In their double file, the trainees left plenty of room for the frequent wagons, carts, and other riders. The farmers and merchants they passed all gave them a friendly smile or nod, though most tended to avoid eye contact with Master Ileom, whom they surely recognized and whose reputation was that of a prickly, unpredictable outlander instead of an adopted son of New Haven. The farms to either side buzzed with activity, even in the heat. The breeze carried a hint of potential rains coming from the south, though the clouds in that direction were scattered at the moment. Rain noted some ripening grapes, and his mouth watered. New Haven had become a renowned maker of wines in the last decade or so, and the closer the vineyard to the fortress, the better the quality of the grapes, or so it was advertised. Kissed by God, some claimed. More manure available, most likely.

When the road began to traverse low, rocky hills with few trees and only the occasional farm, Ileom gave his first command since their departure. "Half bow ready!" he shouted, and it was his voice, not just the command itself, that sent a chill down Rain's spine. A slippery knot writhed like a passel of snakes in his stomach. Ileom seemed deadly serious about this being a real patrol, and he had mentioned bandits. He also appeared frustrated, as if there were something—or someone—they should have found already. Rain had never been in a fight with a determined opponent actually trying to kill him, and a mouth so recently moist at the thought of grapes became parched at the prospect of being proven a true coward. His chest began to tighten, and he started to quiver, but he made himself go on.

They had executed this formation only once, though it was fairly simple. First, their lines elongated. Then, in every pair down the line, one man uncased his horsebow and nocked an arrow after wrapping his reins loosely around his pommel, while his partner moved half a horse-length ahead to provide a lead for the bowman's horse. The one assuming the role of bowman alternated down the formation, left side then right. Rain's partner, another fifteen-year-old named Kyne, was their bowman.

Rain tried not to appear nervous as he heeled Sun Tamer and then checked to make sure he was at the proper spacing. When he looked forward again, Ileom was leading the head of the troop east off the Dunroad, onto an old minor causeway, barely visible. A pair of wagons stopped to allow the trainees to pass, their drivers looking on with confused curiosity. The knot in Rain's stomach tightened.

If they were traveling to Jerel's Altar, they were taking the back way, which made little sense. Rain estimated the village lay approximately five miles farther south, and only a couple of miles off the Dunroad via a good connecting road. East and south they went, though, and more east than south, skirting craggy mounds of scrub brush and boulders, winding through broad gullies, some with tiny active creeks, most without, the entire landscape void of large trees due to dry soil that was more rock than dirt. Besides the movement of the horses, all was quiet. It would have felt peaceful but for the rapid beating of his heart, the tightness clenching at his throat, and the sweat slicking face, arms, and neck.

Ileom soon took to ranging ahead of the group, sweeping forward and back in small arcs, cresting the hills and mostly staying in sight. Whenever Rain got a good look at his face, he saw intense purpose, not that of a master fretting over his dullard trainees. Surprisingly, that provided some comfort. If they found trouble, at least Ileom was with them, and no mere group of bandits could stand against Master Ileom. However, as they continued deeper into what some Sarenites called the 'Rock Garden' for a religious reason Rain couldn't remember—perhaps Jerel's Altar was linked to it—Ileom took on a look of … not desperation, but anxiety. He increased the pace, and he seemed ready to run his warhorse into the ground in his manic search. For what? Did he *hope* to engage bandits? If so, why hadn't he summoned a real Legion patrol? Well, aside from the fact he hadn't trained the Legion himself and they didn't have a reputation of competence.

It was enough of a puzzle that Rain almost forgot to be frightened, until Ileom came charging down a long rise. When he pulled up in a shower of stones, dust, and dry grass, face hard as the mountains, his eyes revealed a light Rain had never seen before. The snakes in Rain's stomach coiled, ready to strike.

"Bows away!" Ileom ordered. "Ready for the charge!"

Kyne must have been nervous, too, because he nearly dropped his bow while trying to secure it. He didn't seem to notice the arrow clattering to the ground, and Rain wasn't about to dismount and fetch it for him. With tight jaw and dry mouth, Rain unlimbered his sword, ready to draw at Ileom's command. Sun Tamer began to paw the ground but stayed in her place. Rain could have sworn she felt … *eager.*

"Double front!" Ileom shouted, then turned his mount to begin cantering back up the hill. More smoothly than Rain would have expected, the trainees formed the two-deep charging wall, nineteen abreast, the jangle of harnesses and creaking of saddles making time with the thudding of steel-shod hooves on the hard ground. Excitement mixed with the tension in the air, and even Rain felt it. They were a formidable force, led by Master Ileom, and they were apparently going to battle. Or was it still just a test? Rain hoped for that … and was ashamed.

The troop crested the hill and paused, horses prancing and straining at their bits. Rain's eyes caught movement in the distance, to the southwest and at least half a mile off. It looked like horsemen, kicking up a lot of dust and circling something. Screams rose faintly on the breeze, and his eyes widened. People were being attacked! He couldn't tell exactly how many horsemen there were, but they didn't seem few in number, and Ileom hadn't ordered his trainees to bring spears or lances, just their short bows and swords. They didn't have full armor or shields, either.

Rain expected Ileom to assign a pair of trainees to race back to the fortress for help, even though it was a good distance away now and any assistance would come far too late. Sweat trickled down his back under his hot leather jerkin, but he still shivered, his breath coming too fast. His heart pounded as his mind raced in no direction and all directions at once. Were they really going to charge? They weren't strong enough—they would all be killed. But those people, whoever they were, those victims of the bandits, they needed help, and—

"Battle spread three!" Ileom bellowed, this time in a voice that could be heard on the moons, and Rain nearly fell out of his saddle.

With spastic alacrity, the trainees separated into three charge walls, one center and two curved wings. Ileom placed himself at the head of the center formation, raised his sword, and shouted again.

"Charge!"

The group let out a war whoop—a rather tremulous one, in Rain's opinion, or maybe that was just his own—and kicked their horses into a gallop, racing down the hill toward their target.

Rain rode in the middle wall, positioned almost directly behind Ileom. That made him feel better, but he wondered what he would actually do when they reached the bandits. Did Ileom believe the enemy would be frightened by their charge and run? Rain prayed for that, pride be damned.

The ground was relatively smooth on this side of the hill, and except for the fact that they had to skirt the occasional stand of bushes or low trees, the three groups made fast time. When they were about halfway down the slope, the bandits noticed the threat. Rain watched in dreadful fascination as they stopped in near unison and formed up—not to run, but to meet the charge! There had to be at least thirty of them, well armed with long swords, axes, bows, and a few spears. He suspected there might be a handful more beyond a stand of trees on one side. As the wind picked up and dispersed more of the dust, he spotted several wagons, most with slain oxen at the yokes, and at least two dozen crumpled gray-brown masses on the ground. Someone on foot began running west—a woman, it appeared—but the bandits ignored her. He detected no other movement among the wagons. Black-winged shapes already circled overhead.

The wind whistled in Rain's ears beneath the short flaps of his leather helm, but his fiery mare seemed to ask for more speed. If he let her run full out, he was sure they would overtake Ileom, and he wasn't that stupid. He was determined to stay as close to Ileom as possible, and he hoped Sun Tamer truly was as fast as she felt, in case they all needed to make a run for it. Lights, how could he think such a thing?

The bandits formed a single broad line but as yet didn't charge. The distance was four hundred yards now, and Rain thought his heart would escape his chest with every cycle of Sun Tamer's pounding hooves. It leaped into his throat as he saw the bows come out. Coolly, it seemed to him, the bandits nocked arrows, waited a second for the range, then let fly. Rain strained to see if any might hit him, nudging Sun Tamer to the right to avoid part of the volley. In a flash the arrows arrived. Rain heard a sickening thud to his left, a scream, and then a trainee falling backward off his horse to impact the ground with bone-crunching force. Several other arrows found a mark, and Rain registered Ileom spurring his mount to greater speed.

He let Sun Tamer run for all she was worth so he wouldn't lose Ileom. Run she did, like the winds of a tornado. Rain felt the battle exhilaration Tashiel often talked about from her studies, and which Ileom had explained multiple times. He drew his own sword—poorly made compared with Ileom's—and raised it, ready to strike.

The next volley of arrows flew, but a sudden whirlwind of dirt and rock knocked the vast majority off target. Ileom seemed to brush one away with his sword, though that must have been a trick of Rain's dust-filled eyes. He blinked, trying to clear them, then realized he had drawn even with Ileom and they were ahead of the rest by a few paces. He dared not slow Sun Tamer, though, and while his body seemed almost frozen with fear, he knew that battle was inevitable, that he would have to do *something*, that he would of necessity fight for his life. Why couldn't the bandits have just turned tail and run?

The bandits put away their bows, took hold of swords, axes, or spears, and charged. Rain tried to mimic a new war shout with his comrades, but his throat was so dry it came out a pathetic warble. Ileom's voice boomed, however, as a powerful, living thing. Rain greedily drew some courage from it, for it heralded invincibility.

He picked out his first target: a thin, long-haired man in mismatched clothes wielding a wicked-looking axe. If that axe fell on his head … He shivered violently, nearly fumbling his sword, then gripped it more tightly and focused intently on the man. He saw no fear, just crazed determination, and as they closed the man gave a yell to make the dead shake. He raised his axe for a crushing strike, and Rain brought his sword over his head in preparation to counter and shunt the blow aside.

Sun Tamer had other designs, however. She suddenly slowed, catapulting Rain's head into her neck. Again he struggled with his sword, which was now in no position to counter anything. The bandit had started his swing, then arrested it when the timing was thrown off. Sun Tamer unexpectedly surged forward, striking a glancing blow to the side of the man's mount with her shoulder. Rain spied wild frustration in the man's eyes as they passed, still traveling very fast, and then he heard the horse cry out in pain and tumble hard to the ground. The bandit screamed as well, in what Rain instinctively knew was a death cry as he was crushed under the animal's full weight.

Shaken by the encounter, but amazed at his good fortune and the prowess of his obviously intelligent horse, Rain slowed Sun Tamer and turned her around. Ileom was still beside him, doing the same. "Well done, Rain!" he shouted, then kicked his mount forward to target another bandit. Rain looked to where Ileom would have met his first prey, seeing only a riderless horse galloping in the direction of the hill. Then he spotted the bloody mess lying on the ground nearby, a large, thick-bearded man with a blood-pulsing stump for a right arm. It took a tremendous amount of force—and skill—to cut a man's arm off clean. He gagged, then remembered his goal of staying close to Ileom. As he dug his heels into Sun Tamer she leaped forward, impatient for the battle. He let out a guttural whoop that surprised him in its intensity, his body humming with a newfound energy, his sword a light extension of his arm.

Sun Tamer again proved her mettle as they closed anew with the bandits, who battled in small, organized groups. She rammed one horse in the flanks with her chest, harder than Rain could have pictured a horse hitting another horse, knocking mount and rider to the ground and likely breaking the bandit's leg. Without pause, she bounded past the fallen pair and whirled to let Rain aim a good broadside swing at an attacking bandit. The force of the head-high meeting of swords reverberated through his whole body, but again Sun Tamer knew what to do, repositioning so that his next blow, swung in a tight arc, struck the bandit in the upper back before he could recover and position himself to counter. Rain felt his blade bite through the man's leather armor and cut flesh, but not deeply. The bandit yelped in pain, and another nimble maneuver from Sun Tamer left him incapable of making an effective parry. Rain executed a thrust this time, aiming just below the man's armpit. His blow struck true, all the way to the other side, and he knew he had delivered a killing strike. The man grunted, then gurgled as he slid from his frightened mount and off Rain's sword to the ground. Rain gagged again as he noticed the man's blood thick and dark on his sword, but Sun Tamer kept moving, which wrenched his mind back to his fight for survival. *Where is Ileom?*

She took him toward another group of bandits battling with four trainees—and, from the looks of it, winning. When he was close, Rain saw Jervin go down under a hail of blows, though he couldn't tell if he had been seriously wounded or just knocked off his horse. Instinctively, Rain let out another whoop to draw the bandits' attention, then hacked hard at the arm of the first bandit he came to, who was turning his mount to face the threat.

The man had fine steel chain covering his forearms, and while Rain's blow didn't cut, he felt the metal crease and the bones break. The man's cry got the attention of more bandits, who divided their attention between Rain and the other three trainees, another of whom went down before Rain had a chance to adequately assess the new situation.

The bandit whose arm he had broken withdrew, and Sun Tamer skittered away from the onslaught of two others. She was so quick, in fact, that Rain nearly lost his seat, grabbing the pommel just in time to save himself. Stars, she was good. Reins were unnecessary, though keeping your balance was. She spun suddenly and charged, slamming shoulder to shoulder with one of the bandits' mounts. The other horse stumbled, unseating its rider in the process, and then scampered out of the battle. Before the other bandit could react, Sun Tamer surprised yet again as she reared up and brought front hooves crashing down. The man didn't see it coming in time; one hoof landed in his chest and the other in his abdomen. Rain cringed at the impact, feeling it in his own bones, knowing the man's death would be excruciating.

Sun Tamer whirled again, a horse possessed, Rain squeezing hard with his legs at the unexpected movement. Someday, he should really learn how to ride in battle so his horse didn't have to do all the work. She charged another bandit, but apparently that one had seen enough. Rain caught a glimpse of fear-widened eyes before the man wheeled his mount south and buried heels into horseflesh. Rain thought for an instant of giving chase, and Sun Tamer bounded forward as if she wanted to, but then he brought the reins to bear and checked her. Surprisingly, she obeyed, and seemingly without complaint. Again he wondered at her. This horse was a hero—could horses be honored as such?

He turned to find three bandits near to finishing off the remaining two trainees he had come to help: Garrett and Jervin. Both fought from the ground, Jervin swinging his large, two-handed sword in wide, frantic arcs. Garrett barely fended off the blows aimed at him, and both were clearly tiring. For a cold moment Rain wanted to see them die, but a deep-seated disgrace at that thought impelled him forward. He didn't yell this time, but heeled Sun Tamer as one of the mounted bandits withdrew a pace from Garrett and readied to throw a spear, his back to Rain. Rain leaned as far forward as he could, sword becoming a short lance. In mere seconds they closed the gap. By the time the bandit registered what was happening, it was too late. Rain thrust his sword into the man's back and all the way through, letting go as he passed. The bandit couldn't even scream as he fell. Rain spared a look for his sword, but then Sun Tamer took over again, avoiding another bandit's charge. Somehow, incredibly, she seemed to know Rain had lost his sword.

She went to a full gallop for a few seconds, then dug her hooves into the dirt, turned back toward the battle, and stopped. It took Rain a second to realize what she expected.

How smart is this horse?

Smarter than he was, obviously. He hurriedly unlaced his short bow from the strap behind his saddle, then snatched and nocked an arrow. None of the bandits had pursued him, and he had a clear shot at one. He aimed quickly, confident in his archery ability, and let loose. The arrow whistled from the string, true in its course, but merely struck a glancing blow off the bandit's back, careening harmlessly to the ground. The man took notice, however, judging the new threat to be significant enough to turn his mount and charge it.

Rain's heart pounded harder as he nocked another arrow. Sun Tamer stood calm as starlight after turning slightly to give Rain a better angle. The bandit moved side to side in his saddle, trying to force off Rain's aim, but Rain waited until the bandit was almost upon him before letting the arrow fly. It punched through the man's neck, causing him to release the reins and fall backward off his charging horse. Sun Tamer danced out of the way, then galloped forward a few paces to put Rain in position for another shot.

Rain downed two more bandits with his bow, Sun Tamer providing a rock-steady platform. After Ileom had eviscerated two other bandits in an astounding fashion Rain couldn't quite describe, the remaining bandits fled south, trampling a comrade in their newfound panic. Sun Tamer didn't try to pursue this time; she knew the battle was over. As she awaited his command, he patted her lathered neck. She was breathing heavily, but not laboring. He focused on her, unable to process all that had just happened.

"I'd love to figure out a way to make you mine," he said, knowing that was impossible. She truly was a marvelous animal. He couldn't imagine another horse he would want with him in battle, not even Ileom's. She had surely saved his life.

"Form up!" roared Ileom, and it was only then Rain fully realized the sounds of the battlefield had changed. The clatter of retreating hooves grew faint, the clashing of horses and men replaced by the moans and screams of the injured and dying. He must have been blocking out those sounds—none of which came from the direction of the burned-out wagons. He watched in numb fascination as the grizzled master-at-arms dismounted and put down a wounded horse, abruptly stopping its screams. As Ileom remounted, the surviving trainees moved toward their leader, some staggering on foot. All wore shocked and exhausted expressions, with several pressing hands to wounds.

As Sun Tamer stepped calmly forward, Rain counted his comrades, his tally ending far too quickly. Twelve still sat their saddles, including Garrett on a different horse than the one he'd started with. Five more stood among them. Jervin limped badly, while two others were only able to walk with assistance. Half their patrol was down, including Brem. Hopefully, most were just wounded and could be healed. But how many dead? Ileom shouted again—something about calling out their names. Rain waited until all the others had spoken, then added his own name as if it were an afterthought.

"We are fewer, but we are triumphant," Ileom proclaimed, though Rain detected a trace of hollowness in his voice. "The bandits have fled the field, and we stand as victors of the day." Ileom had surely said such words before, on other fields in distant lands. Maybe they had sounded inspiring then, but Rain felt no elation. If this was a victory, he never wanted to see a defeat. Or another victory.

"Rain, to me!" he barked. Startled, Rain urged Sun Tamer to separate from the ragged half-circle of men that had formed up. She still moved with skilled grace and nary a sign of fatigue, while Rain felt drained, as if a three-day nap would merely mark a beginning in the recovery of his strength and wits.

Sun Tamer halted in front of Ileom, whose proud bay warhorse snorted his superiority but then whickered and touched muzzles with Sun Tamer. For her part, Sun Tamer stood stock still, as if the large bay stallion didn't exist.

"New Haven hasn't seen a battle like this in fifty years or more, not even on the western borders. Despite your lack of experience, Rain Barynd, your skill and bravery broke the bandits' backs. I hereby declare all here to be Council Guardsmen Third Rank, but you are Council Guardsman Second Rank."

Rain blinked, momentarily speechless, as the full import of what Ileom had said—what he had done—pierced his post-battle stupor. The only thing he could think was that he hadn't done much, that he was undeserving.

"Sir, my horse, she—"

"Performed admirably for her new master, yes," said Ileom, and Rain's breath caught. Had Ileom just given him Sun Tamer as well?

Before Rain could say anything more, Ileom addressed the rest of the new Council Guards. "Split into groups of three and search the battlefield. Tend to our wounded first and disarm any bandits still alive. Address their wounds last, and then we will seek to extract some information. Rain, you will accompany me to the wagons."

Rain nodded acquiescence, then spied Garrett watching him. Along with the usual contempt he always directed toward Rain, he displayed a trace of grudging gratitude, maybe even admiration—though the day Garrett openly respected him the stars would all fall from the heavens.

Rain broke eye contact and turned to follow Ileom, who already had his warhorse moving toward the circled wagons. Rain's heart sank deep as he began to take a more detailed inventory of the massacre. None of the oxen had survived, but that wasn't the most sickening part. Neither was the group of men and women whose bodies lay in a tight clump just inside the haphazard defensive barrier. By the looks of it, they had tried to fight off the bandits using nothing more than long sticks and work knives. No, the worst came when he and Ileom looked inside the first wagon, where four small children huddled lifelessly together, slaughtered like vermin.

Rain emptied his stomach to the side of his horse, then scrubbed his mouth with the back of his hand. Ileom stared at him intently.

"You were scared at first," he commented.

Rain swallowed, thinking back to those initial horrifying moments when it seemed his whole body filled with bile and he could hardly breathe. Well, he had no bile left now. "Yes, Master Ileom," he replied, feeling his embarrassment beginning to show.

"It was your first battle."

Rain nodded, shoulders slumping, then wondered what this had to do with the slaughtered children.

"You did well, Rain. How many did you neutralize?"

Neutralize? He tried to think, but however hard he tried, he kept coming up with the number four—four children they hadn't been able to save. And there were likely more. "Four, I think, Master Ileom." Actually, Sun Tamer herself had dispatched almost that many, despite Rain's inexperience and ineptitude.

"Four," said Ileom dubiously, avoiding any talk of the carnage in the wagon. He guided his mount toward the next in the circle, and Rain followed. "I was twenty before I killed my fourth man. I quit counting soon after that. It should never be a pleasure, or a measure of personal accomplishment. But you did well, and you surely saved some of your fellows."

Rain let the words slide over him, barely hearing, for he could already see at least one dead child in the next wagon. He fought down the urge to vomit again. Why? Why would bandits commit such brutal violence on innocent people? On children? Rage welled, building toward an inferno in an odd way he had never felt before, but then Ileom said, "Revenge is never the right answer, Rain. I learned that the hard way, too."

What did that mean? Why not? He had never heard his hero tell stories about revenge, but it still puzzled him that Ileom could be so calm when he had obviously felt great anxiety to save these people. They continued checking the wagons for survivors, finding none. Eleven wagons, twenty-two slaughtered children—two of them just babies, three young teenagers. Twice more Rain couldn't prevent his stomach from heaving. Fifteen adults had been killed, eight men and seven women who had attempted courageously but in vain to protect their children. The rage came again—if it hadn't, he would have bawled his eyes out right there on his horse.

When they had completed their circuit he looked toward the battlefield, where the others still searched for wounded and stripped dead bandits of their possessions. A couple of the new guardsmen acted gleeful about the second part, which somehow disgusted Rain, even though a portion of him wished those bandits were still alive so he could hurt them again.

"Rain." Ileom's voice was insistent, and it suddenly registered that he had called Rain's name more than once. Rain turned and saluted. "Yes, sir. Sorry, sir."

"The woman who made it away. Can you track her?"

Rain cast about in his mind, confused for a moment. Then he remembered seeing her. "Yes, sir." Rain was the best tracker among the former trainees, having learned the skill from two of his uncles in the deep foothills and forests leading to Istarrea. The woman couldn't be hard to track, anyway. Scarce minutes had passed, she had been heading almost due west, and she was wearing a dress.

Ileom nodded with a grunt. "Go, then. Take an extra mount—we don't need them all. Meet us back at the fortress. We won't stay here long." He paused a moment as if to ensure Rain was listening closely. "And keep her safe, Rain."

With that oddly serious tone, a mantle dropped gently but firmly onto Rain's shoulders. It was the most earnest—and *reverent*—order Rain had

ever heard Ileom give. If the woman's safety was so important, Rain wondered, why was Ileom sending him off alone? He nodded solemnly, then
saluted again before taking one last look at what remained of his comrades.
Perhaps a wagon or two could be salvaged and hitched up to some horses to
bring the bodies back to the city for proper burials. Holy stars, half of their
training group had fallen! Suppressing a shiver, he set to the task of finding
a riderless horse—one from New Haven, preferably. He approached one,
grazing calmly just north of the wagons, and took it in tow.

He picked up the trail easily just beyond the westernmost wagon. The
woman had aimed straight across the shallow valley toward a gap between
hills. He could almost visualize the line of her travel fading into the distance, wondering how far away she was now. Surely not far. He urged
Sun Tamer to a slow canter and casually watched the trail. They reached
the gap, which the woman had followed for a short distance before turning north up a knobby incline. Shortly after topping the hill, her trail of
trampled grass and blood drops intersected the inbound path of the patrol.
She had taken that northwest, the general direction of New Haven City.

After ten more minutes, Rain's admiration for the woman multiplied.
She must have run for a long time without stopping to be this far from
the wagons so quickly.

Suddenly, Sun Tamer stopped dead. Rain let out an "oof!" as he ended
up on her neck, the pommel of his saddle catching him so that his next
few moments were spent looking at the world cross-eyed. But curse this
horse he couldn't—it would be like blaspheming his mother.

"Okay, what is it?" he finally asked with a wheeze. Sun Tamer whickered, and Rain could have sworn she picked up a hoof and pointed to
his right … at a crumpled body lying motionless near a thick bush. "Oh,
no," he whispered as he dismounted and tied the long lead of the spare
horse to his pommel. Dread squeezed his heart as he rushed over to the
body of a woman in a grayish brown dress, eyes scanning for the reason
she was down. Her reddish gold hair shone like fire, but she was turned
away from him. As he knelt beside her he detected movement, ever so
slight; she was breathing.

Not yet daring to rejoice, he carefully took her shoulder and neck and rolled her toward him. When he beheld her face, eyes closed as if in sweet repose, his own breathing stopped. She was young, probably mid-twenties … and the most beautiful woman he had ever seen. His heartbeat quickened, until he remembered that she surely had a husband lying dead a few miles back, and maybe even a child or two. The next thing he noticed was the broken arrow shaft sticking out of her lower left side, surrounded by blood-soaked cloth. He marveled again at her strength and determination.

Her eyes fluttered open, and he nearly jumped out of his skin. Instead of being hazy with pain, they were clear as a finely cut gem, deep emerald in color, and a perfect match for that face. They widened in fear as they focused on him. She tried to struggle, but faintly.

"It's okay," Rain reassured her. "I'm not one of the bandits. We killed most of them." He felt foolish saying that. It hadn't helped her husband or the others. "I saw you make it away from the wagons," he continued, trying to put compassion into his tone instead of boyish confusion, "and I was sent to find you. You're safe now."

The woman blinked, then looked him up and down. She nodded, apparently satisfied with his story, though he still detected a trace of suspicion. She tried to lick her lips in preparation to speak, but they were so dry she had a hard time of it. Rain wished his canteen wasn't sitting behind his saddle. Before he could retrieve it she spoke, her voice a crystal whisper.

"I'm dying." Fear returned to her eyes.

He shook his head forcefully. "No, we'll get you to a healer—we still have a few good ones in New Haven—and you'll be fine." In the next instant, he realized how difficult that would be, given her injury. Could she survive a horse ride all the way to the city? Perhaps he could build a litter. As he looked around, he knew that was hopeless, too, as twisted, stunted bushes were the only source of wood nearby.

She startled him with a sudden, fierce grip on his arm. "It's not important that I live," she hissed through teeth clenched against a new wrack of pain, "but you have a mission. You must find … the prophet. Give him this key …" Her eyes flickered, and he thought she might lose consciousness, but she regained focus. She winced as she reached into a pocket of her dress, then extended her hand to reveal a metal key, smooth and exquisitely made, of average size, bluish-copper in color. "This world … and others … depend on it."

Her voice trailed off as her body slumped, arms falling limply to the ground. The key slipped out of her grasp and dropped into the yellow grass. Rain sagged, too, but then noticed the slight rise and fall of her chest. How long would it last, though? What could he do for her? How angry would Ileom be if she died? And who was this 'prophet' she mentioned? Had she been delirious? She hadn't seemed it. Had she really said the entire *world* depended on the key? And who or what were the 'others'? Was the key a magical talisman of some sort? Those were extremely rare, mostly relegated to fairy tales designed to delight or frighten children. Legends of powerful ancient magic-users were … well, legends.

He picked up the metal piece and examined it. Tashiel had told him something of the making of simple magical artifacts, from her own studies. She claimed the true art of it was largely lost, and only the most ancient of talismans possessed powers worthy of any remark. His eyes usually glassed over at that point in their conversations on magic.

But the key didn't matter at the moment. The woman's life did. What was the trick Tashiel had been trying to teach him, the gathering and fine manipulation of heat? It could be used for cauterizing wounds, even fusing flesh back together. He had been close to achieving it a couple of times, and Tashiel had assured him that he had at least a small spark of magic accessible to him. Most people did, after all, though usually they couldn't attain the required reach. He couldn't think of anything *else* to do. Without such magic, this woman would die. He could start a fire and heat his belt knife, but that felt like it would take too long and be too … imprecise. Could he stop the bleeding inside as well as out?

He placed the key in a breech pocket before gently examining the woman's wound more closely. With his knife he cut away the cloth closest to the wound, then cursed himself as it pulled away with a sticky tug. Blood pulsed slowly around the arrow shaft. He felt around her back and found that the tip had punctured the skin there. He would have to push the shaft through if he hoped to seal the wound, and it would have to be now. Before she bled out. He had to try, no matter how crazy it seemed.

It would have been harder to force the arrow through if she were conscious, screaming and struggling against the pain, muscles clenching. As it was, he still blanched, feeling and hearing flesh tear as the arrowhead broke all the way through and he pulled, turning her on her side.

He took his only bandage from his pouch, balling it up to cover the exit wound as he rolled her onto her back again. He placed more cloth from her dress over the entry point, adding pressure. Then, focusing as best he could, he began the insane attempt at actual magic, at amassing and concentrating heat from the surrounding environment. The goal was to amplify it to the point where it became a knot of dense, contained fire that could also be shaped. He'd seen Tashiel do it, but she had already graduated from novice to initiate in the Magicians Guild at New Haven.

Now, how did it go? First, he needed to open himself up to the space around him, feel it as if it were alive. He must see it, greet it, comprehend it to some degree, and then … it seemed so ridiculous for a moment he nearly lost his concentration completely, but he pressed on, eyes squeezing shut. Whenever he tried this with Tashiel, the attempts made him feel like he was wandering through a deep fog trying catch a greased piglet. The destination existed, but it was impossible to reach. Still, despite so many past failures, he was determined to figure it out.

Heat was plentiful in the area, from sun and earth, substance and life, including himself and the horses. He recited the short incantation of magical focus Tashiel had taught him, repeating it over and over again, first in his mind, then as a whisper, then louder. He became distantly aware that his hands were moving, as if he were physically gathering something into a small pile in the air. According to Tashiel, he didn't need to use his hands, and the verse was just an aid for the initiate, but he wanted so badly for this to work. It *had* to.

His face suddenly felt warm, and his eyes blinked open. Was it working? Amazingly, it seemed to be, though it wasn't nearly enough. He recited the words again, tried to extend the range of his gathering, and then ... yes, it was definitely getting hotter. And he could visualize his destination. No fog surrounded him. It was as if the shock of the battle—and his actions during it—had shifted something inside his mind. How, he couldn't comprehend. But gathering the heat felt almost natural. Had *he* passed out, too? Was he dreaming? No, he couldn't be.

He needed to concentrate the heat further; also make it more pliable, turn it into a tiny tool he could maneuver to sear the woman's flesh shut, inside and out, and stop the bleeding. He nearly lost concentration again as his mind foundered upon exactly how he would manipulate the heat through the wound. It seemed like a natural thing, however, which he could simply do with his hands. Would they burn? For some reason, it felt like they wouldn't.

He reached for his amassed, concentrated heat while striving to gather more—without any words this time—then directed it with his fingers to the woman's wound. He watched in detached fascination as his fiery implement touched her flesh and began to work. He pressed it all the way through, following the path of the arrowhead as best he could, carefully cauterizing the flesh in between and at the point of exit, hoping the damage already done to her organs wasn't fatal ... and that he wasn't doing more harm than good. He had no way to tell for sure, and he wasn't a physician. Finally, he sealed the outer flesh while withdrawing the tool, leaving only a light scar. How had he done *that*?

The woman barely trembled in her unconsciousness. She no longer bled. He scrutinized the tool, which looked like a long, thin rod made of impossibly small cords of twisting molten metal, then stared in astonishment at his hands. They appeared normal, and he felt no pain. He let the heat dissipate, shivering as he realized how cold it had become immediately around his person while he held the tool.

A rush of swirling warm wind enveloped him as he observed the woman's face. Color returned, her breathing steadier and deeper. Shaking his head in astonishment, he rejoiced at her life, at the fact he had saved her. And he had used *magic* to do it! The awe made his skin tingle and his chest swell. Tashiel would be incredibly proud. Or, more likely, she wouldn't believe a word of his story. Unless he could replicate what he'd done. Could he, or had it been a fluke driven by extreme circumstance? He was too mentally exhausted to try again. Ileom might know … if *he* didn't think Rain crazy, too.

They were a long way from New Haven, and the woman appeared very weak. He tried to make her more comfortable before retrieving his canteen. After getting her to drink a little, he carried her over to Sun Tamer, who had stood calmly the entire time, as if fully understanding the situation. Rather than drape the woman over the saddle of the spare horse and tie her in place, he lifted her—after some small struggle with her skirts—into his saddle. Then, gripping the pommel and letting her sag onto his left arm, he swung himself up behind her. With reins and lead rope in one hand, and the other around her waist to keep her back tight against him, he urged Sun Tamer forward.

The ride along the trail passed uneventfully, allowing Rain plenty of time to think about what had transpired so far that day. His first battle, permeated by blood-gelling fear; the fierce courage of Master Ileom—and of Sun Tamer; the loss of half his comrades; the wanton and brutal slaughter of innocent men, women, and children; the lone survivor, who had run an incredible distance with a terrible wound; his use of magic to heal her, at least enough to hopefully get her to New Haven alive; and the crazy things she had talked about in her delirium. The key in his pocket likely fit the door to her house, and he smiled at that. She would be needing it back.

They didn't reach the Dunroad until the sun was close to setting, given the slow pace Rain kept for Sun Tamer. He also wondered how long the healing had actually taken. Time had seemed to stop. But the Dunroad was an important milestone, for the heavily trafficked trade route meant relative safety. The exultation he felt at helping the woman—who continued to sleep peacefully—increased as he realized they would certainly make it back to New Haven that night. He was tired and sore, and the awkward way he had to sit caused some discomfort. Sun Tamer needed food, water, and rest, too. Those were small things, though, compared to a life saved. "Soon," he reassured his heroic horse. "Soon."

After the first two miles up the road, it became a serious mental struggle to keep going, to ignore the stiffness and tiredness, to stay alert. Traffic on the road decreased, and darkness overtook them.

He was surprised, then, when one moment it seemed the journey might never end, and the next they were approaching the great western gates of New Haven. From there, lines of lampposts illuminated the way through the city and into the fortress. It seemed he had been half asleep part of the way, and the woman was still unconscious, but no matter. They had made it, and he would soon be able to celebrate his multiple successes with Tashiel. Her parents might even be impressed. Tall hope, but he embraced it.

Up on the central rise, the western portcullis of the Keep stood open. The great fortress, like the city itself, had no fears of the night, nor a desire to fully rest. The quietest period of any day was the two or three hours before dawn—at every other time, the city pulsed with activity. Rain figured it was close on midnight, still early for most of the habitual revelers, which included many of the clergy. He searched his sluggish mind for where he should take the woman, to whom he should report first. He had tried to think about it along the way, but his focus was frazzled. Were Ileom and the others back? Their progress would be slow with all the wounded, and they might have decided to go to Jerel's Altar for the night. Should he talk to the gate guards? The officers at the Dome of Judgment near the Keep's center had probably left hours ago. What about the Healers Quarter, north of the Keep? That seemed the best idea, and it should have been his first thought. He could make a report to both the Dome officers and the Council Guard adjutant tomorrow. And Master Ileom, of course.

The gate guards motioned for him to pass with little more than a cursory wave of their hands and some ogles for the woman, who they must have assumed was drunk. They expressed annoyance when he ordered them to take his spare mount in hand, by authority of Master Ileom. Grumbling, they acquiesced, and as he passed under the tall stone arch in the elaborate city wall—a perimeter more decorative than defensive—he was tempted to urge Sun Tamer to a trot. The woman was safe, and he was anxious to hand her over to someone else so he could visit Tashiel and tell her his story, even if he had to stealthily wake her. Then get some real sleep. Wonderful, glorious sleep. Unfortunately, bouncing the woman around in her unconscious state would look foolish, so he maintained Sun Tamer's steady walking pace.

"Antara! Antara!" came a quivering male voice to his left. Rain's head snapped toward the sound, and he spotted a man rising from the ground at the edge of a low stone warehouse, eyes focused on the woman in Rain's saddle. More than a dozen other people stirred as well, a few of them in the process of waking. Those already alert wore the same look of worry and hope. They followed the man as he approached Sun Tamer, arms outstretched. They mumbled the same name in near reverence, redolent of the fantastical tales some mothers told their children about spirits who appeared from the netherworld to mock the disobedient.

Rain shortened the reins and brought Sun Tamer to a halt. These were no spirits, and they apparently recognized the woman. He was glad of it. "You know her?" he asked the first man, who now stood near his stirrup, hands nearly touching her dress.

The man peered up at him with tears in his eyes and nodded. "Aye, sir, I do. What kind of fate has brought her safely back to us?"

Rain cocked his head, wondering what the man knew, and how he could know it. "She is hurt. Her group was attacked by bandits to the south.

She is—" He had been going to add that she was the only survivor, but that news could wait. "She will be all right. I am taking her to the healers."

"Bless you, sir," said the man. "We will go with you and attend her. Her name is Antara. She is precious to us."

"Very well," said Rain, not quite knowing what to make of that last statement. But at least he had a name for her. He studied the other people who had gathered around. They alternated their grateful gazes among Antara, him, and the man. Most were middle-aged or older, both men and women, but he spied a teenager as well. The group had swelled to almost thirty, each wearing a white band across their forehead, identical in cut and style. He was sure he had never seen any of them before, nor anyone like them. That was odd. They could be foreigners, but the man didn't have an accent.

He started Sun Tamer moving again. After the first few steps, with the white bands pressing close, he could tell she was becoming a little spooked. And given the well-deserved trust she had earned, an uneasy feeling began building. He urged her to a slow trot, holding Antara tighter. The white bands jogged to keep up, nearly surrounding them. He spotted another teenager in the glow of a passing lamppost, noting a feral eagerness in the boy's eyes that produced a chill.

Something wasn't right. Yes, he was exhausted in mind, body, and spirit. He was probably experiencing battle shock, too, though he'd never felt it before to know for sure. But he couldn't shake the uneasiness, especially given Sun Tamer's obvious and uncharacteristic anxiety. If he could just get Antara to the healers, he could sneak in a quick visit with Tashiel and then find his room in the barracks and sleep for an entire day. Oh, how he looked forward to that, almost more than he had anticipated anything in his young life.

He felt as much as saw the hands reaching toward the stirrups and Sun Tamer's bridle, and in that instant Sun Tamer must have sensed them as well. He grabbed the pommel as she reared, forcing the white-banded mass back. Then he gave her free rein, and she bolted out of the fanatical crowd, neighing defiantly and kicking up her rear hooves in warning to anyone who dared get too close. Rain looked around, trying to get his bearings. They had turned north a short distance back, onto Highbringer Street, which would take them to the Healers Quarter. He couldn't proceed there now, since he had told the white bands his destination. His mind raced, probing where to go. He thought of the Keep, but that would be problematic as well. The healers there—most of them quite old—would likely be asleep, and their assistants would just direct him to the Healers Quarter, while also sending a message ahead. Did the white bands mean her any harm? He almost stopped, chiding himself for a fool, but the feeling that he needed to be completely clear of the white bands—for Antara's sake—came so strongly he couldn't ignore it. Sun Tamer's instincts were better than his, anyway. And she clearly knew one of her riders was still unconscious, for her gallop was one of the smoothest Rain had ever felt.

He finally decided upon Tashiel's home. Hopefully her parents were out, trying to impress their social betters at a well-lit party. They would be none too happy at him calling openly at this time of night, or morning, whatever it was—especially her father—but their home was the safest sanctuary he could think of until he could get everything sorted. His course decided, he turned left off Highbringer Street as he slowed Sun Tamer. He needed to go east, but west first, then south, would hopefully throw the white bands off the trail. Anger flashed at these strange new people. He would find out who they were and why they were in the city, once Antara was safe and he had rested. He was a member of the Council Guard now, Second Rank, so he could actually *do* something about them, especially after he recounted everything to Master Ileom.

His mind turned to what he would say and do when he showed up at Tashiel's front door rather than tapping discreetly at her bedroom window. She would ask why he hadn't gone straight to the healers. But before he could work it all out, he arrived, urgency impelling him to dismount immediately.

It was a groggy Master Dowren, unfortunately, who answered the door. Upon seeing Rain with an unconscious woman in his arms, he straightened, eyes wide.

"Rain?" he asked in a bewildered tone bordering on affront. "What is this?"

Rain hesitated, then answered, "I need your help, Master Dowren. It will take some time to explain, but … may I come in?"

Master Dowren's eyes narrowed in curiosity and suspicion. He leaned his head out, pausing on Sun Tamer's Council Guard trappings as he looked around. Finally he nodded, backing up to let Rain through.

"Is there somewhere I can lay her down?" asked Rain as he surveyed the small living room and adjoining kitchen with table, chairs, and two short, hard benches.

Master Dowren studied Antara briefly before responding, eyes resting a moment on the blood stains. "Yes. I will get blankets. You may lay her near the hearth, and I will start a fire."

"Thank you, sir." Rain hadn't realized how cool it had gotten, though that was normal at night during late summer in the semi-desert climate of New Haven. While Master Dowren disappeared to retrieve blankets, Rain repositioned Antara's weight in his arms a little. She breathed peacefully, eyes closed, with neither whimper nor moan. She was beautiful, Rain noted again. Her hair fell from her face in gentle waves. Her skin was a smooth bronze, her lips a soft, healthy rose.

"I have the blankets, Rain." Master Dowren's entrance startled him out of his trance, and he hoped fiercely the low light of the single small lantern near the front door wasn't enough to let Master Dowren see him blushing. He didn't appear to notice, thankfully, and set to laying out the blankets on the floor near the fireplace. When he was finished, Rain carefully laid Antara down. As he began to rise, he nearly jumped out of his skin for at least the second time that day.

"Rain, what are you doing here?" Tashiel had entered the room, dressed in a soft blue night robe trimmed with chiffon. He turned toward her, his mind furiously calculating the best explanation. He still wasn't ready, but decided a skeleton of the truth was the best option. His gaze alternated between Tashiel and her father, with an occasional peek at Antara, as he tried to tell the short version of the story … or most of it. The process became more difficult when Master Dowren started firing questions, probing for details. Tashiel cast frequent glances at Antara, her expression fluctuating between pity and suspicion. When he finally related the part about the unnerving people with the white headbands, and his escape from them on Sun Tamer, he felt even more exhausted than before. He had judiciously left out both Antara's house key—for obvious reasons—and his use of magic, pretending instead he had been able to make a fire to heat his knife and cauterize the wound. Even so, was the story believable? Things like this didn't happen in New Haven.

"Well," said Master Dowren, sounding somewhat skeptical. "Just by her complexion and how she's resting, she doesn't appear to have sustained serious internal injuries, which is a miracle. I did hear of a patrol having some trouble to the south today, but nothing about battle. You certainly look the worse for wear. How many bandits did you say you downed?"

"Four, I think," he muttered. "Master Ileom was the hero of the engagement, not I."

Master Dowren's eyes narrowed as they bored into Rain's skull. "Has Ileom returned?"

Rain blinked. "I don't know. They may be traveling slowly. We lost several men, and many more were wounded, some badly."

"You mean *boys* playing with swords, don't you?" Master Dowren angled his eyebrows in derision. He had made it abundantly clear in the past he didn't like his daughter roving about with a boy who wasn't learning an occupation with real potential. Soldiering was for those not ambitious or bright enough to learn a gainful craft. Rain's face burned with embarrassment and anger, but before he could reply, Tashiel spoke up. Unfortunately, it wasn't to defend him.

"Why were *you* sent after this woman? Did you volunteer?"

This woman? The words stung. Tashiel scowled at him, eyes casting daggers. Then he understood. Of course she wouldn't use Antara's name. She was jealous. *Jealous!* Suddenly, he wanted to laugh, the whole scene was so ridiculous ... and he was so tired. Dozens of people had *died*, but both father and daughter examined him like he was a little boy who had stolen sweets and didn't want to admit it even though the evidence was all over his face and hands. He looked from Master Dowren to Tashiel, and back again, slowly, feeling the anger building. If they would not accept him, he would go somewhere else, and he would take Antara with him. Maybe out of the city entirely, to a nearby village. Someone there would care.

He let more of that anger enter his voice than was probably prudent. "Ileom gave the assignment. I don't care if you believe me or not. This woman"—he pointed at Antara—"lost her family. She almost died, too, and she needs rest and care. I would have taken her to the healers if I thought it was safe. You can help her or not, that is your choice. If not, I will take her elsewhere."

Never had he stood up to an adult like that; never had he even said that many words in cogent sequence to someone his elder. For a moment, he wanted to cringe and turn away. But he didn't. He kept his eyes locked on Master Dowren while maintaining a solid mask of determination. The appearance of Tashiel's mother by her husband's side didn't distract him, not even when she complained Rain was wearing a sword in their house. He almost broke down, however, when he remembered it wasn't the one he had started the day with. Then Mistress Sereill saw Antara lying on the floor in her bloodied dress and nearly fainted. Master Dowren held her tight to keep her standing.

He met Rain's glare with a stern, unflinching gaze that seemed to last for several minutes. But finally, his eyes turned toward Antara, and when they refocused on Rain a spark of admiration flickered. It was gone quickly, and Rain didn't dare test it.

"She will be safe here, Rain. We are not people to turn away someone in need." Resentment limned Master Dowren's tone at the imagined offense, but Rain didn't bother trying to correct the perception.

"Thank you," he said instead, bowing his head. "I will return to check on her later, and then try to find her kin. Right now I have to report in at the barracks." With a slight note of defiance, he added, "I'll bring you word of Master Ileom when he returns. As a Council Guard Second Rank, I'll be one of the first to know." He turned away before any of them could react to his surprising new station, and in two quick strides was opening the front door.

"Rain, wait," came Tashiel's voice. "I'll … I'll see you off." He didn't turn his head, not caring to see her parents' expressions. He just stepped outside into a darkness lessened slightly by the scant light from the front windows and a streetlamp several houses down the row. When he heard the door close, he finally turned, Sun Tamer's reins already in his hand.

"Rain, I'm sorry," said Tashiel, staring into his eyes. "I shouldn't have doubted you like that."

Rain felt a little startled by that admission of guilt. From Tashiel? She was usually so like her mother, never wanting to admit to anything.

"I shouldn't be jealous, should I?" she added, her eyes a little more earnest.

Rain finally relaxed. "No, you shouldn't." He reached out his hand, and she grasped it tightly in both of hers, relief evident on her face. This was indeed an entirely new experience, one he wasn't sure should make him feel so giddy. He smiled. "In fact, you should be happy, because I left something out of the story."

She tilted her head, giving him a look that demanded he explain quickly.

"I used magic today," he revealed, watching closely her reaction.

Her eyes widened to teacups, and she dropped his hand, her own hands clapping to her face, then her midriff. "What? Are you serious?" A proud smile burst forth. "I always *knew* you had some potential, but you wouldn't believe me, even when we practiced and I showed you how you could do it. What exactly did you do?"

"I gathered enough heat to seal up Antara's arrow wound, inside and out."

Tashiel's eyes widened again, her breath whistling with a hint of disbelief. "You mean you didn't use your knife and a fire? You collected that much heat from your environment and focused it so precisely … as a *beginner?*"

He nodded, enjoying the shock on her face. "I did. Maybe I'll spend some time at the Academy with you." He didn't really *want* to spend any time at the Magic Academy, but it seemed an appropriate thing to say.

Tashiel searched his face for a few moments, and then her broad grin reappeared. "That would be nice, Rain. I'm proud of you. Mother will be proud as well, and maybe even Father. Usable magic talent is rare and brings great honor."

He had pleased her, and yet somehow he felt less than satisfied. Magic wasn't who he was, and he didn't want to please her parents with magical ability. He wanted them to like him for who he truly was now—a member of the Council Guard, a brave soldier who protected the city, not a useless coward of low skill trying to steal their precious daughter. After saying good-bye and receiving an energetic kiss from Tashiel that nearly made him approach Sun Tamer from the wrong side, he was on his way to the barracks, secure in the knowledge that the mysterious woman was safe and that Tashiel was sincerely proud of him.

Only five of the Guard trainees had died, but one of them was Brem, who least deserved it. Rain didn't discover that until late the next morning, after Master Ileom had returned and snatched barely two hours of sleep.

Rain stood tall and somewhat guiltily refreshed in Ileom's cramped office in the heart of the Keep, its slivers for windows making him also feel a bit claustrophobic. He proudly wore a clean burgundy and brown uniform, which had magically appeared at daybreak on the small chest next to his bunk. His epaulets sported two silver stars of rank, and he imaged them gleaming as he gave his official, monotone report regarding Antara. When he recounted how he had saved her—including the part about magic—power surged through his body, adding to his newfound confidence. He had triumphed in his first battle, passed his first test. And healed someone!

Master Ileom deflated him like a hollow loaf of bread.

"You have a long way to go, boy. You survived your initial battle, but more will come—and some will curl your intestines around your toes. Best you keep preparing as fast as you can." His stern tone was dark and prophetic, but Rain focused on one word … *survived?* Was that all he had done, and mostly out of luck? Yes, he had to admit the hard truth.

He was suddenly a relative pauper again, competing with the nobles' sons and losing because of his poor bloodlines. Standing up to Master Dowren must have gone straight to his head.

Strangely, while Ileom seemed happy that Antara was healthy and in good hands, he didn't appear overly anxious about her. He didn't even thank Rain for saving her, and he made no comment on his use of magic! How odd. Concern clouded his eyes when Rain told him about the white bands, though. He wasn't forthcoming as to why.

With a stiff gait, Rain exited the office, pondering where to go. Ileom had given him just two days off—this day and the next—to rest up for a more rigorous training schedule, as if he were still a raw recruit instead of a newly promoted Second Rank Guard. He had hoped for more, especially after an intense first battle, but his dour commander had surprised him yet again.

He thought about checking on Antara, even felt a strong pull to do so, but shook it off amid the confusing malaise of his emotions. Part of him wanted to find his bunk and grab more sleep, but he headed for the stables instead, hoping Sun Tamer would be game enough to take him out of the city today. In his parents' last letter, they had mentioned they would be visiting his uncle in Sheran Village, a short trip north. The subtext, of course, was that their only child might find some time to see them. Perhaps a nice day in the country, especially in an area where the grass grew greener and more trees thrived, would help him order his chaotic thoughts. In any case, it would have to do, especially since Tashiel would be busy all day at the Academy. And he certainly didn't plan to wander around aimlessly in search of entertainment, lest Ileom find out.

Thankfully, Sun Tamer, already quartered in the south stables with the rest of the horses of the Council Guard, seemed healthy and eager for a ride, even so soon after their harrowing adventure. She tossed her head back and pranced when she saw Rain. He had never imagined developing a bond with a horse, presuming such a thing would take months, if not years.

"Easy girl," he said, stroking her neck while a groom saddled her. The man had appeared out of nowhere and insisted it was his job, even snapping a salute before running to grab a saddle from the clean, well-appointed tack room. "We're just going for a peaceful ride in the country. Nothing to get excited about, nobody attacking us, just some rest and relaxation."

He could have sworn she understood him and whinnied contentedly. Shaking his head, he watched the groom give the girth strap a final pull and finger check before securing the standing end. He now recognized the man as one of the Council Guard's more experienced grooms. Pride surged anew in his chest, along with a surreal bewilderment. Was he truly a Council Guardsman Second Rank? Besides the two stars on his epaulets, his formal tabard bore the complex silver compass of New Haven and was crafted of the finest cloth he had ever worn. His riding gloves were new as well, along with the breeches and boots; out of pure luck the cobbler had in inventory an unclaimed pair of boots his size. His feet felt lighter than goose down.

As he tried to tamp down creeping vanity, the horrors of the day before returned. To keep them at the edges of his consciousness, he focused on Sun Tamer. Antara's face somehow floated into the mix as well, though she seemed distant. He promised himself he would check on her later … and give her back her key; he mustn't forget that, nor let Tashiel see the exchange.

He mounted, sitting the saddle with straight back as he guided Sun Tamer out of the stables and into the clear morning sunlight. She was decked out in her own Guard colors and accoutrements, seeming proud of them. A short walk took them outside the Keep's walls to follow the same route eastward out of the city that his troop had used the day before. This time, however, instead of turning south after passing the city gates, he took one of the roads north, toward Sheran. Several fields already showed evidence of the early harvest underway. That was the primary reason for his parents' visit; his widowed uncle could use some help, and their own crops would mature later.

They would be surprised to see Rain. Despite their subtle invitation, they knew how demanding Ileom was. Perhaps Rain and one of his friends or cousins in Sheran could make an excursion deeper into the foothills, harass a grumpy dwarf or two along the way, and return just in time for a celebratory feast with his family coming in from the fields. Then he could return to the city, showing off his status again as he passed the guards at the various gates. He might even ask one of them to fetch him and Sun Tamer some water, and the man would surely do it. They might not for a Guard of Third Rank.

⌒∞⌒

The ride through the gently rolling farmland was pleasant enough to soothe Rain's emotions. He stopped several times to let Sun Tamer graze, or to drink from clear brooks passing under bridges. Her coat shone with a new luster—in part because of the additional grooming she had received as a Council Guardsman's mount—and her step felt light, whether walking, cantering, or galloping.

The countryside grew ever lusher as the land marched slowly upward toward Istarrea and the westward-curving tip of the great continental spine. Rain had never actually set foot in Istarrea, hadn't even come within sight of the border. As a member of the Council Guard, however, an opportunity would come. His world was expanding, and he eagerly embraced it.

He leaned forward and patted Sun Tamer. "What part of Mero Vothas do you come from, girl? Whoever bred and trained you must be famous … at least to people who know about such things."

She didn't respond to his touch or his voice, just maintained a steady, fast walk along the minor merchant road running parallel to the north-aiming extension of the Dunroad a few miles west. At some point in the distant past, it had been decided that the Dunroad would change names and become the Starway as it meandered toward Revalis. Rain thought it kind of silly.

At this time of day, even the minor roads were liberally dotted with the busy traffic of commerce. Rain dipped his head to a liveried wagon train leader, an older man who squinted at him, then blinked. Rain suppressed a smile. Yes, he was young to wear the epaulets of Second Rank.

"I'm from the southeast," came an incongruous feminine voice wafting on the breeze.

Rain's mind went blank. He stared at the spot of mane between Sun Tamer's ears for a full two seconds, trying to process how she could have spoken to him. Then his mind caught up, and he looked to his right, mouth falling open as he fumbled the reins. Antara gazed calmly, even regally, back at him, soft hair blazing in the sun. Her dress shimmered in light blue with darker accents, accompanied by riding gloves and boots of exquisite, softened leather. A narrow silver necklace graced her immaculate neck, bearing an elegant eight-pointed star. Her horse stood taller than Sun Tamer, with broad chest and dark gray coat.

Eyes wide, he swallowed, then managed to stutter, "How are … I mean, how did …?"

"I've been wondering that myself." She studied him as a hawk might examine a particularly plump rabbit. "My wound is healed, and that couldn't have been done by the amateurs in New Haven. I wouldn't even have survived the journey to get to them. To be fair, amateurs are almost all we have left, at least on this continent. Too many mistakes have been made, mainly by greedy pretenders doing more harm than good as they shake people down for their coin. People distrust magical healing as a general rule now, and the true talent continues to wane."

He had only a paltry understanding of that. And he was still trying to process her sudden appearance, dressed like a duchess or a queen.

She clicked her tongue. "So … it must have been you. What is your name, and how old are you?"

He let a snapping of reins nearby distract him, turning his head to watch one of the wagon train drivers urging his charges to maintain a fast gait. They were pacers, not trotters.

After a few uncomfortable seconds, he answered. "My name is Rain Barynd. I'm a member of the Council Guard, Second Rank."

Antara eyed his uniform, offering him a patient look. "I can see that. I'm not familiar with the ranks here, though. And you weren't wearing that uniform yesterday."

Yesterday. A lifetime ago. He had been a baby then.

"We were just … training," he explained, "with Master Ileom, and we didn't expect to come across a group of bandits." That wasn't quite true, based on Ileom's warnings.

Her eyes widened slightly. "Ileom led you toward Jerel's Altar?"

"Yes."

"You were victorious, I presume." She let out a long sigh. "Did any of the children survive?" Her expression showed sadness, but less than he would have expected. It struck him again how differently she was dressed. Night and day, and yet both wardrobes seemed to fit her. He didn't dare ask about it, though.

He looked away briefly again, swallowing as his stomach churned at the remembered images of the slaughtered children. He cleared his throat. "No. I'm sorry. I wish we would've gotten there sooner. We might have saved your—"

"Your arrival allowed me to escape. And I have neither husband nor children."

"Oh." Rain resisted the temptation to ask her about the group and where they had been traveling. It wasn't his place. Instead, he said, "I don't know how you ran so far before collapsing."

"I was motivated."

He nodded, remembering her urgency. Was she referring more to her life or the key, which he still possessed? She had seemed perfectly willing to die to keep the key safe. If her house matched her attire, he could begin to see why.

"You haven't answered my second question. How old are you?"

He blushed. He could lie, except he wouldn't. Not to her. Why?

"Almost sixteen."

She gave an impressed hum. "Fifteen is young. You must be good."

He tried again to guess her age. Twenty-two? A little older? "I've been … fortunate." He felt a spike of shame at how undeservedly haughty he'd been acting since donning the new uniform.

"Indeed," she agreed, a little too heartily. "And clearly you can perform at least one type of healing magic." She pinned him with her gaze, preventing him from disavowing.

"I'm not very good," he said with a self-deprecating shake of his head. "I'm not even sure how I did it. It just … I tried to do what I could."

Her eyes narrowed. "Your will is strong. You exerted more control over the elements than most can achieve after years of study. I was dying. That much I remember clearly. And you didn't just randomly gather heat. Otherwise, you and … was it two horses? … would have gotten awfully cold. Perhaps deathly so."

He didn't know what to say to that. Nobody had ever commented on his will before. His mother had often called him stubborn, but what mother hadn't said that about her child? He had no siblings, his mother unable to bear more children after his birth, so he only had a few cousins to compare himself to. And his friends, but they were all so different. That thought gave him an idea to change the subject.

"I'm heading to Sheran Village. My parents are visiting, helping my uncle with his early harvest. I know a few others there, too."

"Sheran." She seemed to test the word for balance. "I have heard of it. It's not far off this road, correct, just a few miles on?"

"Yes. And it isn't large. Where are you, um, journeying?" He wasn't sure he should have asked, but he had a strong desire to know.

She tilted her head, a faraway look coming to her eyes as she stared beyond him. "I'm not sure, but I will accompany you for now."

His eyebrows rose. "Me? Why accompany *me*?"

"Well, you *did* save my life. And the parents of your girlfriend were kind enough to give me your name. Yes, I already knew it." She winked, causing another instant blush.

"Um … well, shouldn't you return to your people?"

She quirked an eyebrow. "My people?"

"Yeah, the ones with the white headbands. We found some in the city. Sun Tamer didn't like them much, but they knew your name, and they seemed, um, anxious for your welfare."

She gazed forward as their horses plodded serenely along at an average pace, her expression neutral at first. "The white bands. Yes, I'm familiar with them." She pursed her lips, and Rain sensed unease. "They are quite … determined … in their pursuits. You said they knew my name. What name did they give?"

That seemed an odd question. "Um … Antara?"

"Hmmm." Her eyes flashed as she scanned the horizon.

"I had never seen them in New Haven," he offered.

"They are rare in these parts. They come primarily from Sheraya. And I am *not* one of them."

"Oh. So … why are they here?" He cast his mind back to the battle with the brigands and all the brutally butchered bodies of the poor … pilgrims? He didn't remember seeing any white headbands among them.

She hesitated, then frowned. "I wish I knew. Your girlfriend … Tashiel? She can do magic as well?"

The new question knocked him off-balance again, but his answer wasn't long delayed. "She's studying at the Academy in New Haven. She's pretty talented."

"But not nearly as talented as you."

His tongue stuck to the roof of his mouth. Such an assertion seemed inconceivable.

Her light laugh turned his bones to jelly. "She was jealous of me. It wasn't hard to tell when she left the house this morning." She tilted her head again. "Why *did* you take me to her parents' house?"

He shrugged, feeling his face warm. "Well, *I* didn't feel good about the people wearing the white bands, either, and I just wanted to find a place I knew you would be safe until I could figure something else out. Or until Master Ileom could, that is."

"And then you promptly left the city."

"No. I mean, yes, late this morning, but I didn't think you'd be … up and about so soon. And I told Master Ileom everything. This is just a day trip—he gave me two days off—and I was going to come check on you later."

She gave him a teasing smile, and despite a twinge of guilt, part of him thought—or rather hoped—it might be flirtatious, though that wasn't likely. She was too beautiful, and obviously refined. Maybe she was a princess in disguise. His mother had told him a story like that once, from more than a hundred years ago.

"I appreciate that. And I trust you. I don't trust easily."

All he could do was nod, then avert his gaze again. They rode in silence for almost a minute before she posed another question.

"Master Ileom's name is widely known. What do you think of him?"

Rain considered how to answer. He idolized the man and craved his approval, but he didn't want to reveal the true depth of that to Antara.

"He's brave. A war hero, from the stories that are told. And he's tough on the trai ... er, the Guards."

"Hmmm. It's strange that he's here, don't you think, tucked away in tiny New Haven with little of real import to do, away from all the places his expertise could be better utilized?"

"We had plenty to do yesterday. And he travels a fair bit."

She let out a long breath. "Well, yesterday was a rare occurrence, right? This is one of the most peaceful places on Rega. Why would Ileom remain here?"

"Why wouldn't he?" Rain countered. "And maybe it's peaceful because he does."

She rocked her head slowly from side to side, giving that consideration. "I don't know. He is a mystery ... aloof and prickly. He's from Jeveria, by the way, but don't tell him I told you that. It's not any fun being on his bad side."

She ... knew him personally? After acting like she didn't? The mystery deepened. He didn't know how to tactfully pursue that thread, and they weren't far from Sheran. He let it drop, wondering suddenly why she hadn't yet mentioned her key.

Just after turning onto the road to Sheran, which lay two miles east, Antara asked, "Was it tiring?"

"What?"

"When you used magic. When you healed me."

He tried to remember, but the impressions and images remained fuzzy. "I don't know. I guess, maybe. I was already tired. It was my first—" He clamped his mouth shut, not wanting to say 'battle.' But the way her lips twitched told him she understood. He stared ahead, jaw clenched, the clash becoming vivid again, roiling his insides.

"Your first battle." Her tone was cool, and she paused only a moment before asking, "You acquitted yourself well?"

He rolled his shoulders, and they ended up in a hunched position. "I guess so."

"Does Ileom think so?"

He squinted instead of responding, and again she guessed correctly.

"You were promoted."

He nodded, frowning at how self-conscious that made him feel in front of her.

"Did Ileom know about your access to magical abilities? I presume your girlfriend has been teaching you a little, not the Academy."

He shook his head. "No, he didn't know. He does now, of course. And she's been trying. She thinks I have a little potential."

She gave a light chuckle. "Oh, Rain. As I said, you have *considerable* potential. Incredible, actually. Are you sure Ileom didn't suspect?"

Rain swallowed and shrugged, having no idea what Ileom thought of people who could use magic, and wondering why he hadn't shown much reaction when Rain had described its use to him. Antara remained silent for a time, and Rain began to ponder what he would say when he rode into Sheran with Antara beside him. How would he introduce her? He was about to ask where exactly she was from when she spoke.

"Master Ileom knew the group was coming, and that I was with them, but I don't know how he knew we were in trouble. Or that *I* was, specifically. That intrigues me, though I have a suspicion. Things are changing, young guardsman. And rather quickly."

Rain once again felt at a complete loss. He had no idea what she was talking about. "It doesn't matter, does it? We were too late, anyway."

"Not to save the key."

"Is *that* what the bandits wanted?" That only made sense if it wasn't a mere house key.

She pressed her lips tight as if she'd said too much, then pinned him again with those eyes. He might as well have been encased in rock.

"Do you still have it?"

He nodded, then reached for the tunic pocket where it hid.

She held up a hand. "I don't want it back. I gave you your charge. You must deliver it to the prophet."

He gave her a dumbfounded look. "Why me? And which prophet? This continent is crawling with people claiming to be prophets or prophetesses."

She let out a breath touched with exasperation. "I wish I knew which one. Ileom might." She instantly, uncannily calmed. "I'm confident about you, though. Part of me wants to take back the key. It is powerful, and ancient. But I … can't. Again, Ileom may have some insight. He knows that I recovered it … or rather, found it. You'll have to ask him."

He stared at the road ahead for a moment. "Does it have magical power?"

She didn't respond, just sat her horse straighter. Sheran had come into view, nestled between two low hills with well-ordered farm plots surrounding it.

"You may tell them I'm from Misery, in Chalace," she said a few seconds later. "I came north to find my brother, who ran away from home. My father sent me. He is a minor merchant."

Rain glanced at her. He had detected a somber note. He couldn't tell whether the words were true or just a cover. But he knew he was in way over his head.

6

A few minutes later, the first people from Sheran noticed them as they approached the small but busy town with its quaint gardens and clean streets. Rain's village of Mari's Mask was messier and homier, but he appreciated the precise predictability of Sheran. A teenage girl and two younger boys, all carrying laundry baskets, stopped to watch them pass. The town's blacksmith, whose name Rain couldn't remember, looked up, squinted, then stepped free of the awning in front of his shop to get a closer look.

"Rain Barynd?" he asked, eyes taking in his face, then the uniform. He sounded uncertain.

"Yes, it's me," Rain responded. "I'm here to see my parents and uncle."

"Ah, yes ... um, well"—he glanced at Antara and quickly averted his eyes—"I'll go get the mayor."

The man had already turned and headed up the street, thereby missing Rain's quizzical expression. Rain didn't need to see the mayor, who was probably out in one of the fields with the others. Perhaps his parents and uncle were with him?

He noted the growing crowd of children staring at both of them, mostly Antara. He spotted more adults, too, who made themselves visible while continuing their tasks. Sun Tamer snorted. It almost sounded like a chuckle.

"Well, I think we can get down now," he said to Antara.

She nodded, then took care with her dress as she dismounted. When his feet touched the ground, he spied some kind of pants or leggings she wore underneath, then looked away. He'd wondered before why more women didn't just wear pants, though he couldn't deny how radiant she looked in that dress, standing in the brilliant sun as she soothed her horse, which he could now tell was a stallion.

"What's his name?" he asked, nodding toward it.

"Cyclone," she responded, patting his neck. "I'm just borrowing him from the city's stables."

Rain had never seen that horse before, but the stables were large. "He looks fast."

"So does yours. What's her name?"

"Sun Tamer."

The name made Antara blink, as if in surprise, recognition, or both. But then she smiled. "That is a wonderful name."

Rain led Sun Tamer toward the small square in the center of the village, Antara and Cyclone keeping pace beside them. A young boy came up and asked if he really was a Council Guard. His mother shushed him and drew him away. Antara didn't get any direct questions, but several girls whispered excitedly to each other as they watched, accompanied by gasps and giggles.

A dry well stood at the center of the square, a new main well having been dug at a location divined just outside the village. Rain secured Sun Tamer's reins to a post, then scratched his head, wondering what they could do while they waited.

Luckily, the mayor came bustling toward them, flanked by Rain's uncle and parents, all wearing broad smiles.

His mother broke into a run the last several yards. "Rain!" She nearly knocked him over with her high-speed embrace. "What a surprise! And what are you wearing?"

He grinned, then looked at his father, who, along with the mayor and his uncle, inspected the new uniform with unbelieving eyes.

"Well, it's kind of a long story, but Master Ileom made me a Council Guard, Second Rank. Just yesterday."

He enjoyed observing the growing wonder in the eyes of his family, and then Antara jumped in. "He saved my life yesterday. Brigands, south of the city."

His mother gaped, alternating her gaze between him and Antara, taking in her fine dress.

"Who are you?" asked the mayor. "I mean, forgive me." He bowed. "Welcome to our humble village. I am Ordren, mayor of Sheran. We are not accustomed to hosting anyone of such refined … lineage." By his face, Rain wasn't sure the mayor had wanted to choose that particular word. Antara *was* stunning, though. Any man's mind might go blank staring at her, presuming high royalty. Rain blinked, realizing his had.

"My name is Antara. I'm visiting from Ta'Voran, in Minifor. My parents operate a spice-trading business there."

Rain couldn't guess why she had changed her story, but it sounded better than being from Misery, even though he had no idea what Misery—or the island country of Chalace—was really like. At least she hadn't claimed to be a princess or a queen. He didn't want *that* much attention.

"Well, we are pleased you have graced us with a visit," said Ordren, spreading his hands wide and bowing again, as if she had indeed declared noble ancestry.

She laughed. "The pleasure is mine." She looped an arm through Rain's, and he almost flinched at the action. "Rain is my bodyguard for the day—Master Ileom's orders—and he wanted to visit his parents." She gave them a nod as she nudged him.

"Oh," Rain said, "yes, um, Deneac and Yrtsa, my parents. And my uncle, Sesig."

Antara executed a perfect curtsy, even while holding his arm, prompting a cough from his father and a clumsy attempt at imitation by his mother. Rain wasn't sure she had ever curtsied in her life.

After a couple of awkward seconds, the mayor clapped his hands. "We should celebrate later, when everyone has returned from the fields. We can prepare a small feast. And we have instruments. We can dance, right here in the square. Are you, um, staying the night?"

Rain started to say they weren't, but Antara corrected him, which greatly pleased Ordren.

Rain groaned inwardly. He liked the idea of food, his belly rumbling in agreement, but not the dancing. Antara would expect him to join her, and that had *not* been part of Ileom's Guard training. He had done the simple dances of children growing up, but never the adult ones. He had no idea how they went, having paid little attention, always goofing around with his friends instead.

After another long hug and an uncomfortably thorough wellness check by his mother, everyone went back to work except Ordren, who made sure the horses were cared for and then took Rain and Antara on a walking tour of the village and its environs. The man could talk, non-stop. It must be one of the main requirements of becoming mayor.

At the close of the day, and after a sumptuous meal which Rain made last as long as possible, Antara asked that he dance with her only once, and she was very patient. When the number ended, she skittered away to dance with the mayor. Rain realized with a jolt that he hadn't wanted their time to end. But, reminding himself how awful a dancer he was, how many times he'd scuffed her fine leather riding boots—mainly by stepping on her toes—*and* that he had a girlfriend, he retreated to the edges of the gathering just inside the light of the cooking fires and torches, happy to watch while conversing with his parents. That is, when they weren't dancing themselves. He didn't see any of his friends or cousins, unfortunately. Of course, they all had apprenticeships in nearby hamlets, and none of them had known he was coming. If not for the mayor's long-winded tour—and Antara's presence—perhaps he could have found a couple of them.

Ordren and his wife offered Antara a bed, while Rain stayed with his parents at his uncle's place. His mother's oldest brother was a recent widower, and their children had all grown up and left the house, so there was plenty of space. All three peppered him with more questions, marveling at his sudden status as a Council Guardsman and the appearance of Antara; also the inexplicable horror of the barbarous slaughter. When he mentioned he had taken her to Tashiel's house, his mother burst with astonishment.

"You took her *there*? Why?" He had excluded the white bands from his explanations, along with the magical healing. His parents might understand, but his uncle had no love for magic, not after the healers had made his wife's condition worse, not better, leading to her unexpected passing.

He shrugged. "It was late. Her wounds weren't severe, and I thought Tashiel could help with them—you know, because she studies at the Academy. I think Antara really just needed to rest. I left her there and returned to the barracks."

"Well, she looks none the worse for wear," his mother noted, "so Tashiel must have done a good job. Was she ... I mean, does Tashiel know you and Antara came here today?"

He told the truth. "No. It was kind of ... last minute."

"Oh."

"So, Master Ileom tasked you to protect her," said his father, nodding as if that made perfect sense, which it still didn't. None of it did.

"Yes." He supposed Antara's declaration was sort of true. Ileom *had* sent him to help her after the battle.

His father and uncle asked a dizzying new array of detailed questions about the battle itself, pausing several times to calm and comfort his mother, whose face became paler and paler as the recounting progressed, even though he tried to leave out the most horrific parts. In the end, though, she seemed proud, like his father and uncle. That left him with such a warm feeling he slept more soundly than he had in months.

∞

Rain and Antara departed at mid-morning the next day, after a breakfast that could have passed as another feast. The village was completely taken with Antara. Word had spread throughout the night to the outlying farms and several other villages, so the numbers in Sheran had swelled to more than double. Before they mounted their horses, she gave a brief speech appropriate to a monarch, and Rain half-expected people to start pledging allegiance to her. She expressed her deep gratitude for the hospitality she and Rain had been shown, voicing a sincere-sounding wish that she could return someday.

That seemed a dubious half-promise, but the villagers—the mayor and his wife included—crooned with delight.

As the celebrated pair progressed toward the main road, out of sight of Sheran, Antara turned to Rain. "Can you show me the talisman?" After he gave her a blank look, she added, "The key."

Duh. All that food had slowed his brain. He retrieved it, holding it up to glisten in the sunlight. His eyes met hers as he prepared to speak … and in a flash, she wasn't there. And it was dark. And he was on his own two feet. He spun right, then left, trying to make out anything in the inky, cloud-covered night. Had he passed out? Was he dreaming? He poked himself in a few places and felt his uniform. He was still dressed the same. He took a deep breath, noting the crispness of the air. Its scents were … foreign to him. And he couldn't remember ever smelling in a dream before.

His eyes began to acclimate. He found himself in a field of some sort of grain, about quarter grown. Twenty yards ahead stood a fence, made of posts with taut cords running between, too thin to be rope. That must mean it was expensive, so he was trespassing on the land of someone wealthy. Rich people often had guards protecting their homes and property, and he instinctively felt for his sword, letting a small sigh of relief escape as his hand felt the solid, reassuring hilt. Crouching to make himself smaller, he moved cautiously toward the fence. Beyond lay a road of hard-packed gravel, dark and almost perfectly smooth—another sign of prosperity.

After scaling the fence, he stepped onto the road and followed it up a slight incline, then dropped to a kneeling position as he spotted a house, definitely large, with several lights burning inside. Bright lights, which could mean exotic oils. He had no idea what to do. But, he reasoned, if he was indeed dreaming, which was the only logical explanation, he could surely afford to get a closer look at the manor. It rose two stories and boasted a covered porch with square pillars running half its length in the front. Two lights created wide pools of light on the outside, their glow steady and inviting.

It took him several minutes, playing along with the dream and moving with utmost care, to near the manor. He crossed a broad swath of short-cut grass—probably maintained using sheep or goats—and positioned himself near one side. Then he listened intently, noting muted voices and faint music. Multiple instruments fabricated those tunes. Hired musicians? He crept next to a window, noting its crystal clear glass, another luxury. Where *was* he? Why would he be dreaming this? How could his weak, uneducated mind even conceive of it?

Focused light from a hooded lantern suddenly flashed in his eyes, followed by a gruff voice speaking in a tongue he didn't recognize. He instinctively rolled away from the house, then unsheathed his sword, still grasping the key in his off hand. The light followed him, then flashed brilliantly ... and there was Antara, on her horse, under a bright sky, an expression of concern and intense curiosity suffusing her face. She had moved Cyclone up against a motionless Sun Tamer, and she grabbed Rain's arm as he swayed in the saddle.

His head swiveled, disorientation assaulting him in waves. His breath shortened, and he felt himself beginning to sweat. After a few seconds, he was able to calm himself and focus on Antara.

"What ... happened?"

She squinted. "I was about to ask you the same thing. You disappeared in the blink of an eye. Sun Tamer and Cyclone stopped, and we moved to the side of the road. Several minutes passed. I was ready to tell anyone who happened by that you had received an urgent call from nature." She quirked an eyebrow, lips twitching. "Then, suddenly, you're back, clearly dazed."

Confusion danced a raucous jig in his head. He didn't even remember getting off Sun Tamer, much less getting back on. Wait ... *disappeared?*

"Are you all right?" she asked, and the worry seemed genuine.

He thought about that as he examined mind and body, even wiggling fingers and toes and taking the deepest breath he could draw. "I think so. But I had the strangest dream."

"You think you dreamed?"

He shook his head, not hiding his bewilderment. "Yes, I must have. But I was in a place I'm sure I've never seen before. It was night, and I crossed a rich man's fence, walked along a fine road, and came upon a grand manor, which I started to investigate. A guard discovered me, shining a blazing light in my eyes and speaking a strange language. Then I woke up."

She swallowed, and there was no mistaking the nervous glint in her eyes, which dropped to the key. He loosened his grip on it.

"You traveled," she said in a whisper, then seemed shocked she had voiced the words.

"I ... *what?*"

Her eyes wandered in the distance. "Traveled. Physically transported yourself by magical means. And then you traveled back, arriving atop your horse, even though she had moved. Remarkable. But how did you travel with just the key?"

"Just the key?" He gazed at the mysterious talisman, then hastily put it back in his pocket as if it were hot and might burn his hand. Some magical objects were said to be highly unpredictable, having been infused by powerful sorcerers who were themselves unstable.

His voice carried a plea as he looked back up at her. "I don't know what just happened. But maybe you should take it back." His hand fluttered near the pocket.

Her eyes still navigated distant reaches, though she gripped his hand and moved it away. "Your magical talent is powerful, and as yet untamed. Somehow, that must have triggered the key by itself. I have never heard of such a thing ... though, to be fair, this is fairly new to all of us." She again appeared to have said too much.

"By *itself?*" Vines of panic wound around his neck, prickling his skin, slowly squeezing.

She finally rested her gaze on him, which brought a reassurance he couldn't define.

"You don't have the book."

"The book?"

"The key opens a book, which has to be read, and they operate together."

"To … help someone go somewhere, without, um …?"

"Yes." Her eyes began another peregrine journey in the skies as she continued. "Someone has found the book matched to this key, stolen from the Oracle of Sephyr in Jeveria—Ileom is certain of that. We knew they would seek the key as well, but we found it first, down in Mero Vothas."

"You and Ileom are working together?"

"Not by choice. We barely know each other, and his reputation is … complicated. But if this key were to fall into the wrong hands, it could mean disaster for all of us."

Rain scrunched up his face. "How?"

Antara fixed him with a gaze more serious than any his parents or even Ileom had ever achieved. "Think about it a moment. Remember what Ileom has been teaching you, which I'm positive goes well beyond what it takes to be a Council Guard in tiny, sheltered New Haven."

He closed his eyes, then popped them back open. "Do you mean …?" His imagination ran wild. "They could move armies and supply trains? Or assassins? They would be impossible to counter."

"Not impossible. Fortunately, there *are* limits to what the key can do. But very difficult, yes. Any general would kill to get his or her hands on such a tactical advantage."

Rain swallowed, his mind trying and failing to grasp the full magnitude. There were so many dangerous possibilities. "So … where did I go, or was it random?"

She stared at him for several seconds, eyebrows drawn down, then seemed to make a decision. "The key transported you to another world—not anywhere on Tenris. And it wasn't random. We must find Ileom."

Rain and Antara began their search for Ileom at his office in the Keep. Not finding him there, they began the process of scouring all of New Haven, both inside and outside the fortress.

They came across Tashiel near the Academy, on an errand for one of the Master Mages. Seeing Antara with Rain, she turned a strange purplish color. She looked aghast at Antara's dress, as if it were the most repulsive thing she'd ever seen.

"We have to find Master Ileom and give him some new information," explained Rain, lending urgency to his tone, hoping she would understand it was 'business.'

"I'm sure I don't know where he would be," she responded tartly, pointedly ignoring Antara, "but my parents and I will expect you for dinner."

"Yes, of course. As soon as we find Ileom, I'll come over."

That seemed to mollify her somewhat, along with his impressive new uniform, which she felt by running a possessive hand down his chest, and they continued their search.

They found it impossible to get an audience with Chestan the Eminent, Holy Priest of God's Favor and the supreme governing authority of the city, despite several protestations from Antara, including one whispered into the ear of the Master Secretary. They were finally allowed to see one of the other members of the Council of Eight—the least influential and respected of them, unfortunately—a hunch-backed man in his late eighties with beady black eyes and tiny spectacles named Elidim. His office, high in the Sun tower, was elegant but cluttered, mainly with ancient books and strange-looking artifacts. Rain didn't even know how to describe some of them. One was a skull, but it looked odd in its proportions. It was also a light green.

After Elidim's aide showed them to a pair of plush chairs and exited, the aged priest steadied his gaze on them from across his messy desk, tilting his curly-whiskered chin down to see over the top of his spectacles.

"You have an important message for Captain Ileom, I understand?"

Antara had asked Rain to let her do most of the talking, and he was perfectly happy with that arrangement.

"Your Eminence, I am here at Master Ileom's invitation. As you know, my caravan was attacked near Jerel's Altar, and …" her voice cracked as she blinked through tears "… no one else survived."

After a slight pause, Elidim nodded. "Yes, I heard about that unfortunate incident. Terrible business. Master Ileom is quite incensed."

It was hard to tell if the attack bothered Elidim or not, and it had been far more than an 'unfortunate incident.' Rain had never met one of the High Priests in person, had only heard a handful of sermons from them. They were said to commune with God and his Witnesses through the ethereal servants, which some called angels, and that sometimes they were difficult to understand because their thoughts existed on a higher plane. Trying to make sense of that always confused him.

Antara sniffled, seemingly unaffected by the lack of empathy. In fact, her face reflected the utmost respect, even awe. It looked odd on her.

"He vowed revenge," she said, "and he has a lead on where to start looking for the person who ordered the attack." She took a deep breath, eyeing the high priest carefully. "As you probably know, I was on a secret mission, traveling to Istarrea. That mission has been compromised. I need to return to my people as soon as possible, and I should carry whatever information Ileom has found back with me."

The pause lasted much longer this time, and Rain wondered which 'people' she had made up for this performance. Elidim's eyes closed as he thought, eyeballs rolling around in random patterns. After a few seconds, Rain suspected he'd fallen asleep and was already dreaming. He *was* old.

Finally, his eyelids trembled, then snapped apart, causing Rain to lean back involuntarily. His eyes shone with an amber light as he fixed them first on Antara, then on Rain.

"You are a member of the Council Guard. Sound the alarm. The enemy approaches."

Rain froze. "What enemy? Nearing the city? *New Haven?*" It was inconceivable. Nobody attacked New Haven … except the incredibly rare group of bandits.

"Yes, and do it now." Sternness fired his brittle voice. "Start with the Academy. We will need their magic, as much as they can muster."

Ileom had explained scenarios like this to his trainees, but those were academic exercises. Real soldiers rarely had to deal with obeying orders that didn't make any sense, right? And he had been a Council Guard for less than two days! He glanced at Antara, and the alarm in her eyes, followed by a sharp nod, was all the motivation he needed. He unstuck from his chair and bolted for the door, leaving her and Elidim to deal with the rest of the Council. Wait, were they just trying to get rid of him? He paused, then realized how ridiculous that sounded. Why give him such a momentous order? There were far more plausible ways to do it.

"*Now*, Rain," reiterated Antara, and that got him moving again.

The Academy wasn't far, but only if you were a bird. It was in a different tower, which meant he needed to descend far enough to cross one of the delicate arching bridges, then climb again. Upon reaching the great hardwood doors of the Academy, etched with so many lines of archaic script he wondered if anyone could read both doors in a full month, he pounded on the lacquered surface.

"By order of High Priest Elidim, mobilize for the defense of the city!"

He waited for a response, but none came immediately. He knew the mages had ways to observe him standing before the door. Were they confused, too? They had never seen this particular Council Guardsman before. Nor someone so young in the Second Rank.

He was about to shout again when one of the doors opened inward on well-oiled hinges—whether by manual or magical means, Rain had no idea. A tall man in the dark, blue-gray robes of a Master Mage emerged and stood calmly before him, clasped hands nearly hidden in wide, silver-embroidered sleeves. His broad silver belt shimmered in the light of a powerful orb floating just above his left shoulder. Rain squinted as the man spoke.

"Who are you, young man?" The way he said 'young man' inferred 'child.'

"Rain Barynd, Master Mage, newly promoted by Master Ileom."

"And he sent you?"

"No, Master. He has apparently left the fortress. We—me and the woman who survived the bandit attack yesterday at Jerel's Altar—met with High Priest Elidim, trying to find Master Ileom. It was Elidim who ordered me to sound the alarm."

The man glanced around, seeming puzzled. "I hear no bells, no horns."

Rain's neck grew warm. "I was told to come here first, without delay. The High Priest said the enemy approaches."

"What enemy?"

"I'm sorry, sir, I do not know. I'm just following his orders." Rain lowered his eyes, hoping it would be enough. He itched to be away, toward the sentry posts, then the barracks. They would listen. Well, he was almost sure they would. *Would* they? And did they even really need to? The longer he stood in front of the Master Mage, the more foolish he felt. A confused old man—probably senile, which would explain his lower standing among the Eight—had given him a preposterous-sounding order. But what else could he do?

"Very well. I—"

"Rain, what are you doing here?" Tashiel's voice made him jump, and he looked up to see her standing by the Master Mage, dressed in her light brown trainee robes with the simple corded belt of black.

"I … had a message to deliver … from High Priest Elidim. Antara and I were meeting with him when—"

"That *woman*." There was no mistaking the acid in her voice. She narrowed her eyes. "What were you doing with her? Still 'searching' for Ileom?"

Rain's eyes widened. Not only did he not have time to tell the story, he didn't *want* to tell it. Not ever. Suddenly, he too felt the enemy coming, whether as a real, physical threat or not.

"Yes, we haven't located Master Ileom yet. And Elidim sent me here."

"High Priest Elidim," corrected the Master Mage.

Rain blinked at him. "Yes, the High Priest." He bowed low, in part to avoid Tashiel's glare. "I must go now, to warn others."

"Of what?" Tashiel demanded.

Rain shifted his bow toward her, which he'd never done before, but it seemed appropriate in the shadow of the Academy. The gray stone of the walls loomed darkly. "That an enemy approaches, according to High Priest Elidim. I'm sorry. I must be on my way." With that, he began running through the tower, planning his sequence of stops. He was fully committed now. He ignored Tashiel's cries to turn back.

⟨∞⟩

Less than an hour later, as the sun reached its mid-afternoon mark, soldiers and mages of New Haven stood together atop the battlements of the Fortress of the Four Stars for the first time since well before the births of Rain's parents. He hadn't thought to ask Elidim from what direction the enemy would come, but since the Dunroad lay to the west, it made more sense that an army would approach from there, especially if they had siege equipment.

The fanciful outer wall of the city, unfortunately, was unsuited to hosting defensive emplacements or troops, so most of the Sarenite defenders had set up on the western side of the Keep, with some on the north, south, and east as well. A few thousand citizens from the city had been allowed inside, but then the doors had been shut.

The ancient High Priest hadn't shown himself yet. Nor had any of his companions or their leader, Chestan 'the-not-so-Eminent-in-an-emergency.' Master Ileom remained curiously absent, too, meaning that Master

Sarnick, a much younger man than Ileom who had never seen real combat, commanded the troops.

Rain had joined Kyne and two other new Council Guards on the east side, high above the gates. He had hastily donned plated armor, well oiled and in pristine condition, over his crisp uniform tunic. Mismatched greaves protected the fronts and backs of his legs. In the chaos of the storeroom below the barracks, he hadn't found gauntlets or a helm that would fit, but a guard protected his sword arm.

He wished Brem were with them. But Brem was gone, while Garrett still lived. Maybe God and his Witnesses knew something he couldn't grasp, but it didn't seem a fair trade.

"You're *sure* that old geezer Elidim wanted everyone to mobilize?" asked Kyne. "Do you think it was a drill maybe?"

Rain gave an exasperated sigh. This was at least the twentieth time Kyne or a passing officer or mage had posed some variation of the same question to him. "I told you, I'm sure. And I don't know. I wish Master Ileom were here."

"Where could he have gone?"

Rain shrugged. "I have no idea. It's like he vanished into thin air. Nobody knows where he is or where he might be."

"How many members does the Legion have now?"

"About two hundred and fifty, I think. And we only have a hundred. The mages never tell anyone how many they are, and not even Tashiel will give me a hint, but there have to be at least thirty, plus their initiates. A messenger was sent north to Istarrea, too. They'll send help."

"If we need it," boasted Kyne, then smiled. "By the way, has your girl-friend shown you how proud she is of you making the Guard?" He winked at the others, and they laughed. Rain tried to laugh along, without giving an answer, but he probably just made himself look stupid. They took it as some sort of crude affirmation and laughed harder, until one of the officers of the Legion standing nearby snapped his fingers and glowered at them.

They quieted, but Kyne still snickered softly. "What's it like to kiss her when she uses magic?"

Rain's face lit on fire, and Kyne had a devil of a time containing himself … at least until a pair of booms sounded, followed by impact tremors emanating from the other side of the fortress. Rain swallowed hard as he joined every other soldier in staring west across the Keep. Several more booms followed, producing similar crashes.

Colorful arcs of smoke painted the sky, one after the other and sometimes in groups, each heralding fire and death, causing the stones of the mighty fortress to quiver. Counter arcs flew from the battlements, the mages of the city responding. If the enemy had come from the west, through the barbarian lands, where were the Istarreans from the border forts? Perhaps the attackers had traveled from the south, and then turned east, but how would they have passed through Mero Vothas? It seemed surreal that New Haven City was under assault of any kind. What could be the purpose? Was it the talisman?

The Legion officer shouted orders, directing the men to the western side. Easier said than done given the complicated architecture, but most responded with promptness. A few delayed, terror-struck, one man claiming in a high-pitched voice that someone needed to keep watch on the eastern side as well. Several of his companions joined the refrain. Rain ignored them as he and the other Council Guards raced along the quickest path to the ground level so they could cross the Keep and climb atop the higher western battlements.

As they sprinted through the Grand Courtyard, next to the Yard of Petitioning, he could have sworn one of the towers swayed briefly, but that was impossible. The bones of the fortress were incredibly strong, reinforced by old, enduring magic. They could never fall. Or so he had been taught.

Just before they entered the base of one of the western towers, Rain heard a thundering, unmistakable voice. "Rain! Rain Barynd! To me!"

His mind stumbled, followed by his feet, and he nearly planted his face in the stone. Turning on one knee, with a hand to the ground, he spotted Ileom striding toward him with the largest sword Rain had ever seen resting on his shoulder, a massive two-hander that seemed to absorb the light of the sun and then reflect it through its owner.

Rain hastened to obey, meeting his master amid a sea of guards, legionnaires, and poorly trained militiamen rushing toward the walls and towers.

Ileom laid a heavy, gauntleted hand on his shoulder. His armor looked new, some of the finest Rain had ever seen, polished to a high sheen. "I need you to carry a message to the Istarreans in the northern forts. Their comrades to the west have been completely overrun, and this enemy is powerful, with new weapons we haven't seen before. Istarrea will need to call up its reserves and every bit of magic it can muster." He removed his hand and reached for something tucked behind his belt. "The scroll in this tube contains more details. Get Sun Tamer and go to the postern door on the north side of the eastern gates. Hurry. Ride fast. You must not delay."

Tongue temporarily tied, Rain saluted and took the scroll case. Ileom's hand returned to his shoulder, squeezing hard. "You will have opportunities to prove your bravery again before the day is done. You must remember your promise to Antara to find that prophet. The talisman she gave you is far more important than you know … and is likely why this enemy came. They *must* not have it."

Rain's hand twitched toward the pocket where the strange key nestled. He already had a fair and unsettling idea of the key's importance. He yearned to hand it over to Ileom, but he knew what the response would be.

"What prophet?" he asked instead. "How do I find him?"

Ileom's gaze rose to the walls as another massive blast echoed. He frowned, his eyes blazing. When he fixed them again on Rain, their heat was palpable.

"That is your task, not mine. I have work to do here. I have some surprises for this enemy—things I no longer need to hide—and the central tower will not fall. I'm also not accustomed to repeating orders."

Rain swallowed, taking another quick look at those rushing to the defense of the city. He realized he viewed it as *his* city now. It had always seemed to exist at a distance, even when he was inside, training to be a defender. In just two short days, his world had been stood on its head.

Despite confusion and uncertainty threatening to overpower him, he saluted again, then raced toward the south stables and Sun Tamer.

Strangely, he could almost sense her anticipation. And then it hit him squarely how dangerous his mission was. If this enemy had overrun the border forts and were attacking the city with such obvious fury in search of the talisman, anyone fleeing with clear and unpanicked purpose would become a priority target for their inevitable scouts and skirmishers. Well, it shouldn't be too hard to appear panicked, since it was so close to the truth. He tried to swallow again, but his throat had gone dry.

Nobody was watching the postern door, though plenty of frantic people passed him rushing in all directions. He managed to flag down one poorly equipped militiaman to make sure the outer door was secured after he exited. The man couldn't seem to decide if Rain was crazy for wanting to get outside the protection of the Keep's impregnable walls of legend … or cowardly but wise for fleeing. Either way, he asked at least twice if he could join him. After another round of crashing and shaking lent some credence to the latter, Rain informed him in a confident voice that he had an important mission to perform for Master Ileom, who would rally the defenses, and the man complied.

Sun Tamer maintained an impressive calm as Rain led her through the trembling, dark corridor to the outside. After the militiaman had locked and buttressed the door, Rain wondered if it would matter. Based on a new crescendo of sky-splitting cracks along the entire western side of the city, the enemy would certainly breach soon. He heard far fewer responding magics from the masters of the Academy, and New Haven didn't possess any working ballistae or trebuchets—just polished display pieces.

He shuddered as realization dawned that the unprepared city would likely be lost. Ileom had promised the Sun tower wouldn't fall, but how could he guarantee that, and what purpose would it serve, anyway? Was there a secret underground escape tunnel? He'd never heard rumors of one. Besides, where could it lead that would make any difference? What would happen to Tashiel and her parents, and all the other people in New Haven? What was already happening to them? As he peered down the slope from the Keep into the eastern part of the city, he noted hundreds upon hundreds of people fleeing along the streets. Absolute bedlam reigned as they piled up, trying to squeeze through the eastern gates with whatever they could carry on their backs, along with the few animals that weren't quartered in the Keep's stables. A few were nimble enough to climb over the wall. Once beyond, the panicked mass of humanity became a geyser, scattering multiple directions, but mainly straight east toward the foothills. He sprang onto Sun Tamer's back as the muscles along his spine tightened. Part of him wanted to go back, to fight and die with the other soldiers. That notion still seemed impossibly foreign to him. And he had his orders. He was a Council Guardsman, Second Rank, and Master Ileom himself had set the task. The troublesome talisman burned in his pocket.

He guided Sun Tamer carefully at first through the growing throngs, though it was slow going. So he let her take more of the lead. She didn't go berserk like she had during the battle with the bandits, but she aggressively moved people out of the way, sometimes with a warning snort or whinny, sometimes with chest or foreleg. In a couple of instances, Rain felt guilty as people stumbled and cast him terrified, disbelieving looks. He didn't have time to explain that Master Ileom's message *must* get to Istarrea, along with the key.

They had just passed through the outer gates and broken free of most of the milieu when Rain froze. Antara approached from the area south of the gate, riding Cyclone and staring calmly but intently at him as people streamed around her.

Sun Tamer turned and trotted toward them without any prompting from Rain, neighing to warn people not to cross her path. When they were close, he asked, "How did you know where I was?"

"I saw Ileom speaking with you, and then you ran straight for the stables. You also have the key, and he knows that. He obviously sent you out of the city, as he should have."

"Yes, he did." He didn't elaborate. Nor did he ask how she had reached the outer gates first.

"Well, I'm coming with you. North, I presume?"

He nodded, and Sun Tamer turned parallel to Cyclone, the throng of panicked New Haveners giving both horses a careful berth as they began to canter toward the foothills.

They passed the first road heading north—the ring road. The second was the one they had taken the day before to get to Sheran. Another, farther on, plied its own path northward, with better cover from hills and trees. That seemed the best option. The traffic east hadn't lessened, the general ruckus increasing as if people felt they were far enough from the city to talk—or shout or scream—without the as-yet-unseen enemy overhearing and targeting them. A few began to comment on Rain's armor, weapons, and fine horse, openly wondering why he wasn't defending the city. Antara told him to ignore them, but it started to get under his skin. He almost responded a few times, but Sun Tamer and Cyclone moved faster than the crowd.

After making the turn north, the way opened up, and they could let the horses gallop for stretches. Rain craned his neck to witness tall plumes of smoke rising from the Keep and the western side of the city. It seemed the entire area might soon be ablaze, and his mind couldn't begin to comprehend it. At the first walking pause, Antara spoke. "I assume Ileom has ideas for the Istarrean mobilization, but what else did he ask you to do?"

He gave Antara a frustrated look. He sensed she already knew the answer. "He mentioned the prophet again. No name, no location, no sect. How am I supposed to find him?"

"Or her. I've been thinking about that, recalling some of the histories I've studied, and it doesn't have to be a man."

"Right, so the ocean is now double the size," he said with a moan.

Antara cast her gaze over the few heads bobbing around them, including several children who seemed to have cried themselves out as they shuffled along with their parents, most of whom had been shedding their own tears. "This may sound strange to you, Rain—or maybe it won't—but God caused your path to cross with mine, and I suspect Ileom had a hand in helping to orchestrate it. I don't know him as well as I should. And I don't know the answer to your question. But I *do* know you have been chosen for a reason. It won't be easy, but you will never be without help from somewhere."

He didn't feel nearly as comforted by that as she probably hoped. Not at all, in fact. It was just something else he couldn't fathom at the moment.

Screams erupted in a new chorus less than a quarter mile ahead of them, and Rain stood in his stirrups to improve his view. As he feared, elements of the enemy army had rounded the city, spreading out and hacking their way through frightened citizens, asking questions of a few and searching the fallen.

Not surprisingly, the majority were meanly dressed barbarians. But some were not. The strangers wore light-green uniforms with no discernible armor, and while a few carried swords, bows, and long spears like the barbarians, most possessed magic, wielding large, strange-looking wands that spit death with alarming efficiency.

"We have to get off the road!" yelled Antara. "Follow me!"

Rain tore his mesmerized gaze from the awful scene of macabre mayhem, noting that their only viable path sent them southeast. Cyclone and Sun Tamer broke into a dangerous gallop over uneven terrain, and Rain heard a shout from the direction of the attackers. He looked back to see several of the mages turning their oddly constructed wands toward him and Antara. He tensed for the impact of the magic, feeling more for Sun Tamer than himself.

Antara called out a phrase Rain couldn't understand, and a bluish sheen hazed his vision, both ahead and behind. Impacts from the mages' weapons pelted it, but nothing got through, and the horses increased speed at Antara's urging. Amazed, he stared at her back as she leaned low over Cyclone's neck, flaming hair rippling wildly in the wind of their swift passage.

After at least two full minutes, he thought they might be clear, but upon cresting a small rise he spotted a smaller skirmishing party less than twenty yards away, made up of a dozen barbarians accompanied by two of the green-clad soldiers, both with startling blond hair. They seemed just as surprised as he and Antara. As the one with a wand moved to bring it to bear, Rain drew his belt knife and threw it, instinctively forming heated winds around the blade as he willed it to fly fast and true. A loud thunk into the chest of the armorless mage signaled success, but the other attackers spread out to trap them.

Ignoring the shock at what he'd just done with a simple thrown dagger, Rain drew his sword and aimed Sun Tamer for two of the barbarians, each of which brandished a wicked-looking hooked spear. He thought to throw his sword like he had his knife, but there were two of them, and they were ready for the charge. Instead, he brought Sun Tamer up short and vaulted to the ground, swinging in compact, powerful strokes on light feet to fend off the spears and engage the bodies of his assailants. A quick slash wounded one barbarian badly in both legs, sending him to the ground, and after another parry, Rain ran the other through, just below the sternum. He paused only to be aware of his surroundings, then jumped back onto Sun Tamer's back.

Antara had done … something … to a group of barbarians nearby, along with the other green-clad soldier. They staggered as if drunk and weak, weapons aimless. Had he heard something, like a small clap of thunder? She pointed to the escape route she and Rain had just created. As one they urged their mounts forward, aiming east, and after another pair of minutes, with the distant sounds of the city's death throes fading rapidly, Rain finally slowed Sun Tamer. She didn't act tired, but any run over unfamiliar territory, especially off-road, carried considerable risk of her breaking a leg.

Keeping the horses at a fast canter, they progressed several more miles until they had penetrated deep into the forested foothills. They hadn't detected any pursuit, nor had they come across any other unfriendlies. At last, after crossing a small stream—barely a trickle given the lateness of the season—Antara called a halt, stating the horses needed some rest. Rain agreed, though he still felt nervous.

"Where's the nearest town from here?" she asked after kneeling at the stream and slaking her thirst with a cupped hand.

Rain tried to place their position using the maps in his head. "Maybe two miles, northeast. Transcend."

She stood, eyebrows raised. "That's the name of the town?"

He shrugged. "I didn't pick it."

She chuckled, and he was amazed he had gotten her to laugh. He noted again how beautiful she was … this time after besting numerous enemies in battle … and how useless a thought that was for him to acknowledge.

"You have magic," he said, instantly picturing Tashiel, probably trapped in the dying city. He felt sick.

"Of course I do. Why wouldn't I?" She added a small smile to the tease, but must have noticed the emotion in his eyes. She drew nearer, a look of empathy on her face. "I'm sorry, Rain. Your world has just been shattered. Mine once was, too, and I'm not talking about the bandit attack. None of that group of pilgrims were my family, or even my friends. In fact, most were white bands in disguise."

Rain gave a dull nod, finding himself struggling mightily against a pounding dread centered mostly around Tashiel and her parents, but also his own family, who were dangerously close to the city. Somehow, a logical question broke through the thick, dark surface and demanded attention.

"Is that why you didn't protect them?"

Her lips set in a hard line. "No, it isn't, and I didn't expect to put them in any danger. I should be dead, too, and not by a bandit's hand. One of the white bands suspected who I was—perhaps I was careless in some of my inquiries—and drugged my food. I don't believe they knew I had already stolen the key from more of their compatriots near Arxhana, in Mero Vothas, switching it for a duplicate. And I had hidden it on my person with a simple magic." She pointed at the armor covering his tunic.

"They had pilfered it from the Guardians of Heaven in Jeveria, a dangerous group to cross. They were planning on meeting up with that group of white bands you saw in New Haven to continue a search northward for the key's linked book. I'm not sure how I woke up, but when I did, it was too late. I was barely able to save myself in my weakened state. The rest of the drug wore off as I ran, and then I knew I was dying."

Rain felt a headache coming on. "So ... what you said to Elidim. You really are ... a spy?"

She nodded. "Sometimes."

"Were you bringing the key—I mean, the talisman—to Ileom?"

"Yes. And together we would search for the prophet. And that book."

He gave a confused shake of his head. "So why do I still have it again?"

She shrugged. "I don't fully understand that myself, but I've never been more certain of anything in my life. Being so close to death was only part of it. Ileom isn't unfamiliar with such things, either."

"Oh." The headache localized near his temples. "So, who exactly *are* the white bands?"

A dark look crossed her face. "A group of cruel religious zealots from Sheraya. Servants to Queen Givyren, who has become extremely fanatical herself."

"And the bandits?"

"An unforeseen complication," she replied, frowning. "I'm not sure who they are, or where they came from. Mercenaries, perhaps. I *will* find out, though." Her lips tightened again as she folded her arms and stared grimly into the distance. Cyclone snorted softly as he looked over, but then returned to munching on grass with Sun Tamer.

"So ... how did Ileom know where you were?"

She made him wait several seconds before responding. "You don't need to know that yet."

"Who *are* you?" The words came out almost a whisper, as if part of Rain preferred not to know. Ever. The question also sounded silly in his ears—she wasn't going to reveal her true identity to the likes of him.

"I am a lot of things. And yet not enough. Not nearly enough, Rain Barynd. And far too blessed."

That sounded both vague and ominous. His head throbbed. "Who, um, sent you?"

"I can't tell you that, either." Irritation flared in her eyes, but he couldn't tell if she was upset by the question or the answer.

He looked away, taking a moment to process everything he had learned so far. Antara was a spy, and Ileom was far more than a war hero. She could use magic. All this trouble had rained down on peaceful New Haven because of a magical artifact that looked like a key. And he had unwittingly used that key to visit … another world? There really were inhabited planets among the stars? More fairy tales.

"I'm on your side, Rain," she said with an earnestness that surprised him. "There are powerful forces in this world who would use that key for evil—to amass power and subjugate everyone else. I've seen what that looks like. This continent has remained relatively free of such things for many years, unlike Akris, but … well, you just witnessed that the tides are shifting. Precipitously."

He gulped, then scrunched his brow. He knew little about politics and thrones, so he changed the subject. "You protected us with your magic back there, and you used words."

She took a small step toward him. "It helps me sometimes … to focus, and to feel the urgency for my magic. Some magic-users can *only* perform with the help of certain phrases or gestures, but that is only because they have leaned on that crutch too much."

"Oh. Um … can Ileom use magic, too?"

She studied him intently for several seconds. "Yes, but that's all I'll say."

He expelled a breath in frustration that unexpectedly boiled over. "You told me what you felt about me keeping the key. But I don't understand that. It would be safer with you and Master Ileom. If he survives, that is." His face abruptly burned with shame, at both the outburst and not being at New Haven to help. Or to die trying.

Her gaze became even more intense. "He will. I can almost guarantee it. And not only did I pass you the key, it has responded to you—*without* the book. I cannot stress that enough, Rain. That is something *I* don't understand, and by itself it means I can't take it back now. I'm not sure I could be trusted to, anyway."

"What? Why?"

She knitted her brow, her eyes green sparks. "Never mind. That's not for you to worry about, guardsman."

Feeling humbled, he asked, "How bad are the Sherayans? They're right in the middle of the Five Kingdoms, which have been allied for at least a hundred years, right? They keep the eastern warrior kingdoms in line, and foreign invaders off our shores. According to Ileom."

She let her eyes wander, clearly considering how much more she should tell him. The loudest explosion yet reached their ears, and after a glance in the direction of the city, hidden by the hills, she seemed to make a decision. Her expression softened.

"I told you the landscape has shifted, some of it due to gradual processes, some of it suddenly. Sherayans in general have long believed Jeverians, Broenites, Vrieslanders, and Sajinai to be heretics from the 'true church,' violators of the Great Oath they once shared, but they tolerated them. Groups like the white bands, who call themselves Shepherds of the Ascension, wielded relatively little influence. That began to change with Givyren's succession to the throne fifteen years ago, and it has accelerated recently. The white bands are the most fanatical group among the Sherayan Holy Conclave, which is itself distinguished for its zeal among all the factions of the Great Church. These so-called 'shepherds' are utterly ruthless toward anyone they perceive as standing in the way of their divinely appointed mission to lead humanity to the next plane of existence. And most of the moderates who previously blocked their path have been swept aside in a torrent of religious passion."

"Which is why they creeped me out. Sun Tamer, too."

Antara nodded, then considered Sun Tamer for a long moment. "Yes. Well, if they were to obtain both book and key—and they have a reasonably good line on where the book is—they would terrorize this world. Other worlds as well. All in the name of 'holy' progress. Does forced conversion sound pleasant to you?"

He shook his head. "They … don't have anyone who could travel with the key alone?"

Her eyebrows drew sharply together. "As I told you, that isn't supposed to be possible. Those who forged that key—whether from this world or another, and a very long time ago—also created the book that went with it. It is quite clear from everything we've uncovered that neither works without the other. Until now, that is."

He gulped, tempted to start digging a very deep hole for the talisman. "So the white bands, once they have the key and the book, will give it to their queen, who will then … try to take over all of Rega?"

"Yes, without hesitation, by bouncing back and forth from that other planet to wherever she is familiar with here, likely causing havoc there, too—or gaining additional allies to join her in the plunder. Which is why we must keep that key from her. Queen Givyren claims she rules apart from the Church, but she could be a white band herself. She would throw her full support behind zealots across the continent in starting a Holy Crusade to unite Rega under the iron authority of the Church, with her as Empress and High Priestess. Picture hell, only worse. With the ability to move key elements of their armies quickly, the Sherayans would be exceedingly dangerous. And they've started wars of conquest before."

Rain stared at the ground, the implications too large for him to fully grasp. "Ileom says they practice dark magic, too, especially the warrior mages of the Hearkendoom."

She huffed. "There's no such thing as 'dark' magic. It all comes from the same source, to be used for good or evil based on our agency, which God holds inviolable—frustratingly so, sometimes. The magic can be wielded for dark purposes, twisted into cruel abominations, encouraged and enabled by the Pretender, who achieved great power before he was cast out of God's very presence."

Rain looked back up, blinking several times. His parents believed something similar. "You know far more than I do about these things."

She grimaced. "I don't know nearly enough. And we're both in for some rude awakenings. The Sherayans are only part of a much larger problem. We saw a glimpse today."

Rain pondered that a moment, amid new rumbles from the direction of the city. "The white bands aren't linked with these new invaders?"

She shook her head. "I don't think so, but we know almost nothing about these men in the light-green uniforms. Rumors, really. We've never been able to place a spy with them, which didn't worry us too much, because we thought they were peaceful. Hermits, mostly, from west of the barbarian lands, hidden in the mountains. They must really want that key back."

His eyes widened. "*Back?* I thought you said the white bands stole it from the Jeverians."

"I did. That part I am sure about. However, I cannot say for certain where the Jeverians obtained it, only that the Guardians who were protecting it are quite incensed." Intense concentration marked her brow. "Perhaps *they* hired the bandits. If they had sent their own, you might not have survived the encounter. Even Ileom fears them ... to a degree. And they him, of course. In any case, recent rumors describe these so-called hermits as traveling by key and book, from some time in the distant past, and they are clearly willing to kill in their search for something they deem extremely important—your key, whether it was originally theirs or not." She looked away again, seeming frustrated.

"Where are you really from? And who sent you?" His intense desire to know overcame the hesitation to ask again.

She blinked at him, then gave a slight shake of her head. "Not yet. And we should move on now, to this fascinating place called Transcend." With that she turned and walked to her horse.

Sun Tamer and Cyclone seemed refreshed, even after only a few minutes' rest. Sun Tamer's tranquil eagerness to continue the journey lifted Rain's spirits ... until he noticed smoke rising high in multiple directions, including that of Transcend. How far had the enemy army already advanced? Would they pillage and burn the entire country?

"We must hurry," said Antara. "They must know the key escaped the city. They will be scourging the land."

"How would they know?"

She gave him a bleak stare. "I ... do not know." Head lowered, she kicked Cyclone and galloped off.

Despite Antara's desire for haste, she exercised caution in guiding their approach to Transcend. The smoke in that direction thickened for a bit, then began to dissipate. That could be good or bad. Either townspeople were successfully fighting the fires, or there wasn't much left to burn. Rain didn't pray much, but he hoped it was the former.

The view of the town that finally greeted them dashed his meager hopes. The sounds and smells, too. Death assaulted his nostrils amid the crackling of fires and popping of embers. A hellscape he scarcely could have imagined confronted him, with or without a belief in eternal judgment.

They stopped, surveying the morose scene. Only a few homes had completely burned to the ground, but more would follow. Bodies littered the street, all of them perfectly still. Children—even babies—hadn't been spared the massacre, and he suppressed the urge to retch, remembering with vivid clarity the butchery at the wagons. Who could be so evil? And how?

"Hopefully some of them escaped," said Antara, her voice filled with sadness.

"It doesn't look like it," said Rain in a hoarse whisper.

She angled her chin up the street. "Some made it away. Look at those who fell. The old, the feeble, the very young. Those who weren't fast enough to flee."

Rain's eyes paused on a pair of adult bodies, crumpled near a child's. "And those who refused to leave them behind."

Antara sighed deeply. "Yes, them, too."

"If they're just searching for this cursed key, why kill these people?"

"Because they're wicked. A special kind of hardened evil, rigorously nurtured in a vacuum of selfishness and hubris, masked by false altruism." Her next words caused Rain to shiver, coming out as almost a snarl. "They're focused on their objective, but they *enjoy* killing anyone or anything within reach, rationalizing it as necessary 'collateral damage.' Their mission, of course, if accomplished, will allow them to murder far more people. We should keep moving."

Rain was about to accept the suggestion, but hesitated. "We should see if anyone needs help." His level look belied nervousness that he had spoken so boldly. She returned his gaze, finally nodding.

"All right. But be careful. In addition to the fires, it's possible they left a spy or two behind."

Rain wouldn't have thought of that. It was becoming clearer every day—no, every hour—how much he had to learn. Trying to calm his nerves, he dismounted and unsheathed his sword. Then he walked toward the nearest house, wholly intact except for the front door hanging askew on a single hinge. He thought he detected a hand on the floor in the dim interior, just a few feet short of the threshold.

He did a quick search of the home, sword held ready before him. He found just the one body, an old woman who could have been his great-grandmother, slain as a savage afterthought. He moved on to the next house. Antara remained outside, leading the horses as she studied the streets and the fields beyond.

He searched a dozen more homes, finding nothing new and finally vomiting. After his stomach had emptied, it filled with a boiling anger. He wished he could flush out a spy, so he could split the man in two. He was sure he could do it, given the rage coursing through him. And his magic; he wouldn't forget his magic.

At the next house, he detected a slight scuffling sound, rejoicing at the same time his gut clenched. He kicked open the door and rushed inside, figuring the enemy wouldn't expect that given how cautious he had been. He set his feet, tensing for thrust, swing, or parry, then blanched. The tip of his sword dropped to the floor as a young girl looked up at him with fear-stricken eyes, hands held pleadingly before her.

"No, please," she croaked. She began sobbing, repeating the phrase several more times. Then she collapsed onto the corpse of a middle-aged man wearing the half-chain of an Istarrean soldier. What was *he* doing here? Was he related to the girl?

Antara appeared in the doorway. "You found a survivor."

Rain nodded, then looked again at the girl, whose sobbing continued, though softer.

"We're not here to hurt you," he offered. It sounded hollow. Antara measured her steps, then knelt before the girl.

"What is your name?" she asked, her tone more comforting than anything Rain could have achieved.

The girl sat up, sniffled, and wiped her eyes. "Jerise."

"Do you live here?"

She looked around, as if the place seemed unfamiliar. "Yes."

"How old are you?"

"Nine."

"Is this your father?"

Jerise's eyes dropped to the man, and Rain noticed the slight movement of his chest. His eyes widened as the girl shook her head.

"He's alive!" Rain moved to his other side and started examining him. He had taken a nasty head wound, probably damaging one eye. The broken shaft of an arrow protruded from his armor, near his heart, accompanying another hole in his chest where an arrow or bolt had apparently gone all the way through. Such force was hard to imagine, even from a crossbow. Several slashes scored sword arm and both legs, and a great deal of blood pooled beneath him, though not enough to indicate a major artery had been severed. It was a miracle he still lived … but he would soon die.

Rain glanced up at Antara, and she nodded. "Try," she whispered.

He swallowed, more anxious than if he had indeed encountered a spy, and struggled to clear his mind. He focused on the man's face, with its short, peppered beard, well-trimmed mustache, and slightly crooked nose. He appeared peaceful, which meant Rain was almost out of time.

He took a deep breath, then closed his eyes and concentrated on gathering heat. It came much easier than the first time, given the flames and embers nearby. The number of wounds the man bore nearly overwhelmed him, but he decided to focus on the head first, since the arrow clearly hadn't pierced the heart, then work his way down as fast as possible. It took long seconds for the fire tool to appear, and for him to gain control and begin repairing—as best he could figure out—the damage to the man's skull. He wasn't skilled in anatomy beyond the basics of battlefield first aid, so it was slow going, and he grew ever more frustrated as he sensed the man's life slipping away.

More heat bloomed nearby, but in some part of his mind he knew it wasn't a threat, so he maintained focus. When he felt he could move on from the head, he looked at the chest wound nearest the man's heart. He started upon realizing the arrow shaft was gone. Had he done that without knowing? How did this magic work, exactly? After removing the breastplate, he discovered that *both* holes in the chest had been sealed. He surveyed the injuries on arms and legs, finding the same with all of them. He examined the man's body again, even reaching carefully underneath the torso to search for damage. His hands came away slicked with blood, but he hadn't felt any abnormalities.

Amazed, he sat back on his heels, fists on the floor. He felt tired, but not as much as expected. Perhaps he was learning, though he didn't seem to be aware of it.

He looked over at Antara, kneeling next to Jerise, who had apparently fainted. Antara wore a mask of dumbfounded fascination, but instead of staring at him, her eyes focused on Jerise. Her lips parted, as if she were about to say something, but then closed.

"What?" Rain asked. Panic gripped his heart. "Is she okay?" He scooted over to face her small body, prepared to start again.

"It was her," Antara said, shock dominating her tone.

"What do you mean?"

"You healed the head wound, but she did everything else, and incredibly fast. She even … did a bit more on his head, especially the eye."

"She *did?*" He stared, slack-jawed, at the girl's now serene face, remembering the bloom of heat. "How?"

Antara took a deep breath, one hand on her stomach. "She watched you for a few seconds, and then she … I guess she mimicked you. But I've never seen such intuitive power and talent in one so young. Or knowledge. I haven't even read about a close example." Their eyes met, and she added in a voice tinged with awe, "I've met two magical prodigies, the likes of which the world hasn't seen in at least two centuries, in two *days*. Nobody in the Order will believe me."

"The Order?"

"Never mind." Her voice had returned to normal, brooking no objection.

Rain turned back to the man and laid a hand on his chest, which rose and fell much more significantly than before. Steadily, too. It was a miracle. *Another* one. He was living in a folktale cloaked by nightmare. And if he was the prodigy Antara claimed, the old stories said he'd more likely go mad or meet an untimely death than become a real hero. Perhaps being a farmer wouldn't have been so bad after all.

Antara examined Jerise intently, then lifted her head to lay it on her lap. The girl didn't appear to be hurt—just exhausted. That made sense if she had indeed healed a man so near death.

Rain finally stood, still uncertain what to think or feel. He needed to find some water and wash his hands, but then a thought popped into his head.

"You said the men who did this are evil, and you said it like you knew for sure. But you just told me you didn't know much about them."

He hadn't meant to sound accusatory, but he was having a hard time processing everything. She didn't seem to mind, luckily. She just turned her head to regard him with calculating eyes as one hand stroked the young healer's hair.

"The evil is obvious. But yes, we know more about this group than I let on, though it is difficult to tease out the full truth from them. Rumors describe a great power hidden among the Teeth of Grayshadow, possessing exotic magics of incredibly dangerous capacity. We assume most are hyperbole, especially because our early attempts at contact were rebuffed with extreme politeness." Her eyes closed for a moment, as if she were sifting memories. "More recent intelligence hints at a desperate struggle for control within their society, lasting more than two years, but nobody paid it much mind since it was closely contained. We have been planning to send someone again to assess, but now ... well, it is apparent which way that struggle went, and that the victors are not content to mind their own business any longer. How they convinced *any* barbarians—much less some of the larger tribes—to join them is a mystery, and an important one. The barbarians enjoy plunder, when they can get it, but not wanton slaughter. It is not their way, as they believe their gods would be displeased with such cruel, wasteful, and cowardly behavior."

She sounded much like one of the tutors Master Ileom often brought in to 'train up the minds' of his novices. As he considered her words, she removed Jerise's head from her lap and gently laid it on the floor so she could rise. Then she searched the rest of the house. When she returned carrying a bulging knapsack, Rain—now standing—gave her his best brave and determined look, counting on his Guard uniform to lend it additional credence.

"Will I be expected to join the, um, Order?"

She gave a slight shake of her head, revealing little with her eyes. "I can't tell you. And not without Ileom's approval, anyway." She quirked an eyebrow, as if to say, "Any other premature questions?"

He swallowed and reforged his pride. "Well, it's critical we get Ileom's message to Istarrea, as fast as possible." He realized he was stating the obvious, but she nodded as if he had said something sage.

"What message for my people?" The weak, masculine voice caused them both to jerk and stare as if at a ghost. The Istarrean soldier had awakened. He sat up with a groan, then felt at his head, chest, and various other parts where he had taken injury. His eyes became wide as the twin moons at full. "And how am I alive? Or *am* I?" He gazed at Rain, then Antara, his expression haunted.

Antara answered him. "You are very much alive, sergeant, thanks to the healing ministrations of a member of the New Haven Council Guard … and this young girl here."

The man blinked at Rain, then directed a confused look at the girl. "Who is she?"

Antara raised her eyebrows. "You don't know her?"

The man shook his head, still staring at peacefully reposing Jerise. Then he tested his legs and stood, turning to face Rain. He saluted, which seemed so utterly odd Rain nearly lost control of his jaw muscles. "I am Haran Goth, Sergeant at Arms in the Southern Border Command. Since I am in your country, I am in your service."

Rain barely remembered to salute in return, then glanced at Antara. She smiled, seeming to enjoy his fresh discomfort.

"How," Rain asked the man, "did you come to be here, um …?"

"Haran Goth."

"Yes, sorry, Sergeant Goth."

"You can call me Haran if you like."

"Oh, okay. Well, I'm Rain Barynd, and this is Antara …"

"Antara will do," she said, nodding respectfully at Haran.

Haran bowed to her as if she were a queen. "Without your arrival, Mistress, I would be dead. That is clear to me. After a lone messenger from the western forts arrived yesterday morning at our border with New Haven, nearly dead, I led a small mounted scouting force south. We were attacked, then hounded for many miles. Today, we heard from one of your own messengers that the city of New Haven had been assaulted, so we tried to hurry north with him and report. We were not fortunate in that regard, instead driven farther south by a most confounding and ruthless enemy who wielded powerful magic. They must have ensorcelled the barbarians into helping them."

"That's an interesting word to use," said Antara, "but it is nearly impossible to force a man's mind to your will through magic. Even if it *could* be true, I believe I would have felt it when we encountered some of them."

Haran bowed again to her, deeper this time. "I am honored by your wisdom, sorceress."

Sorceress. Yes, clearly she was that. But she appeared more regal than magical, as if being a mere sorceress was beneath her. At least it seemed so to Rain, but what did he know? New Haven's magic-users weren't considered all that powerful, and while just two days ago he had been in awe of the things Tashiel could do, he wasn't any longer. Jerise made Tashiel look like a day one novice. In that instant, he realized with a mysterious sense of surety that the world—not just Rega, but all of Tenris—would never be the same, and in ways he couldn't hope to comprehend.

"Rain. Rain? *Rain.*" He blinked, realizing Antara was addressing him. He stared at her feet, blushing.

"Rain, we have to leave, keep making our way north. You'll need to carry Jerise. Haran can ride with me."

Rain nodded, stooping to lift the small, peacefully sleeping body. No terror marred her face. They exited the house and approached the horses, Haran taking Jerise while Rain mounted, then settling her against his back. Rain kept hold of her crossed wrists at his stomach to keep her in place. They were so small. Riding wouldn't be easy as long as she slept, but he would manage.

He waited while Antara and Haran searched the remaining few houses, returning with somber faces. Antara took to the saddle, helping Haran up behind her, and they departed the smoldering ghost town. Cyclone and Sun Tamer picked their way carefully through bodies and rubble, ears twitching as nostrils flared. How long before the survivors could return to bury the dead? Or would they return at all? A mile out, as they followed a minor path, Rain called ahead to Haran.

"How many men did you have? I didn't see any of them in Transcend."

"Is that the name of the town?"

"Yes."

"We were separated. Scattered, really. There were ten of us, plus your messenger. I lost my horse nearby, killed by a bolt from one of those strange wands. At least he died quickly. As for me, I fought as best I could, but fell. I don't know how I made it into the town. I must have crawled."

Silence reigned for a time, and then Jerise began to stir. Rain heard her gasp, then scream. She cut it short, perhaps realizing it was dangerous to make so much noise, but her breath came in quick, sobbing convulsions, her entire body quivering.

Sun Tamer stopped, and Rain patted Jerise's hands. "Relax, we're safe. We're heading for Istarrea, and then we can figure out what to do next, how to find your family."

He cringed as that hint of a promise left his lips. Her chest heaved as if she were preparing to wail, but then she said in a slobbery stutter, "They're … dead. I saw them. My … my parents, my brother and sister. Our two dogs. All dead."

Rain glanced forward. Antara had stopped and turned Cyclone sideways.

"I'm sorry," Rain said, knowing his words would do little to fill the void.

Antara brought Cyclone closer. "Jerise, can you tell us how you healed Haran? How you knew how to do that?"

Apparently, the serious question caused Jerise's mind to move in a different direction, and she calmed a little. "I'm … not sure, but my father was a physician. He served several villages, and sometimes he took me with him. I … saw what your, um, guard was doing, and I knew I could do it, too. I saw where the man was hurt, and I wanted to help him so badly, especially after watching my … family …" Her voice trailed off, and Rain was amazed she didn't start sobbing again. He would have.

"How did you remove the arrow?" asked Antara, her tone soothing.

"I … dissolved it, I think. I didn't know what else to do."

"You *dissolved* it?" There was no mistaking the shock in Antara's voice.

Jerise buried her head in Rain's back, crying softly. She didn't answer. Antara looked at Rain, but all he could do was give a slight shrug. Seeming almost shaken, she wheeled Cyclone back around and led on. Now that Jerise was awake, they could move a little faster, and Rain asked her if she could look behind them once in a while and tell him what she saw. She squeezed him tighter, not wanting to do that, and he didn't press.

Despite Rain expecting a roving band of demons and barbarians to pop out of the trees beyond every rise and around each bend, they encountered no one but the occasional small group of refugees. All of them begged for news, but Antara and Rain could tell them little. No, they didn't know the status of this particular village or that, other than Transcend. No, they didn't know if the Keep at New Haven still stood. No, they hadn't encountered the enemy in the last several hours. And no, they couldn't say if the Istarreans were coming to help. Haran looked deeply embarrassed every time they answered that question.

They camped for the night, off the road under the boughs of a great tree, keeping a rotating watch. In the morning, Antara insisted on doing some scouting first. When she returned a short time later, reporting she had found nothing of concern, they started off again.

After a long day, a second anxious night, and another long day, they neared Istarrea as dusk deepened. While this border didn't boast stout forts like that with the barbarians, the military presence was visible and numerous. Clearly edgy, too.

"Halt!" came a gruff command from somewhere behind a barrier of timbers bristling with anti-cavalry stakes and creased with arrow slits. The man behind the voice sounded little older than Rain. They stopped, thirty yards away in the fading light.

"Identify yourselves!"

Antara straightened, her mien imperious. "I am Antara of Ta'Voran. Rain Barynd, Council Guard Second Rank from New Haven, accompanies me, along with Sergeant at Arms Haran Goth, one of your own, whom we found wounded but were able to heal. We rescued a young girl as well. We carry a message from Master Ileom Mystrevan for the Council of Four. One of you may take it to them, or we can deliver it ourselves. What updates do you have?"

A soldier emerged from behind the barricade, carrying a torch, his gaze and gait wary. He stopped when he was still ten yards away.

"There is little news. We have been ordered to seal the border. Every unit has been mobilized, and reserves are being called up."

Haran grunted, then dismounted somewhat clumsily from behind Antara. He took a few steps toward the soldier and straightened his back. "The very depths of Akell disgorged her prisoners. They roam the land like festering boils."

The soldier swallowed, backing up a step. "You ... were injured by them?" Dried blood covered much of Haran's uniform. He had reattached his breastplate, too, and the punctures in the armor were impossible to miss.

Haran grunted again. "Aye, nearly killed. Healed only through the use of magic. Discovered by these fine people. We encountered a few refugees, but not many. This new enemy has little mercy."

The soldier, who was indeed young, maybe twenty, saluted. "Our captain is checking other areas of the border nearby. You should speak with him. You can wait here."

Haran raised an eyebrow, but then nodded. "Very well. Let your captain know that—"

"I am here," sounded a booming voice, issuing from a tall man atop the most beautiful warhorse Rain had ever seen, besides Sun Tamer and Ileom's beast from the gods. He emerged from the trees, almost like a wraith. He pulled up near his soldier, eyes fixed on Haran.

"Haran Goth?"

Haran saluted. "Yes, sir."

"I have reports that you abandoned your post, and several men followed you. What have you to say to that?"

Haran frowned deeply. "I led a sanctioned scouting mission—*toward* the enemy, not away from them. As far as I know, all my men are lost. I, alone, survive."

"Convenient."

Haran threw his shoulders back. "You may outrank me in some situations, but in others you do not. I will not have my honor questioned by you, especially in front of your men. I would hear these accusations in full, and challenge those who made them."

The captain returned his stern glare, apparently unmoved. "I am ordered to arrest you. You will stand trial before the Quorum of Nine. You may make your appeals to them."

Antara moved Cyclone forward a few steps, pinning the captain with a glare. "I care nothing for your petty politics," she said, her voice sharp-edged crystal. "And I charge you, captain, with personally delivering a message from Master Ileom of New Haven to the Council of Four—*not* the lower Quorum of Nine—at best speed. Take more than one horse if needed, but if I find that this message didn't reach them by the morning, you will be hanged forthwith."

Her authority rang among the trees and defensive emplacements, the captain struggling to suppress astonishment. He squinted at her, then looked at Rain, hands twitching on his pommel.

"Master Ileom, you say? From Jeveria?"

"Yes, and you are correct in presuming the message doesn't just come from him."

Fear flashed in the captain's eyes. He studied her and Rain a moment longer, and then nodded. "I will deliver the message by morning. You will stay here until I return. My men will provide for you. Shelter, food, water."

"We will stay if we choose," she responded with imperial aplomb. "Our path is uncertain."

Their path didn't sound uncertain to Rain. They had made it. They had delivered the message. He was happy to camp near Istarrean border defenses, which included magic-users. What was she trying to do? He jerked as Jerise gasped, then spotted the finely etched metal tube given to him by Ileom … *floating* in the air toward the captain, whose face went slack. Rain tapped his pocket where the scroll had resided. How had Antara gotten it out of there without him noticing? And with magic!

In slow motion, the captain reached toward the tube, then hesitantly grasped it, as if it might shock him.

"You have your orders, captain," said Antara. "There is much to do before this enemy obtains too great a hold. I know I can trust you. Now go."

The man regained some of his composure, then bowed from the saddle before spinning his mount and disappearing back into the trees in a flash of hooves, shouting for someone to procure a spare horse. His soldier stood somewhat dumbfounded, uncertain what to do. Rain could imagine his confusion.

Antara let her eyes fall upon him, and they were kind.

"What is your name, soldier?"

"Destry, Mistress, er, Your Eminence."

"And that of your captain? It was rude of me not to inquire it of him."

"Regnis. Captain Regnis."

"He is a good captain? Stern but fair?"

"Um, yes, Your Eminence, he is."

"Good. I sensed it. We will camp with you tonight. You have provision for the horses, too, I presume."

"Yes, yes, follow me." He seemed eager to be moving, and he led them swiftly beyond the barricade, through a thin stand of trees, and into a broad clearing hosting an expanding cantonment. Several soldiers and camp workers lighting torches stared at the group in surprise, but nobody questioned them. Destry showed them to an open space, then promised to fetch a tent and men to set it up and care for their horses. He didn't comment on Jerise, who clung tightly to Rain's back, even as he dismounted. She was light, so it wasn't difficult.

Full dark was soon upon them, but by that time a large tent had been erected, divided in the middle, and they sat before a small campfire that chased off the cooler air. Destry made sure they enjoyed a hot meal, and promised no one would bother them. His demeanor felt like an odd mixture of obeisance and wariness.

"Should we keep a watch?" Rain asked, glancing at both Antara and Haran.

Haran shook his head as Antara answered. "No, we are safe here. But for how long, I do not know."

"We could cross the passes, head for Broen," suggested Rain. "It's a larger country."

Antara gave a slight frown, staring into the fire. "I had thought of that, or perhaps even traveling through Broen to Jeveria. If we could fly, we could have hopped over the Miracle Mountains from New Haven and gotten there much quicker. It might be good to counsel with the Oracle of Sephyr and First Regent Rosgan, but that course feels … hmmm … weak. My purpose isn't to run from this threat but determine how best to confront it."

Rain let his confusion show. "And wouldn't the Oracle and the First Regent of Jeveria help us figure that out?"

She pursed her lips. "Perhaps. Perhaps not. Mirenia I trust, but several deep rifts cleave the Church in Jeveria. How she is holding it all together, I cannot imagine. I fear spies there, too. We must not underestimate the dangers posed by this new enemy—and Sheraya, and maybe others. The invasion of New Haven wouldn't have been undertaken without careful forethought, including information from other nations on this continent. These new adversaries aren't just evil. They're cunning. They have a plan." Her eyes locked onto Rain, and he could almost feel the talisman burning in his pocket. Digging that deep hole sounded appealing again. Destry could easily procure him a shovel. And how was Antara on a first-name basis with First Regent Rosgan of Jeveria? Rain hadn't even known her name was Mirenia.

"Can I see the talisman?" she asked.

Rain's eyes widened, and he glanced at Jerise, then Haran. The old soldier stared thoughtfully at him. Jerise's eyes blossomed with curiosity, a portion of the fear and horror having receded with a warm meal and a sense of safety. Emotionally, she was probably still in shock, though.

"Are you sure?" he asked Antara.

She nodded curtly. "Yes. They are part of this now. I don't know why." She held out a hand.

Rain swallowed, then retrieved the talisman and passed it to her. Her hand twitched, but she took it and brought it close, eyes roving its surface as she rotated it. Then she laid it against the bare skin near her neck and closed her eyes. She murmured a few phrases Rain didn't recognize, and the hair on his arms rippled. He thought he detected something swirling around the talisman, like tiny red and blue sparks, or miniature shooting stars. After a few moments, she breathed heavily, sagging a little. She offered the talisman back to Rain, her eyes at once resigned but determined.

"I thought perhaps I could bind it to me now that it is out of immediate danger, as you've been hoping, but it is as I expected—it has chosen you, Rain. Something far beyond my ken is at work here, though I am loathe to admit it."

Rain hesitantly took it back, staring dumbly at the metal, warm to his touch. How could an object 'choose' him? And why? They needed Master Ileom. Surely *he* would know what to do.

"I encased it in a protective field," she continued, "one that should shield it from scrying. I think the enemy must somehow be able to sense its general location, at least sometimes. If so, they know we headed north, and maybe even that we have crossed the border."

"But you saw nothing when you scouted yesterday," noted Rain. He was pretty sure he had never heard the word 'scrying' in a factual conversation.

She raised an eyebrow. "Did I say that?"

Rain thought back. "Well, um, no, just that you found nothing to concern us."

She nodded. "Correct. But I found signs of our enemy in the area. I should have done then what I just did to the talisman, but at least I created some false markers, which seem to have confused them a bit."

Haran rubbed his hands and frowned, looking between them. "They will attack here next."

"I doubt it. This enemy is obviously formidable, but Istarrea is far stronger than New Haven, and invading her would also elicit a powerful response from nations like Broen. They *will* seek to track us, however. I have no doubt they already have spies in Revalis, and they can surely get scouts across the border."

Haran blinked, clearly hoping she was right about Istarrea's allies but wrong about the spies. Rain felt the same. He squinted at her.

"You said earlier our path was uncertain. Are you thinking of heading *south*?"

"Actually, I thought about traveling northwest, across Istarrea, then taking a ship from Loshan across the southern edge of the Ice Sea into Hammerfell, or maybe down the western coast of Rega to Arsellis. We are still at least a month from the ice floes. But that doesn't feel right, either."

"It sounds fine to me," said Rain, but as the words passed his lips he knew they were wrong. He clamped his mouth shut and gazed into the dancing flames, perplexed at how he could possibly feel that way. Haran added another piece of split wood to the fire.

"You may choose," said Antara after a few seconds. He looked up at her in surprise.

"Me?"

"Yes, you, and not just because of the talisman. Well, primarily because of the talisman."

That *frosted* key. Anger flared in his gut, along with another tidal wave of grief. His parents were more likely dead than not because of the cursed artifact. Tashiel and her parents almost assuredly so. Probably Ileom, too, despite what Antara claimed.

Antara must have seen it all in his face. She slid her camp stool closer, then rested a hand on his wrist. His skin tingled at her touch, which smothered a portion of the sorrow. "Listen carefully, Rain. God—who is as real today as he ever was, despite the splintering of the faith by so many grossly imperfect religious leaders—has entrusted you with something.

He never does so without proffering the help required, even if it comes after much difficulty. If you are willing, you will succeed."

He shook his head, eyes fixed on the ground. "I don't understand how that works."

"You will."

Her assurance brought little comfort, but rather than drown in a pit of his own ignorance, he thought of another question that had been bothering him. "How does your mission extend beyond Rega?"

Her fingers looped under his palm, and she squeezed. His young heart fluttered. "There are many forces at play, that is true. Including on Akris. Unfortunately, I don't fully comprehend it yet."

"The people of Akris are always fighting with each other. That's what the traders say. Mainly The Golden Empire and …" He couldn't remember the name.

"Kent, which is no more, save for a few scattered holdouts. Some still resist Emperor Creegan, mainly the City States of Belyshar, but that won't stop the emperor from directing his gaze across the ocean at Rega."

"But Kent—"

"Was too strong? Yes, we believed that, too. Something changed, though, and recently. Then we learned more about this talisman, which may be related in some way. If God intends to further brighten the picture, I hope he does so soon."

"She," interjected Jerise, who hadn't said a word since they'd asked her about the healing.

Antara removed her hand from Rain's, placing it with the other in her lap and sitting straight. She smiled at Jerise, her countenance spreading more warmth than the fire. "You are both correct and incorrect. We will save that for another time, though, my dear."

Jerise looked away shyly, then scooted her stool closer to Rain and wrapped her arms around herself, rocking slowly back and forth as she stared into the fire. Haran cleared his throat, gaze resting on Jerise a moment in concern before he met Rain's eyes.

"I will accompany you, wherever you go. My life is bound to yours, and I will defend you to my dying breath. I am a widower, but I will ask Destry to send word to my children, who are all grown. She is coming with us, too, correct?" He nodded toward Jerise, and Antara answered his question.

"Yes, she is. She is perhaps the most remarkable healer this world has ever seen, and she has a purpose in everything that is coming."

Jerise hugged herself tighter, eyes still locked on the flames, her rocking more pronounced.

Rain thought his heart might have stopped beating at the internal gonging of a massive bell. A mountain might as well have been dropped on him, too, the full magnitude of the prior days' events finally manifesting in the gravity of Antara's words ... and Haran's. What was happening? A seasoned soldier from Istarrea had just pledged his service ... to *him*? A skilled sorceress with powerful political connections was willing to let *him* choose a course to protect an ancient talisman that had transported him to another world? And those who also sought that magic included the Sherayans, some mysterious new group with incredibly destructive magic from beyond the barbarian lands to the west, and essentially the entire continent of Akris? How was he to know what to do? He was just Rain Barynd, humble son of artisans and farmers from Mari's Mask in the tiny, peace-loving nation of New Haven. Council Guardsman Second Rank or no, he was far too small.

He stared in utter stupor at Haran, then at Antara. "Can we sleep on it?" he asked meekly.

Antara smiled. "I think that's a splendid idea."

11

"So, have you decided?"

Antara's question stopped Rain short as he entered their small camp the next morning, having just returned from speaking with Destry, who had promised to secure them two more horses.

"Yes, I think so," he said, bowing slightly.

"Stop bowing to me."

"Yes, m'lady."

She rolled her eyes. "And don't call me Lady."

"Yes ... um ... okay."

"Do you *think* you've decided, or are you sure?"

His eyes darted several directions, all of them in avoidance of her probing gaze. "Well, I ... um ..." An image of Ileom popped into his mind, and he finally swallowed hard. "Yes, I am. Mero Vothas." He looked at her, tentatively.

She stared at him for only a moment, then nodded firmly. "Very good. Back through the fire to Mero Vothas it is. We'll all have horses, correct?"

"Yes, m'la—, um, ma'am."

"Antara. You will call me Antara. It's really not that hard. I'm not your regent." She said it in a voice that made her sound like, well, his regent.

Rain bobbed his head, then escaped to find Haran and Jerise and let them know they would be leaving as soon as Destry brought the horses.

Jerise had accompanied Haran as he toured the camp and spoke to a few of his countrymen. The sergeant needed clean clothes and new armor as well. Rain returned with them twenty minutes later, and shortly thereafter Destry and a groom arrived, leading their four mounts, Sun Tamer and Cyclone with heads held high. The other two looked sturdy and healthy, though they paled in comparison.

After they had all mounted, and Destry and the groom had helped them secure packs and saddlebags bulging with provisions—plus their tent—Rain thanked Destry and took the lead. Antara had insisted. Haran brought up the rear.

"You're heading east," noted Antara after they had passed beyond the outer perimeters of the war camp. "Will we travel among the dwarves for a while?"

Rain glanced back at her. "That was my thought. I think we'll have a smaller chance of running into enemy spies there."

She nodded. "That is wise. The dwarves deal more swiftly and sharply with spies than most peoples."

She came even with him, then turned and narrowed her eyes. "Are you thinking of going underground?"

The thought hadn't crossed his mind, but Haran overheard and piped up from behind, "That might be a good idea. Living with the dwarves for a while would be better than dying."

Antara twisted toward him and arched an eyebrow. Cyclone kept marching along, though his ears twitched toward the conversation. Sun Tamer's, too.

"Despite the stories," she explained, "very few of the dwarves live underground, and only for short periods of time on a rotating basis to access the deeper mines. They are children of the sun as much as anyone else, including the elves. Their mines are extensive, though, and you can travel many miles beneath the surface before re-emerging, which can be useful. Unfortunately, few maps exist, and those are closely guarded."

Rain gaped at her. "Elves are *real?*" He had always assumed they were mythical beings, like dragons.

Antara laughed. "Yes. They are few in number, though, and far more secretive than the dwarves."

Rain scrunched his brow. "Where do they live?"

She gave him a mysterious smile. "I have only a vague idea of two or three locations, and even if I knew for sure, I couldn't tell you. I've made certain … oaths."

That spiked his curiosity further, but there wasn't anything he could do about it. He had other questions about them, though. "Is it true they live forever?"

She laughed again, more heartily. "No, but that's a fun rumor, and they allow it to proliferate. They do live longer—about fifty percent longer than humans and dwarves—and they're as strong as the dwarves, pound for pound. A greater proportion of them are adept with magic, too; perhaps that and their somewhat longer lives first gave rise to stories of immortality which have survived the centuries."

"Have you met one?" asked Jerise. She had moved her horse forward until she was almost in between Rain and Antara.

Antara became suddenly somber. "I have met several. They seek a new sanctuary."

Rain didn't know what that meant, and he didn't want to ask, but Jerise did. "Why do they need a new sanctuary? Are they not safe anymore?"

Antara gave her a motherly smile. "I don't understand all the reasons, my dear, but they clearly don't feel as safe as they once did. Perhaps you will get to meet some of them, and they can explain it. They will be interested in you. I would like to be there for that."

Rain tried to remember from the stories whether elves were skilled at healing. He yearned to know, but he still held his tongue.

Haran had moved closer as well, and they traveled in a tight bunch. The horses didn't seem to mind. "What if the dwarves think we're spies?" he asked.

Rain had met quite a few dwarves growing up, and he didn't expect them to be overly suspicious—not of their group, anyway. He thought Antara might laugh again, but she gave Haran a respectful nod.

"Dwarves are guarded in their interactions with outsiders, and rightly so, but I doubt they would see our small troop as spies. It's the Mero Vothans I worry about."

Haran gave that some consideration, then asked, "Why the Mero Vothans?"

"With more enemy attention directed this way, they will already have received a large influx of refugees. While they are not an uncompassionate people, there are limits, and they generally like to keep to themselves, anyway."

"But we are only four, well provisioned, and we have a purpose."

"Which is what? How much can we tell them?"

He nodded almost immediately. "I see your point. We are still only four, however, and we can pay our way. Last I checked, they were happy to take a person's coin."

She raised an eyebrow.

"I convinced the paymaster in camp to give me forward pay, since I would be on ... a special mission ... with you."

"That was resourceful, Haran. Rest assured I will have access to funds wherever we go. Perhaps my worries are misplaced." She gazed forward, and they rode on in relative silence, the horses spreading out again with Rain at the head.

Three hours later, with the sun nearing its zenith in a sky splotched with scudding clouds, Sun Tamer snorted and tossed her head. Rain raised a hand to call a halt, but Jerise didn't know what his gesture meant and almost ran her mount into the back of Cyclone.

"What is it?" she squeaked, fear lacing her voice.

"Someone is coming. Sun Tamer doesn't seem too alarmed, but we should dismount." He hesitated, glancing at Antara, worried he had sounded too commanding, but she was already sliding off her horse. When they were all on their feet, Haran with his newly provisioned sword drawn and a protective arm around Jerise, Rain walked ahead, searching for a place off the path from which he could get a better view. He found a small hillock and scrambled to the top, then knelt to watch and listen.

When the sounds became clearer, they certainly didn't indicate an enemy presence. Soon he spotted the first person, haggard and dirty, pulling the lead ropes of a cow and two goats. Several more people followed, men and women, very few children. Some carried small packs, and a pair of women pulled a two-wheeled cart piled high with an assortment of cargo. He spotted half a dozen sheep and one more cow, along with a trio of mangy, hungry-looking dogs. All told, eighteen people plodded along, seemingly oblivious to the constant bleating of the sheep and goats, the occasional yapping and whimpering of the dogs. As they got closer, Rain could distinguish the haunted stares, occasionally flushed with pain, both physical and mental.

He rose from his semi-concealment and ambled down the hill toward the group, trying to appear non-threatening. The first person to see him flinched, though, despite his Guard uniform, then fell to his knees and began sobbing. Others in the group cried out in panic, searching for a place to run.

"It's okay, you're safe!" he called out, realizing how foolish such a guarantee sounded. How did he know they were safe? The enemy could be lurking behind the next rise, or galloping toward them in a thunder of hooves with lightning lancing out before them. He slowed his walk, making sure to keep his hands up and away from him.

The man regained his feet, eyes glassy, then took two tentative steps forward.

"Do you have news?" he asked, voice breaking. "Have they gone? Have they been defeated? Can we return to our homes?"

Antara appeared beside Rain, as if out of a mist, but the man didn't flinch this time. Her voice could have soothed a wounded bearcat. "The enemy was not defeated, but the Istarreans are mobilizing a stronger defense. Our destination is Mero Vothas, which holds more opportunity for us. Perhaps more security as well."

The man blinked, then wrinkled his forehead as he stared at the ground in front of her. "Can we … join you?" he asked meekly. "You look like you could provide some protection."

Rain almost chuckled, mostly to release his own tension. Just the two of them? Haran and Jerise hadn't arrived yet, but even with Haran added to the mix … these people must be incredibly desperate. Antara regarded Rain, her expression thoughtful. "What do you think, Council Guardsman?"

The man bobbed his head at Rain and whispered, "Please."

Both the request itself and the way it was delivered felt decidedly strange. The man had to be in his forties, and Rain was fifteen—uniform, sword, and large stature or no.

He had no idea what to think. He had heard of refugee situations before, in lands far away. Technically, he was a refugee now, too. But he had a mission, and how could a ragtag group of hungry wanderers fit in with that? He gazed at Antara, eyes pleading for advice.

"We could use their help," she said.

Rain blinked. Their *help*?

She turned to the man. "What is your name, good man?"

"Arosh, m'lady," he replied, bowing.

"I am Antara, and this is Rain Barynd." She then addressed Rain. "They have animals and a few provisions, and they know how to forage. In return, we can provide the protection they seek, with both magic and sword." Arosh's head jerked up at the word 'magic,' awe and relief filling his features.

"Yes, well, that … um, sounds good," stuttered Rain.

She smiled at Arosh. "Have you any who need healing?"

He nodded energetically, his entire visage transformed. "Yes, m'lady, several of us. Nothing major. Those who—" his eyes dropped again, his mouth snapping shut.

"You had to leave some behind who couldn't keep up as you fled."

After a moment, he nodded, face reddening.

"Perhaps we can backtrack and find a few of them?"

He looked up again, seeming confused. "But the enemy …"

"Didn't kill everyone. Though they are still looking for something, their search has spread out. They are wary of a robust Istarrean response as well."

His eyes widened, and he nodded dumbly. Then he turned around to look back at the bedraggled line of stunned humans, all staring either at him or at nothing at all. "We go with these people," he said in a voice just below a shout. "Back the way we came."

After a few confused murmurs, the members of the small caravan began to turn themselves around. It wasn't easy with the cart, but Rain jumped in to help get it redirected. After he returned, Antara stepped up behind Arosh and touched his elbow. The man twitched and paled before recovering.

"The healings," she reminded him. "We can rest here for a while." As she turned, Jerise and Haran emerged from the trees, leading the horses. Antara motioned Jerise forward, then nodded at Rain to proceed as well. She approached an older woman with a bloodstained sleeve, turning her over to Jerise as she moved on to examine a pre-teen boy.

Rain considered Arosh first. "Are you injured?"

The man still seemed befuddled at what was happening. "I ... uh ... my shoulder, but not badly."

Rain examined his shoulder. He didn't see any blood. "Dislocated?" he guessed.

"Yes, it'll be fine. Others are more badly hurt."

"You popped it all the way back in?"

"I think so. I can move it a little."

Rain wanted to ask more questions, because he didn't know exactly what to do. Healing Antara's arrow wound had seemed straightforward to him, because he could see it. He hesitated, almost turning away, but then laid a hand on the man's shoulder and closed his eyes. Perhaps applying some heat would help, he reasoned.

As the heat began to build, he was able to visualize some of the things Jerise must have done with Haran's healing. She likely probed the injuries first, using some of the knowledge gleaned from her father to know how to address the damage. And maybe ... the sudden insight astonished him. She had also communicated with her patient at some level below—or above—conscious thought. Haran's body had told her how it used to be, and she had made the corrections to bring it back to proper form and function. In theory. But could *he* do that?

He refocused, trying to understand the man's injury. After several seconds of intense struggle, he was about to give up, but then he caught a glimpse, somewhat fuzzy, of the damage inside. A picture formed of what the healthy bones, muscles, and ligaments should look like—also vague, but somewhat discernible. He reached for the heat he had gathered, then grabbed the man's shoulder with both hands and levered it in a direction he could sense was the right one, while applying the heat inside. A soft pop followed, and he let the magic-laced heat do its reparative work while he tried to determine if he had achieved what he needed to. He finally resolved that he'd done all he could, though it had felt like swimming in dark waters.

The man groaned, and Rain removed his hands, opening his eyes. Part of him worried he hadn't helped at all and might even have made it worse.

The man dipped his head. "Thank you, it feels much better."

Rain wasn't sure he believed him. "Are you sure? Wind it around. Do you have full motion?"

The man gave him an uncertain look, then complied, slowly, eyes widening in surprise as his arm moved in completely normal rotation.

"Does it still hurt?"

"Maybe a little, but it feels much better, and … stronger. Thank you." He bowed.

Rain let out a breath he hadn't realized he'd been holding. "Good. I'm not nearly as skilled at this as"—he nodded toward where Jerise ministered to a young woman's arm, Antara closely observing—"well, she is." The man followed his gaze, then gawked.

"How old is she?"

"Nine."

"And she …? This is a miracle." He fell to his knees, hands on his thighs, head trembling.

Rain backed up a step. "Don't kneel to me. I'm not anyone to reverence. We've barely survived ourselves. Perhaps … um … God is watching over us." He couldn't believe he'd just encouraged someone else to have more faith. He'd never done *that* before. He had his own to worry about.

The man rose but kept his head bowed. "Well, either way, I am in your debt, and your service. You and Antara and … the others."

"Um, thank you. Jerise is the young healer. Haran is the Istarrean soldier whose life she saved when we found them."

Arosh nodded. "Amazing. So, Mero Vothas?" He seemed to roll the sound around in his mouth for taste. "We will accompany you to the end of your journey … or as far as you will allow us."

Rain's eyes found Jerise and Antara again, moving down the line. Exclamations of gratitude and joy punctuated the air. Then he considered Arosh and his offer. "Welcome, and we will have to see. We don't know what tomorrow will bring." That sounded appropriately like Ileom.

⌇∞⌇

"You? Rescued *me*?" Ileom glared at the scrawny wizard in his ridiculous robes patterned to look like a pile of autumn leaves with silver-gilded tips. Tenedrast was one of his least favorite among the Council, and he had never bothered hiding it.

Tenedrast squinted at the polished stone floor of the poorly lit anteroom of Ileom's quarters in the Order's isolated, high-mountain keep, fast on the intersection of the borders of Mero Vothas, Jeveria, and Sajin. After a moment, he looked up, bold annoyance crinkling the corners of his eyes. "Can you think of a better description?"

Ileom growled. "I could have escaped that trap on my own. I came prepared. And the central tower still stands. I made sure of that before I left the city."

"Of course it does. Nobody on this world possesses the power to break it. But since you successfully triggered the mechanism, it is also sealed now; it couldn't protect you if you returned." Tenedrast glanced at the great sword strapped to Ileom's back in its special scabbard that allowed him to draw it quickly to the side. "That artifact is powerful, to be sure, as is your armor—and your magic—but this first contact was hotter than we expected."

"Hotter than *you* expected," Ileom corrected. Tenedrast had a knack for the abstract, but the practical often escaped him. "Why did you even come? Why not Avrenor or Thirena? They are the most familiar with our

112

progress there. Of course, they wouldn't have foolishly risked an artifact even more powerful than the sword." He narrowed his eyes to reinforce the rebuke … and in warning of any possible dissemblance.

Tenedrast took the hint, taking a deep breath before his shoulders suddenly slumped, the flickering lamplight making it more dramatic.

"Avrenor is dead. Thirena's life dangles by a thread. The healers are grappling with an insidiously twisted magic … and they are failing."

Ileom's eyes widened as his chest constricted. That explained the abrupt halt in communication. He let his gaze bore into the wizard, who somehow maintained eye contact. "When did this happen? And *how*?"

"Two days ago, while you were still, um, 'clearing the back trail,' I believe you put it, for your young acolyte. And drawing far too many of the enemy toward you. At least one of the assassins came from the ranks of the Order. He had been here in the Keep five years."

Ileom's mind raced to identify everyone in the Keep who had resided there for that period of time. Unfortunately, he visited infrequently, and he didn't know everyone. "Who? And again, how? It would be nearly impossible."

Tenedrast breathed deeply again. "We believe they used a different type of artifact, previously unknown to us, to briefly suspend the outer protective wards. Activated from inside, of course. They overpowered the personal protective enchantments of Avrenor and Thirena with unusual ease as well. They assaulted Avrenor first, in his chambers, then Thirena as she crossed the High Archway alone. The attacks came within a minute of each other, giving the Sentinels little time to react."

A low growl formed at the back of Ileom's throat. "Some of the assassins escaped?"

Tenedrast nodded. "Three, yes."

"And the traitor?"

"He is dead, which is unfortunate. I would have treasured the chance to talk to him."

"What was his name?"

"Creygin, an artificer. Quite skilled. He hid his magic well, and it was formidable. The old strength is indeed accelerating its return."

"And Avrenor's communicator artifact?" He already knew the answer.

"Is missing. Probably stolen. Useless without the paired match you hold. At least as far as we know."

Ileom clenched his jaw, staring hard at the gray walls, as if he could see through them to find a solution. This was incredibly frustrating news. He had heard the name Creygin, but only once, in passing. Was he from Rega, or had he come from Akris? And how had he and his fellow assassins obtained an artifact that could interrupt the enchantments of the Keep? The Order was in danger of losing the battle of control over the old talismans that kept popping up at regular intervals—not just in Rega, but across Tenris. Their unpredictable power caused a growing avalanche of chaos.

He put a hand over his eyes, rubbing his temples with thumb and fingertips. "I presume this new artifact is uncatalogued?"

Tenedrast gave him a deeply troubled look. "Agrancik and Vellinar have examined the residues of the magical breach as well as they could, and made an entry. None of the archives show anything similar."

"Any idea where it might have come from?"

"No, but we are investigating. The only plausible explanation at this point is that the Tahn Arganda discovered it."

Ileom gritted his teeth. Akris. Emperor Creegan. "They're on their way, then. They took two of us out of commission, and they've already sown great division among several nations on this continent. They must believe it is enough, especially with these new allies."

Tenedrast considered him solemnly for a moment, and Ileom felt a strange connection pulse between them. Another unwelcome surprise.

Finally, the wizard spoke again, his tone filled with dread. "I fear they are right."

After retracing the refugees' path for a few miles and finding a dozen corpses but no survivors, Rain and Antara led their somber but more determined group eastward, deeper into the foothills, gaining significant elevation. They traveled three days, passing through human, dwarven, and even mixed villages, most of which hadn't as yet been slashed by the claws of the enemy's invasion force. They encountered no unfriendlies, which Antara interpreted as a good sign that her shield around the talisman was working.

Amid that relief, Rain wondered if the refugees might be able to join one or more of the villages, at least temporarily. The area seemed relatively safe, and while the winter would be colder, the land was good, the forests teeming with wild game.

Arosh and the others unanimously chose to continue with them, however, and Antara was unabashedly pleased by it. In fact, her mood remained optimistic even when a brave Istarrean scout shared news that the city of New Haven had indeed fallen and that few had escaped alive. Rain's thoughts turned to Tashiel, her parents, and Ileom—also to his parents, so close to the city with his uncle, unless they had for some reason headed home the day of the attack. When would he be able to find out their fate? The scout had no information on Sheran or Mari's Mask.

His unease grew when, two days later, now traveling south, they encountered another group of refugees in much worse shape than the first group had been and with almost no supplies. They numbered twenty-seven, including young children, and they had all but given up. Two men lay on hastily constructed litters, near death. Jerise attended to them first. Rain healed several broken bones and puncture wounds, along with some nasty gashes that had become infected. Antara again stayed close to Jerise. She didn't attempt any healing herself, and at one point Rain caught a look of extreme frustration suffusing her face.

An hour after the healings had concluded, Rain crouched on a small rise, scanning the landscape as he tried to shake off some fatigue. They still hadn't encountered any enemy scouts or skirmish groups this far east, but he worried their luck wouldn't hold, especially with the appearance of the new refugees. Unless Antara was right that they were focusing mostly northward and had lost track of the talisman. He didn't dare latch fully onto that hope yet.

"Rain, sir, we are ready to move out. All of the newcomers have been fed, and we've made sure they have adequate coverings for their feet. Lady Antara asked that we let you know."

He rose and stared dumbly at Arosh, wondering again at the strange circumstances. "Thank you, um, Master Arosh. Lady Antara can lead out. I need to do a bit more scouting."

Arosh, who was growing more confident, though he always deferred to Antara and Rain, gave a sharp nod and retreated toward their growing camp. Almost fifty people now, which was hard to comprehend. Rain spent another minute on his observation, then gave a low whistle. He had just discovered that Sun Tamer would respond to it and come to him. She emerged from a small stand of trees. Amazing.

He took her north and west for nearly half a mile, extending his radius from the camp. Then he carved a rough semi-circle among the best cover he could find. He was glad to have Sun Tamer's senses added to his own, and they progressed with relative confidence until the wind turned to their back, negating her keen sense of smell for what lay ahead.

He slowed her pace, pausing more frequently to listen. He didn't feel any kind of premonition, but recent memories enjoined heightened awareness.

He finally angled her southeast, on a line calculated to intercept the trail of their now moving camp, noting that the sun had neared its zenith. The air still carried a brisk tingle, but it would warm somewhat over the next three hours.

Then he did receive a premonition—unmistakable, like cold water drenching his heart. He stopped Sun Tamer, drew his sword, and instinctively readied a fire arrow from the surrounding air and ground. Wait, how had he done *that*? And so quickly! He could see it hovering next to his head, awaiting his command.

A slight rustling came from ahead and to the right. Sun Tamer heard it, too, turning her head and flicking her ears. Without thinking, driven by jitters, he launched the arrow toward the sound, throwing additional heat into it and willing it to—explode?—yes, explode on contact. That could be useful. In this case, however, he would probably only fry a rabbit. And raise a whole lot of ruckus that would terrify those in the caravan. Potentially draw unwanted attention, too. *Idiot.*

The explosion came just after a loud crack sounded. He felt a projectile—*a crossbow bolt?*—whizz past his head. He ducked, then kicked Sun Tamer into motion as a man screamed. Thankfully, his fire arrow had done some damage. Unless it was a hunter, perhaps even some poor refugee trying to forage, afraid of an armed man on a horse. His heart quailed as Sun Tamer crashed through a thicket into an area where he hoped they could get a better view.

Two green-uniformed enemy soldiers appeared, one on fire, flailing his arms in a vain attempt to slap out the flames until his friend forced him to the ground and into a roll. Upon hearing Sun Tamer snort a challenge, that man turned, reaching to retrieve one of the large, odd-looking wands from the ground. Rain was already leaping from the saddle, hitting the ground and rolling to regain his feet. The man was too far away to engage directly. Instead of trying to conjure another fire arrow as the man raised the magical weapon in his direction, Rain's body performed an action he had drilled hundreds of times under Ileom's tutelage. He spun his body and launched his blade with what he hoped was just the right torso leverage and wrist motion to make it impact point first on target with sufficient velocity. It was a difficult skill to master, especially with a sword, but even Ileom had once admitted Rain was pretty good at it.

The tip would have impacted squarely, but the man had good reflexes. He turned his body and let it fly by, surprise and anger flashing in his eyes. The distraction allowed Rain to close on him. That had been the other part of the drill—cast your sword, then sprint after it. He tackled the man, throwing his full weight behind his shoulder and into the man's gut as he drove him into the ground. Air left the wizard in a wheezing rush while Rain pushed onto his knees, grabbed the man's own dagger, then fended off the feeble resistance of his arms to ram it into his side, aiming for the heart. Shock painted his assailant's features, and Rain knew he had struck true when the light in the man's bright blue eyes flickered, then winked out.

Withdrawing the knife, he turned to the enemy scorched by his arrow. That man had stopped thrashing, and he hadn't risen. Rain approached with care, then recoiled when he saw the man's face, or what was left of it. His hands and arms, too. Almost all the flesh had been burned away. What had he done? He definitely hadn't cast natural fire. The good news was that two enemy combatants lay dead, and they couldn't take news back to whoever had sent them.

He took a moment to retch, which was becoming an embarrassing habit, then located his sword and returned to the wizard he had killed with the dagger, wiping it off to note it was made of perhaps the finest steel he had ever seen. The man's small pack, sitting nearby, contained some provisions and a few artifacts Rain didn't recognize. He picked up the wand as well, observing how abnormally long and heavy it was, made mostly of dark metal and with strange wooden handles. Had Tashiel mentioned metal wands before? How did they work? Antara would know. She had already plainly demonstrated the deficiency of his education. Ileom hadn't dwelled on such things—he just taught trainees how to fight with the weapons they had … and yelled a lot.

Sun Tamer seemed to nod at him in admiration as he approached her, standing majestically just a few yards off. He squinted, then shook his head as he stuffed the wand in the saddle bag—what would fit of it, anyway—shouldered the small pack, and mounted. He put them back on course toward their group, which couldn't be far off.

He spotted Antara first, cantering alone in his direction, her face a mask of determination. She dug her heels into Cyclone's flanks, calling back to Haran to keep the caravan moving. Cyclone lived up to his name when she reached Rain, rearing and spinning after they came to a thunderous stop.

"You encountered the enemy?" she asked, her voice tight.

He nodded. "Just two of them. Both dead."

She calmed Cyclone further, then nodded. "Take me to them."

Before complying, Rain reached back into the saddlebag and proffered the wand he had captured. "I took this from one of them. It's heavy."

She grasped it with one hand, testing its considerable weight as she examined it. "Wood and metal, combined. And with odd protrusions ... handles?"

Rain shrugged. "He held it with two hands. It's almost a mage's staff. Those are rare, aren't they?"

She nodded, lips pursed, still fixated on the strange object. "I will need to study this, but it may be beyond me. I know one person I can trust who might be able to tease out its power, though."

"It launched a magic projectile at me," he said, remembering the near miss with a suppressed shiver. "At least, I think that's what it was."

Her eyes narrowed, and she nodded down his trail. He obliged, pivoting Sun Tamer and leading them toward the battle site. After a few paces, with the powerful staff settled behind her pommel, she asked, "How did you defeat them?"

He tried to recall the details. It had happened so fast, and some of his movements had been automatic. "We heard them, and I launched a ... um ... fire-blossom arrow? It exploded, and we were able to close. One was burning; the fire arrow ended up killing him. The other I engaged with sword and knife before he could bring that staff to bear again. He was strong, and a good fighter." Had he said that last part to impress her?

"Hmmm … you can already judge a good fighter?"

He realized how foolish that sounded. "Well … that is … yeah, I guess I really can't yet. He was better than me, though. I got lucky." He was sure *that* was true, even though the battle had ended so quickly.

She stared forward a moment, then pierced him with those coruscating emerald eyes. "It is not luck, I think. You are skilled, and God has a purpose for you. If he expressly does not wish you to die at this time, by the way, you will not die, as long as you are trying to do what's right."

He tried to take that as comforting, but it far surpassed his comprehension.

"Don't let that make you overconfident," she added in a warning tone, "lest your ego grows to crush your usefulness and he must choose another."

That was a distinctly uncomfortable sentiment, so he kept his eyes on the path ahead, not wanting to think too hard. They soon came upon the corpses, the one still smoldering, nearly unrecognizable as human. Antara dismounted and approached the charred remains first. She knelt, reaching out a hand and closing her eyes for a few moments, but not actually touching the body.

When she rose, wonder tinged her expression. "You did this with an arrow made of fire from the surrounding air? That *exploded?*"

Rain didn't understand it, either.

"You're definitely like Jerise," she added, "just in different ways. I've heard of pairs like you from the past—naturals with amazing ability, found close to each other—but it's been hundreds of years. The signs have been pointing to it, but still…" She raised a finger. "Again, don't get a big head."

On the contrary, Rain suddenly felt small and disoriented. He should be more … grateful, at least. That's what his mother would say, right before his father reinforced it. He stared at the misshapen lump on the ground, forcing down another urge to vomit. Then he looked at the other man, slain by a mere dagger. Sightless eyes aimed at the sky, shocked anger frozen in his chiseled features. His open-faced helm had fallen off, revealing light-brown hair. The blue of his eyes had deepened in death, and no scars marred his visage. From his build, he didn't seem like a mage. He was a warrior, nearly as large as Ileom, and yet he hadn't hesitated to wield the wand. Two cloth emblems had been sewn into his uniform, one on each side of his nearly closed collar—a four-pointed golden star inside a silver circle on a background of purple, an expensive color.

"Take his tunic," said Antara. "His boots and gloves, too. And search his pockets."

Rain nodded, then set to work on the grisly task. He had never pictured having to do such a thing, and he hoped it didn't become a common occurrence … or that nobody ever had occasion to do it to him. He finished two minutes later, having found only a few unfamiliar coins and some folded sheets of an extremely stiff paper covered in a foreign script. The boots and gloves seemed of extremely high quality, as did the tunic.

As he packed the things in his saddle bags—after Antara had briefly perused them—she commented, "It says something that this army is outfitted so well."

"Except the barbarians," Rain noted as he kicked his leg over his saddle. He turned Sun Tamer on a course to intercept their party again.

"Yes," she mused, swaying softly as Cyclone walked alongside. "But I'm not sure they're trying to make allies of the barbarian tribes. They may just be using them as disposable mercenaries, perhaps under threat. They're clearly ruthless enough, and they've injected that cruelty into the barbarians to some degree."

"War is hell. Even good men will do brutal things when fighting for their lives, or the lives of their families."

"That is wise coming from one so young." It sounded like a genuine compliment.

"Master Ileom taught us that. Drilled it into us."

She nodded, eyes gazing far away. "He has seen much."

"Yes, well, unfortunately, he's not here, and I wish he were."

"Me, too, but I'm glad we at least have you." She didn't look at him, and he was grateful. She would have caught him staring open-mouthed, red-faced, and cross-eyed. He might even have drooled a little.

It took five more days of slow but steady travel to reach the Mero Vothan border, marked by a series of rounded stone altars spaced about a hundred yards apart. Some of the stones were quite large and would have required teams of animals to move them. Since they weren't on a common road, they didn't see any border guards, but Antara advised them there would almost certainly be patrols.

They had progressed at least another five miles before they encountered the first Mero Vothan soldiers, a group of ten mounted men led by a captain capped by a brightly plumed helm. The troop blocked their path, the captain raising his hand in a commanding gesture as he ordered them to halt.

Rain and Antara, side by side, waited calmly as the crimson-topped captain approached, his men spreading out as they unlimbered short lances.

Before the captain could address them, Antara raised her chin. "Do we appear to be a threat, good captain?" The word 'good' could have been replaced with 'foolish' and fit her tone better. Rain didn't think it wise to antagonize the man.

The captain scowled. "You are strangers, and some of you may be enemy soldiers trying to infiltrate these lands."

Antara made a somewhat exaggerated show of turning and displaying their humble group. Then she returned the captain's scowl. "I am the Lady Antara, of Ta'Voran, and I can assure you no enemy has tagged along with us. I am leading these poor families to a place of refuge, where people are kinder than those they have recently had the misfortune of meeting."

The insult cracked like a whip, and the man barked in offended response, "We have taken in thousands of refugees, and already they are causing trouble. By orders of Chief Magistrate Corvellum Dynast, we can take no more at this time. So, you either return north, head straight east until you reach the River Eln, or feel our steel."

"The River Eln is in the mountains," she retorted with iron-tipped words of her own, "and the cold already begins to bite there. The enemy still patrols parts of New Haven and may even occupy the city. So, you're offering us three different ways to die?"

"The barbarians and their handlers have left the city, most of them returning to the west, though a few still cause mischief across the countryside, for reasons known only to them. I have my orders, and you're not the only ones suffering." He studied the group more closely. "In fact, you seem better off than most. Did you put down your wounded?" The sullen glint in his eye added additional venom to the affront, but he didn't get the rise out of Antara that she had gotten out of him. Rain was certain she was about to tell him they had a skilled healer among them. It might get them in.

But she didn't. She just clicked her tongue. "Very well then. We will return directly north to the border and find a place to camp there. You may send two of your men with us, if you wish, to make sure we do as I've said."

Without realizing it, the captain was now partially under her command. It was astounding to witness. He nodded. "Yes, indeed I will. And I will pass that way myself in two days' time."

"Order an extra requisition of rations as well," she said calmly, as if she were speaking to her maidservant. "You can bring it with you and we'll enjoy it together."

He blinked, obviously unsure how to respond. After a second, he tipped the rim of his helm, whirled his horse, and retreated, calling out the names of the two men who would accompany them.

"What just happened?" asked Rain.

"I am not completely sure," replied Antara. "But we have two more soldiers. That's useful, right? And if the captain brings some extra rations …"

"Foraging here will be difficult, I agree. Game is more plentiful farther north, where there is more water."

She smiled. "We have done well so far. And I will help a little with that now. You'll be pleased, I think."

The natural question was about to trip off his tongue when the two Mero Vothans trotted their horses up, giving them both salutes. Salutes!

Within minutes Antara had everyone organized—professing it to be under Rain's direction, of course, which was still ridiculous—and moving back toward the border, the two Mero Vothans ranging ahead and behind, for all the world acting like they were riding scout for a royal caravan.

After the group crossed the border, the two soldiers spread out, searching for a suitable site with adequate cover and access to water. Within an hour they returned, claiming success. Antara turned to Rain, who shrugged and nodded, and they followed, coming to the chosen location just before dusk. A small spring marked the eastern edge of a broad clearing, with a large number of mature trees surrounding the area and marching down a gentle slope with the spring's effluence. It looked perfect, though Rain still felt uneasy about being anywhere in New Haven. They needed to continue south, and soon. He was sure of it.

Ileom took his time studying the recently discovered Tahn Arganda base through his sight enhancement artifact in the bright rays of midday. It was already quite large, as he had feared. Others like it probably lined this eastern coastline of Chalace, and he would bet at least one squatted along the western reaches of the Isle of Valkyris, though the unusual magical properties of that strange land mass would make it difficult for them. Tenedrast was scouting the islands of the Lady's Travail with a smaller group; he would likely find a newly constructed camp or two there as well. When Emperor Creegan finally ordered the full invasion, it would be massive. All the surviving spies agreed on that, and Ileom was staring at evidence.

"How long do you think they've been here, sir?" asked Captain Drydan of the Order's Sentinels, who had just approached, the snap of his salute audible.

Ileom let the magic of the artifact fade, then lowered the device—a narrow, glassy rectangle for which he hadn't yet commissioned a suitable housing he could strap to his head. He turned to the young but promising officer he'd chosen to lead the fifty-five men he'd brought with him. Drydan's brown field uniform looked freshly laundered. That would change, as this terrain wasn't easy to scout or patrol.

"At least a month. Their defensive perimeter already has some fallbacks built in, and I counted more than a dozen permanent structures. They're preparing it to grow, too. This base will probably triple in size and house ten thousand men, but it will take them time to bring enough ships here from Akris and establish a steady supply route. I'd say six months."

"Won't naval patrols from Arsellis and Kyatera intercept some and turn them back?"

Ileom grunted. "I don't put much trust in the arsies and katydids. Their reach into the Calfar isn't nearly as extensive and secure as it once was. And the ships might be coming from both directions."

"The route through the Dreijan Deep is much longer for them, and more treacherous."

"They would dare it. At least until they feel they don't have to anymore."

Drydan nodded, staring in the direction of the base, which could barely be seen with the naked eye. "Do you think any of them have spotted us?"

Ileom followed his gaze, tempted to re-engage the artifact. "No, probably not, but you'll take some men closer. Creegan's cronies need to know someone is watching, and they'll be hesitant to provoke anything at this point."

The captain accepted that assignment stoically, not mentioning the high risk.

Ileom continued. "Word of our presence needs to get back to this mysterious new General Inzeal, in particular, who doesn't appear to be present in this camp. I doubt he's still back in The Golden Empire, though. I'm almost certain he's somewhere close by."

"Perhaps he was one of the assassins," offered Drydan.

Ileom grumbled an indeterminate response. He really had no idea. It rankled him beyond reckoning that he knew so little about this man. Half the spies the Order had sent to gather more information on him had disappeared. "When we convene this evening with your squad officers, we'll discuss how to coordinate the additional scouting that needs to be done, along with contingency plans—not just for us, but for the key and book we requisitioned from the Keep to get here. The key has almost recharged, and we can use it in an emergency, but it can only take a few of us at a time. And it must not fall into the hands of Inzeal."

"Understood, sir," said Drydan, then frowned slightly. "That other place we passed through to get here when we traveled using the book and key … do we have any idea yet where it is, or what it's called? That was just my second trip."

Ileom gazed skyward, as if he could see deep into the stars beyond Tenris's blue mantle. With the sight artifact—and enough combined magic—several of the Order thought it possible. "No, and none of the silver doors in that cavern have opened for us. It is a mystery I'd like to solve, but with reluctance." Actually, one door *had* opened, but the captain didn't need to know that.

Drydan nodded. "I noticed the lights were dimmer this time, and starting to flicker. Might that affect our return?"

Ileom narrowed his eyes. "No. The place might go dark, but it will still be there. That's all I can tell you, captain."

"Yes, sir." Drydan saluted again. "I can report that our camp perimeter is set, and both sentry and training rotations have been initiated."

Ileom's right eye twitched as he nodded. "If we have to fight on this trip, then we have failed. But the battle will come soon enough, so get your mind and body right. Your spirit, too."

After three weeks, the refugees had something that could be called an organized camp. Rain credited most of that to Haran … and Antara, of course. Thanks to her, they weren't starving. One of her abilities allowed her to track animals, and even to calm them a bit, which made hunting ridiculously easy. It seemed almost unfair … until his belly reminded him he was hungry again, an all too common occurrence.

A few folks had complained that making thread out of animal sinews to patch together hides for shelters seemed uncivilized, but their objections didn't last long. They soon had roofs over their heads to protect them from increasingly inclement weather, and the pole structures were made to be portable.

The Mero Vothan soldiers had pitched in admirably with everything, including throwing up some earthen embankments to provide places of redoubt in case they were attacked. Androl and Chaigen—the one tall and thin, the other built like Rain but shorter—accepted Rain's suggestions, too, even treating them as orders … as long as they felt Antara approved. Initially, she nodded when they openly sought her assent. Now she just smiled. She had stopped trying to convince them they didn't need to look to her for affirmation on everything.

"I think it's hilarious, by the way."

Rain nearly thumped his head on a low-hanging branch at Antara's voice coming from right behind him. He hadn't heard her approach while he examined one of the crude spears he had made to increase their armaments.

His cheeks warmed as he turned. If they were red, hopefully she would attribute it to the coolness of the air. It was still morning. "What's hilarious?"

"That Androl and Chaigen salute your commands but still glance over at me. What did you send them to do a few minutes ago? I couldn't quite hear it."

How well could she read his mind? It was no longer a question of if, and she was better at it than Tashiel. "I sent them to Haran for some of his sword training. He's very good. I want him to assess them, too."

"Oh." She tapped her chin, seeming interested. "Why not assess them yourself? You've been trained by one of the very best in the world."

He doubted he met the qualifications of trainer, Ileom's tutelage or not, but different words sprang to his mind. "Because they would look to you before every move and hurt themselves."

She laughed. "My, you're developing a sense of humor. That's good in a commander."

He definitely blushed this time. "I'm not a commander. I'm fifteen."

"Almost sixteen, right? And more mature than most. History tells of good commanders as young as twelve."

"Well, I'm not them, and this isn't history."

"Aha, but we're *making* history." She winked, which seemed at odds with the gravity of her tone. "I can feel great events coming, and we need to be involved."

"Which means we need to move *south*." He snapped his mouth shut, not sure why he'd said it with such vehemence. Embarrassment, most likely.

She nodded. "Yes, I agree. But we must wait until that Mero Vothan captain—what did he say his name was? Ogre?—comes by again."

"Toreg." She hadn't forgotten the man's name. She liked to make fun of him, and everyone in camp knew it. One man had even carved a likeness of the captain astride his horse—quite well done, too—and placed it atop a pole stuck in the ground at one of the entrances. People liked to salute it, then imitate him doing something silly like boastfully excusing himself to use the latrine.

"Ah, yes, Toreg. It will be nice to have another pair of soldiers, plus some additional provisions and weapons."

Rain raised his eyebrows. He still couldn't believe the captain had agreed to her latest request. "The two new soldiers will just replace Androl and Chaigen."

She tilted her head. "Will they? I think I've convinced our two new friends to stay with us. We can tell Ogre that Androl and Chaigen will return a few days later, and then … they'll stay. Which will give us plenty of time to convince the new guys it's a good thing." Her eyes glittered as she smiled, and his heart lurched, as it did a few times a day. He could never tell if she actually flirted with him; he presumed it was just her personality. She had told him she was twenty-five, so he was too young for her to consider. He shouldn't be thinking about that, and he didn't want to be anyone's toy, either. That reminder usually diverted him, at least for a while.

As if their conversation had acted as a magical summons, a shout came from a man patrolling the southern perimeter with one of Rain's pitiful spears.

"Mero Vothan soldiers!"

Rain glanced at Antara, then trotted in that direction, passing their large, stone-encircled central cooking fire. He heard her begin walking briskly behind him. He reached the perimeter just as Haran, Androl, and Chaigen arrived, along with another refugee sentry. The two spear carriers proudly planted the butts of their semi-weapons in the rain-softened earth and stood straight, throwing their shoulders back. Androl and Chaigen no longer snickered when they did things like that. The two Mero Vothans moved to flank Rain and Antara, who had caught up. Haran stood slightly to the side, hands clasped behind him as the horsemen came into view around a rocky hillock.

Captain Toreg led his double line of riders to within a few paces of the group. Rain counted thirty men, many with overly large, bulging saddle bags. He spotted extra cavalry spears, bows, and swords as well, more than expected. Maybe Antara would feel the need to show Toreg some respect now. Perhaps that's what she had wanted Toreg to aim for.

"Greetings, Captain Toreg," said Rain, stepping forward.

Toreg blinked, having surely expected Antara to speak first.

"Greetings, Guardsman Barynd," he responded with a slight dip of his head. His eyes scanned beyond him. "Your camp looks impressive, and you have kept your word."

Antara stepped up beside Rain, her voice a mellifluous flow of appreciation. "It appears you have kept yours as well, captain. I am impressed."

Toreg bowed deeply from his saddle, and Rain thought he caught him blushing.

"Thank you, m'lady. Included are some gifts from the provincial governor, who hopes circumstances will allow him to meet you soon. Cloth, thread, fine leather for shoes and boots, even a few dyes. Some proper cookware, too."

Antara bowed her head, holding it for a full two seconds. That had to cost her, but Toreg *was* being quite generous. "That is very kind. Please convey my thanks to the governor and his wife."

"His wife passed a year ago," said Toreg, the implication clear in his voice. Rain groaned inside.

"Well," said Antara smoothly, "I am doubly thankful then for the trouble he has gone to on our behalf." Rain tried to figure out if the response was clever or not. She didn't seem taken aback. Of course not. She had seen a lot more of the world than he had.

Toreg cleared his throat. "I brought three additional men to stay with you. They will help Androl and Chaigen patrol this section of the border. Your camp, in fact, is important to controlling this area, which is why we brought so many additional weapons, plus a few spare mounts."

Rain blinked in surprise, wondering if Antara had done the same.

"Thank you, Captain Toreg," she said, the breathless touch of gratitude riding her tone surely intended to have an impact. It did, making him squirm in the saddle. He seemed at a loss for words for several seconds, then whirled his horse and started shouting orders for his men to proceed to the camp and begin unloading.

Antara touched Rain's arm as they moved to the side, and he caught a hint of deviousness in her smile as she said in a soft, intimate voice, "This is working out nicely. It seems I didn't need to convince Androl and Chaigen to stay after all." The smile disappeared, replaced by … something else. "Thank you for ensuring we could all be here."

It was Rain's turn to thrash about for a response. Her compliment, infused with emotion, seemed sincere. He knew she credited him with saving her life, though he still didn't feel like he had done anything heroic or extraordinary in the process. It had mostly been luck with an ability he didn't understand. Plus Ileom's training. And more luck.

Before he could come up with anything, she turned and started walking toward the camp, Androl and Chaigen trailing her like loyal hounds. Those two wouldn't have needed *any* convincing. Rain watched the train of horsemen pass by in single file, then observed the bustle directed by both Haran and Antara. Toreg piped in occasionally, making it sound like the camp was preparing for an imminent visit from Chief Magistrate Dynast himself. Rain studied Antara most closely, wondering again how much she knew of which he was utterly ignorant. A mountain likely couldn't hide it all. Nor would it dare make the attempt without her approval.

On a chilly night several days later, Rain broke his entranced stare into the fire to notice that he and Antara were the only ones left sitting around it. She was relaxing just a few feet from him, on a real chair, newly fashioned, flame shadows dancing across her face as she gave him a penetrating look. Had she said something? He couldn't recall.

"What is it?" he asked.

"I've been thinking about the talisman. I know you traveled … unexpectedly … but can you recall anything you may have thought or felt in the moments just before, or even after?"

The memory gave him a headache, and she'd asked this several times already. "No. Everything was normal, and then … it wasn't." He gazed at the crackling embers again. "I'm not even sure it really happened. Sometimes I worry that, um …"

"That you're not well situated in the head?" She stated it as a physician would, which made him believe it might be a real diagnosis.

He blinked, then focused on her again. "Am I?"

She smirked. "You're fine, Rain. I was there, remember? I saw you leave and come back. I'm almost certain I know what happened. I felt the magical nature of it, too, though I can't quite describe it. I was already familiar with some of what the talisman could do. Now I'm wondering if … well, if we can study it together. Perhaps we can unlock more of its secrets."

How did one study a magical artifact? He pulled it out of his pocket, staring at it for several seconds in the flickering light. Images of blood and fire filled his vision, surrounding the faces of his parents and Tashiel and so many others, followed by disorienting views of another place, completely foreign and impossible to comprehend. A place where he had been powerless and utterly lost. He squeezed the key hard. Then he threw it in the dirt.

"I don't want it. I can't do this. This is for you and Ileom, not me. I need to go find my parents … and look for Tashiel if I can get into the city."

She gazed at the key, making no move to pick it up, her demeanor calm. Then she stared at him for so long he had to avert his eyes. She was so still he couldn't even detect her breathing.

"So, you haven't given up. You just want to brave a different challenge."

"What?" He had just told her he was giving up. He couldn't have said it more clearly.

"You're willing to wade back into danger to find your family and girlfriend. There is much to admire in that. Tell me, though, what do you think your chances of success are alone?"

He shrugged, leaning forward with elbows on knees, not looking at her.

"Our job is not to go back and look for survivors," she continued. "Others are mobilizing to do that, primarily the Istarreans, following the protocols in Ileom's message."

He looked up, eyes widening. "You read it?"

"Of course I did. It wasn't difficult to get it from you during the night and bypass his seals. He knows I can do that, by the way, so I doubt he was worried about me reading it. In fact, he probably expected it."

He looked down again. He couldn't bring his eyes to rest on the key.

After several seconds, she added, "Our mission is much larger than you can possibly imagine, Rain, and it involves the lives of untold millions of people, *including* Tashiel and your families. Do you trust me?"

He closed his eyes, then opened them as he raised his head. "How can I? I barely know you." That sounded weak and foolish.

"We have already passed through several intense experiences together," she responded. "If another one were to occur right now, would you worry that I wouldn't have your back? That I would run, or even worse, betray you?"

"Well … no, I guess not."

"You *guess* not? You'd best be sure. Have I given you any reason to believe I'm not trustworthy?"

"No, but—"

"Correct. And I understand. This is much larger than a boy from New Haven would ever expect. Your world was small and stable. The rest of Tenris, I'm sad to say, is not like that. And peace never lasts indefinitely—anywhere. The current threats have been building for a long time. You, Tashiel, and your parents would have had to face them one way or another, eventually. With me and Master Ileom, you can do more for them than on your own or with anyone else. But you have to be patient and determined."

She was right. He had been sheltered, living in New Haven. He wasn't well read, either. Ileom had shocked the trainees recently by requiring them to start studying history. Rain had only known folklore and fairy tales, mostly. Plus warped rumors from traders and travelers, obviously meant more to entertain than inform. Even a country rube like him could tell that, but the stories were easy to enjoy while living in relative peace and prosperity. And to think that not long ago he had been frantic about losing a practice sword bout against an even more spoiled trainee.

"The time will come when you will be able to personally attend to your parents, Rain. Until then, you can serve them far better by staying the course we're on, by accepting the bigger challenge. I presume that is what they would want you to do."

He glanced at the key, but still didn't pick it up. Finally, he looked at her and said with a resigned exhale, "How are we supposed study the talisman?"

He detected the hint of a smile. "I've been thinking about that. I'm going to show you something. It's quite difficult to do. I will form a solid strand of air, and then I want you to gather heat, shape it into something like a fire arrow, or a healing tool, only much smaller, then wrap it tightly around the strand of air without touching it."

He squinted. "Without *touching* it? How tightly?"

Her slight grimace wasn't reassuring. "A blade of grass would fit between—flat—but nothing larger."

That sounded impossible, but he didn't say it out loud. "What will it do?"

"In theory, I can take control of the combined strand—your magic and mine—and feed it slowly into the talisman, delving it. We can leave it on the ground, because it will get hot."

He raised his eyebrows, resisting the urge to throw his hands up. "I can barely see your magic. And I'm not great at controlling mine." *My magic.* That was still bizarre to contemplate. "I'm not sure how I'll be able to do what you just asked."

She gave him an encouraging nod. "Just try, and keep trying. You'll get better at it. I don't expect you to be successful on the first attempt."

He grunted. "That's good, because I won't be."

She clicked her tongue. "Not a great attitude."

He scrunched up his face, rubbing his eyes with his palms as if that might improve his ability to detect her magic. Then he looked around to make sure nobody had come out of their tents. "Okay, go ahead."

"I just did."

He searched near her, eyes and mind straining to locate the strand of air she had conjured. He needed sunlight, he decided. After a few frustrating seconds, he thought he detected it. She kept it remarkably still. Of course she did. She was far more experienced. He took a deep breath, then gathered heat to form a shaft much thinner than the arrow had been. He tried to make it malleable as he moved it slowly toward her thread. After a long minute, he got it wrapped around twice, though not even close to tight enough, and then came a soft pop as it wiggled. His thread rebounded and disintegrated, sending a small wash of heat across his face.

"Not bad for a first try," complimented Antara. She sounded sincere, but he had his doubts. "Keep going."

Over the next two hours he made dozens of attempts, until fatigue clawed at his brain and he started to see mirages.

He finally shook his head in defeat. "I can't. I'm sorry."

She didn't seem nearly as disappointed as he felt. "That's all right. These things take time. We can try again tomorrow. Hopefully we can make some real progress before we move on from here."

"When will that be, do you think?" They'd had a few conversations about it, with Haran and Jerise included, but they hadn't arrived at a decision. It usually came down to getting to know the three new Mero Vothan soldiers better and being able to trust them. Two of the newcomers were hard to read.

"Soon, and before we do, I want to travel with you, using the talisman. I have an idea on how to trigger it."

He suppressed a shiver. "To the same place?"

She nodded.

"How? I'm guessing it just took me to a random spot."

"Perhaps. But it may have a memory."

His eyebrows rose again. "Really?"

"In a sense, yes, like writing something on a tablet. It's there, recorded, for someone who can interpret it."

"Oh." He would have to trust her on that. For now, he just needed sleep.

⌒⌒

Ileom kept close watch from a distance with the sight artifact as Captain Drydan and four men broke their fifth camp and moved to a new location even closer to the enemy base. They had been at it for weeks now, observing the steady progress of the Tahn Arganda encampment, which included the occasional arrival of more ships laden with men and beasts, plus materials and provisions. Ileom had detected a pattern in the enemy's scouting, and it eased his mind a bit; as hoped, they clearly knew Drydan and his men were there and didn't want to provoke an engagement. Not yet, anyway.

None of the other Sentinel teams scouting in different directions had found anything. Also good. But the number of ships now anchored in the bay gravely concerned him. He had already traveled to the Order's

Keep once with an update, and news was spreading to all the capitals on the continent.

The initial reactions, of course, varied. Most took the threat seriously, while some didn't believe an actual threat existed. And still others, like Queen Givyren of Sheraya, acted with purposeful indifference. The Order's spies hadn't yet intercepted a direct communication between Queen Givyren's government and the Tahn Arganda, but there were plenty of signs she knew what was happening … and what her role was expected to be. Ileom had floated the idea of arresting her for treason to her own country, but the reliability of political allies within Sheraya was currently at a low ebb.

At noon of that day, Ileom ordered the two soldiers with him to send a mirror flash message to Drydan, then withdraw toward the main base camp. Ileom followed only after Drydan and his men were more than halfway back themselves, staying alert for any tails. He detected none. He finally walked into the camp late in the afternoon, after checking in with the two sentries in overwatch positions—one on a hillock, another in a tree. Drydan rose from a camp stool and desk, where he had been making some notes on a map, and saluted.

"Captain, it's good to see you and your men back safely," said Ileom in greeting.

"Thank you, sir." Drydan's uniform still looked clean, though Ileom wasn't sure how.

"Your final report will be ready by the morning?"

"Yes, sir. I'm including a detailed mapping of the encampment and its environs. It was easy to determine where they plan further expansion. They have an impressive tree-cutting operation. We were spotted several times, though we observed no strong reactions."

Ileom nodded. "I noted that, too. It appears you were not followed, either."

"We tried to be careful when we extracted, though your additional precautions were wise."

Given his experience with Drydan, that wasn't flattery, though one could never be sure. "No sign of General Inzeal?"

"No, sir, but we believe one of his top lieutenants is there, newly arrived just last night."

Ileom waited calmly for him to elaborate. He himself hadn't noted anyone of high import, but most of his time had been spent tracking the movements of the enemy patrols and checking the coastline in this direction.

"He is a shorter man, but the decorations on his tunic represented a hundredweight in gold and silver. We saw him look our way once, but he didn't act concerned."

Ileom pondered that a moment. "Well, there's no way to know if he's a competent leader or a good actor. Shorter, you say? How tall?"

"At least a foot shorter than you, sir. And not as broad. His medals must have weighed as much as he did."

He had never heard a joke from Captain Drydan before. Of course, he rarely joked himself. Some people were brave enough to tell him he should, to improve his esteem in the eyes of his men. But he had long felt comfortable that his success on the battlefield provided all the respect he needed to continue to be effective.

He gave Drydan a tight smile. "Anything you can say about his features? Perhaps one of our spies has seen him before and knows something of him."

"One of my men got close enough, I'm not sure how. Light-brown hair, no apparent baldness, legs a little longer than normal in proportion to his body. Decent build, no paunch. Mid-forties, we guess. He walks fast, always in a hurry, but calmly. His gait appears athletic to me. He is likely a skilled fighter."

"Hmmm … that is helpful. Anything else of interest?"

"As you noted, they don't appear to have any horses yet, and they're manufacturing cavalry spikes to carry on their invasion flotilla."

"Their cavalry will come later, if they intend to use any at all for the initial thrust. If I were them, I'd bring my own horses after establishing a strong foothold. If I needed cavalry before then, I'd have trained cavalrymen with me and steal some horses, especially if Mero Vothas is the point of entry. Less than optimal, since the horses would be trained differently, but I'm sure they already know we are … less than prepared."

Drydan nodded, pensive. "Yes, sir, you are probably right. They have, however, just erected two sizeable structures, partially hidden from your vantage point, that appear to be barns for large animals. Between them, they could hold at least two hundred head. Warhorses as large as those of Holnevia."

That was interesting, but Ileom didn't know where to go with it yet. Inzeal was surely working on some surprises, but what could this one mean? Unless … it couldn't be, could it? His eyes shot toward the skies, which were slightly overcast.

"Help me rouse everyone off duty. We move now, every man with an arrow nocked, at a fast jog. Tents and anything else heavy we leave behind. Stay close to the trees. We don't stop until we reach our secondary camp, where three of the other scout groups should have already gathered."

Drydan's eyes widened as he glanced heavenward. He wasn't privileged to the high-level secrets Ileom knew. To his credit, he didn't question. He just turned and obeyed, spreading the message quickly. Within a minute they were moving, with Ileom—the only one without a bow—in the lead.

He wondered how long they had. He also kicked himself for not seeing an airborne attack as a possibility. No such threats existed on Tenris, but on Alave they did. Agrancik had assured the Council of the Order that the likelihood of such a threat being transported to Tenris was extremely low, but even the honest opinion of a trustworthy man could be deeply flawed if the source information was faulty.

Halfway to the secondary camp, still five miles distant, he increased his pace, his concern growing. He also sent his best runner ahead to deliver a warning, telling him to leave sword, bow, and light armor behind. He trusted the man was in stellar shape.

After four more miles, he wished he himself were better conditioned, and he felt his old leg injury begin to manifest. It had been healed, but not fully, and his body still remembered it, which had made hobbling in front of his New Haven Council Guard trainees as the wounded war hero less acting and more recall.

Still, he pushed himself harder, alternately encouraged and distressed by the fact that he heard no sounds of battle, no men screaming in pain or terror. He was either on time or far too late.

A minute later, he spotted the first two golden blurs streaking from the clouds toward the camp, followed quickly by a dozen more. He shouted the charge, a surge of adrenaline allowing him to reach and maintain a full sprint. The first sounds of battle rang through the crisp air. The sunlight was beginning to fade, but griffons saw well in the dark.

As his group burst into the camp, he noted in the chaos that his runner had arrived, giving the defenders at least a little time to organize. Bows sang as spears aimed skyward to fend off attempts to breach their positions from the air. Unfortunately, the hides of the griffons were tough, their claws sharp, and the men on their backs had crossbows, which they used effectively from altitude.

Ileom drew his massive, two-handed sword. It was lighter than it looked, but still weighty. Then he jumped, landing heavily as he unleashed a burst of magic into the earth, which responded by hurling a massive blast of dirt, rocks, and debris upward at the attackers. His enhanced battle shout got their attention, too. After some of the dust settled, a threesome wheeled and dove at him.

Using another earth enhancement, and timing it just right, he surprised his attackers by vaulting thirty feet into the air with a push, swinging his sword in a mighty arc that lopped the massive head off one of the griffons. The shock on the rider's face was worthy to be etched in steel, and for an instant he wished he were an artist and could make it so.

He landed lightly, then pushed up again as the other two riders tried to wheel away. With a sharp slash he raked the side of the nearest rider and severed his restraining straps, also damaging one of his griffon's wings. The man tumbled to the earth to join his companion, who appeared to have broken his back and at least two limbs in his fall. The third rider successfully ascended, pulling out a small horn and blowing urgently into it.

That was clearly a signal to either regroup or retreat, for the attack halted, the remaining thirteen griffons all rising, some more slowly than the others, one carrying a dead or unconscious rider stuck with a pair of arrows. Ileom studied them from the ground, noting that three of the monsters would probably be out of commission for a while. Two were riderless, so he and his men had taken out three or four total riders, and those were valuable assets. The number of hours of training they must undergo had to be extensive.

He turned, looking for Captain Drydan. When he spotted him, Drydan trotted over, his face pale. Ileom pulled out his sight artifact and handed it to him as he infused some magic into it. "Here. The magic charge will last about fifteen minutes, and it will pierce the clouds. It's also not affected by darkness. Track those griffons; make sure they leave."

Drydan stared dumbly at the artifact, then looked back up. "Griffons?"

"That's what they're called, yes, and they're not from this world. That's as much education as I can give you right now. Go."

Drydan recovered his usual composure as he saluted and ran toward the nearest small hill. Ileom watched him until he placed the artifact before his eyes. Then he turned toward the closest defensive emplacement. Several men there had fallen, including three wounded being hastily tended. He had never become fully accustomed to the sounds of men in extreme pain, as some soldiers claimed they had. He moved on to the next group, offering what direction and encouragement he could, then the next, and finally the fourth and final, at which point he had his assessment. Five dead, twelve wounded, six severely. Against fourteen griffons, each double the size of a large warhorse, and skilled riders. His Sentinels had done well. Of course, if he hadn't arrived to provide a powerful assist aided by magic, the damage would have been much worse; perhaps his men would all have ended up dead or captured. No wonder this new general wasn't concerned—Ileom and his men hadn't watched the skies, which hadn't been cloudless for a single moment since they'd arrived. Summer had passed, and while it didn't rain much in Chalace, the clouds were ubiquitous in autumn and winter.

He addressed one of his lesser captains. "Berin, we need to get out of here, but I can only take six with me at once, then allow time for recharge.

I will bring back a healer from the Keep on my first return. Make sure we still have an adequate defensive posture. Drydan will be back shortly. It will be a long couple of days, but hopefully the enemy is hesitant now."

The captain, seeming only somewhat unnerved, saluted, and then Ileom used his magic to make two arcing jumps to the place from which Drydan watched to make sure the enemy was still retreating. Thankfully, they were. Then he bounced toward the spot where he had secreted the key, followed by the one hiding the book, the growing fatigue of his fast run and liberal use of magic—especially the earthstorm—still masked sufficiently by adrenaline and determination. He had lost five good men today. He would *not* lose any more.

15

"So soon? Do you think that is wise?"

Rain blinked at the mild remonstrance. Antara had given him another difficult, uncomfortable task: pray, ponder, and follow his feelings about when they should violate their commitment to Captain Toreg and abandon their 'strategic' encampment. He had just told her what he felt. Strongly. They stood just a few yards behind her tent, out of view.

"I don't *know* if it's wise," he said. "I'm not very good at this. But it's what I feel."

She nodded, but her piercing eyes still made him uneasy. "Very well. I'm convinced now that all our new Mero Vothan friends will follow us and keep confidence. Haran can see to the preparations."

He considered her use of the phrase 'our new Mero Vothan friends.' And her tone. It made everything feel much more permanent. What was she planning? Then he wondered what he should be doing while Haran was getting everything prepared. Parade around pretending to inspect? He'd seen Ileom do plenty of hard-eyed scrutinizing, but he wasn't Ileom. He might as well sit down and carve a figurine out of wood for all the good he would be over the next few hours, but Antara had other ideas.

"Wait for me here. I'll be back in a few minutes. Then we need to find a place to practice while our people prepare. You feel we need to move, and that is good, but *I* feel we need to make this breakthrough soon."

Clenching the fist she couldn't see, he finally looked away after a weak nod. The whisk of her skirt, tailored from some of the new cloth in deep blue and light yellow, marked her departure. He found an old stump on which to sit as he questioned his feelings … and his sanity.

He heard her return to her tent after speaking with Haran, then emerge shortly thereafter. When she came around to the back, it took him a moment to process what he saw.

She quirked an eyebrow. "What? Don't women ever wear pants here?"

Truth be told, he'd rarely seen it, but he just shrugged.

"Well," she stated, "pants are useful, and I find them more comfortable to travel in. So, let's go. Haran has the preparations underway. I know just the place we can work."

He nodded, then followed her lead. She led them past the camp perimeter, over a small hill beyond the spring. After a few minutes, he knew the place she had in mind, an odd circle of ancient stones set at the bottom of a shallow bowl. It seemed a good choice, though in a way he couldn't articulate. Had he sensed magical energy there?

She slowed as they approached the circle, until they walked side by side. Then, between one step and the next, a large, opaque oval appeared just before them. He didn't have time to avoid it, his only reaction a surprised yelp as she grabbed his arm and pulled him through. He whirled to see that the oval had disappeared just as suddenly, then realized they were in a completely different place, nothing at all like the area of weathered stones.

He looked at Antara, who seemed pleased. "What happened?"

Her eyes twinkled. "We traveled. You and me, together. Amazing."

His eyes widened. "But how? And where?"

"I'm not positive on the where, but while you've been trying to refine the weaving of your threads, more successfully than you think, by the way, I've been learning things, too. Every time you employ your magic, there are ... manifestations ... from the talisman. Very subtle, but real. And strange. I've never encountered such profound, complexly simple power."

"Complexly simple?"

"I know. It doesn't make sense to me, either. There is a divine link."

"Oh. Well, my parents believe everything has a divine link."

She nodded, her expression thoughtful. "Yes, that is true. You have good parents. But feeling that from an inanimate object is quite rare."

Still utterly lost, Rain couldn't argue that they had indeed traveled somewhere. And he resisted the urge to correct her by saying he had *had* good parents; he was convinced now they were dead. He looked around, taking in their surroundings. At least it was daytime this trip, though rain threatened. They stood in the middle of a field of grain of some type, just as he had before. The shoots were still fairly young. Up ahead ran a fence, which seemed eerily similar, and beyond that a road. His breath caught as he realized they were in *exactly* the same place. He glanced at Antara, and she correctly interpreted his surprise.

"This is the spot?"

He nodded slowly, still trying to wrap his mind around it.

She seemed both satisfied and unsurprised. "Which way did you go? You said you found a house—a manor, rather."

He pointed at the fence. "I crossed that, then turned right and walked up the road, over the crest. It isn't far."

"Excellent. Not much of a crest, but I'm still glad I wore pants." She winked, then motioned for him to lead the way.

He started out cautiously, head swiveling as he examined the relative flatness of the landscape. The field was massive, much larger than any he had ever seen, and in all directions he spotted others just as large—some grain, others corn, several with shorter, leafy plants. Clusters of trees decorated his vision as well, and he spied houses in the midst of several of them. Not villages full of people to work the farms, just single houses, along with large barns. And some of the fields were round, with odd wheeled structures lancing out from the middle. The field he and Antara occupied sported many large wagon wheels

CROSSROADS OF AWAKENING MEMORY

arrayed along its length, metallic-looking and connected to each other by an incredibly long pole.

He stopped and turned to her. "This definitely looks like another world."

She nodded, and he noted a hint of wonder in her eyes. "Yes, it is. And we need to find out more about it. I'm pretty sure you can trigger a return if we get into trouble. Consciously, this time. That place we found with the strange, ancient rocks on our world—coincidentally close to our camp, don't you think?—it gave the key a temporary ... boost, which should linger for a bit."

"Pretty sure?" Those two words wrestled in his mind.

She put her hands on her hips and smirked. "You're a soldier. Pretty sure is the best you can beg for sometimes, am I right?" Her colloquial comment, delivered in a rogue accent, hit the mark. And he didn't want her to think he was afraid.

"Yes, okay." He strode toward the fence, then halted to peer closely at it. The posts were sturdy, and the four sets of cords running between them—no, braided metal wires—carried small spikes placed at intervals. He'd never seen anything like it. How long would it take a blacksmith to make something like that, enough to encompass such a massive field *four times*?

He found that the wires had decent play in the middle between posts, and so instead of climbing over as before, he held the two middle strands of thorny wire apart, creating an opening Antara could crouch down and step through. She nodded as if impressed. When she was on the other side, she did the same for him. One of the spikes snagged his tunic, and he heard a small rip. It almost bit into his flesh as well. She could have warned him back in the camp what she was planning—he would have worn armor to this place.

They stepped up onto the road, and he noted again how firm it was. It also had solid white lines painted almost perfectly straight on each side, with an interrupted yellow line down the middle. So odd. He began walking along the yellow line toward the top of the gentle rise. From there, they should be able to see the manor.

Before they crested, a shrill sound from behind—as from a large bull's horn, only sharper and higher in pitch—made him spin. What he saw defied description. A monster with two massive eyes bore down on them, though it was slowing. The sound repeated several more times, until Antara yanked him by the arm and hustled him off to the side of the road. Rain stared in fascination as the monster, which had four wheels like a wagon, only smaller and fatter, rushed past, growling. He spotted a bearded man, enclosed behind glass and wearing something black over his eyes, staring at them as it sped by. He was shaking his head and frowning. He probably thought they were idiots. Or maybe he wanted help escaping the monster? Rain was too confused to give it proper thought.

The wagon monster didn't stop, but continued on, picking up speed. Rain blinked several times as he realized how fast it must be going. Even the swiftest horses under harness couldn't possibly bring a wagon to such speeds.

He shook his head at Antara, whose eyes still followed the strange animal. Finally, she turned to him. "Well, it clearly didn't pose a danger to us. It warned us it was coming, then passed on by. And that was a human riding it, protected by a seemingly impervious structure."

"A blind human. Or at least one who didn't want to see much."

"Oh, he could see just fine. He wore something over his eyes to reduce the glare of the sun. I've seen similar things on our world, made of glass and then tinted somehow. By the elves." She winked. "I think this road is for creatures like that. Notice how it stayed on one half, between the yellow and white lines. We should walk along the verge, outside the white."

Rain agreed, and soon they topped the hill. The house stood just where he remembered, surrounded by tall trees, most of them deciduous, but with a pair of thick, towering pines, too. The manor was impressively large, two stories tall, though it didn't appear as elegant as he remembered. Peeling paint marred many of its surfaces, and some of the glass looked quite dirty in the daylight.

They approached carefully, coming even with the structure so they could see more of what surrounded it. A pair of wheeled beasts sat near a side entrance. Another building with a massive door rose farther back. Antara touched his arm, and they stopped. The beasts occupied most of Rain's attention, until he heard a familiar noise. A large black dog bolted from the back of the house, bounding toward them as it barked a warning.

When it had nearly reached them, Rain went to one knee and held up a hand, ordering the animal to stop in a gruff tone. The dog complied, sitting on its haunches, and then stared devotedly at Antara, not Rain. Of course. A shout from the manor caused it to bark once more, in a different tone, almost as if in apology to Antara, before it turned and scampered back to the house. Rain rose as he spotted a man standing on the front porch, then lifted a tentative hand in greeting. The man said something that sounded apologetic after giving the dog a quizzical look. The voice sounded similar to the one he'd heard on his first visit.

Antara started walking toward him, and Rain hesitated before following.

After they crossed the wide strip of green grass, softer than any Rain had ever felt, she gave a slight bow. "Hello. My name is Antara." She gestured at Rain. "This is Rain Barynd. It is a pleasure to meet you."

The man gave her a baffled expression. He glanced at Rain's sword, then his uniform tunic. He started speaking, but it was pure gibberish.

Antara placed both hands to her chest, face apologetic. "I'm sorry, sir, I can't understand you." Then she raised one hand and mimicked taking a drink, raising her eyebrows expectantly. The man nodded, then retreated through the open door and motioned them to follow.

"Clever," whispered Rain.

"I know. I really want to see what's inside."

Rain could only describe the basics of the interior. Chairs, a long sofa, tables, dishes, some pictures on the wall, a large rug. A small lamp was attached to the ceiling, but it didn't look like a chandelier. The windows let in plenty of sunlight, so it wasn't lit. Other light invaded the space, too, from a panel hanging off one wall, which also emitted noise. It was like … a window to a distant place. He could see and hear other people through it, in miniature. The man was using magic! Rain blinked, glancing at Antara in alarm. The man had gone farther inside, to a different room.

"Relax, Rain. I don't recognize the magic, but it appears harmless, just like that wagon beast that passed us. Nobody here has any reason to hurt us."

"As far as we know."

She chuckled. "Yes, as far as we know."

The man returned with the water in a crystal goblet. Antara took a generous drink and handed it to Rain, who did the same. The man cocked his head and gave them another odd look, then brushed a fly away from his face. He said something else, apparently in the form of a question.

Antara gave him an embarrassed smile, then nodded in appreciation as she handed back the goblet. "Thank you. We'll be going now." She took Rain by the hand and led him outside, not letting go until they were back on the road, heading toward the field. His hand tingled well after she had let go. He barely heard the dog whining as it watched them leave.

"That went well," she said as they ascended the hill. "He clearly thought we were strange, but it was all so fascinating. They have some amazing things in this world, but we need to get back. I'm pretty sure time is passing normally for us, though I'm not an expert on such things. Also, that mysterious boost from the stones on our world will be wearing off soon. I don't want to be trapped here, do you?" She laughed, and he stuttered an incoherent response.

She brought them to the place where they had arrived, the line tromped in the adolescent grain making it easy. Then she took a deep breath and smiled at him, almost flirtatiously. "I figured coming back to the same spot might be easier. You may need to hold the key this time, and then think of the place we left from." He complied, and she closed her eyes, humming softly. He was almost as shocked as the first time when the oval appeared. They stepped through, into the middle of the circle of stones, not next to them. Antara nodded as if that made perfect sense, looked up at the sky to note the position of the sun, which hadn't moved much, then started off toward the camp.

When they arrived, they found everything ready, faster than expected, with the few children playing around the burned-out campfire and among the wheels of their single wagon, cobbled together from salvage discovered on foraging trips. A few of the boards displayed the burn marks of their former demise, but the patchwork conveyance was sturdy enough, and a huge help for their move.

Antara's gaze settled on Haran, who was speaking with Androl. The grizzled warrior stopped and turned as they approached, bowing slightly to Antara.

"We are ready, m'lady ... sir." Rain caught slight suspicion in Haran's eyes when the older soldier glanced at him. He didn't know what Antara had told Haran about them wandering off together, and he tried not to blush at what the sergeant might be thinking, sworn to his service or not.

"Very good," said Antara. "Thank you, Haran." She seemed—or pretended to seem—unaware of his veiled concern and curiosity. She addressed Androl next. "And our soldiers understand their scouting patterns?" There was more behind that question, which Androl clearly understood.

"Yes, m'lady." He, too, spared a glance for Rain. "We worked it out with Commander Barynd a few days ago. All the contingencies are set, and we have our stories ready if we're discovered. We'll keep to minor roads, of course."

Rain winced at his use of the title 'Commander Barynd,' but Antara acted like it was the most natural, logical thing in the world. She had let the phrase drop from her lips just the day before, in the hearing of Androl, and he had, as she had surely expected, adopted it. To please *her*, of course.

Rain almost gave an embarrassed eye roll, then sensed Antara's gaze upon him. He turned, catching her expectant expression. He cleared his throat. "Thank you, Captain Goth, Captain Emerin. We'll move out, then. Lady Antara and I will take the lead."

He caught a slight raising of eyebrows from Antara at his off-handed promotion of the two men to captain, but it made sense to him, especially since she had similarly elevated him to commander. They would have to work out their specific rank orders. Or would they? They had seven total men, Rain included. Why in the world did they need to think about multiple ranks?

Fortunately, Chaigen showed up with Sun Tamer and Cyclone, saving him from further awkwardness. He and Antara mounted, and he tapped

Sun Tamer with his boot heels to commence a trot toward the front. They had ten horses now, two pulling the wagon. Because of Antara's ability and Toreg's helpfulness with provisions, they had amassed a significant amount of salted meat, along with some flour, dried fruits, and a variety of wild tubers. It wasn't a fancy diet, but it sufficed. They also had ample waterskins, filled from the spring, and the Mero Vothans had helped plot a course that would give them access to water along the way, even as they passed through dryer regions.

Their destination wasn't fully clear to Rain. Somewhere south and east, still north of Arxhana, the Mero Vothan capital, seemed to feel right. It would have to be far enough from Crystal Mirror Lake that they wouldn't be seen as encroaching, yet close enough that they could interact and trade as needed—and not just with the dwarves. That balance was something Antara obviously understood much better than he did. And then … then he was supposed to search for a prophet. Somehow.

Re-crossing into Mero Vothas felt less climactic than Rain had expected. The land wasn't any different on the other side, and no Mero Vothan guards mustered to harass them. He kept a sharp eye out, though, and they always had a pair of Mero Vothans scouting.

After the first several hours, the trip assumed peaceful uneventfulness. They had food and water, and they were all in good health. How many refugees wandering around New Haven could claim the same? His heart constricted at the thought. Antara had convinced him again not to go looking for his parents—or their remains. She showed empathy, but she clearly cared a great deal more about that precious talisman and the 'higher' purposes wrapped around it. Her subtle flirtations were probably meant to keep him close. And curse him if it wasn't working.

He vowed he would return soon, though. He had to find them, or at least discover what had happened to them.

On the third day, Antara interrupted his further ruminations on the fall of New Haven, wearing that regal dark blue and yellow skirt again. She had just returned from speaking with the members of their small caravan, taking Jerise with her to make sure everyone was feeling well. Haran roved up and down the line, checking on things and getting updates from men and women alike. Androl kept busy overseeing the scouting. All of which left Rain with little to do except … ruminate. It was making him anxious, even knocking him a little off kilter.

"Another group of refugees has followed us. They're about half a day behind, all on foot."

Rain gave her a blank look, taking a moment to process what she'd said. "Our scouts found them? How many?"

"Fifty-seven. They have no small children among them. They are led by two Council Guardsmen, it appears, since the scouts report they are dressed like you. They aren't in great shape, especially since they take little time to forage, not wanting to fall too far behind us."

"How do they even know we're here?"

She shrugged. "They must have scouted earlier, and our trail isn't hard to follow."

He pondered the new development as Sun Tamer continued plodding along. She seemed to be getting bored, too. Then a thought sprang to his mind. A faint, desperate hope danced a jig. Was it possible his parents were part of that group? The slightest chance was enough.

He wheeled Sun Tamer off the road, causing Cyclone to rear slightly before Antara followed. "You want to go meet them right now?" she asked.

"Yes. Our group can stop here for a bit, can't it? I'll tell Haran and Androl."

Receiving no objections from her, and surprised he'd said it so assertively despite the hedge of an interrogative, he quickly found the two captains and let them know his intention. They accepted it calmly and brought the train to a halt, announcing some short-range foraging missions.

Antara requested to accompany him—acting oddly meek—and they let Sun Tamer and Cyclone run a bit. Sun Tamer relished the chance, and it became a competition. Rain had to rein her in several times and make her walk for stretches. Cyclone seemed livelier, too, and Antara commented how exhilarating it was to feel the speed and strength of their mounts. Was it pretense, or did she really experience the pure joy of it like he did?

Within an hour, they spied the other refugee group in the distance. Rain could already tell it was a ragged, tired bunch. Probably near starving. One of their Mero Vothan scouts appeared from behind some trees on foot, startling him. The man hustled up.

"I've been keeping an eye on them, sir, m'lady." He ducked his head toward Antara.

"Thank you, Greshin," she said. "They need food and water. Take Yorel and make haste to our people, who have stopped. Bring back as many provisions as you can carry on your horses. Bring Haran and Jerise, too. If you can be back here before nightfall, you will save some lives."

Greshin saluted and raced back into the trees. Moments later, he and Yorel bounded away on their horses, speeding toward their temporary camp.

"Our people?" said Rain, realizing too late he had uttered it out loud. He'd been wanting to find the right time to question her about it, though.

Antara gazed at him with soft determination. "The more we say it— and act like it—the more true it will become."

"But … why does it need to become true? We just need to get them to a safe place, right?"

After a barely perceptible shake of her head, she replied, "I don't think so. The world is changing, Rain, and that change will accelerate further. It already has for New Haven, but no country—no people—will be left untouched."

That warning continued to sound far more ominous than his simple mind could comprehend, so he just gave her a bemused look and heeled Sun Tamer toward the refugees.

As they got closer, he squinted, surprise tingling the back of his neck. At fifty yards he was certain, and he didn't know whether to groan or laugh hysterically.

He stopped Sun Tamer just ten feet from the two Council Guardsmen, their uniforms barely recognizable, dirty and with multiple bloodied tears. The Mero Vothan scouts had sharp eyes.

They blinked up at him, recognition dawning as uncertainty filled their expressions.

"Garrett, Jervin," he said, uncertain how to modulate his tone.

He felt Antara's eyes on him. After a moment, Garrett dropped his gaze to Sun Tamer, and he mumbled, "You still have your horse."

Rain despised Garrett, bloody uniform or not, and that emotion seized him momentarily. He had to remind himself with great effort that Garrett and Jervin had obviously passed through hell. He scanned the line of refugees, several with their eyes pegged to him and Antara in hopeful pleading, but most staring downward, waiting like they were cattle. One had plopped onto the ground, staring sightlessly into the distance.

Rain swallowed, his throat suddenly dry. "We can help. I—that is, the Lady Antara and I—have two men fetching provisions. They should be back before nightfall."

Garrett's eyes went wide in desperate disbelief. "You … will help us?"

"Of course." He gave a sharp nod, then dismounted and approached his two beat-up nemeses. "Do you have any wounded among you?" That was clearly a silly question.

After a pause Garrett replied, "Yes." He glanced up at Antara. "Is she a healer?"

Rain shook his head. "No, but I can do some minor healing, and we have another healer much better than I am. She'll be here with the provisions. Show me who I should tend to first."

Garrett stood dumbfounded, until Jervin nudged him. Rain remembered Jervin had been wounded at Jerel's Altar, and he looked him up and down. "Your leg?"

"Healers in New Haven took care of it before …" He didn't continue, just adopted a confused, disbelieving look.

"Follow me, Rain," said Garrett. "I mean, um …" He looked at Antara again.

"Commander Barynd," she supplied helpfully. Rain cringed while his chest puffed out slightly of its own accord.

"Okay. Um, Commander, please follow me. We have several injured. Others took wounds that were too severe. We … well, we had to …"

"I understand," said Rain, a sudden surge of empathy warming his boastful chest. "This is what war looks like, just as Master Ileom described it. I wasn't prepared, either. And it's definitely worse than Ileom's yelling."

His small attempt at humor fell flat. Garrett just nodded without expression, then led him toward a woman a few horse lengths back leaning heavily on her teenage daughter. Her ankle appeared twice its normal size, wrapped in bloody bandages torn from her tattered skirt. Rain had her sit, and then he knelt, struggling to focus until Antara appeared next to him and laid a gentle hand on his shoulder. After wondering what Garrett would think of *that*—and feeling foolish for caring what Garrett thought about a beautiful, elegantly dressed woman touching him—he was able to concentrate. Within a few minutes, he felt satisfied the woman's ankle was nearly as strong as before it was injured.

She let out a joyous exclamation once she realized it, hugging and crying with her daughter. Garrett shook his head in wonder and guided them to the next person. Soon, Rain wished Jerise were already with them. Some of the injuries he could only partially heal, especially the head wounds, but he did his best. He ministered to thirty-eight people, some with multiple maladies, and by the time he finished he was almost completely spent. He didn't know how much time had passed. Low clouds blanketed the sky in a sullen gray, and the light from the sun behind them had dimmed considerably.

"And you?" he finally asked Garrett, who blushed.

"Mine can wait." He looked away, then backed up a step and bowed to Antara.

Rain turned to her as well. "I'm exhausted."

She clicked her tongue in sympathy. "I can imagine. Come, we can sit and rest near the horses. I've gotten everyone else situated. The others will be here soon."

He glanced around. Indeed, she had. The mood, of course, had improved dramatically with the healings. Most of the people glanced their way frequently with a smile or an uttered blessing.

"Our little community is expanding," she said in a low voice when they had seated themselves semi-comfortably on the verge of the minor road, where the grasses were thicker. Garrett and Jervin had planted themselves twenty yards away.

Rain grunted. "We can help them, but we don't need them."

"We *have* helped them," she corrected. "And we might very well need them. Garrett and ... Jervin, is it? ... obviously aren't two of your favorite people, but they are soldiers, trained by Ileom."

A low growl escaped his throat.

"Why don't you like them?"

"It doesn't matter."

"I see. Well, treat them fairly, Rain, as a commander should."

"I won't treat them at all. If they join us, Haran and Androl can deal with them."

"And you will ignore them."

"Correct."

She gave a tsk-tsk. "They must have treated you very poorly. But war changes a great many things."

He didn't respond to that. She was right. But she was also wrong.

16

Agrancik Rezanprey fixed his over-large eyes on Ileom after a quick shake of his head. "I do not know what has happened. If General Inzeal has acquired griffons from Alave and brought them to Tenris, it is a troubling mystery." Ileom deepened his glare, but Agrancik didn't wilt. Was he holding something back?

"Not just griffons, but trained riders," said Tenedrast, seated with them at a round hardwood table of rich, swirling hues in a private chamber high in one of the Keep's soaring silver towers. "Obviously, a second key linked to Alave has been discovered and is in play. Is Inzeal perhaps from your planet? Is that why we know so little about him?"

The question of Inzeal's origins seemed to make Agrancik deeply uncomfortable. "I cannot say. If he *is* from Alave, he would have changed his name. And I have not seen him here to know if I recognize the face."

"We are riding blind into a hurricane," growled Ileom, gazing through one of the tall tower windows at snow-covered Witches Peak in the far distance.

"Griffons are tricky to handle. He cannot have brought many."

Ileom's eyes pinned the so-far trustworthy alien human again. "We don't know that. You will have to go back to your planet and assess, taking one of the Order with you as the full Council agreed."

"It is not that simple," protested Agrancik, the only modern Order member not from Tenris. "And it sounds as if you don't trust me."

Ileom let a low rumble escape his throat again. "At the moment, I don't trust *anyone*."

"That is true," offered Tenedrast. "Even on his best days, in calm times, he doesn't trust me. Antara, maybe. Avrenor, who is now dead."

Agrancik shifted his gaze between the two, letting a solemn moment of remembrance linger, then spread his hands before him on the table. "I am afraid that my book is not functioning properly with my key. I believe I can return, but I cannot be sure where the key will take me."

Ileom had suspected that for a while. "Why didn't you tell us?"

"I was trying to fix it. I have so far been unsuccessful, even with Vellinar's help. Perhaps if Antara could assist? She is best at these types of things."

Ileom turned to Tenedrast. "Have you been able to locate her?"

The mage shook his head. "She has masked the talisman Rain Barynd possesses, and for some reason she is not allowing herself to be scried through our normal means. I do not detect a permanent absence of her presence, though."

"She's worried about what powers the enemy possesses that she isn't aware of," Ileom supplied. "I am, too. You were at least able to locate her briefly just inside the Istarrean border, correct?"

"Yes, but that was some weeks ago. I doubt she would have stayed there."

"That is where we must start, though. They likely headed deeper into Istarrea, perhaps over to Broen. Or maybe west, across the Ice Sea." He stared at Agrancik until the man squirmed in his chair. "All three of us will go, using the cavern key, and you will bring your Alave book and key. I will inform Markydis, who can let the rest of the Council know. If we can't find Antara and Rain quickly, you and I will go to Alave, wherever the key drops us."

Agrancik glanced at Tenedrast, obviously weighing both the risk and the off-procedure demand. Ileom hadn't intended to volunteer himself to accompany the Alavian to his home planet, but he suddenly felt strongly about it. Finally, Agrancik nodded. "Very well. I am anxious to discover and repair the anomaly, so that I—or rather, we—can also assess the danger on *my* planet."

"Your *stable* planet, where everything is under control." Ileom hadn't growled this time; instead, his tone was smooth as a sheet of ice.

Agrancik's countenance finally fell. "Again, I am sorry."

∞

The roads through the lightly populated upper hill country of Mero Vothas, hard against the Miracle Mountains, were mostly poor to nearly impassable, especially with a wagon, but they managed. A few magical assists from Antara helped, along with the felling of dozens of trees. She could place a shield underneath the wagon's wheels, strong enough to bear its weight for the few seconds needed to traverse a tougher obstacle … as long as the horses were able to cross it first; not even she could get them to set foot on an invisible surface. Rain couldn't blame them. Seeing the fully laden conveyance roll on magically hardened air was distinctly unnatural.

Rain caught several dwarven scouts tracking their progress, but they never ventured close enough for him or Antara to speak with them. They made Garrett and Jervin nervous for reasons they wouldn't disclose.

Their Mero Vothan scouts were effective in keeping the group's profile low, alerting them when to stop or change course to avoid potentially uncomfortable encounters. Rain was grateful for them, and he expressed that to Androl as they entered their third week of travel since leaving the camp.

"We're just doing what we promised to do," Androl responded, craning his neck to look up at Rain riding Sun Tamer. Rain dismounted to walk alongside him.

"What do you think Captain Toreg will do when he finds out?"

"*When?*" Androl sounded genuinely surprised.

"Yes, when. He'll eventually find out. He has to."

Androl angled his eyebrows in deep thought. "Not necessarily. Things are still in chaos, with refugees crawling everywhere, especially in the lower areas. We're a noticeable group, but one of many, and nearly in the mountains. We're also more than two hundred miles south now, well outside his area."

"But the border camp."

He shrugged. "He might eventually find it abandoned, if he crosses the border to check up on me and the others—or to deliver a message to Antara, I suppose—but he won't know why. The enemy could have chased us out, for all he knows. Or we might have ventured toward New Haven City. And he has a lot of other things to worry about."

Rain pondered that a moment. "But what if one of your men returns to wherever Toreg is based and lets him know? Or finds another way to get him a message?"

Androl cocked his head, frowning. "Betrays us?" The surprise seemed doubly genuine, and by 'us' he likely meant 'Antara.' "I doubt *that* will happen. We have had many discussions on it, and we are agreed. Lady Antara has asked me about this, too."

Rain nodded, letting his eyes sweep across their path. It had rained the day before, but not hard, and the road in this section was better than most they had traversed in recent days. It felt good to walk. They would stop soon, with sunset only about an hour off. Antara was out with a hunting party, and given the abundant wildlife in these greener environs near the first peaks of the Miracles—plus her skills—they would return with plenty of fresh game.

After a few minutes, he spotted a pair of dwarves watching them from atop a distant, rocky knoll. He indicated them with his chin.

"Do you think any dwarves will bother us?"

Androl let his gaze rest upon the watchers for a moment. "Not likely. The dwarves are peaceful."

"Unless they're being invaded."

Androl chuckled, one of the few times he'd done that around just Rain. "I suppose that's true. They are said to be fierce, doughty warriors."

Rain wondered about that. Had they fought anyone recently? Ileom had described to him and the other trainees the challenges to a fighting force presented by prolonged peace. Armies gain potency through battle experience, and when they go long stretches without anyone to fight, they lose much of their edge, especially as the veterans retire and are replaced by fresh recruits.

Training helped, to be sure, especially if conducted by seasoned soldiers, but the real thing was different. Rain himself could now attest to that.

"What if they do harass us? What should we do?"

Androl studied the dwarves again. "We aren't making any threatening moves. They also must realize we aren't an easy target. They're good at sensing magic, by the way, even from a distance."

Rain turned to him and blinked. "They are? You mean when it's being used, or …"

"From a great distance, they can tell if it's being used. If they're close—maybe fifty yards or so—they can sense the ability. At least, that's what I've been taught."

"Jerise has been performing more healings along the way, including for the horses."

Androl nodded. "Yes. The dwarves will know we have magic-users among us. And strong ones. I'm not sure they can tell what kinds of magic we employ, though. Lady Antara can master air. You, fire. Others, earth or water. Some, the very rare ones, a little of everything."

"Like Jerise." Yes, he had noticed. At first, her healing had been dominated by heat, but she had been adding the other elements, more and more of late. It made her far more effective and efficient. She had vastly outshone him in healing before; now he was a speck at the bottom of a deep ravine.

Rain mused on that a minute longer, then asked, "Aren't the dwarves resistant to magic?"

Androl grinned. "Who told you that?"

"Um … I don't know. That's what I've heard, though."

"Well, I've never heard that, just that they don't have many magic-users among them."

"Neither do we."

"We have more than they do."

Rain wasn't sure about that, but how would he know?

Androl changed the subject. "How much farther, do you think? We'll pass Crystal Mirror Lake in another two or three days."

Rain mulled that over. "Maybe the same distance beyond the lake? It feels like we'll know the spot when we come to it."

Androl nodded. "You are a praying man?"

Two things about that question gave him pause—the reference to being a man, and how often he really prayed.

"I … need to learn it better," he finally replied.

"Hmmm … as do we all. I was not raised to pray much, but I'm beginning to believe we need it."

Rain had no pertinent wisdom to offer, so he stayed silent. They continued marching along, the soft ground occasionally yielding a squelching noise.

He was lost in contemplation when his head snapped up at the sound of an approaching rider from up ahead. It was Antara, and she had Cyclone at a full gallop. Rain immediately mounted and urged Sun Tamer forward.

Cyclone came to another of his whirling stops before Sun Tamer had taken more than a few strides, and then Antara spoke in a calm but urgent tone, loud enough for Androl to hear, too. "We encountered a sizeable party of dwarves up ahead. They wish to speak with you, Rain."

"With *me*? Why?"

"They recognized your uniform, and they have received a report of your battle exploits."

"My *what?*"

"When you killed those two soldiers. A dwarf or dwarf-friend must have been watching."

"Oh." This was yet another first. "Well, should we take Androl and Haran with us?"

She gave her head a slight shake. "I don't think that will be necessary. And these dwarves don't seem hostile."

"Okay. I'll follow you."

After giving a nod that covered both him and Androl, she turned Cyclone and galloped off. Sun Tamer leaped after them as if it were a chase, mud spatters flying behind the two horses. Rain caught the spray from Cyclone's hooves until he steered Sun Tamer off his line a bit and pulled her back. She didn't like that. He was certain she wanted to get ahead and spray the stallion back.

A few minutes later, Antara slowed Cyclone to a trot, and Rain moved Sun Tamer up beside them, wiping dried splotches of mud from his face and uniform. Some had clodded in his hair, too. He scoured the landscape, noting nothing of interest until they had passed through a stand of trees. Then Antara brought them to a halt, and he counted more than thirty dwarves, at least half of them armed with broad axes. A few carried bows as well. At their head stood an imposing dwarf in a belted, dark-blue tunic with golden emblems on both sides of his chest. The rest were dressed in rugged dark browns and grays, except for a female dwarf standing next to the one in blue. She wore a silky gown of saffron and emerald, bordered at the hems with small, multi-colored stones. Her belt and thick necklace appeared to be pure gold, and both she and her male companion sported several exquisite, bejeweled rings.

The dwarf leader raised his hand in apparent greeting. "You are Rain Barynd, of the New Haven Council Guard?"

Rain nodded, hands twitching on Sun Tamer's reins as she nickered. He was about to dismount, thinking it the courteous thing to do, when Antara tsked loud enough for him to take note.

"And you are the protector of Lady Antara?" asked the dwarf. His over-large ears twitched.

Rain didn't turn to see Antara's reaction to that query as he re-settled himself in the saddle. "Kind of. We've protected each other."

The dwarf lowered his hand and wrinkled his bulbous nose. "Where are you taking such a large group of people, including several other soldiers?"

It was a fair question. "We plan to pass by Crystal Mirror Lake, and then hopefully find a place we can settle."

"Permanently?"

Rain glanced at Antara, who stared primly back at him, before he answered. "Well, yes. New Haven is not safe."

The dwarf wagged his thick brown beard. "It is safe now. The enemy has retreated fully, back beyond the barbarian lands."

"We have heard rumors, but how do you know this for certain?" asked Antara.

He puffed out his chest. "We have sent many scouts. Our horses—ponies, you like to call them, though they are merely thicker and sturdier, like us—are not fast, but they have great endurance. Most of those scouts have returned, and they all report the same thing. So, you can return to New Haven."

Rain had no idea how to respond. Should they turn around and go back to New Haven, see how many had survived, start to rebuild? Part of him keenly desired that, of course. But … he had his mission, which stealthily lodged more firmly in his mind every day.

As he floundered, Antara replied, "We have a purpose for being here, Master … ah …"

"You may call me Rastifellen."

"That is your short name?"

"Yes."

"Very good, Master Rastifellen. As I said, we have a purpose, and I am a member of the Order of the Fallen Moon. These refugees have come to us, and they are under our watchcare."

Rastifellen narrowed his eyes. He clearly recognized the reference to the Order, which meant she hadn't made up the name, though perhaps he suspected a pretended connection. Whenever Rain asked her for details, she gave him crumbs.

The dwarven man stared for long seconds at her, then at Rain. Finally, he turned to the woman beside him. They shared a weighty look, and then she said to him, "It accords with the recent pronouncement from the Circle. And I sense no danger from them. They may pass." She turned her gaze on Antara, as if to both emphasize and question the 'no danger' part.

Antara gave her a solemn nod. "Great danger *is* coming. All good people must prepare to stand against it."

The woman maintained her eye contact, even as she gave a slight bow. "Indeed. Are the elves aware, too?"

Elves again. Rain hoped shock didn't show on his face. It was still hard to believe.

"Yes, they are, and many are gathering, though I know not where."

"As are we," said Rastifellen, "though the Order has not formally requested an emissary from us yet." Rain couldn't tell whether he sounded offended.

"Consider this the formal request," said Antara, maintaining her sober tone while lifting her chin a little. "I will even write it up. Your emissary will be welcomed."

The man's bushy eyebrows came together as he folded his arms across his chest. "You can indeed provide a writ?"

Antara nodded. "I can, and I will, once I return to our wagon. I have my seal with me."

The man turned to the woman again, then took a deep breath. "Aristomili, are you thinking what I am thinking?"

She cracked a smile for the first time. "I can seldom tell what you're thinking, as you're often confused, but I agree we should take them to the valley. They will be safer there. At least for now."

The *valley*? Rain looked at Antara, who returned his gaze and smiled. She broke the connection as Rastifellen cleared his throat.

"Upriver from Crystal Mirror Lake, there is a hidden valley. Few know of it. It is protected by means of a very old magic, and for reasons we don't fully understand the climate is much milder than the surrounding area. The United Dwarven Kingdom claims it, but it is considered sacred. We have not allowed anyone to live there for more than a hundred years, not even of our own kind."

"Until now," said Aristomili. "We have felt it coming, and our scouts have been watching your group closely."

After a pause, Antara turned to Rain and said, "Well, Commander Barynd?"

Still feeling confused, he tried to gauge the dwarves' expressions. What did they think of her, a member of the Order of the Fallen Moon, which they obviously respected, asking his opinion? Why did she keep elevating him?

The answer came, though, from a place so deep he felt like it began at the center of the world. The moment loomed profound but passed quickly, feeling a little like heartburn. He nodded at Rastifellen and Aristomili. "Yes, that is the right place." He blinked, startled at his own answer, and how it had come. What was happening to him? Was his descent into insanity increasing in speed?

"I agree," said Antara firmly. She made a formal bow to the dwarven leaders from her saddle. "We accept your kind and most gracious offer. Night has nearly fallen. Would you join us for a meal?"

Based on the dwarves' guarded expressions, it was a bold invitation. But then Aristomili laughed heartily. "Of course we will! Rasti might claim it'll kill him, but I won't complain if it does." She winked, and Antara returned the laughter. Rain tried to laugh along, but it came out more like a coughing fit.

Rastifellen rounded on her, face turning red. "Well, *Aris*, it was not I struggling to hide my constipation the last time we shared a meal with humans."

Aristomili's cheeks blossomed with color. She cast a fleshy finger at his nose, nearly poking him. "You would do well to mind your tongue, my dear brother, lest it end up in your ear."

They were *siblings*? Was that better or worse than them being spouses? Would a fight erupt among the dwarves present?

Antara guided Cyclone forward until he stood just a few feet from the pair. They both swung their glares toward her.

"I am aware of your dietary norms," Antara said. "We cannot match them, but we can come close. Do not fear to repast with us, for you would do us much honor."

Rain couldn't have come up with such a diplomatic response if he'd had a week to prepare. He studied the dwarven reactions; happily, the party seemed mollified by her words, the two leaders finally nodding their full and united acceptance.

"We will come," said Rastifellen. His grumpy scowl turned mischievous. "But my sister might need your healer, who is clearly powerful."

Before a real fight could break out, Antara spoke loudly. "That is splendid. By your leave, we will ride back swiftly so that the preparations may begin." She turned Cyclone, and with a glance at Rain, they were on their way.

"What happened?" asked Rain when they were well out of earshot. He had to yell for the wind rushing by.

She didn't turn her head, but the turbulence around them lessened considerably. He couldn't see that magic, but it allowed her to speak in a normal voice. "For a dwarf to address another dwarf by their doubly shortened name in the presence of non-dwarves is a great insult."

"Can *we* call them by their, um, doubly short names?"

"Yes, because that is practical, and dwarves are very practical ... unless they're playing insult games with each other."

She let the magic dissipate and they rode on, soon reaching the caravan. After Rain called a halt for the day, Antara issued orders to women and men alike regarding the preparations they would need to make. Soon, their little community buzzed like a beehive with excited activity. Rain caught countless expressions of wonderment that they would get to meet—and even dine with—a distinguished party of dwarves. He and Antara hadn't even told them yet of the dwarves' promise regarding the magical valley. He assumed they would be happy at that, too, though he started to harbor his own doubts. They would be isolated. Why had he decided so hastily?

Much later, after the dwarves had dined with them amid an ebullient mood and then settled nearby for the night, he was finally able to ask Antara about it.

"This place," he began, not sure how to articulate his feelings, "it ... seems like you've heard about it. What will we *do* there?"

"I don't know, Rain, but we'll figure it out."

"Have you seen it?"

She demurred, offering a mysterious smile. "Just pray, and be grateful."

The dwarves departed the next morning, except for two guides, who Rastifellen claimed were among their mightiest warriors, though they didn't appear particularly strong or fierce. The average dwarf was only a few inches shorter than a human, and these two were no exception. Nor did they exhibit a noticeable martial aspect. Before noon, these guides led them off the road and onto a narrower path, which they claimed would be wide enough for the wagon to traverse, though tight in spots.

Rain wondered when they would cross the border into what the dwarves considered their territory, but he didn't dare ask. Such lines didn't exist on any human maps he had studied. He had bigger problems to dwell on, anyway, and spent much of his time struggling with his feelings. The responsibilities kept increasing, while his ability to handle them stayed the same. At best. He had prayed, or at least tried to, but it was hard to tell if it had done any good. He didn't say anything to Antara about that, and she didn't ask.

The terrain became more rugged, and their progress slowed. However, their forays to find food met with increasing success. Antara remarked that they might not even need her. She spent a great deal of time speaking with the dwarves, peppering them with questions and listening intently to their answers. They remained patient with her near-constant queries, probably because she mixed in a fair amount of flattery. Despite her efforts, though, she couldn't get them to give her their names.

By the fifth day of travel on their new path, they were in the mountains proper, and the air had grown significantly colder. They hadn't been hit with any precipitation, fortunately, but patches of snow decorated the landscape. While winter was still many weeks off, Rain expressed concern to Antara that people might begin to freeze. He didn't think he would be able to gather enough heat to help.

She laughed lightly. "There is plenty of heat all around us, including deep in the ground, and you're stronger than you think. You also don't know what true cold is. None of us has experienced it. You can learn to gather heat from farther away. Remember, too, that you are only gathering, not destroying. The heat does not disappear. It just dissipates, available to be gathered again. It is said that, long ago, the best mages with your talents could cycle the heat continuously, so that the cold couldn't displace it. That must have been taxing, although more people could access magic back then, sharing the burden. We will squeeze more people into each tent, and you can infuse larger rocks with heat to help us pass the nights more comfortably. Thanks to Captain Toreg, we also have enough clothing we can wear in layers to help us through the days when we are active. Do not worry."

Rain had already tried injecting heat into rocks, all the way through, and it was relatively easy, depending on the type of rock. Antara said she knew which kinds of rocks held the heat better, and there was no shortage of stone in the mountains, so his anxiety subsided.

Two days later, at about mid-morning, they topped a ridge and began descending into a narrow bowl. At first, it appeared much like other places they had traversed, but Rain soon noted a marked rise in temperature. He trotted Sun Tamer up to where Antara talked with the two dwarves.

"Where are we now?" he asked her, though his question was directed at the guides. He still felt nervous talking to them, though they seemed friendly enough.

She broke off her discussion and smiled at him. "We're here, Commander. The warmth you feel is real, and it's a permanent feature."

"How?" he asked.

"I do not know. Hot water running close beneath the surface? I don't feel any magic at work here." She turned to the guides. "Where are the hot springs you told me about?"

One of them pointed ahead and a little to their right. "We are not far. They are hidden in a fold in the land, and breezes clash above them, spreading the steam. That is the old magic, and you may not be able to feel it."

Antara pursed her lips. "Hmmm ... not without some study and practice. But I *will* find it. So fascinating already, this place."

Rain strained his eyes, and he thought he spotted a bit of that steam. He couldn't be sure, though.

A few paces on, one of the guides threw up a hand. Sun Tamer reacted instantly, nearly throwing Rain onto her neck.

"What is it?" he asked.

"We must wait," the dwarf said without turning. He kept his hand in the air.

After a couple of minutes, Rain wondered how long he could hold his hand up like that. Apparently quite a while, for it remained still as stone.

Finally, he slowly lowered it, then motioned them to follow as he and his companion continued on, veering left. Rain felt disappointed, wanting to see the hot springs first, but he had no choice but to accept their direction.

The slope lessened, and twenty minutes later the guides led them into a broad glade, as verdant as any Rain had seen in spring. Both guides stopped, raised their hands high for several seconds, faces aimed skyward, then let them drop.

Rain almost fell off Sun Tamer. A chorus of gasps filled the air behind him. Dozens of pristine buildings had suddenly appeared, nearly filling the green glade, organized across a perfect grid of impossibly smooth streets made of crushed rock glazed over with a transparent material.

The buildings were fashioned from precisely cut stones in varying shades of tan and gray. At least half boasted two stories. The tops were squared, with no peaks or towers, and the windows were broad and plentiful, some with shutters, some with glass, some sporting both. Shutters and curtains displayed a host of subdued colors that somehow seemed sharp. Flowers and small bushes decorated street edges, window boxes, and gardens.

Antara dismounted, then moved to stand next to the guides. Rain followed suit.

"What is this place?" she asked, voice tinged with awe.

"This is one of the sanctuaries," said a guide reverently. "As Rastifellen and Aristomili said, it hasn't been occupied for at least a hundred years. Its magic is older than the bones of the mountains, and even the members of the Dwarven Circle understand only a small portion of how it works. That is all I can say. This is your new home, if you choose to accept it."

Rain raised an eyebrow as he studied Antara. Did she sense anything odd or potentially dangerous? He didn't, but his mind was still trying to catch up. She returned his gaze after a moment, then nodded to the guides.

"We accept and are most grateful. This good fortune is beyond imagining. God has truly revealed his hand in this."

Both dwarves squared themselves to her and bowed, eyes remaining fixed on her. They could have been twins, Rain finally noticed, though perhaps it was a trick of the light. "Indeed he has," said the other one when they straightened. "You will find plentiful stores of food here, along with seeds. The land can be worked year-round, and wild game is abundant, especially beyond the edges of the valley. Animals you bring here can stay, of course, and they are safe. As are you, as long as you abide the rules of the sanctuary."

Antara gave them a respectful, acquiescing bow in return. "What are the rules?"

The one who had first addressed them took a small step forward. "First, I will tell you our names, after apologies for the secrecy. I am Didremigar." He gestured at the other. "This is my brother, Nostramidas. We are of the Inner Watch; hence the need for discretion. You may call us Migo and Midas, if you wish."

Antara's eyes widened slightly, and her nose pinched, subtly screaming surprise. She took a long, slow breath as she studied them. "Why do you reveal yourselves to us? To my knowledge, no member of the Order has known the name or likeness of anyone in the Dwarven Inner Watch for at least seven decades."

Midas stepped up beside his brother. "The Circle can read the signs as well as you. The incursion into New Haven was the beginning of much greater trials ahead—a clear warning bell. And, if our information is good, the Crossroads governing travel between kindred worlds have awakened, heralding a chaotic but ultimately cleansing climax of linked destinies." His fiery gaze flicked to Rain, piercing him.

Rain could almost feel the talisman warming in his pocket. *Linked destinies?* Migo patted his brother on the shoulder, winked at Rain, then continued. "My brother is very dramatic, though he is correct. But regarding your original question, Lady Antara … the rules of this valley are simple, as are the penalties for violating them. The first rule is that you defile not the name of God. I presume you are aware that what we call the 'Old Magic' was divided into Light and Dark. Light Magic, championed by the Creator, protects this valley. Your governance process for this rule must be robust, or the natural consequences will follow, far more quickly than in other places on this world." His eyes remained on her until she nodded, then switched to Rain until he did likewise.

"The second," chimed in Midas, expression still intense, "is closely related to the first: you must establish your laws in accordance with the words of God recorded in the First Revelations."

"I am familiar with those," assented Antara. Rain wasn't, but he nodded anyway. He felt newly overwhelmed by how little he understood.

"The third," said Migo, "is to honor agency. These people are not *your* people—they are God's children, each divinely powerful in their own right. They must be able to participate in their own governance, not be ruled by the foolish fiat of the arrogant."

Rain blinked at that. Didn't the dwarves have a king? And how did robust enforcement of laws against defiling the name of God square with honoring agency?

"And the fourth," said Midas, "is to expand this place for others who will come and wish to abide the rules and stay. It is indeed a place of refuge, but also of preparation for the battles that await, both physical and spiritual. Daunting is the task; do not underestimate it." His eyes displayed twin fires again.

Rain took an involuntary step backward. Surely Master Ileom should be here, not him. The weight of the 'simple' rules laid out by these clearly important and knowledgeable dwarves suddenly felt like an avalanche thrashing him down a rocky slope. He still hadn't even turned sixteen, and in truth he was a mere Council Guardsman of tiny, obliterated New Haven. He had discovered some magical ability, but what of it? Besides that cursed talisman.

Without thinking, he withdrew the key and held it out to Migo and Midas. "Here is the traveling talisman we have. Do you want to safeguard it?"

Antara gasped. When he looked at her, she was frowning deeply while avoiding his gaze. Migo and Midas hadn't allowed a shadow of reaction to cross their faces, which seemed remarkable.

"That is not yours to give away," Antara finally said in a stern but tremulous tone.

"Why not? This ... Dwarven Circle, or the Order of the Fallen Moon ... it belongs with one of them."

"Because you need to take that key to the prophet."

His frustration and uncertainty burst free again. He couldn't help it. "Why me? And what prophet? I would just be giving it to him—or her—and someone else can do that. Maybe this prophet is one of the dwarven leaders. Migo and Midas can take it to them." He sounded like a toddler throwing a tantrum, and his cheeks flushed. He didn't lower his eyes, though.

She pursed her lips, her mien darkening further as she focused intently on him. Her voice no longer quavered. "You are to find the prophet or prophetess yourself, though you may have a companion. That accords firmly with the prophecies and signs." She glanced at Migo and Midas, who nodded grave agreement. "And I'm not so sure that you will need to relinquish the talisman. You may very well be the proper, *permanent* bearer of it, surprising as that may seem, even to me."

"But I don't *want* it," persisted Rain in frustration, nearly barking. "I have no idea what to do with it. Surely there are others who could use it better, like Master Ileom."

Antara's tone transformed from lecturing to imperious, shocking him to his toes. "You will do your duty, soldier, and I can safely speak for Ileom on this. He, too, is a member of the Order, and we are aligned in our purposes. There are plenty here, including me, who can provide assistance as needed. Ultimately, you have your agency, and God *can* find another, but if you cannot trust him in this, neither can you lay claim to the promises."

Though Rain wasn't at all clear on what those promises might be, something shifted inside, and he felt the weight largely disappear, which stunned him anew. How long it would last, he couldn't say, but he took a deep breath before nodding toward her, then at Migo and Midas, adding a small bow. He noticed the minor noises of people and horses behind them, all patiently waiting.

"Thank you, Migo and Midas," he said. "We will do our best."

To Rain's surprise, that seemed to satisfy them. Migo announced, "We will go now and leave you to your work. We have much to do ourselves, for the worlds are in commotion."

Worlds. Rain's tiny peek at that other world he and Antara had visited pulsed brightly in his mind.

⚮

Three days later, Rain, Antara, Haran, Androl, and Jerise met in an upper room of the town's largest building, situated near its center and facing a broad, shallow fountain filled with milky, warm water. Rain had dared Androl to taste it, and the bold Mero Vothan had proclaimed the water delicious and refreshing. Given everything else in the town, it aligned. It might have magical powers, too, though Antara couldn't detect any.

Rain no longer wondered why Jerise was invited to their meetings. Though just nine, the impact of her growing healing abilities couldn't be discounted, and with the trauma of her village's destruction fading, a vivacious personality had begun to emerge, along with a unique sharpness of mind. She was so smart Rain felt embarrassed sometimes.

Antara alternated between being a doting sister and a ferociously protective but demanding mother to her. Haran, of course, proclaimed himself her permanent protector, sworn to Rain's service or not. That bond grew daily.

Antara had called the conclave, and they waited for her to begin. Rain wavered between leaning forward to rest elbows and clasped hands on the beautifully finished oval table, or leaning back to place his hands in his lap. He tried both, at least twice, then settled on the latter.

A smile twitched at Antara's lips as she noticed, and he averted his gaze to Jerise, who was whispering something to Haran. Androl sat still as a statue, hands on his thighs, in the attitude of studying one of the large paintings on the walls. This one depicted an enormous fish with broad wings, vaulting above the water in the act of closing its mouth around a fully bearded man in a white, red-belted robe, surrounded by a halo of light and holding both hands out to ward off the attempt. An orange orb glowed between those hands. Very strange.

"Well, this has been an eventful few weeks," Antara finally began, "and God's grace smiles on our endeavors. Now that we are largely settled into our new home, it is time we turn our minds toward how we govern under the rules of this hallowed place. As far as I can determine, we are under no immediate military threats here, but people must eat, and work, and learn. The recent obedience forced by dire necessity will wear off, and we will all behave like ... well, normal people again."

"You should be the mayor, or duchess, or whatever," said Haran. "The people will choose you. They respect you, and you will judge equitably."

Antara's gaze sharpened. "Androl, Rain, is this what you believe?"

Rain nodded immediately, catching Androl's similar reaction out of the corner of his eye.

"And how about you, Jerise?" She acted the doting sister at the moment.

Jerise glanced up at Haran, then also nodded. "I agree."

"Hmmm ... well, I don't." Antara swept her eyes across the group before continuing. "One person, even if chosen, should not make all the decisions—that seems basic from the requirements we were given."

Rain still didn't fully understand any of the rules, even after a pair of long conversations with Antara, but he didn't have a logical counterargument.

"We must also look immediately toward expansion and preparation," she continued. "I know you didn't expect that, and neither did I, but events in the world are indeed accelerating, faster even than the Order had anticipated. Rain, you and I should travel to Arxhana. We may discover important things there, and we can recruit. I need to get a secure message to the Order as well, and there are those in the capital I can trust with that."

Rain inwardly groaned. He had no desire to set out on another journey so soon. This place was incredibly comfortable, and he'd had enough adventure to last him a good, long while. If he must leave, it should be to head north and seek word about his parents and Tashiel. And this mysterious prophet or prophetess, though his commitment still wavered.

Antara must have sensed his hesitation. "We can achieve more together than apart, Rain, and all will be accomplished in its due time."

In its due time. He had heard that phrase before, and it always meant, "You can't have it, so stop whining about it." He nodded acquiescence, then stared at the table as Antara continued.

"Haran, do you have some candidates for a town council?"

The grizzled veteran nodded. "Aye. Several names. I'm sure Androl does, too."

"Good," said Antara. "Between your two lists, let's come up with a final group of ten and then let the people vote on which five they want to represent them. All five will be equal in authority, with decisions made by majority vote … and *not* subject to my approval. No council member will occupy the role for life, but we can talk later about the amount of time they may serve. And I *mean* serve."

Haran raised his eyebrows before offering a thoughtful nod. Androl agreed immediately, as usual, and they began to lay out the names and discuss them. Haran saved Jerise's name for last.

Antara tapped her lips, pensive. "When do you turn ten, Jerise?"

Jerise glanced around tentatively. "Um, next month."

"Well, entire nations have been ruled by people younger than you—with the help of advisers, of course."

Jerise gazed up at Haran, who nodded with a smile. Then she turned to Antara. "Okay," she said meekly, then adopted the precocious grin she had started to flash recently, glancing at Rain. "As long as Rain has to share the pain, too."

Antara's entire face brightened, outshining the sun. Rain didn't like it when she did that; both his brain and his knees went mushy each time. "Haha, splendid. Yes, he will, though I suspect his role will be different." Her demeanor had changed to that of mother, so proud of her daughter. "You should be in the final group, Jerise, and I'm sure the people will elect you as one of the five. If not, so be it."

After they had finalized their list of ten, which included Haran, too—Antara refusing a nomination for herself—she steered the conversation toward how they could help the people prepare physically, mentally, and spiritually for the stiffer tests to come. An intimidating task, but somehow Androl and Haran seemed excited about it.

Finally, Antara focused on Rain. "Have you been to Arxhana, city of a thousand winds?"

He shook his head. Of course he hadn't. He hadn't been *anywhere* outside of New Haven before.

"Well, I have, a handful of times, though I'm sure things will be different with refugees swelling its population. Magistrate Dynast might be more difficult to entreat under present circumstances, but speak with him we must. That should be our first task. Do you agree?"

Why would she ask him that? He had no idea about any of this. The chief magistrate was essentially a king, and that's all he understood about the man. He nodded dumbly, and she added, "There may be others on the High Court we should contact as well, but we can assess that as we draw close to the city. We should leave in the morning."

That was soon. He wanted to explore more of the town and its environs—enjoy this amazing haven, which was both safe and luxurious. The houses all had running water, provided from the springs at a higher elevation and regulated by some complicated mechanical means. The farm implements looked impressive, and none had rusted. Jerise revealed that was accomplished by emplaced magic, which she compared to how she had learned to set a healing process in place with a metered dose of additional power that would run out over time. That allowed her to move on to the next patient more quickly. She really was brilliant. And *nine*. He wondered if something similar could not only protect a sword from rust, but maintain its sharpness as well. Maybe even prevent it from breaking.

They held the vote that evening, and sure enough, Jerise was selected as one of the five, along with Haran. The townspeople rejoiced, until Antara told them she and Rain would be leaving for a time. Rain knew they wouldn't miss *him* much, but Antara … to many of them, it must feel like having a foot or a hand amputated … or maybe the head. She was the real leader of the group.

She inspired everyone—including Rain to some degree—with a masterful discourse on the blessings they had received and how they must become more worthy of them by learning to work together in faith, harmony, and charity. Haran added some words of his own, at Antara's request, and then the one-time refugees returned to their new homes in the mountain paradise, each a veritable palace replete with unimaginable comforts. And the food stocks … the ambrosia and nectar of the heavens, their provenance a magic Rain couldn't even begin to imagine. Antara had cautioned that no more provisions would just appear—they would have to work for them. Nobody could complain.

☾∞☽

They left early the next morning, and even Sun Tamer and Cyclone seemed atypically reluctant. Androl had discovered a small cache of good oats, so Rain made sure to bring a couple of sacks with them.

In studying one of Androl's maps, Rain had been shocked to learn that their new location put them only about halfway between New Haven and Arxhana as the bird flew. The world—even their continent of Rega—was so much larger than his young mind had ever imagined. Antara suggested they travel southwest at first in order to intersect the Caravan Road, which met the Dunroad a little north of the coastal city of Calertus, Mero Vothas's third largest city, rumored to be one of the most beautiful cities in the world. The Caravan Road would make the rest of the trip to Arxhana faster. They had no need for stealth, so Rain didn't object. Their horses would want to go fast no matter the terrain, and good roads were safer for them.

The lake and hill country of Mero Vothas seemed more tranquil than anticipated. They encountered no refugees, and the rote behaviors of the inhabitants implied that the invasion of New Haven had happened too long ago and too far away to be of significant consequence. Since neither he nor Antara *looked* like refugees, everyone treated them with respect, even deference. Rain no longer wore his Council Guard uniform, but he probably looked even more distinct. Antara had asked one of their tailors to make Rain a uniform in dark green with silver trim that would have been more appropriately worn by a prince. It didn't itch, but felt like it should.

To those who asked, Antara explained that they had recently crossed the mountain passes from Jeveria. That elicited additional admiration for their well-dressed bravery, as some of the passes were already treacherous with the approaching winter.

By the time they reached the Caravan Road, the temperature had become considerably warmer than just outside the hidden valley, and Rain's uniform began to feel hot. He wore a newly made white shirt underneath his tunic—also commissioned by Antara—and he finally decided to expose it, even if that bothered her. His expectation of a comment lasted at least a mile before he understood she wasn't going to say anything. The shirt was pleated, and it blazed like a diamond in the sun. He was cooler, but realized he didn't look any less preposterous.

She finally spoke again after a small caravan passed them on the other side, heading northwest. It would likely end up turning south to reach the docks of Calertus.

"I've told you a bit about the chief magistrate, Corvellum Dynast. The Second, actually—his father had the same name."

"You mentioned he has a connection to the Order, but you didn't say what it was."

"Didn't I?" She scanned the sky, brow furrowed. "I thought I had. I know I didn't tell you the names of the Mero Vothan High Judges, and you need to memorize those. The feeling grows stronger that we need to engage with some of them, though I think we should do that after we meet with Dynast."

"Okay." He didn't call out her deflection.

"The first is Astin Goldeneye."

"That's his real name?"

"Yes, it is. If I recall correctly, his great-great-grandfather had a glass eye, an unstable mind, and lots and lots of money, so that became the family name. Master Astin seems more reasonable than some of his pro- genitors, so we may start with him."

"Well, at least it's an easy name to remember."

"True. Mavris Chesop and Amaria Threvensgood are cousins, though they don't look at all alike. Significant rumors surround that, as you might expect."

He raised an eyebrow, and she caught his expression.

"The rich and powerful aren't the most faithful, if you get my meaning."

"Oh." He should have gotten that right off—he wasn't a complete country rube. "Are they worth talking to?"

She shook her head. "I'm not sure. Mavris is shrewd, and Amaria cruel; together, they form a spike garden. But the other woman on the Court, Chantress Hightower, is newer, younger, and I believe more rea- sonable. The other two men, Dieron Markiess and Grigzim Runshael, have close ties to Dynast. Sometimes I think that's good, and sometimes not. They are both fabulously rich, and preserving that wealth drives much of their decision-making. Again, that isn't always bad, but in some cases it's devastating."

"Do I need to memorize these now?" he asked, letters jumbling around in his head in dozens of different arrangements centered around the easily remembered Goldeneye and Hightower.

She laughed. "No, not right now. We'll review them again when we reach the city." Her face suddenly went blank. "Don't look back, but we're being followed."

He almost did anyway, eyes widening as his pulse quickened. "How do you know?"

"A trick I learned from someone in the Order. It lets me see behind me, like in a mirror."

Rain blinked. "You've been doing magic? Why couldn't I sense it?"

She smiled. "This trick is subtle. If you focused, you could, but I've noticed two men about fifty yards back maintaining that distance and letting their eyes rest on us far too often."

"Highwaymen?"

"Perhaps. Won't they be dismayed if they try something." She winked, and then her mien grew grave. "Or they could be something else entirely. I checked the mask on the talisman before we left, but … at the next way station, let's find a secluded place so I can check it again."

With that, she urged Cyclone into a slow gallop, Sun Tamer keeping pace. They traveled several miles that way before Antara slowed again. She didn't look back, but she appeared focused. Rain finally caught a glimpse of her wispy 'mirrors.'

"Well?" he asked after nearly two full minutes.

"They're farther back now, but they didn't lose us. They're definitely following."

"Great. But they're not soldiers?"

She pursed her lips. "They may not wear uniforms, but they're soldiers all right."

The evening had reached at least its third hour before they stopped at a way station to rest. Several dozen other travelers crowded the same space, consisting of two large open-sided shelters and a store of provisions for livestock. The two men didn't join the group, according to Antara. She checked the talisman and seemed satisfied, but they kept a watch, alternating every hour or so. They started out early again, after making sure the horses had gotten enough to eat and drink.

After a few minutes, Antara announced that the same two men had appeared behind them. Rain ached to get a glimpse. A few miles later, he couldn't stand it any longer. He halted Sun Tamer, claiming he needed to re-check one of her shoes. Antara raised an eyebrow but didn't comment. As he performed the check and fiddled around in his saddlebags, he stole some good peeks at their two shadows. One, a tall blond man wearing common but well-tailored clothes, had gotten off his horse, too, ostensibly to retrieve some food hidden deep in one of his bags. He reached up to hand something to the other man, also tall, but broad-shouldered and dark-haired, with the squarest jaw Rain had ever seen. The man nodded in thanks and raised the morsel to his mouth. His eyes betrayed him, however, for they flicked to Rain and Antara without any apparent purpose.

Rain remounted, satisfied.

"Did you see what you needed to?" Antara asked.

He blushed a little. "Yes."

"Good. You need to be able to recognize them. I don't think they'll cause us any problems on our way to Arxhana, but once there, the game changes."

Great. Back into the fire.

"I thought we could stay at one of the nicer inns I know there," she continued as they got the horses moving again, "but that may not be wise. There is another option, however."

She went quiet, until he asked, "What's the option?"

She turned and smiled coquettishly, speaking more softly. "We'll stay with the chief magistrate, of course. He owes me a favor—well, not directly, but he'll understand."

Rain whistled, causing Sun Tamer's ears to flick toward him. Then he cringed. "I won't know how to act."

She waved a hand. "Nonsense. Just act like a soldier, which Ileom taught you well, and say thank you a lot. You'll be fine."

Rain shrugged, unconvinced. "What if we can't stay there?"

"Then we risk an inn. But Corvellum won't deny us. Trust me."

It took another four days to reach Arxhana, the broad skyline of the unwalled capital both more and less than what Rain had expected. The area hardly seemed to live up to its nickname 'city of a thousand winds,' though maybe it had reference to something else. Antara claimed not to know. The sheer numbers of people and the magnificence of many of the structures left his mouth agape, though. It was like the city of New Haven and its Holy Keep of the Four Stars replicated multiple times. Unfortunately, up close it was quite dirty, and with its seams almost bursting with Sarenite refugees who hadn't risked returning home yet, it was also noisy, with lots of shouting from Mero Vothan guards trying to impose order amid the enhanced cacophony.

Antara kept her chin high as they passed through the outskirts, a perfect vision of the visiting dignitary whose job it was to ignore such chaos. Rain kept his head on a swivel, as much out of curiosity as any concern for danger. The dirt and gravel road turned to fitted stone, and at the first major intersection in the city proper, Antara led them left to enter a sea of palaces, large and small, loud and subdued, all immaculate. The stones of this street were smaller, containing shimmering specks, the crowds much diminished due to an increased number of guard patrols. The way curved slowly to the right, remaining almost perfectly flat.

Suddenly, she reined in Cyclone, coming to a stop. Rain reacted too slowly, having to turn Sun Tamer to face them. Her ears flicked rapidly.

"What is it?" he asked, eyes scanning behind her. She didn't have to answer, because he spotted the two men who had been following them, about a hundred yards back. They stuck out like a gangrened limb. They, too, had halted, glancing around in a failed attempt to appear nonchalant.

Rain urged Sun Tamer into a trot toward them, part of his mind aghast at what he was doing, and he heard Antara whirl Cyclone to follow. He also sensed as well as saw a shield form before him, maintaining its place as he moved. After he had closed more than half the distance, the two men trained their focus on him, separating their mounts a few feet.

He brought Sun Tamer up five yards short, Antara joining him a second later. Since he had instigated the approach, he didn't wait for her to speak.

"Who are you, and why are you following us?"

"Who are *you*?" retorted the blond one, disdain plainly evident. "You travel with a dangerous woman."

Antara took over. "I do not recognize you. Therefore, you are suspect. Speak your purpose quickly, or suffer the consequence."

Rain had never heard such a coldly threatening tone of pure authority from her. He already knew she was dangerous, and part of him felt for those two men. Unless they had magic, too. His gut clenched in anticipation of a desperate fight.

Nervousness swept across their faces, quickly suppressed. They glanced at each other, and then the blond replied to her. "We are emissaries of your father. He sent us with a message for you. It is time to come home."

Antara moved Cyclone another step closer. "You are new, and apparently not well trained. Why did you not approach me and relate your business, instead of skulking behind in such an obvious fashion?"

They tried not to seem embarrassed, but they clearly were. The blond cleared his throat. "We planned to wait until you found a suitable place to stay. Then—"

"You didn't tell us your names," she interrupted. Rain would have turned to jelly under that glare, which had switched to the dark-haired man. The shield strengthened … and … were those *spikes* extending from it?

"Relax, Antara," said the dark-haired one, his tone softer now. "We aren't here to force anything."

"Which you couldn't."

He gave a grudging nod. "Which we couldn't. Please release your attack shield."

"I will not. Your *names*."

Annoyance flashed in his eyes, but otherwise his expression remained neutral. "Very well. I am Merloc, and this is Uthrid. You don't know us because we are rarely seen. We travel far and wide protecting your father's interests."

"You are spies and assassins. And Uthrid is a very odd name." She quirked an eyebrow at the blond.

After a brief pause, Merloc nodded. "We have those skills."

"Why does my father want me to return? We are not … aligned. He knows that."

Merloc took a deep breath. "He wishes to change a few things, and he requires … excuse me, *desires* … your help."

"You both have magic," she said, ignoring the strongly implied demand.

They looked at each other again and Merloc replied, "We do, useful for our work, though it is weaker than yours."

Her face hardened. "And a tiny candle when compared to his." She didn't have to gesture toward Rain. Their eyes widened slightly as they snapped to him. He almost grimaced. She had just placed a massive target on his back, made worse by the fact that he had no idea who would be aiming for it, besides these two hard-looking men. That other planet suddenly seemed appealing. He could get lost there.

"You may tell my father three things," she continued. "First, his preparations for what is coming are woefully inadequate and misguided. Second, his steward in Mero Vothas apparently sold one of his favorite steeds to New Haven, inexplicably." Her eyes flicked to Sun Tamer, and Rain shifted slightly in the saddle, unsure what to think about that revelation. "And third, I will indeed return, but I cannot say when. I have other things I must do first."

"He will not like that," said Merloc.

"Okay, four things," she replied with tart acidity. "The fourth is that what he likes or dislikes is of no consequence, either to me or to this world. There. You have your message. Now go. And if I see you again, there will be no discussion. In fact, you have *precisely* ten seconds to be out of my sight."

Rain himself shivered at that deadly promise. Clearly, Merloc and Uthrid took it seriously as well, for they spun their mounts and kicked them into a gallop, ignoring the shout of a pair of city guards to slow down.

When they had disappeared around the bend, the clicking of swift hooves fading to a light, echoing staccato, Rain turned to stare open-mouthed at Antara.

"I never want to meet your father." He wasn't sure why he'd picked that to say first, but he meant it.

She returned his gaze, her mien having undergone a complete trans-formation, becoming almost deferential again. "And I never want you to meet him. I'm sorry I can't say more about who he is … or where I'm from. Not yet. It's … messy."

Messy. Was that the technical term? Was it better or worse than 'complicated'?

Her visage altered again, putting her clearly back in charge. She steered Cyclone back up the street, Sun Tamer following without any prompting. At length they came to the opulent lane's end, where it opened into a broad circular plaza sprouting a small bunch of tall, narrow trees in the center.

The size and grandeur of the palace beyond made Rain's mind stutter. Most of it rose three stories, with several towers reaching much higher. Two of those glittering squared spirals flashed hints of azure. The New Haven Keep was—or used to be—just as magnificent, but this seemed more exotic. And to think that Arxhana was considered one of the lesser capitals on the continent!

A fence of finely worked iron bars between massive square stone pillars surrounded the palace, but the wide gate onto the plaza stood open. At least a dozen guards filled Rain's view, and he didn't doubt many more were readily available. These didn't wear the drab gray-and-tan livery of the city guards but rich burgundy and deep brown, with gold trim. Their polished, bronzed helmets gleamed in the midday sun, the tips of their tall, tasseled horse spears seeming sharp enough to pierce stone.

Antara led them right through the gates without a pause, delicately extending a hand to the first guard who approached her as she bid him help her down. The man kept a straight face while complying. Two other guards took position near Rain, their spears angled in high ready position.

"Thank you, good man," said Antara as she alighted onto the fine, reddish paving stones leading to the palace's main, porticoed entrance. "We have traveled far, and with some difficulties owing to the invasion of New Haven." The guard dipped his head, eyes expressing understanding as she continued. "I am Lady Antara. The chief magistrate is not expecting me, but he knows me. We carry a message of some urgency for him, and we may not be safe staying at an inn in the city."

Why tell them so much? wondered Rain, though he was a poor judge of the situation.

"M'lady, Magistrate Dynast is not here. He is at the Regency Complex, attending to various administrative matters."

Antara nodded. "Of course, as would be expected. I presume you have a guest suite available? Or, we can wait out here in the sun while you send a messenger to him." She said it in the sweetest voice, but the implication was clear.

Another guard separated himself from a larger group and approached. His tunic sported two white cords looped over one shoulder. He bowed to Antara.

"I have seen Lady Antara before. I can vouch for her and will personally escort her and her companion to one of the guest suites. M'lady, we will task three men to your security and convenience."

Antara smiled graciously. "Splendid. We didn't bring much with us, and we are very tired. Take especial care of our horses, sergeant. They are heroes." That was true.

The sergeant bowed again, then called for two men to handle the horses. Rain dismounted and followed Antara as the man led them through a massive set of gem-encrusted double doors and onto a floor that shone like a sea of glass. Rain tried hard not to gawk at the décor, but Antara gave him some excuse by pointing and commenting favorably on several fine artistic features, noting which were new since her last visit.

It took them a full two minutes to arrive at their suite, which looked out on a lush garden replete with a pond stocked with golden fish. Rain felt like one of those fish ... only thrashing about on dry land, unable to breathe. The luxury was difficult to absorb, even after the wonders of their new village in the dwarven valley. He hesitated to sit in one of the plush, artfully decorated chairs, for fear he would ruin it in some way.

After the sergeant left, closing the door to the suite's entrance foyer behind him, Antara let out a long breath. "I was a little aggressive. We're lucky that guard remembered me."

"But you *have* been here, right?"

"Once, yes, though I was with others, spending most of the time in the background. I'll have to remind the magistrate who I am, and who I accompanied. He will not remember me."

"But ..."

"I know. I exaggerated a bit. It was a risk."

He nodded, then wandered toward one of the interior doors.

"That's probably a privy," she called out in a helpful tone, and suddenly his body decided that's just what he needed. He refrained, though, just checking it briefly before exploring the three bedrooms, each with its *own* privy, plus two sitting rooms and a small audience chamber. His entire extended family could live comfortably in that suite, feeling like kings and queens.

"Everything is in order?" she asked when he returned.

He nodded, then sat on the edge of a chair.

"Good. Well, we must be careful, even inside the palace. Those men sent by my father are certainly connected to other spies in the city. I cowed them temporarily, but we don't know what my father directed them to do if I refused to return immediately. There are a number of possibilities, most of them unsavory."

She said it so calmly. He nodded in faked understanding, without having any idea how to wrap his mind around it.

"You have a question? Not about my father, mind you."

He had many, but anything he could articulate? He thought for a few seconds, wishing he had taken advantage of one of those privies already.

"Do you still believe Ileom is alive?" His pondering had gotten him nowhere, but that question popped into his mind afresh.

Antara stepped toward a window overlooking the garden, gazing out at it. "Yes, I do. He rarely underestimates a situation, and even then, he is more powerful and resourceful than you know. Which reminds me that I need to compose that message to the Order and arrange for it to be sent. I should do that before the magistrate either returns or sends for us. Oh, and he barely has a limp, by the way."

"The magistrate?"

"No, Ileom."

Rain leaned back in the chair without realizing it. "Huh. So why ...?"

She chuckled. "I don't really know, but I mean to ask him about it. Tease him, really. I guess he thought it should be part of his persona in New Haven, like he was a spy or something. He is *not* a spy."

"Oh." Such was the extent of the response he could come up with.

"Make yourself at home, Rain. I'll be back. I need to find some good writing supplies and a particular courier among the staff here I already know I can trust. Don't get into any trouble."

He suddenly realized he had leaned back, so he shot forward again to the edge of his seat. "I won't."

She gave a light laugh that sent rolling vibrations up and down his bones, then exited the suite. He raced for the nearest privy.

Rain had no idea how long Antara would be. After thirty minutes, nobody had checked in on him, and he had noticed earlier that one of the rooms had a door onto the garden. He stepped through it and instinctively took a deep, refreshing breath, causing the pungent smells from at least a dozen varieties of flowers to overpower his sinuses. He suppressed a sneeze, worried someone might hear and investigate. Or worse, see if he needed anything. At least his ridiculous regalia seemed to fit with the setting.

He wandered a few paces deeper, marveling at the immaculate maintenance. It was almost a painting. He spotted an ornate bench embraced by three manicured bushes, but he had been sitting too much, so he kept walking. Somewhat absently, he took the talisman out of his pocket and studied it again. It still appeared in every regard to be a key—exquisitely crafted, to be sure, but just a key. He almost laughed. *Just a key!*

At that moment, light flashed around him, and his knees nearly buckled. When he could focus again, he found himself standing in that man's house in the other world. *How?* He hadn't even thought about it. Well, he kind of had. That new target Antara had branded him with burned between his shoulder blades, as if it extended to this planet. A dish clattered to the floor without breaking, and then he noticed the man and a woman gaping at him from two chairs facing the window box on the wall. The black-bordered box produced a great deal of noise—*people cheering?*—and when he looked he saw tiny figures running around on a green field with white lines, wearing strange but colorful uniforms.

The couple continued staring at him, and then the man slowly raised his hands, shock replaced by fright. The woman seemed to swoon for a moment, on the verge of fainting, but then raised her hands as well.

Rain hadn't drawn his sword, but he realized they must feel threatened by his sudden appearance, armed as he was. He put both hands out, palms up, and said, "I'm sorry," knowing they wouldn't understand the words. Then he raced out their front door and accelerated to a sprint, aiming to get back to the field where he had appeared the previous two times. A big metal monster almost hit him as he crossed the road, and after an angry squeal it made that familiar high-pitched horn sound. Yelling followed, and he quickened his pace further, dashing up the minor incline as he gulped in the alien air.

He leaped the fence with a hand on a post, then kept running to the approximate spot in the field. He skidded to a halt and turned in a con- tinuous circle, holding the key in his hand and trying to focus. *Go! Jump! Travel!* The words started in his head, but he began chanting them aloud, at greater and greater volume.

Nothing happened. He began to panic. Why wasn't it working? And why had the key brought him here *again*?

Minutes passed, and he noticed this world's sun close to setting. Then another metal monster approached, with large lanterns on top flashing a blinding red and blue. Two men emerged, dressed in dark blue uniforms bulging with all kinds of odd-shaped equipment, shouting and holding something in their hands that they pointed at him. He would have called them knives, but they were too thick and blunt. Stubby wands? He knew by their tones they were serious, that they viewed him as a threat. So he surreptitiously dropped the key in the shoots of grain and raised his hands, taking a few steps toward them as they crossed the fence, until they started shouting louder. One of them was almost frothing at the mouth. Who did they think he was?

Within moments, one of them had moved behind him, placing his wrists in steel manacles which felt cold and sharp.

The man then grabbed the back of his tunic at the neck with one hand, the connection between the manacles with the other, and urged him forward with more force than was necessary. The other man held two of the fence wires apart for his partner, and then Rain, to pass through. The first man removed Rain's sword from its scabbard and led him toward the monster on wheels. He opened a strangely-shaped and rather small door with a glass window, then guided Rain into a soft seat, talking all the while. After the door was shut, the two men conversed outside for several minutes, inspecting his sword a few times. Even if Rain had known their language, he wouldn't have been able to hear them well enough from inside the beast's belly.

Finally, they both entered the beast through doors farther forward, a glass partition separating them from him. A few seconds later, the beast began to move. Rain's first thought was how many shapes and colors of lights shone from the inside, on polished surfaces facing the men. The second was how fluid the conveyance felt. Powerful, too. They picked up speed swiftly, soon traveling far faster than Sun Tamer could. They went for several miles, turning only once, the sky darkening rapidly, until they came upon a town or village, with buildings of brick, stone, wood, and even metal. And the lights! *So many lights.* How could they maintain that many fires or obtain that much oil? And why would they need to? The town was much larger than he first thought—clearly a city. Tens of thousands must inhabit it. The monster took two more turns before slowing as it approached a large building glowing with light from dozens of windows. Lamps on poles outside bathed the grounds as well.

The two men pulled him from the beast, a bit more gently this time, perhaps because he hadn't resisted at all, and led him inside the building, where it seemed like full sunlight shone. He almost needed to shade his eyes. *At night!* And one of the doors had slid aside automatically. Magic?

They must have noticed him marveling, because one of them scratched his head with a look of mild confusion. A woman at a tall desk behind thick glass started speaking to Rain, but all he could do was shrug and shake his head, feeling and probably appearing utterly helpless.

One of the men touched the sharp edge of his sword and expressed surprise. Had they thought it was fake? It didn't look like a practice sword, wooden or not. Unless they weren't familiar with swords? He hadn't seen anyone else here carrying one so far. What a strange world.

The two men removed his sword belt, then searched him for other weapons, finding the dagger from the invader. They also peered into his small bag of coins—which caused more confusion—and opened an old note from Tashiel he'd almost forgotten he still carried. They handed everything to the woman through a small opening in the glass, after which a loud buzz sounded. They led him through another door with a thick glass window, down a long hallway, and along a side corridor until another buzz preceded the opening of a third door. After a second short and pointless interview, this one conducted by a grumpy-looking man with a balding pate, they made him stand still. A different man flashed a tiny beam of light in each of his eyes from some sort of magical device, looked him up and down again, and led him to a small room with a thick and fantastically expensive metal door. After removing his manacles, the man departed, the door clanging shut behind him. Rain found himself alone in the brightly lit, solid-walled cell with a narrow cot and what appeared to be an open privy in the corner. A basin protruded from the wall, and he guessed from what he'd seen in the dwarven village that it offered running water.

It was all so amazing, and yet ... he was a prisoner. On a strange planet, unable to communicate, all alone. And he no longer possessed the key. He prayed it remained safe in that field until he could find a way to retrieve it, even if all he could ever do with it again was melt it down for the precious metals—presuming they were worth anything here.

⚬

After several hours, during which he discovered how the incredible water basin and latrine worked, he yielded to sleep, finding the cot surprisingly comfortable. When he awoke, he discovered that a small metal tray had been passed inside. It sat on a thin slab suspended on the inside of the door at about waist height. Enticing smells wafted from it, but he wasn't that hungry yet, so he ignored it.

A little while later, the door slowly opened, and a paunchy, mustached man entered, accompanied by a slender young woman, dressed almost identically, and yet … not. The man peeked around the edge of the door to note the untouched tray of food, giving a small shrug to the woman. He then motioned Rain to stand and extend his hands. He placed manacles on his wrists again, keeping his hands in front this time, which was far more comfortable. The pair led him out of his cell and down a short hallway, into a small room with metal table and chairs. It dawned on Rain that he had never seen so much metal and glass in his life. Expensive glass, too. Crystal clear. The man closed the door and showed him to one of the chairs, while the woman pulled a thin, gray metallic slab from a black leather bag with handles. After sitting next to him, she set the slab on the table and proceeded to split it in two along its thinnest dimension, swinging the top piece up along a hinge on the long edge. An inner surface sprang to life, making Rain twitch. The woman noticed, furrowing her brow.

She spoke slowly, fingers tapping on the other interior surface, decorated with dozens of alien symbols. Her actions somehow made the other surface alter in appearance. He was strongly reminded of the window box on the wall in the strange house, though he hadn't seen those people do anything to make the images change.

A man's face appeared out of nowhere, nearly filling the window and causing Rain to involuntarily lean back. The man started talking, and the language sounded different from what the other people had spoken to him. Rain frowned, then looked at the woman. She said a few words, and based on the tone she had asked him a question, eyebrows raised. He thought he understood what she meant. He shook his head.

She tapped a few more times, fingers flying, and a woman's face popped up in the window, babbling in what was apparently a third language. Again, he had to shake his head at the proffered query. Rain listened as the process continued, baffled at how many languages existed on this world, and how different most of them sounded from each other. None of them sounded any-thing like Regan Common. They must have gone through at least a hundred before the woman put the pieces of the metal slab back together. It contained powerful magic, though he sensed nothing from it, just a slight humming noise.

She asked a different question, gesturing toward him and then moving her hand near her own mouth, as if mimicking something coming out of it. Ah, he got it. He nodded, stated his name while placing his hand on his chest, and proceeded to briefly describe who he was and where he was from. She stopped him with a raised hand, opened the magic slab back up, tapped on it several times again, then angled it toward him. She had conjured it into a mirror, because he saw his own face. She nodded for him to continue.

He recounted his training as a Council Guard of New Haven, to ex-plain why he carried a sword. After further prompting, he launched into the recent invasion, how the Sarenites had tried to fight it off, and how he had escaped at the orders of his commander. He left out Antara, Haran, Jerise, and all the other refugees as he detailed his journey through the hills and finally into the mountains. Then, skipping both the key and the dwarven city with its Old Magic, he described the trip to Arxhana, the incredible suite he was given next to the garden, and ... He trailed off at that point, staring down at the table and shaking his head.

"I don't know why I'm here now, and I don't know how to get back." The intensity of his own emotion surprised him, and he blinked several times rapidly. How *would* he get back? Could he?

The woman studied him for a few moments, eyes wide, expression soft. Then she sat back and spoke with the mustached man for several minutes, doing most of the talking. He seemed to object to some of the things she said, but she appeared successful in overriding him, at least as far as Rain could tell. He was so lost.

They returned him to his cell, removed the manacles, and encouraged him to eat by bringing a fresh tray of food, though he still wasn't hungry. As they left, the woman started up another fast conversation with the man.

Several more hours and another nap later, the woman returned, this time with two uniformed men, different than the first pair. Strangely, they didn't manacle him before leading him outside the building. It was morning. He gawked at the number of metal monsters rolling around, all with humans inside. Where were they going in such a hurry? They placed him in one of the front seats of a pearl-colored beast, and then the two soldiers or officers had a conversation with the woman, their tone serious, eyes darting frequently toward him. They didn't trust him, and yet the woman did; that was clear. Finally, the woman entered the beast from the other side, sitting next to Rain and pulling the door closed, a strange-looking wheel like one might find on a seagoing vessel situated in front of her—only much smaller and without the protrusions to keep it from spinning out of control.

She smiled reassuringly at him, then placed a hand on her chest. "Hannah," she said. When he didn't respond, she repeated it. Ah, Hannah must be her name. Duh, he had done the same for her.

He thought he could pronounce it. He pointed at her and said, "Hannah," then pointed at himself and said, "Rain."

"Rain," she repeated, eyes curious as she tested it out a couple more times. Her grin broadened, and then she turned her head and pushed on something with a finger, causing the beast to rumble. Really, it was more of a purr, like that of a large cat. She touched another button, did something he couldn't quite see with her feet, and turned the wheel as the beast started forward. His eyes widened. Was she *controlling* it?

He split his time between watching what she was doing and observing their surroundings through the remarkably clear glass windows. It looked to be late spring or early summer, with leaves full on the trees. The air outside had been warm but not hot. Then he noticed that the beast was somehow blowing cooler air onto him. He didn't smell anything different, and the woman seemed fine, so he relaxed.

She made the beast turn several times over the next few minutes, finally stopping it next to another building on a busy street. Special skirts on both sides of the road were filled with people walking. The explosion of color and variety in their clothing made him feel a lot less conspicuous about his own. Some people even made Antara look plain. Well, not plain, but not a queen, either. The woman got out, came around to his side, and opened his door, beckoning him to exit the beast.

He complied, then let her lead him inside the building, made of reddish-brown brick with windows trimmed in yellow-painted wood. They proceeded down a short hallway, and she looked around, calling out a couple of times. A rotund man with a completely bald head and a face full of hair appeared through a doorway, his face instantly expressing recognition. He glanced at Rain and gave a friendly smile, barely blinking at his attire.

Hannah spoke to the man for a few minutes, and while his expression revealed curiosity at several points, he didn't seem concerned. Finally, she patted Rain on the arm to get his attention, and gestured that he should follow the man. He nodded, then bowed to her.

"Thank you for your help. I don't know exactly what you did, but it appears I am in a better place."

She smiled, but he could tell she was frustrated at not being able to understand him. Then he followed the man, who wore a short-sleeved shirt with no buttons that had been splashed randomly with several colors of dye. On both sides. He also bore a tattoo on the back of one forearm. It looked like an anchor with a rope wrapped around it. The man turned when they reached another doorway, smiling again. Noise came from beyond the door, including laughter, though somehow the timbre was a little off.

When Rain stepped through, he noted two sets of bunkbeds along one wall of a small room with a narrow window. The walls were painted a lighter shade of yellow. Three of the beds were currently occupied by males close to his age. All of them were smaller, though. They sat on the edges of the beds, staring toward the opposite wall, where another of the window boxes hung, suspended by steel arms and connected to dark ropes disappearing into the wall. The man pointed to a bed, one of the top bunks, then raised a finger as if asking him to wait. He disappeared for a minute and returned carrying a small, flimsy-looking sack, which he handed to Rain. In it, Rain spotted a variety of things he didn't recognize, along with what looked like a change of clothes and a miniature loaf of bread inside another sack, this one transparent! He blinked, then looked up and nodded, uttering his thanks.

The man pointed at each of the boys, uttering a word for each one, presumably a name. Rain couldn't immediately memorize the sounds. The man then pointed at him.

"Rain Barynd," said Rain. All three scrunched up their faces. His name sounded strange to them. Of course it did. He gave a slight shrug, then climbed the ladder onto his bunk, turning to sit cross-legged and stare at the window box, which spouted nonsense amid a head-spinning jumble of images.

The man spoke to the other boys for a minute, obviously explaining to them that Rain didn't speak their language—and maybe even that he was dim-witted. He couldn't care about that, though. He needed to figure out how to return to that field, find the key … and hopefully get himself home. If that was possible.

The boys ignored him, so he eventually lay back on his surprisingly soft bunk—with a real mattress!—and closed his eyes. He couldn't sleep with his mind spinning so fast, not to mention all the noise in the room. But at least his body felt relaxed, and he was pretty sure he was safe for the moment.

Some time later, with the box displaying a different multi-hued flavor of confusion, Hannah came into the room and called Rain's full name—she had remembered the sounds, impressively well. She held up his small coin bag and the old note from Tashiel, which she must have retrieved from that other building. That was kind of her. He felt extremely lucky that nothing except the sword and dagger had been permanently kept from him so far. There were apparently good people on this world.

She beckoned him off the bunk, and he followed her down the hall to a door emblazoned with a strange sign that looked kind of like a man. She urged him to open it and enter, and inside he found a latrine area. Thank goodness. He hadn't known how to ask. He was doubly grateful she didn't follow him inside. The area was immense and even had some privacy barriers, plus multiple wash basins with running water.

When he returned, she led him to a smaller room with another desk, wooden this time, with two chairs set up next to each other on one side.

He noted she had tied her straight brown hair in a tail behind her head. He couldn't decide if that made her appear older or younger, though she was probably a bit older than Antara. She had her folding window slab with her again, and she opened it up after they sat. Then she began showing him images, startling in how real they appeared, pointing at each one and waiting. He caught on to what she expected, and he began naming the images—at least those he could recognize. Many were things he had never seen before. After he named them, she also named them, pointing to what looked like writing above or beneath. Their language. She was trying to show him their language and learn his. But how long would it take to learn an entirely new language? He didn't need to, anyway. Or did he?

She produced some impossibly thin paper and a small rod that she clicked. She set the paper on the table and handed him the rod. When he stared at her blankly, the rod resting lifelessly in his palm, she took it back and wrote some text on the paper. *Oh, a writing utensil. Duh.* He nodded, and they began again. He had never written much, and his form wasn't great, but he did his best. She often wrote the equivalents with a second rod next to his scratches, even though he could see them on the slab's brilliant surface.

After more than two hours, it seemed she could tell he was getting frustrated, though he tried not to let it show. She stopped, scrunched her eyebrows for a few seconds, and then brightened. She rose, motioning him to follow as she turned to leave the room.

She led him back outside, onto the skirt of the street. She had shown him a similar picture, but he couldn't remember the name associated with it. Just then his stomach rumbled loudly. He'd taken a few drinks from the water basins, but he still hadn't eaten anything since he'd arrived in this unbelievable world. She stopped and turned, concern etching her face as she looked him up and down. Then she nodded sharply and continued, finally arriving at the pearl monster she had brought him in, which had moved to a different spot to rest, one that wasn't along the street. He stood motionless and uncertain until she opened a door and ushered him inside.

She got in from the other side again and began the intricate set of steps that would encourage the beast to go where she wanted.

A few minutes later, she pulled up to a large sign filled with static pictures and words in a dazzling array of colors. The sign started speaking to her. He shouldn't have been surprised. She spoke back, carrying on a short conversation, and they rolled a few yards farther on to stop next to the side of a building. Shortly, a window opened in the wall. Hannah handed a small flat object to a person inside, who, after a few seconds, returned it. Then came a large bag, along with what looked like two transparent canteens, thin and columnar. She gave the bag to him but placed the clear canteens into circular slots between their seats. He hadn't noticed those before. She moved the beast forward again and stopped, pushing a button that seemed to have no effect, though she brought her knees up higher.

Smells of warm food wafted from the bag, which felt like parchment. She looked at him and nodded toward the bag, but he didn't want to be presumptuous, so he just stared back at her.

She squinted, then smiled and sighed, placing the bag in her lap. Then she grabbed one of the canteens and twisted a cap in a solid color. After handing it to him, she nodded encouragingly. It must be water. He took a sip, and it tasted pure, like a high mountain stream. He gave it several more swallows, but preserved the rest. After he placed the canteen back in its slot, she reached into the bag and pulled out an object enveloped in more paper. She unwrapped it, revealing a savory-smelling sandwich of some type that clearly included meat. His mouth watered as she handed it to him and nodded again, speaking softly.

He took it in both hands, then bit into it, slurping in the juices that tried to escape. The burst of flavor was heavenly. The sandwich included some sliced vegetables and a type of leafy plant that added texture. The bread itself was bland, but everything else tasted perfect. Beyond perfect. He chewed quickly, swallowed, and took another bite. Before he knew it, he had devoured the entire sandwich, at which point she handed him a small, open-sided box crammed with some other kind of foodstuff. He began pulling out long pieces and wolfing them down. They tasted somewhat familiar, and they were hot and salty. He soon found he needed more water, and he gave her a questioning look as he pointed to the canteen. She laughed, then nodded, and he took another drink.

When he had finished the small box, she handed him a large wafer of some type, half-sheathed in much thinner parchment, like paper. Only rich people got paper, so she must be very wealthy. He bit into it and realized it was sweet, kind of like a pie, but more solid. He consumed that, too, took another drink, and put his hands in his lap.

"Thank you," he said, and it was heartfelt; he hoped she could tell from his expression. He was still hungry, but that meal had helped immensely.

She smiled again, opened the other canteen, and took a couple of sips. After placing the cap back on and setting it in its hole, she proceeded to manipulate the beast again.

He tried to observe carefully where she was going, looking for anything he had seen before. He thought she might be taking him back to where he had been found, and his heart leaped. Was she going to let him go? He wondered if she would get in trouble, but that didn't concern him much. His desperation to get back rose to a surprising fever pitch.

Eventually, they did indeed drive by the field, then the house where his sudden appearance had frightened the man and his wife, and several miles beyond. She kept looking over at him, but beyond the manor and that particular field, nothing held much interest for him. She finally turned around, and as they passed the field again, he locked his eyes on it. She slowed, then brought the beast to a full stop. He looked over at her and blinked rapidly several times. Perhaps she recognized how important the field was to him.

She got out of the beast, closed the door, and looked toward the field. After a few seconds, he opened his own door using the same procedure she had used on her side, then walked around the metallic monster to stand at the edge of the road, facing the fence. He took a step toward it, then glanced at her, hoping she recognized the request for permission in his eyes. After a brief hesitation, she nodded for him to proceed.

He carefully climbed the fence, trying to gauge his location. Then he set off toward the area where he had dropped the key. He looked back as he heard her climbing over, but kept going, increasing his pace. He started searching among the thickening shoots, bending low and scanning the ground, barely registering Hannah's arrival. It took at least ten minutes before he found the key, lying on its side, nearly invisible. With a joyful sigh, he picked it up, the relief quickly followed by a new wave of soul-crushing skepticism about being able to make it work. But at least he had it again.

Hannah appeared at his side, and as he turned he realized a tear had leaked to scurry down his cheek. Her eyes exuded empathy and curiosity as she stared at the key. He doubted it could mean anything to her. Smiling sheepishly, he shoved it in a pocket, suddenly realizing he hadn't changed out of his clothes in two days and hadn't even washed his face. He must stink by now, at least to her.

That was a minor concern, though. He didn't know what to do next. He had hoped that his desperate desire to return, coupled with touching the key, might take him back, but he hadn't detected even the faintest flicker of the talisman's magic. With no other option, he returned to the beast with Hannah, who guided it back to the building with the bunk room and the loud window box that so fascinated the three boys.

She left him there, speaking for several more minutes with the bald man before departing. Deflated, Rain lumbered up the short ladder onto his bunk. For a long while he stared at the surface of the window box, hardly noticing when the others left and came back throughout the rest of the waning afternoon. He followed obediently when the bald man led him to a larger room with long tables, where many boys had gathered for a meal. His body said the food was just as good as what Hannah had given him, but his mind had a hard time accepting it.

After dinner, the man showed him a place where some of the boys were exercising, mainly by lifting weights that looked as precisely formed as a fine suit of armor. He had no interest in participating, but he was bursting to get back to the latrine.

Upon returning to the bunk room, Rain watched and listened to the window box with the others before finally succumbing to sleep.

Ileom had never traveled to Agrancik's home world. Only one other member of the Order had, and Avrenor was now dead. The trip hadn't been as easy as hoped. The book associated with that particular key, discovered five years ago by Agrancik's late wife—an archeologist and historian on Alave, not a sorceress—required a great deal of magical power under normal circumstances, along with a lengthy set of recitations that set Ileom's teeth on edge. Given that it was indeed malfunctioning, as Agrancik had claimed, the process was twice as arduous. But they arrived, and apparently in the place Agrancik intended, so he couldn't complain.

They alighted on the rounded top of a hill enclosed by a tall wooden palisade, weathered with age, amid a forest of towering pines. It was late morning, mid-summer, with wispy clouds dancing lazily in the heavens. Agrancik promised him their march to civilization wouldn't be long, and that it was mostly downhill. He also indicated they could return to that spot on griffons. Ileom felt a little nervous about that, and it wasn't because of the heights. He wished he could have brought Trump Sounder, his massive two-hander, which now bore a tiny, magically inscribed notch near the hilt for its first griffon killed. Walking around with it here, though, would make him look too militant for an ostensibly peaceful mission.

Agrancik whistled as they strode along a winding path near a gurgling stream. Normally, Ileom would have found that annoying, but too many other issues pressed upon his mind. The grave dangers Tenris faced seemed to morph and multiply daily, and now Alave might be in serious trouble as well. He was certain the Order was missing something critical. While the griffons posed an acute problem, at least they were known now. Well, somewhat.

"You don't seem concerned," he noted.

Agrancik turned and smiled. "My friend, I am always concerned. But it often pays for me not to be so."

Ileom grunted general agreement with the sentiment but countered, "There is no reason to hide it from *me*, however. Especially on this mission."

Agrancik's smile disappeared. "True, my brave friend. The appearance of those griffons does indeed distress me, deeply. Something unexpected has happened, though I cannot guess whether it is a small issue or a major development."

Ileom had no feel for this world, nor whether his god presided over it. That particular blindness would bother him, and he hadn't anticipated how much.

"We should assume a major development."

Agrancik stopped, humming low, his mien worried. He seemed reluctant to meet Ileom's eyes. "Now that we are here, my assurances at the last Council meeting sound weaker. I believe you are correct, my friend."

Ileom thought he trusted Agrancik, but how well could he really know a visitor from another planet, even after five years? He was human, yes, but from a culture entirely foreign to Ileom. Was he acting?

"How should we approach this then?" he asked his alien friend.

Agrancik tucked his thumbs behind his belt. He had worn a long tunic and slightly puffy pants for this trip, native to his homeland. He could be mistaken for a Miniforian. "We can trust the man I told you about, who lives in the village near the bottom of this valley. We should wait until nightfall, though, as we discussed, and contact him in secret. He will be able to arrange a conveyance to take us to my capital, where we can approach another contact."

Ileom squinted, thinking through that again. The blindness suffocated him, and he nearly growled. It didn't feel right, though admittedly he was an impatient man. "Or, we stay a day with him, see what he knows, then send *him* to gather more information if needed. And we approach him openly. Nobody will recognize me, nor suspect I'm from another planet."

Agrancik pondered the radically altered proposal with impressive composure. "Your fine armor marks you a warrior of high rank. That red cloak reinforces it."

Ileom shrugged. "So it does. But you can vouch for me, so people don't feel threatened."

Agrancik worked his mouth for a moment, then nodded. "You are more experienced in the Order, and I cannot come up with a valid argument against your plan. Plus, we might pick up on some subtle reactions to our arrival."

Though a little surprised Agrancik had agreed so quickly, Ileom felt better, and they continued. The Alavian didn't whistle during the remainder of their journey through the valley—an added bonus—which brought them to the village in the middle of the afternoon. Ileom hadn't noticed much in the way of wildlife as they descended, except for the plentiful birds decked out in a unique variety of colors.

The village didn't appear all that mysterious. Most of the buildings were of wood, though some incorporated stone. More scrollwork decorated the surfaces than what he was accustomed to, and the steep peaks of the roofs had slight curves to them. He'd seen such styles before in Har'Batil and the eastern half of Vriesland.

The cuts and colors of the clothing, too, weren't overly odd, though they shimmered differently in the light. He glanced again at the sky, which displayed the familiar hue of blue.

"Over here," said Agrancik, switching to his own language. Over the three years Ileom had worked often with the man, he had learned his language at least passably, along with Avrenor, who had picked it up faster. Ileom had wanted to make this trip that entire time but had never gotten around to it, just as the rest of the Council hadn't yet found the time to study Agrancik's native tongue.

He followed as Agrancik veered toward one of the larger structures, two stories of dark brown with a peaked wooden door. Yellow and orange flowers nodded from a window box.

Agrancik knocked lightly and took a step back. He bowed low as the door opened, then greeted the tall woman framed in the entrance. She was elegantly dressed, unlike the other people in the village, who for the most part wore what looked like common work clothes. Her blue velvet dress nearly touched the floor, accented by a thin, cream-colored sash over one shoulder that gathered at the waist and continued past her knees as cords ending in tassels.

She clearly recognized Agrancik, giving him a lesser bow in return. Her smile seemed tight, but there was warmth in her eyes. Ileom didn't know how to read that.

"Lady Brentia, it has been too long."

"Or not long enough, depending on your viewpoint." The warmth in her eyes remained, causing Agrancik to chuckle.

"I never bring enough good news, that is true. Is your husband here today?"

"Yes. He is composing a letter in the study." She backed up a step, welcoming him inside, her gaze passing only briefly over Ileom. This clearly wasn't the first time Agrancik had brought a stranger with him.

"This is Master Ileom, one of my foreign colleagues," he said as she closed the door. Ileom nodded to her, maintaining eye contact, and she returned the gesture. He preferred to speak as little as possible, knowing he would sound clumsy. His gold and black tabard was artfully designed but carried no writing on it. Neither it nor his longsword in a plain scabbard should elicit conversation. Nor should the cloak. And his armor wasn't *that* fancy. Just extremely well fashioned for its purpose. Magically enhanced, too.

Lady Brentia led them toward the back of the house, which was deeper than Ileom had expected. She showed them into a room, where a very tall, clean-shaven man paced as he reviewed a document held in both hands, mumbling to himself. He looked up as they entered, eyes widening as they fell upon Agrancik. His lips burst into a wide grin, and he set the paper down as he rounded the edge of a desk and clasped Agrancik with both arms. "My friend, welcome back!"

Agrancik bowed low to him as he had to Lady Brentia. "I hadn't expected to return so soon, but the seasons are sometimes unpredictable."

The man nodded several times at that. "Indeed, they are." His eyes sparkled at his wife. "Thank you, my love."

She smiled and left, and the man gestured toward a set of elegant but well-worn chairs. "Please, let us sit. I have many questions for you." He hadn't given Ileom more than a passing glance, just like Lady Brentia, but perhaps it was the custom to wait for the introduction.

After they were seated, Agrancik gestured. "Jehorim Anastavria, this is my colleague, Master Ileom Mystrevan."

The alien man finally studied Ileom, his straight, gray-streaked, shoulder-length black hair brushing against the soft, light-gray fabric of his unadorned tunic with hidden buttons or clasps. "It is a pleasure, Master Ileom. You are from Tenris?"

Ileom shot a glance at Agrancik, whose smile cracked. "We will discuss this," he said in Regan Common.

"I know," said Agrancik.

Ileom then answered Jehorim in an even tone. "Yes, I am." His first three words spoken to a stranger on another planet in an alien language. Agrancik had told him they spoke many tongues on Alave, though most were quite similar to each other.

"Welcome. A friend of Agrancik is my friend, too. You are the first otherworlder I have seen. Can I assume this visit is not just for pleasure?" His eyes flicked to the armor.

Ileom's mind double-checked the translation, and he nodded. "Yes. We have some important questions." He stared at Agrancik, who took the hint and cleared his throat.

"There has been a troubling development on Tenris."

Jehorim scowled slightly. "How troubling?"

"Someone has transported griffons there from our world and is using them in battle."

Jehorim's eyebrows rose as he leaned forward. "You have proof of this?"

Nodding, Agrancik turned to Ileom, who answered, "I killed one. More than a dozen attacked my company. They had riders. Several of my men were killed."

Jehorim breathed deeply through his nose, then started tapping his fingers on the desk as he gazed at Agrancik. "This should not be possible. Better griffons than dragons, of course, but still a grave occurrence."

Ileom wondered if he'd understood correctly. "Dragons?" he repeated, hoping he'd pronounced it right.

Agrancik stared solemnly at him. "Yes, and I apologize. I acknowledged to you and Avrenor that our histories align somewhat regarding dragons, but I didn't see the need yet to reveal their current existence here. They are rare, partly because of the great enmity between them and the griffons, which have grown quite numerous and are more easily controlled."

Ileom searched Agrancik's eyes for several seconds, his own face a mask. "We have no dragons on Tenris," he finally said, addressing both men. "I believe they are … what is the word?"

"Fables?" offered Jehorim.

"No." The word came. "Extinct. Which is why they are fables. They may have existed long ago, but they do not now."

Jehorim rubbed his jaw, exhibiting intense curiosity. Agrancik regained his attention by clearing his throat.

"Have you heard anything, my friend, that would suggest how this could have happened?"

Jehorim frowned, staring at the wall for several seconds. "I recently dismissed a snippet of information coming out of Sistrayn. The young prince is quite ill, and the king has been absent from most of his regular duties, presumably attending to his son. Shortly before that, the castle's chief stablemaster was killed in a training accident. It involved horses, not griffons, but the circumstances are strange. It is not much to go on, but perhaps Sistrayn is the source of this intrigue. I am the first you have told?"

Agrancik nodded. "Yes, but I must relay this information to others, including our queen and her court."

"I will take care of it."

"I would prefer you travel to Sistrayn and investigate," said Agrancik. "You have more connections there than I do. I myself will make an appearance at the queen's court."

"Very well." Jehorim glanced at Ileom. "Should our friend remain here? We will take good care of him."

Agrancik raised his eyebrows at Ileom, awaiting a response.

Ileom studied them both for several seconds, considering, then announced, "I will journey to Sistrayn with Master Jehorim. I need to witness the possibilities there myself."

Agrancik showed no reaction, but Jehorim blinked in surprise. After a moment, he dipped his head. "Very well, then. Our trip will be swift. You're okay if we travel by *maersik*?"

Ileom didn't know that word, so he looked to Agrancik for a translation.

"An old word for dragon saddle, with a different root. He's proposing you travel dragonback."

It was Ileom's turn to blink, and he forgot to switch back to the alien language. "He just said dragons are more dangerous than griffons."

"Yes," said Agrancik, another apology twitching at his lips, "indeed they are, to the wrong people."

Welcome to a new world.

⸎

Agrancik departed thirty minutes later in a small carriage summoned by Lady Brentia. Curiously, it was pulled by something that appeared half horse and half ox, with a stubbier version of a horse's head and neck accented by horns extending to the sides. Its magnificent fur was thicker than either animal's, its hooves cloven twice instead of once. The carriage itself was painted a deep golden brown, the wheels made of a bronzed metal.

Shortly afterward, Ileom found himself trudging through the woods trailing Jehorim, wondering how far away they kept a dragon, as well as what it looked like and how they kept it. Dragons hadn't existed on Tenris for, what, a thousand years or more? The people of that time assumed they had gone extinct, but had they instead … *left*? A mile into the march, and at least three hundred vertical feet upslope, they arrived at a circular enclosure a hundred yards across, formed by thin, arching steel beams connected by heavy cables and sitting atop a stone foundation. A fully covered section took up about a third of the space, and Ileom noted the pair of wide entrance doors made of heavy metal bars, secured by pins as thick as his arms. The rest of the area inside appeared much like the forest floor around it, though with fewer trees.

Four dragons relaxed in different parts of the enclosure, curled up like sleeping cats. They weren't as massive as he had expected, but still plenty large, easily outsizing the griffons by two. Jehorim didn't whistle, but he hummed as he lifted the pins out of the way by means of a pulley system and pulled the doors all the way open on well-oiled hinges. Ileom's mouth went dry as all four beasts lifted their heads and fixed piercing golden orbs on him.

Jehorim turned to Ileom and offered a reassuring smile. "Don't worry, Master Ileom. This enclosure is to protect them from griffons, not prevent them from escaping, although even a score of griffons would have trouble with four fully-grown dragons."

One of the creatures stood on four legs, partially unfolding its wings before tucking them back. It seemed fearsome in a more penetrating way than the griffons, and Ileom had to focus on calming his breathing and heart rate. That annoyed him.

They stepped inside, and Jehorim closed the doors, securing them with a smaller horizontal pin from the inside.

"You said you do not have dragons on your world?"

"No, not any longer. We have stories."

"And in the stories they are much larger?"

Ileom squinted, surprised at the Alavian's perception. "Yes. Some of them can talk, too, and breathe fire. Even do magic."

Jehorim nodded, smiling. "Yes, stories do tend to exaggerate, especially the longer they exist. Our dragons are not so … terrible. If they were, humans would not be the dominant species here, and I suspect the griffons would be extinct or subjugated."

"So … these are just animals?"

Jehorim chuckled this time. "I wouldn't say *that*. They are more intelligent than the others, and though the truly feral ones are frightening to deal with, these creatures here are quite accommodating. They eat less than you would think, too. I'm not sure why, and they are true omnivores, whereas griffons are not."

"So, they're kind of like bears."

Jehorim quirked an eyebrow. "With wings. And much sleeker. Less grumpy, too, though quite particular. You'll like them. Let me introduce you."

Ileom nodded, and they moved toward the creature that had stood. Its amber scales glittered with silver highlights. Jehorim reached out a hand, and the beast touched it with its nose, sniffing softly. "Go ahead," he said. "Extend your hand. He knows you are no threat, because you're with me."

Ileom did so, maintaining the position until his hand had been touched and smelled. Then he turned to Jehorim. "Humans hunt them, too?"

Sadness flickered across Jehorim's features. "Yes, occasionally, in some parts of the world, anyway. My country doesn't, and I know the beasts appreciate it. They are very loyal, by the way, though if trust is broken, their fury is sharp and swift."

That sent a chill down Ileom's spine. He looked up into the creature's golden eyes. "Do you name them?"

"We do. They seem to name us as well, though we haven't quite figured that out."

"And they are not magical?" He had noted a strange gleam in the creature's eyes, and something niggled at the back of his mind.

"No, they are not, as far as we know."

"But perhaps they can *sense* magic?"

Jehorim rubbed his chin, studying him intently. "Perhaps. Magic is extremely rare here, all but nonexistent. Agrancik is … an anomaly."

"Hmmm … so magic was eradicated?"

"Essentially, yes. For good or ill, I cannot tell."

"The only way to expunge it is to kill all who wield it. Is that not for ill?"

"It depends on the nature of the wielders. And not when it will surely drive you mad with power lust."

Ileom gave a low chuckle. "That is true here, too?"

"In almost all cases, yes."

Suddenly, Ileom realized how well he could speak the language, even using words he didn't think he remembered. That felt decidedly odd. Where had he come up with the word for 'expunge'? Or recognized 'anomaly'? He focused again on the animal and said, "He knows I can wield magic."

A few seconds of silence followed. That statement clearly made Jehorim uncomfortable. But Ileom could sense the dragon had understood what he'd said, or at least the gist of it. *How* he could tell that, he wasn't quite sure. The key lay behind its eyes.

"You can do magic?" Ileom detected more than a hint of worry in Jehorim's voice.

"Yes."

"And ... you do not feel strange here?"

Ileom shook his head. "No, I do not. I am curious to see what my magic can do here, but that must wait. I will ask Agrancik first, of course. I believe he is trustworthy." He stared into the dragon's golden eyes again. "What is his name?"

"Lagronizeth. In our ancient tongue, it means Sky Dancer."

"He is a strong flier." Ileom could feel that, too, somehow.

"Indeed." Just then another dragon, silver and gray, ambled up to stand next to the first. It fixed its aureate eyes on Ileom, and he reached out his hand again. There was hesitation this time, but the dragon finally leaned forward for the touch. Ileom let go the breath he'd been holding.

"And this one?" he asked in a near whisper, almost spellbound. "What is its name?"

"She is called Meriswethin. The closest translation is one who smothers fire."

"Flame Slayer."

"Yes, I suppose that works."

"Why was that name chosen?"

"I do not know. She came to us with that name etched into the scales of her forehead. The writing has since faded, but the name remains. Someone here tried to change it. Meriswethin took exception."

"Do you think she would carry me?" He squared himself to Jehorim after asking the question.

Jehorim seemed perplexed for a moment as he considered Ileom and the two dragons. "My first thought would have been Lagron," he began slowly, "but I do believe Meris would carry you."

"Trust me, you are not as surprised as I am." He turned to stare at Meris, or Flame Slayer, again, and she dropped her snout slightly. Ileom mimicked the action, then blinked as a presence flickered inside his head. He heard a sharp intake of breath from Jehorim. When he met his eyes, the man's jaw had dropped a bit.

"You can *link* with her?" Jehorim asked.

Ileom wasn't sure what that meant. It didn't feel like a link—nothing usable, anyway. He shrugged, his skin tingling. "I feel something, but I can't define it, other than to say that it came from Meris."

"Very few on this world—if any now—can link with a dragon, though much is written of it from long ago. I am jealous, because I cannot, not even with Lagron, who knows me well."

Ileom breathed deeply, then studied Meris again. "Well, she seems eager to go. I think she realizes we aren't just here for a social visit."

"Indeed. Lagron, too. I will have them saddled, and we can depart. There is enough light left for us to make it to Dansgren, where we can pass the night."

"And how much farther from there to … what is it called?"

"Sistrayn. We will go to the capital, Hahnril. King Taryn and Queen Juless rule there. Chief Minister Milcross will be part of any discussions as well. He handles all the administrative needs of their kingdom."

"Taryn. Juless. Milcross. They are friendly?"

"Yes."

"And they will not suspect where I'm from?"

"No, they will not. A scant few people are aware of the ability to travel between our two worlds."

How many was a 'scant' few? Ileom looked forward to pinning Agrancik with many related questions at some point during this visit. "Well, I had no idea you possessed dragons here. I wish Agrancik had mentioned it. But I'm anticipating this trip as much as traveling between worlds."

Jehorim gave him a gracious, though thin, smile. "You will not soon forget the experience."

Ileom couldn't tell how high they climbed into the clear afternoon expanse, Meris following Lagron until they leveled out and evened up. He had never felt anything like it. From the sharp wind in his face and the rapidity with which landmarks fell by the wayside below, he knew they traveled at incredible speed—faster than the swiftest hawk.

The saddle was a complex affair, with additional straps to make sure he couldn't fall out. Instead of a pommel, a wide semi-solid surface rose nearly to the level of his chest, the cantle doing the same behind him, allowing room for two riders. Instead of a bit, the reins connected to small contraptions on either side of the dragon's head, part of a complex bridle. A pull would cause a small arm to tap against the skull, just below the ear. Jehorim had given him brief instructions regarding what different sequences of taps meant, but he couldn't remember them all. The Alavian had added that voiced commands also worked, though in some circumstances the sounds wouldn't reach even the dragon's sensitive ears. He had mentioned the lost art of linking again, which theoretically allowed rider and beast to communicate at a basic level, particularly about flying.

There was no good way to use a sword from his seat, and even a long spear would be cumbersome—and risky. He saw no seating to emplace a long lance. Bows would be awkward, too, though crossbows could be effective if one managed a quick reload mechanism from the saddle. The dragon itself, of course, was a weapon. The sharp, thick claws on fore and hind feet hadn't escaped Ileom's notice, and some of the teeth were longer than his fingers. A pity they couldn't breathe fire, ice, acid, or other elements described in harrowing drama in the legends, but transporting warriors swiftly across a battlefield and performing quick strikes from above presented significant advantages. If he had a hundred dragons, and he took them to Chalace …

That line of wishful thinking soon ended. Emperor Creegan already had griffons, which were far more numerous and whose beaks were apparently powerful enough to pierce a dragon's scales. Any enemy would soon adapt to the threat of dragons, anyway, especially since they weren't the colossal, invulnerable leviathans of lore. He had already worked through a few ideas on how to counter the griffons—even without magic.

They reached Dansgren, or rather, a dragon enclosure near it, after dark had fallen. Jehorim explained they were still in Azrimain, the country both he and Agrancik hailed from, though the border with Sistrayn was close. Many of the town's lights remained hidden among the mountain trees, so he couldn't tell how large it was. A tiny village supported the enclosure, and he and Jehorim stayed the night at the home of one of the trainers. Ileom remained mostly quiet during dinner and the chats that followed, his ability with the new tongue having diminished a bit during the flight. Maybe his brain had gelled in the high altitude. Jehorim introduced him as a visiting foreign military consul, and the trainer accepted it without question. The conversation remained safely on mundane topics throughout, and Ileom had no trouble sleeping, especially since his mind knew that when he awoke, he would be able to fly with Meris again.

They rose early, skipped breakfast, and departed, the chilly air quickly penetrating the thin cloak wrapped rather uselessly around Ileom's torso. It got better when the sun was fully up, and thankfully the clouds were sparse.

He felt Meris's presence again, perhaps a little stronger, though he couldn't be sure. He tried focusing, reaching out in his mind for that peculiar entity, which seemed to exist in an entirely new plane of his consciousness.

He thought he detected some stirrings, but after several hours of strenuous mental exertion, he gave up. He could have slept again, if he let himself.

He barely heard Jehorim shouting, trying to get his attention. His head jerked, and he followed the direction of Jehorim's pointed finger, marveling at the large, gleaming city arrayed in a valley below them. The lower end of the vale emptied onto a broad, fertile plain that disappeared into the distance, where he caught the vague outlines of other cities, one of them nearly as large. Riding dragonback was like having a mobile mountain lookout. The view was incredibly useful … and stunning.

They must be approaching Hahnril. As the dragons descended, he noticed that the gleaming surfaces of the city were white stone, speckled with a silvery substance used in much of the construction. Hahnril easily rivaled Jeveria, Ashamadi, or Gran Sheran in splendor, with Ashamadi and Albelai the only capitals on Rega that were significantly larger. No walls surrounded the city, but the valley itself possessed many defensible features that would give any attacker great pause. Unlike Arxhana. Why those fools had never built a decent wall dumbfounded him. Their cavalry was fearsome, true, but the city had still been overrun many times in the past. Even if that past lay quite distant now, history had a cruel, merciless way of repeating itself. And it soon would.

Jehorim and Lagron spiraled them downward, and Ileom noted a small castle as their likely destination. A single pair of guards patrolled its high walls, and a flat area on one of the square towers appeared large enough to accommodate both dragons landing at once. The dragons' feet had barely touched its surface when a door in a small structure at one side of the tower opened. Two men hustled out, each hefting a large bag on his back, which they plopped in front of the dragons and opened. It wasn't half-rotting meat or week-old produce, thankfully.

"Very hospitable of them to feed our mounts straightaway," said Jehorim. "And someone nearby has a keen eye, since we weren't expected. They know these dragons, of course."

Ileom grunted an acknowledgement as he worked through the complicated straps, finally extricating himself and dropping to the tower stone, which Meris helpfully brought closer. Her back wasn't much higher than a horse's when she crouched like that; she was just wider and longer. Her claws clacked as she shifted, sniffing at the bag and then burying her snout in it.

"Come, my friend," said Jehorim. "We must announce ourselves." He led the way toward the still open door, and the two men—apparently un-armed—fell in behind, neither saying a word. They descended a set of wide circular stairs that conveyed them to a broad hallway leading along one of the castle's primary walls. Full-size exterior windows—not arrow slits—looked down upon the city below. The other side featured a course of pillars reveal-ing a luxurious fountained courtyard. Colorful tapestries hung between a few of the pillars, depicting beautiful landscapes or strange creatures. None portrayed anything martial in nature, and only one featured people.

At the end of the colonnade, an arched entryway led them into a room of calm activity, with about twenty people in smart uniforms of purple and gray sitting at various tasks or moving about. Two of them glanced up from papers ordered in neat stacks on a long shared desk. Jehorim stopped to give a short bow. "Who is the captain on duty?"

"Captain Ilders," one of them answered. "He went to the pri—um, he will return soon."

"Very good, thank you."

Jehorim showed Ileom to some chairs along one wall, while their two escorts melted into another part of the castle. They hadn't been sitting more than a minute when a man walked into the room from a different hallway, immediately spotting them. He didn't seem to recognize Jehorim, and he frowned.

"You have business here?" he asked gruffly.

Jehorim rose smoothly, again giving a slight bow. "I am Jehorim Anastavria, of Azrimain. I am known to the regents and seek an audience with them. I bring an emissary with me, whose name I can reveal only to them, on a matter of some urgency."

The man's frown lessened. "I have heard your name before. I will make the request." He spun sharply and left the way he had come, long strides causing the click of boots on stone to fade quickly.

Ileom had also risen, but sat when Jehorim resumed his seat.

"It shouldn't be long," Jehorim said, smiling. "This is a peaceful part of the world, so the regents allow their ministers to make most of the mundane decisions. They will be happy to entertain a matter of relative import." He added a wink.

Ileom nodded, surveying the room again. Nobody paid them much attention, though his armor drew the occasional curious glance.

"The dragons have both taken a liking to you," continued Jehorim. He didn't lower his voice, clearly intending the comment for the benefit of those working in the room. A few heads twitched in their direction. "Perhaps the regents will allow us a more extensive tour of these lands."

Ileom grunted, not wanting to speak.

"The harvest here is expected to be excellent this year. In Azrimain and many other countries as well. We have been well favored." He continued to talk—about crops, the weather, and progress toward universal literacy, which he noted was being led primarily by the churches. That perked Ileom's ears. He also described some new breakthroughs in metallurgy and metal fabrication. Ileom would need to witness some of those things to understand them, but the impression was already growing that this world was a bit more advanced, technologically speaking, than Tenris. Agrancik had never indicated such. Was it because he hadn't wanted to boast, or was he carefully guarding secrets to protect his home world? Ileom supposed he couldn't blame him, to a degree. The Order was ostensibly designed to operate in an open and honest atmosphere beyond such tendencies, but its primary concern was Tenris, not Alave. Perhaps that would change if—or rather, when—the two worlds became more intertwined. It was only a matter of time now.

The one-sided conversation lasted nearly an hour before the captain returned. He raised his chin slightly, then swept an arm behind him. "They will see you now. Please follow me." His tone had become much more respectful, and he even acknowledged Ileom with a nod, though he didn't ask his name.

They proceeded along the hallway and down two flights of stairs, then followed a path through a lush, beautifully manicured garden and under a large archway into the castle proper. The ornamentation and interior architecture fit the status of a prosperous nation—or at the very least a proud ruling class. Paintings in gilded frames adorned the walls, and fine carpets, mostly in red and brown tones, stretched from edge to edge along the floors—even inside some of the rooms they passed. The ceilings were textured in fanciful patterns, often accentuated by soft coloring, and the braziers cast a bright, steady light to guide their way. Ileom couldn't help but be impressed, though he had visited similar places.

They finally arrived at a pair of two-story doors, arcing outward near the top and then back in to form a convex peak, like a half-moon blade. A pair of guards in deep purple uniforms, armed only with short swords— long knives, really—turned to tug on the bronzed handles as the party approached, the opening requiring little effort and generating almost no noise. The captain bid them farewell and retreated.

Inside, at least two dozen pews lined each half of a long, high-ceilinged room. At its end, in an apse, several tall-backed chairs on a dais faced the pews, three of them occupied. Several more guards were spaced around the room.

"This is the Royal Church," said Jehorim in muted tones as they passed through the doorway at a reverent pace. "The regents hold some of their councils here, passing many judgments. We are honored guests if this is where they brought us."

Ileom could distinguish the two regents by the thin crowns they wore. Otherwise, they were dressed rather plainly, the queen sporting a sash similar to that of Lady Brentia. The Chief Minister was a different story. He obviously took his wardrobe seriously. The air wasn't cool, but he wore at least three layers of upper clothing, in complementary shades of purple, green and gold. A long, gold-trimmed cloak hung from the top of his chair, and gold ornamented his neck and most of his fingers. People in positions of power who tried so hard to be noticed rarely impressed Ileom, but he tried to withhold judgment on this planet's cultural norms and traditions.

Jehorim lifted his chin when they stopped at the bottom of the three short stairs to the dais, more than was necessary for looking up at their hosts. Ileom followed suit.

"Jehorim, my friend, welcome," said King Taryn. "You honor us with your visit, though I understand it is not pleasure that brings you here."

"It is always a pleasure to be here," said Jehorim smoothly, lifting his chin even higher, and then it clicked for Ileom. Bowing signified your station was higher, and the lower you bowed, the higher it was. Which meant Agrancik enjoyed significant status. Ileom had seen something similar to the chin-lifting to signify respect or obeisance, particularly in Kyatera. Some called it 'baring the neck.' Either way, bowed or lifted, the neck was exposed. And he had another point to make with Agrancik, who hadn't mentioned any of this.

The queen laughed. "You are too kind, as usual. But you have brought us an intriguing guest."

"Indeed. This is Master Ileom, an emissary from—"

"I came from another world, through a magical portal. And I understand your son is quite ill. My best wishes for a full recovery."

The regents stared in stunned silence for a moment, but then King Taryn recovered a bit. "Our thanks. Today has been one of his good days. You ... didn't come here because of him, though."

"No, I did not. Griffons have been secretly transported to my world from this one, and we have no creatures that can counter them."

He kept his eyes locked on the trio, sensing Jehorim stiffen next to him. They hadn't talked about if or when to make this revelation. It had just felt ... right, and the urgency of the situation on Tenris burned hot. He hoped he had said everything with the proper emphasis in their language.

The queen recoiled in her chair, and the king shot a glance of pure shock at Jehorim. Chief Minister Milcross seemed to have lost control of the orientation of his eyes, even going cross-eyed at one point.

"Jehorim, is this all true?" said the king. "You know I trust you, but this is a tale from an old, dusty book."

Jehorim spent an inordinate amount of time clearing his throat. "Your majesties, we in Azrimain have known such portals exist for only a short time, and our understanding is still primitive. We have discovered access to just one, and a high-ranking member of our Argent Council has been visiting the world to which it leads. Queen Viera believes this discovery portends great things … but ominous ones as well. She is preparing to convene several world leaders, including yourselves, to discuss the implications, dangers, and opportunities, but the appearance of the griffons on Master Ileom's planet is a potentially grave development for both our worlds. Hence our visit. Agrancik is at this time visiting Queen Viera to discuss the matter with her and the Regent's Court."

Queen Juless leaned forward and narrowed her eyes, keeping them focused on Jehorim. "We have the most griffons, so you decided to check here first." Her eyes started to flick to Ileom but stopped, as if she were afraid of his countenance. He couldn't decide whether to be pleased or worried that he had just created an international incident on Alave. Actually, he hadn't: Queen Viera and her secrecy had. As had Emperor Creegan and whoever was helping him here.

Jehorim kept his chin high. "We received intelligence that some may have come from Sistrayn."

Ileom resisted raising his eyebrows. They hadn't discussed being so direct about *that*, either. How would these royals react, especially if they were involved somehow?

"Intelligence from whom?"

"I apologize, but I cannot say."

King Taryn started to rise, anger flashing in his eyes. He glanced at Ileom and resettled himself before addressing Jehorim again. "We are allies."

"Indeed," said Jehorim contritely, "we are. But nefarious forces have attempted to divide us before. We cannot be too careful."

Taryn turned his gaze to Ileom, lifting his chin slightly, which was a surprise. "I can assure you, Master Ileom, that if someone has stolen any of our griffons and taken them to your world, we will find them and punish them."

Ileom raised his own chin. "We would be most grateful. I slayed one, by the way, but I had to use magic to do it."

This revelation nearly caused Milcross to spill out of his chair. The king and queen took it more calmly, though their lips parted slightly. Ileom detected real fear. That was good. Or horribly bad.

After a few seconds, Taryn asked. "What is your world called?"

"Tenris. I am from a nation called Jeveria. We face a growing threat from across the oceans, and the griffons have made it worse. That is why I came. I am the first emissary from Tenris to set foot on Alave."

"And not the last, I hope," said Juless, seeming to have recovered her composure. She hadn't lifted her chin, but neither had she dipped it.

Ileom nodded a few times, then wondered if that might confuse them. "There is much we can learn from each other, I am sure."

"You will dine with us tonight?" asked Taryn.

"Yes, I would be honored. But, if I may, I wish to see some of your griffons first."

Milcross, once he had recovered his well-dressed wits, called two assistants into the chapel, ordering one to make the travel arrangements and the other to organize a small repast for the royals and their guests while they waited. Then they moved to a small dining room connected to the chapel. In impressively little time, they had eaten and were ready to depart. Queen Juless remained behind to supervise the dinner preparations, as did Milcross, who had other administrative matters to attend to.

When it was time to leave, a brilliant black carriage picked them up in front of the castle, pulled by four actual horses, not the strange hybrid Ileom had seen in Jehorim's village. Two royal guards accompanied them, though it seemed mostly for show and protocol since they were armed so lightly. The swift but smooth carriage ride lasted about an hour, taking them well beyond the city's outskirts and deep into the less populated forest of the upper valley. King Taryn asked only basic questions about Tenris, and Ileom was circumspect in his answers. Jehorim remained mostly silent. When the horses stopped, Taryn announced they had arrived.

The first thing Ileom noticed after exiting the carriage was a barn with upper and lower doors, similar to the ones Captain Drydan had described on Chalace, though larger. A series of smaller barns flanked it, surrounded by pastures filled with various kinds of animals. Food for the griffons.

Taryn led them through the lower doors on one side of the nearest barn, then into a small office space filled with ledgers and occupied by two people, a man and a woman. Both jumped to their feet, faces nearly pointed at the ceiling.

"Be at ease," said the king. "We have guests, and I wish to show them our finest griffons. They have all returned from today's training?"

The man threw up an odd-looking salute, having relaxed slightly. "Yes, my liege, and they have already eaten and been groomed."

"Very good. I will show our guests around myself."

"Um, my liege?" began the woman, clearly distressed by his proposal.

"It's all right. I am not a combat rider, but I know all the protocols."

The woman swallowed, saluted, and then arched her neck toward the ceiling again. Ileom almost chuckled.

Taryn strode briskly out of the office, turning down one of four main corridors lined with wide, high stalls on each side. Thick, full-length, steel-banded doors fronted the stalls, featuring iron-barred windows about halfway up.

"Well-fed griffons, properly trained, really aren't so dangerous," explained Taryn as they passed several doors. "They look it, though." He smiled as Ileom peeked inside a few stalls, noting the large beasts either standing or lying down. Their feral eyes and sharp beaks plucked at the raw, recent memory of the loss of his men. He itched to reach for his sword and test his magic on this world. He'd already felt its stirrings, familiar and pure.

The king stopped. "Here," he said, gesturing, "is my favorite. The most majestic creature I have ever laid eyes upon."

Ileom moved to where he could see inside the stall, hearing a rustling. The massive head came into view, the beady, intelligent eyes sweeping across them, then returning to Ileom. The beast gave a maddened shriek and butted its head against the door with such force the entire wall shook.

"Whoa, Charpak, settle," said the king, acting calm but a little surprised. "Just visitors, and they are my guests." He smiled almost lovingly at the animal, raising a hand and moving closer to the door. Charpak shook its head and made some loud huffing noises, dividing its attention between Taryn and Ileom. Its body calmed, but not its eyes; pure hatred pulsed from them.

It was then Ileom realized two things. One, he had raised a foot, unconsciously preparing to employ a defensive magic through the ground. Second, the griffon had clearly been injured recently. It favored one side, including the wing.

Ileom lowered his foot slowly, catching the king's curious glance. "I doubt setting my feet better," he covered with a tight chuckle, "would have done any good had he broken through that door." He tried to make sense of what he had just seen. Had this griffon recently traveled to Tenris and been sent back to recover from a wound, or could it somehow sense he had slain another griffon? Did the smell of griffon blood still linger on him?

Taryn glanced at Jehorim, then gave Ileom an appraising look. "And yet you prepared to stand, instead of retreating when Charpak expressed his anger, misplaced though it was. I have not seen such a reaction from someone who is not an expert on griffons, and rarely from those who are."

Ileom pondered an appropriate response. Instead of deflecting the praise, as he normally would, especially in the presence of royalty, he said, "I have faced situations more fearsome, though I wish it were not so." There, that should give the king pause, especially if he were part of the scheme. He didn't detect evil from Taryn, but sometimes it was devilishly difficult to tell. People like Emperor Creegan and General Inzeal were great deceivers, too. Perhaps, if Ileom could find the right angle, he could persuade Taryn and his wife to help the Order and its allies *repel* the coming invasion of Rega. A tantalizing thought, though the odds were low. Such an arrangement would take months to negotiate, since Taryn's country possessed no obvious motivation for making any sacrifices for Tenris. Well, besides the potential of preferred trading status with an entire continent on another world—and without having to deal with Creegan's strangling despotism. Ileom would not deceive them with empty promises, but he would fight for real ones based on the natural, incontrovertible advantages of human liberty. And it *would* be a fight. The fractures among the nations of Rega were growing … and the Order was beginning to mirror them.

Taryn's troubled expression made Ileom think perhaps he had made a mistake. He had wanted to instill curiosity, even a little concern, but not outright fear. The look passed, and Taryn turned toward the griffon again, reaching his hand through the bars in the door to lay it on the wickedly curved beak. Ileom watched in unsettled fascination as the king soothed the beast with his touch and a few soft words. Part of him wondered if the king might be invoking some subtle form of magic from this world, similar to Antara's abilities. Or maybe it was a connection akin to what he had felt with Meris, which occupied a place of bizarre preeminence in his mind.

"Come," said Taryn after a few seconds, starting to walk again, "I will show you more of these marvelous creatures, and some of our training areas for them and their riders."

"Most griffons," noted Jehorim, "will accept multiple riders."

"One at a time, of course," laughed the king.

"Haha, yes. But there are a few who seem to bond with just one rider. You had one of those once, is that right, your majesty?"

Taryn kept moving, adding a nostalgic frown to his expression. "Yes, indeed. He was magnificent, but he was already quite old when we bonded. Retired from active duties. He died almost ten years ago, and none of his progeny show the same interest in me."

"Griffons are quite fickle," agreed Jehorim with some sympathy in his voice. "Dragons, too, though we understand more about griffons."

"Aye, that is so," noted Taryn. "And we know even less about why they hate each other so much. I suppose it's in their nature." He halted for a moment, eyes finding Ileom. "We haven't hosted any dragons for quite some time, though occasionally people like Jehorim and Agrancik—who I presume is the member of the Argent Council who has been visiting Tenris?—bring some by to visit." He glanced at Jehorim, who nodded uncomfortably. "Rest assured, the griffons of Sistrayn are never allowed to roam free, so we aren't the problem. That is supposed to be true all over our world, by strict adherence to formal agreements."

"But you use them in battle," stated Ileom.

The king frowned again, his eyes seeming genuinely sad. "Occasionally, and unfortunately, yes. But those nations which host large sky battalions have enjoyed relative peace with each other for several decades, and those who do not are hesitant to provoke us. It has served us well."

"Do any wild griffons exist?"

"A few, yes," admitted the king. "They are scattered, though, their ranges small. And most wild griffons are not suitable for riding, much less battle training."

The remainder of Taryn's tour was exhaustive and detailed, taking in the entire housing complex, three different training grounds—including one next to a tall cliff with a wide pond huddling against its base—and the small town supporting all of it. An impressive setup, logistically and militarily, and Ileom's fears of a large-scale incursion by such a force grew. Was that impression intentional? Taryn, near the end, must have sensed it, for he laid a reassuring hand on his arm.

"Do not worry, my new friend. We will find the source of the griffons that have appeared on your world. There is a governing body charged with doing inspections in accordance with our agreements, and I will send a personal message to them with some suitably pointed suspicions. They are good at what they do. Within the month, we will have some answers."

Within the month. Could he wait that long? They had paused near the entrance to the barn where the tour had begun. Jehorim gave the king an appreciative nod, then faced Ileom. "King Taryn is right. Will you be able to stay?"

Ileom scrunched his brow. "Probably not, but Agrancik can bring word. Or perhaps I will be able to return."

"That is good," said Taryn. "And now, we must get back. Dinner will be waiting, and I promise you it will be spectacular."

The shadows had grown long, but Taryn assured them the carriage was equipped with lanterns if it got too dark for passengers or horses. Ileom felt like it had been a productive trip, and he prepared himself to reciprocate as much as possible with a view to finding that persuasive angle with Taryn and Juless. But how long could his otherworldly origin remain a closely guarded secret now? Things could quickly spiral out of control in that regard.

He reminded himself that he didn't need to know everything for it all to work out. God would supply what lacked, if he truly trusted him. Of course, that triggered another level of worry. Were enough people on Tenris sufficiently courageous and faithful to merit God's assistance? Had they grown too indifferent to his presence, or annoyed by his rules? Those rules were strict, but also liberating. Too many people didn't let themselves understand that. And so many were pampered beyond belief, at least on Rega. He wondered how true that was in this part of Alave as well.

The carriage set off. Ileom became lost in his ruminations as Taryn and Jehorim engaged in a lively conversation about Queen Viera and her Regent's Court, until he was jolted back to the present. Horses screamed as men shouted, and the carriage came to a violent halt, nearly overturning. He noted a great flapping of wings and the rending of flesh. The screams and shouts abruptly stopped. He looked to Taryn and Jehorim, whose faces had paled, locked in surprised and fearful expressions.

"Griffons or dragons?" he asked.

Both men seemed perplexed for a moment, and then the king answered, "I heard no battle cries, but the sound of the wings was that of griffons. Which means we have a much larger problem than you feared. I am sorry, my friend. Truly. Perhaps whoever it is wishes to take us, or maybe they will kill us. I wish there were a way to get word to someone, but I fear there is not."

The world outside the carriage had gone eerily silent, and Ileom spied nothing of import through the side windows in the semi-darkness. Had the attackers killed the horses, drivers, and guards, and then left? Perhaps others would surround them on foot? Ileom wasn't inclined to wait and see … and strangely, he felt his own god calling him to act, even on another world. That realization nearly froze him, but then impelled him to greater confidence. He drew his meager sword, wishing again he had Trump Sounder, then grabbed the door handle.

"What are you doing?" Jehorim asked. "The carriage is strong."

Ileom gave a curt nod. "It is also a coffin." He threw open the door and leaped to the verge of the roadway, raising his sword to shield his head from above, looking about for threats as he moved around the back of the carriage, then up the other side, saving an examination of the carnage among the horses and humans for last.

A bestial cry of pure fury pierced the air from above. He spotted a trio of griffons bearing down on him, having vaulted the surrounding trees in ambush. Charpak led them, carrying a man in dark armor with full face shield bearing a long black lance with a wicked tri-pronged tip.

They had him dead to rights, so he reacted instinctively, trusting that the connection to his god here meant more than one thing, as the magical stirrings had indicated. Most of the trees were pines, and reaching deeply into his well of power, he stripped at least two dozen of their needles, launching a hail of thousands of tiny missiles at the griffons and their riders, hoping to at least distract them for a moment.

It worked, causing the beasts to shriek and veer off course, whirling in the air as they sought to identify their attacker. He made an earth-boosted jump to the top of the carriage, readying his sword and praying for additional strength. One of the griffon riders got his mount under control and dove at him, while another had already alighted on the ground at the side of the carriage, perhaps to strike inside. Ileom spun, launching his sword through the air at the diving griffon with all the force he could muster in the turn, then leaped toward the grounded griffon and its rider, catching them by surprise.

As the diving griffon screamed in pain and its rider released a shocked yell, Ileom crashed through the grounded rider's weak defense of raised arms. He impacted the man's armored collar with his shoulder, feeling a satisfying crunch. Then he pushed off the griffon's haunches with a free hand and twisted in the air to land on his feet, praising the old sword master who had drilled him endlessly on various ways to maintain such balance. Turning nimbly, the griffon swiped a taloned claw at him, and he barely jumped back in time to avoid it. He raced for the trees with enhanced strides, using his magic to split a mature pine and separate a long war staff from its hardened core. It flew into his hand as if magnetized, and he turned again to face the threat.

But the remaining rider, mounted on Charpak, had seen enough. He clearly didn't know what Ileom was, and with two of his companions wounded and lying on the ground, one pinned under his very dead griffon, the rider called out a signal. In response, the riderless griffon plunged its long, sharp beak into its hapless rider, hopping over to do the same to the trapped rider and then leaping into the air to join its companion in fleeing the scene.

After Ileom was certain the two griffons were gone, he approached the carriage and rapped on the door, noting that one of the wheels had taken enough damage that it would need to be replaced. Though they didn't have horses, the course was mostly downhill, so his earth magic could have helped roll them most of the way back.

"It is safe now, I believe."

After a second, King Taryn opened the door, peeking his head out before jumping to the ground, fear still etched on his face. Jehorim followed without a word, and they checked on the fallen riders. They were indeed dead.

"We will learn nothing from them," stated the king in a tone of pity and disgust.

"Who are they?" challenged Ileom, the battle rush still partially active. "Do you recognize them? What uniform do they wear?"

Taryn blinked, then crouched and stared at one of the men more closely in the dimness after removing his face shield. Ileom cast a light orb to help him—far weaker than what someone like Antara could conjure, but clearly impressive to Taryn just the same. "I do not recognize him, and that uniform looks only vaguely familiar. He is not one of ours, if that is what you are asking." He looked up at Ileom, eyes hardening.

"The lead griffon was the first one you showed us," said Ileom. "Charpak. They came from that camp."

"I know," the king said, frowning. "I recognized his cry. Something is very wrong. Jehorim, any ideas?"

Staring into the sky, Jehorim jerked his head toward them. "What? Oh, no, I have never witnessed such a thing, and I am deeply troubled. They attacked *you*, the king!"

Ileom studied them both, letting his mind work as his body calmed. "Well, whoever sent them will be upset when the king shows up at the castle, won't they? They knew we were here."

"They may return in greater numbers," warned Jehorim.

Ileom gave a grim nod. "Yes, they may. Which means we have a long and tiring march ahead of us. We must move fast, staying away from the road. I hope you are both in good shape."

Neither looked out of shape, exactly, but each gave him a less than confident nod before wincing at the sight of the slaughtered horses and guardsmen.

"Come, we cannot tarry." Ileom didn't worry how it looked that he was giving orders to a king in his own country—on a different world. He led them off into the trees in the general direction of the city, calling back to ask Taryn for directions from time to time. The light grew poor after he extinguished his orb, the moonlight weak. They wouldn't arrive by supper, certainly, but hopefully before the tolling of a new day.

Several hours later, they had nearly reached the outskirts of the city when a search party found them. The queen had sent out dozens of men on horseback. She had also implied that the newcomer was to blame for whatever might have befallen the king, so the welcome Ileom received was harsh until Taryn could convince his men to back down. Ileom had retrieved his sword with great satisfaction from the chest of the dead griffon, but he didn't think of trying to fight his way free. He could be diplomatic, no matter what Antara often said.

"You must forgive my men," said Taryn after they had entered the castle, which had reached a state of near panic. "Such danger as that which interrupted us tonight is rare in these lands, and they weren't certain how to handle it."

"I wish our lands were as peaceful as yours," quipped Ileom, hoping the king would catch the irony. A 'peaceful' place didn't transport war griffons to another world to aid the beginning of a major war. Nor did it produce a harrowing, near-death experience for its first off-world visitor within two days of his arrival. He was tiring of boasts of peace, which seemed emptier by the moment. He hoped Agrancik was faring better.

The queen expressed immense joy upon seeing them, though she kept her delight at being reunited with her husband to a proper maximum. And she gave Ileom a glare, maintaining it even after Taryn's explanation and praise of Ileom's heroic actions. Ileom deflected, not wanting to appear boastful in front of an upset Juless.

Taryn insisted they eat, though Ileom was anxious to begin the return journey, even though it was past midnight. Part of him wanted to stay and learn more, but he had already discovered where at least some of the griffons had originated. Mission accomplished. This was Agrancik's planet, and he could marshal the resources to drive a potential solution to the problem. As long as Ileom got him the information. He *must* make sure Agrancik knew, and he couldn't let himself trust Jehorim alone with the task.

After they had dined on somewhat dry, re-warmed food—still tasteful and not all that exotic—Jehorim convinced him to stay until the morning, when they could depart bright and early. Ileom agreed, but he slept fitfully, his anxiety over the griffons growing, both in ways he could explain and those he couldn't. In addition to apprising Agrancik of the situation, he needed to return to Tenris as soon as possible and begin making additional preparations for the griffons. He had fought them twice now, and he had some new ideas.

When they awoke in their shared room, protected by what Taryn labeled his elite guards outside the door, he noticed that Jehorim looked as anxious as he himself felt.

"My friend," Jehorim said, "perhaps we should have left last night as you preferred. My apprehension has grown throughout the early hours of morning."

"Mine, too," grunted Ileom, "but I am a guest who does not know your world."

Jehorim raised his chin slightly. "You are most gracious. Come. We will gather some victuals for the journey from the kitchens, and then we can ascend to the tower where the dragons await us."

Taryn arranged a squad of ten men to see them off, and Ileom couldn't decide if they were there to make sure he and Jehorim actually left or to provide the honored protection Taryn and Juless claimed to impart. Or maybe assassinate them. After a few uncomfortable moments with zero exhibited threat, he shrugged it off, though he felt even more eager to take to the skies.

That anticipation soared as they passed through the door onto the tower top and he strode toward Meris. A second later, he stumbled as a steel crossbow bolt slammed through his enhanced armor and into his back. He turned in shock, reaching instinctively for his magic and passing what he could into the stones, which rippled and knocked the guards off their feet. Two toppled over the edge of the tower. He tried to take a deep breath, but it caught, and he felt the magic slipping away with his consciousness. The bolt hadn't penetrated deeply, but it must have been poisoned. As he crumpled to the ground, he heard the dragons roar as they leaped into the air amid the shrieks of approaching griffons; his last wish was that the two magnificent beasts would be able to escape. Of Jehorim he saw and heard nothing.

A week passed for Rain, each day filled with confusing interactions and frequent visits from Hannah, who continued learning his language. He was picking up bits of theirs as well, and he found some consolation in going to the exercise room, even learning to run on a magical contraption that moved beneath his feet. His bunkmates stared at the window box in their room for hours on end, occasionally getting into arguments over it that Rain couldn't understand. Sometimes they were allowed to go to another room where they gazed even more intently at a different window box with several other boys. They took turns holding strange-looking objects, moving hands, arms, and even entire bodies in sudden contortions as they gritted their teeth in concentration, often grimacing, laughing, or shouting. It was frequently so disorienting he had to close his eyes and block it out.

He tried many times to get the key to transport him home. It could, he had convinced himself to hope; he just couldn't find the right focus. He even gathered heat in tiny filaments to feed into it, as Antara had shown him. While the magic actually seemed to be absorbed, the attempts had no discernible effect on the key, which had a mind of its own. Did he just have to wait for it to take him back? If so, how long would that take? He became more and more determined that once he returned, he would divest himself of the key for good—maybe bury it a mile deep, even if it took him a year to dig such a hole. It was a curse, no matter what Ileom and Antara said.

He learned his bunkmates' names: Jared, Elfred, and James. They all seemed about his same age. He couldn't converse with them yet, or comprehend much beyond a few words and phrases. They tried to tease him, he could tell, but apparently he didn't respond as they expected; plus, he was bigger and stronger than all of them, so the ribbing subsided and they kept their distance. Jared, especially, was quite a bit smaller. Rain didn't care about them, though. He just wanted to get back to his world … and entomb that infernal talisman. Maybe travel to an active volcano in the Fiery Whelps and toss it in?

On the tenth day of his confounding imprisonment, Hannah took him and Jared to lunch at a small building filled with mouth-watering smells. Their meals were delivered on hard trays but flimsy plates, and Hannah ate hers—a pile of leafy greens with vegetables and what looked like cooked bird meat—with a fork that weighed no more than a feather. How was that possible? He and Jared had food they could eat with their hands, which suited Rain perfectly.

After the meal, she guided her beast to a much larger structure that contained none of the same scents. Instead, it brimmed with all kinds of exotic items—odd-looking wands, bouncing balls of various shapes and sizes, two-wheeled contraptions, and more clothes and shoes than he had ever seen in an entire village, maybe even a small city! So many colors and varieties—how could one find what was theirs? He got a headache watching Jared perusing everything. Didn't he know which kinds were for him? Jared definitely expressed positive reactions toward certain items.

Hannah led Rain to the shoes, stared at his simple but sturdy Guard boots for a moment, then spoke to a young man, who also examined his boots with a critical eye before disappearing behind a wall. He came back a minute later carrying several boxes, and Rain's eyebrows scrunched as he stared at Hannah. She smiled, then gestured at his boots. It seemed she wanted him to take them off. He didn't like removing his boots when he wasn't sleeping in a safe place. No soldier did, unless it was necessary to dry them out and clean them to keep your feet healthy. Besides well-maintained weapons, sound feet and hands were a soldier's most important tools. Except maybe sight and hearing, of course. Master Ileom said it was the mind, but if you couldn't see, move, or hold a weapon—or were trapped on another *planet*—what good was your brain?

He had come to trust Hannah, though, so he relented, noting the slight puckering of her face as he removed the boots. She backed up a step, too. Jared had wandered over, and he said something in a shocked tone, sliding away, but he also laughed. Yes, his feet probably stank to them. Was that not normal? He had kept his socks clean, and had even washed himself once that week under an amazing mechanical waterfall—clothes and all, except the boots, of course. He had used their soap, too.

The youth gave Hannah an uncertain look, but she reassured him, grabbing a pair of socks hanging nearby and handing them to Rain. His own needed mending; he admitted that. And the ones she gave him felt so thick and soft he wondered if they were real. He put them on after snapping an impossibly tiny cord connecting them to each other, then accepted a pair of boots the young man handed him. They were surprisingly heavy, and appeared so solidly made he blinked in surprise. They had laces woven through metal grommets, which meant they must be abominably expensive. After a questioning glance at Hannah, he put them on and laced them tight. The young man knelt down and felt around the edges, especially near his toes. He looked up at Hannah and said something, and she gestured for Rain to take them off.

He shrugged and complied, and the young man handed him another pair of boots, identical to the first. They fit more snugly, and then he realized what was happening. His jaw nearly dropped. Only nobles or the very wealthy ever had shoes that fit them perfectly—the rest got as close as they reasonably could and lived with it, happily, building the necessary callouses.

These were boots for a master like Ileom, or a king. Was she proposing to give them to him? How could she do that? Was she some kind of noble in this world? Had he become her ward or charity project? He quickly decided he wouldn't feel shame in that, as long as he got to keep the boots.

Hannah squealed in delight. Then she had the young man place his old boots in the box and hand it to him. They went through the same process for Jared, only he apparently didn't want boots. Instead, he ended up with shoes much lighter and softer, decorated in garish colors with dizzying designs. How a cobbler had dreamed up and produced such a creation Rain had no idea.

After that, Hannah had them try on—like princes!—pants, shirts, and what she called 'jackets,' which were light coats. Rain had no concept of what he 'liked' among the various options presented to him, but before long he and Jared were dressed in all-new clothes, making him feel even more like an alien than before. He stuck with plain designs in dark colors, while Jared looked like a performer in a traveling show. As they walked out of the building, Rain's primary focus became how comfortable the boots felt. They were amazing. He could walk for weeks without his feet hurting.

He had wanted to ask about the many knives and inexplicably complex bows with small pulley wheels he saw—no swords or spears, curiously—but he didn't know how. He'd spotted several racks of large, strange-shaped wands similar to those used by the enemy that had attacked New Haven, too, and that both worried and fascinated him. Should he have pointed to one to see if he could have it? Hannah hadn't taken them into that section of the building, and she hadn't shown any personal interest, either.

After returning to the inn—which only hosted young men and a few boys, so it had to be a kind of orphanage—the routine of Hannah learning his language continued. She had recently begun opening different windows inside her window box to display people doing various things like talking, laughing, walking, running, eating, and sleeping. Rain did his best to describe each action so she could piece more of the grammar together. He knew she was magically inscribing the sounds because she was able to make her box repeat them. It was the strangest thing he'd ever heard. Coming from the box his voice sounded different … and not attractive.

Another ten days passed, mostly following the same routine. Hannah started conversing with him in his language. The sentences came out horribly mangled, and her pronunciation was poor, but on most things he could figure out what she was trying to get across. She was definitely smart. She also tried to express images she showed on the box—including text in Regan Common—so he could correct her. A voice from the box helped her sometimes, which nearly startled Rain out of his chair the first time. Who else was magically linked into their conversations? Jared also began showing interest, hanging around outside the room until Hannah finally invited him to join them.

At the beginning and end of each day, when he could find a space with relative privacy, Rain focused on the talisman, continuing to pursue every option his young mind could summon to connect his magic or his thoughts with the obstinate key. He begged, pleaded, commanded, reprimanded—nothing worked. Not even so much as a hint of positive energy. He might as well have carried a rock back from that field. Had the key broken somehow? It appeared whole. Maybe it had run out of energy, but hadn't he infused it with more? He had used enough heat to make it glow, more than once. Was Antara's type of magic necessary for a repair or recharge? Did someone here possess that? If so, how would he ask?

Another ten days passed, and he finally decided to give the field another try, hoping that eventually the place would trigger the key to act. So when Hannah came the next morning, he undertook communicating something of his own to her for the first time. He was sure it sounded awful. "Go to field and home" was about the extent of it, with a look of pleading for emphasis.

Hannah frowned at first, but after he'd repeated it twice, she seemed to understand. "Okay. I know you want to go home, and somehow that field is important. I don't understand how, but we'll go to the field." She said it once in her language, which she called English, and then in rough form in Regan Common.

He understood the English version better, surprisingly, and while the hopelessness of his situation still exerted a strong pull, he felt a rush of happiness. There was a chance. It thrummed inside him like a living thing, at least until they entered the monster to begin the trip. Jared insisted on coming with them, which cheered Rain a little, but doubts began to burrow their way in, lodging deeper and deeper. He had learned that the beast was an inanimate object—like his key, only fantastically more complex—and that while it could do magical things, it was not properly 'alive.' Even though it spoke sometimes.

By the time they arrived at the fence along the road, his hope had mostly died, flickering weakly. He imagined how embarrassing the scene would be. Then he realized that part of him had resigned himself to being trapped here for the rest of his life. That attitude would be shameful to someone like Ileom. But if it were indeed true, he'd have to begin caring about how he could impress people and achieve things on this world, just like he had aspired to be a member of the Council Guard and it had actually happened, albeit in an unexpected and undeserving way. Hannah might help … if she wasn't just using him to further her own ambitions. A cynical thought, but it matched the gloomy mood settling thickly upon him.

He trudged across the field, the toes of his new boots dragging, shoulders slumped, heedless of how much grain he was smashing into the soft soil. Hannah tried to offer some encouraging words in both languages, a few of which he understood. Fittingly, the sky was gray, the clouds low and scudding amid blustery winds, as if they, too, drew close to mock his utter impotence. He finally stopped, turning in a circle, gripping the key tightly in his right hand. He wouldn't cry. He would … NOT … cry. He was a man now. Yes, he'd seen men cry, but not over something so painless and trivial. So he was stuck here. But he was alive. He was healthy. He ate more each day than he ever had, and the variety was astonishing. He had clean, well-mended clothes, amazing new boots, and two people whom he might—though probably not—eventually be able to call friends.

He let his arms fall and stopped turning, heart suddenly calm, eyes taking in the vast views of the softly undulating landscape filled with farms and trees. And then something inside snapped. He arched his neck and screamed at the clouds with every bit of air in his lungs. His eyes closed, and he screamed again. This time he started feeling dizzy, but he didn't care. He shouted a third time, calling out desperately to God, feeling his knees go weak and his body start to spin toward the ground.

His breath came heavy; he thought he might have passed out for a second, but then he lay still, eyes shut, mind numb. He didn't care how Hannah and Jared were reacting. It didn't matter. Nothing mattered. Not even the boots. They could just leave him in the field, where he could sleep until the dream finally ended or the harvest came.

Through the thick fog of his predicament, he heard his name. Hannah's voice, and he detected alarm. Well, of course. He had fallen. She was a kind person.

The alarm turned to panic, and curiosity got the better of him. He opened his eyes, staring up at a suddenly blue sky, and scrambled to his feet. His breath left him again, but for a completely different reason. They were in the castle garden in Arxhana. But *how*? He hadn't *done* anything! He'd wanted it badly, but that wasn't new.

He focused on Hannah, her eyes wide as the wheels on her beast. Jared stood next to her, body trembling as his head swiveled to take in the new environment.

Rain's heart sank. Somehow, he'd just made it *worse*. He was home, but he'd trapped two strangers in his world, one of them perhaps the nicest person he had ever met.

"Antara?" he asked tentatively, spinning again. "Antara!" He moved toward the door to the guest suite they had occupied briefly, tried the handle, and found it locked. Then he heard swift movement from one side of the garden. Mere seconds passed before several guards rushed into the space, some with spears lowered, others carrying drawn swords. Jared gaped at them, grabbing Hannah's arm. She quailed, then looked pleadingly at Rain as he stepped between her and the guards.

"It's all right," said Rain to the Mero Vothans, arms extended, palms forward. "They're with me and the Lady Antara, and they pose no threat."

One of the guards recognized him, his face screwing up in confusion. "Why are you *here*? Where did you come from?"

It dawned on Rain how much time had passed. "I … had to leave … but I'm back. Where is Lady Antara?"

The guard came closer, sword still drawn, its point gleaming. "She couldn't account for your disappearance, so we escorted her out of the castle. She has met with the chief magistrate, by his grace, but I do not know where she went after that." He squinted, eyes hardening. "You said you returned. How did you get back in?"

How to explain *that*. If he were in this man's boots, he wouldn't believe a word out of his mouth. He had just begun a stuttering attempt when a sundering crash came from somewhere nearby, followed by an earth-splitting bestial roar, unlike any he had ever heard. The guards spun toward the sound, one of them shouting a challenge. Then a strange golden beast, significantly larger than a horse and with massive, powerful wings, burst into the small clearing, eyes wild, head jerking back and forth. A man sat astride it in a special saddle, holding a long spear and carrying a crossbow on his back, splitting his attention between controlling the animal and assessing the situation. He was clearly confused.

Rain's open mouth froze as he stared at the scene in bewilderment. The beast attacked the guards with a ferocity he had never witnessed from beast or man, using curved beak and front claws in a thrashing fury. If the rider hadn't been strapped in, he would have been tossed off its back in the first few seconds. To their credit, the brave and well-trained guards brought spears to bear in a bristling defensive position and called for archers, even after several of their number had already fallen. Rain recognized the danger Hannah and Jared were in. He found them cowering behind an insignificant tree that the monster could surely turn to kindling in a single swipe.

He rushed over to them, crouching as he put himself between them and the desperate battle.

"Danger," he said in a loud whisper, in English. It was probably the most unnecessary word he had ever uttered. He motioned for them to move away, grabbing Hannah's upper arm as she hesitantly rose. They began running, but then he heard the twang of bowstrings snapping in rapid succession. He stopped and turned to witness the effect, noting the rider slumping in his saddle, body flopping around like a pin-cushioned doll as arrows bounced off the animal's hide. The distraction of the arrow swarm allowed a pair of guards to get closer. As the creature gathered itself to leap into the air, spears thrust with powerful force pierced its chest from two sides, sinking several inches deep and then snapping off as the beast spun, a blood-curdling bellow bursting from its gory beak. It tried to fly, rising a few feet in a tornado of flapping wings, but then dropped to the ground, balancing on wobbly legs before collapsing onto its side. Rain heard bones in one of the wings shattering, and he cringed.

Hannah and Jared had halted, too, standing right behind him. He raised a hand to them. "Wait. Please." Then he noticed the fire arrow hovering in the air near his own head, ready to launch. Hannah's eyes had transfixed on it. Jared didn't seem to be focusing at all. A wet spot had blossomed around his crotch, though.

Rain tried to give Hannah a reassuring smile as he commanded the arrow to dissipate. He couldn't tell if she felt better or worse, but he motioned her to stay with Jared before rushing toward the group of soldiers, aiming for the nearest one that had fallen.

An adrenaline-fueled growl and raised spear stopped Rain in his tracks. "What are you doing?"

"I have some healing ability," Rain said. "Maybe I can help. Do you have other healers nearby?"

"We've sent for them. What do you mean *you* can heal?"

Rain floundered in his response. "I ... I'm not very good, but I can try. Please let me try."

The guard straightened after glancing at a trio of soldiers examining the winged horse eagle to ensure it was truly dead. One of them rammed a spear into its throat, then twice more.

"That man is gone," said the guard.

Rain didn't need more than two seconds to confirm. Sightless eyes aimed skyward. Half the guard's chest had been ripped away. He suppressed an emetic urge, then searched for another fallen soldier. He spotted one moving slightly and detected a low moan. The man's leg was ruined. He wished Jerise were there. He glanced at the standing guard, and at a slight nod moved over to the wounded man.

He was already gathering heat again as he knelt. Examining the wound, he decided the only thing he could do was stop the bleeding. Again, some-one like Jerise was needed. He fashioned the heat into tools to cauterize, stabilize, and then knit some of the bone and tissue. It still looked like a hopeless mess when he was done, but at least the man would probably survive. He had stopped moaning, and his breathing had steadied a bit.

Rain looked up in apology. "That's the best I can do. He needs a real healer, but he won't bleed out."

The guard, who had followed with his spear still angled menacingly, inspected what he had done. He gave a grudging nod. "Very good. Let us see if others can be helped."

A total of eight guards had fallen. Three were dead, and another would soon follow from a massive gut wound Rain couldn't possibly hope to stanch in time. The others he was able to help, just enough to keep them alive. Then, curiosity drew him toward the beast and its rid-er. The increasing crowd of guards had removed the ill-fated man from his harness and dragged him a few feet away from the dead animal. Occasionally a soldier would stab the winged menace again, or spit on it, or kick dirt in its face. A small group of guards sat on the ground nearby, staring disconsolately at nothing. Ileom had described that stare. Their minds had been overwhelmed by the event, though in time they could recover with some help.

The rider wore a thick leather cap with flaps, lined with fur. That made sense. If he was flying very high, it would be cold, like in the mountains. The rest of his clothing was thick leather as well, nearly black with a few armor plates. He had been punctured by three arrows and scored by sev-eral more, the one through his neck apparently just missing the carotid artery. Surprisingly, he was still alive. Rain's eyes widened. If Ileom were there, he would say, "This man could be useful."

He knelt beside him, and a different guard approached. "What are you doing? Do you know him?" The accusation was clear.

Rain looked up, shaking his head. "I've never seen anyone dressed like this, or any beast like that." He pointed. "But if we can talk to him, that could be useful. I might be able to heal him, so you can … you know, take him into custody for the chief magistrate and interrogate him."

"I saw you heal some of our men."

Rain grimaced. "Not very well, unfortunately, but hopefully they'll live." He looked down at the rider, remembering the first time he had healed, on pure instinct. Arrow wounds were simpler than the hellish mess caused by the beast's rending beak and gashing claws. He focused, gathering the heat, probing, pushing, and knitting as best he could. No bones had been broken, miraculously, though several were fractured. The major organs were intact. The man was lucky. Or unlucky, depending on what the Mero Vothans decided to do with him. Where had he come from?

A shuddering intake of breath announced Rain's success. The man tried to sit up, but a spear butt in the shoulder from one of the guards, several more of which had gathered around during the healing process, forced him back down. He glanced around, studying them, cold eyes failing to mask his fear. He spoke a few phrases, and Rain blinked, looking up at one of the guards.

"Did you understand any of that?" he asked.

The guard shook his head, surveying his companions. Rain focused on the rider again. The words weren't English, either, but something entirely different. The man stared back, clearly aware of the language barrier, which oddly seemed to make his fear lessen. Then he turned his head toward the dead beast, and his jaw clenched. He focused on Rain and spit out an angry stream of ugly words. Rain kept his face neutral, wishing again that Antara or Ileom were there. And Jerise, but especially Ileom. He would know what to do, and the Mero Vothan guards would recognize his authority.

Rain rose somewhat unsteadily to his feet, remembering Hannah and Jared again. He couldn't see them, and anxiety spiked. Had the Mero Vothans taken them somewhere already? The two hapless visitors from the other world would be terrified, especially being unable to communicate well with men carrying swords and spears ... *and* after witnessing a dead flying monster lying in its gore amid a no-longer-pristine garden.

He found the first guard he had spoken with, conversing with a captain in urgent tones. He waited until the captain noticed him. The man flicked his eyes to him and scowled.

"Who are you?"

"My name is Rain Barynd, from the Council Guard of New Haven. I came here ... um, a few weeks ago ... with Lady Antara. I can't explain how I am here today. It involves magical powers I do not understand. But Lady Antara might. Or Master Ileom Mystrevan."

The man blinked, his frown deepening. "I'm supposed to believe you just popped into existence here, in the middle of the castle gardens?"

Rain shrugged. "I know it's hard to believe. I can barely believe it myself. But I and two others—the woman and the boy with her—arrived from another place ... where they do not speak the Common tongue of Rega."

"Another continent?" The man's brow furrowed.

"Yes." That was certainly true.

"And the beast, with its rider?" asked the guard.

Rain shook his head. "I've never seen them, or anything like them. We were as surprised as you, as I'm sure you could tell."

The captain thought for a moment, glancing between Rain and the guard standing next to him, and then nodded. "Yes, you did seem shocked by it. But there could be more than one reason for that."

Rain didn't know what to say, so he just tried to appear as innocent as possible.

"You speak the language of the woman and the boy?" asked the captain after an awkward silence.

"Only a little. And the woman can speak some Regan Common."

"We need to talk to them."

"I know. I will try to explain to them. Can you send for Lady Antara, too?"

The captain glanced at the guard. "Find out where she is." The guard saluted and jogged off.

"Come," said the captain in a stern voice, turning and striding in a different direction. They had gone at least twenty yards through thick foliage before Rain spotted a shaken Hannah and Jared. They huddled together on a stone bench, speaking softly with each other, surrounded by four Mero Vothans. Hannah seemed to be trying to console Jared, and probably herself, too.

She looked up in startlement as they approached, nearly rising but remaining in place out of obvious fear of the guards. Her eyes leaked panicked apprehension when they fell on the captain. The man's sword was sheathed, but he looked angry. After a moment, she shifted her gaze to Rain.

"This is your home?" she asked in English, her voice nearly breathless. He nodded. "Yes. Kind of."

She blinked, and then the captain spoke. "What nation is she from?"

Rain cast about in his mind for the word "nation" or "country" in English. They hadn't discussed the topic of nationalities yet.

"What country?" he asked, pointing at each of them.

Hannah looked confused for only a moment, then answered, "The United States of America."

Other than the word "the," none of it meant anything to Rain, and he couldn't repeat it. She said it again, seeming to sense that. Then she said her name, looking at the captain and placing her hand on her chest. She said Jared's name, too, gesturing at him. Then she added, "We come in peace."

Rain wasn't sure what that meant in English, and his slight scowl triggered some frustration with Hannah. "We do not fight, Rain," she said in Regan Common.

Rain turned to the captain. "They are peaceful. I can vouch for that, having spent about four weeks with them. I still can't pronounce the name of their country, and it is far from here."

The captain crossed his arms, studying all of them for nearly a full minute. Then he addressed Rain. "They don't seem to pose any threat … unless they are magic-users?" One eyebrow rose high, and his stance widened slightly.

Rain shook his head, spreading his hands before him. "I … doubt that. I haven't seen or felt them use any magic, though their nation produces things we cannot make, which are definitely driven in part by magic."

"So, they might be a threat."

He shrugged. "Um … yes, I suppose so." His heart sank at admitting that. He knew they were harmless, but how could the captain be sure?

"Well, I need to make a report to the Commander of the Watch, but I will return. In the meantime, all three of you will be guarded in one of the servant rooms. You will not be allowed to leave for any reason. Is that clear?"

"Yes, sir," said Rain with a sharp nod. The man turned to go, then snapped his eyes back to Rain.

"I understand you did some healing among my men. You are young to wield such magic."

Rain hoped none of the Mero Vothans had seen his fire arrow. "I'm new at it. I hope I helped save at least one of them. More experienced healers can finish the work."

The captain squinted. "Yes, well, thank you." Suspicion still tinged his voice, but it had lessened. He turned and shouted an order, at which a quartet of additional guards came running over. He gave them their instructions, then moved on, heading toward the front of the castle.

Rain looked at Hannah and Jared, genuine remorse in his eyes. "Sorry. Come, please." He gestured and they rose, expressions hesitant. He addressed one of the eight guards surrounding them.

"Lead on. We will come quietly. They do not speak our language well."

The man frowned, glancing at Hannah and Jared, then pointed at three of his companions. "You three bring up the rear. Let's go."

Time dragged in their locked, windowless room. Rain figured dusk must be approaching. Three guards stayed inside with them, with more beyond the door. He had spent the time trying to reassure Hannah and Jared that everything would be all right, but he had a hard time getting clear points across in either language. The two unintentional visitors remained quiet for the most part, making comments once in a while to each other about the frightening strangeness of the situation. It appeared they were becoming more suspicious of him, too.

Finally the door opened, and in swept Antara, dressed in royal blue slashed with red, flanked by two captains, including the one Rain had spoken to. Her noble façade cracked a bit as she took in Rain, who had jumped to his feet in his new garb, but she recovered as she studied his companions, seated together on a small bed. She took a chair to one side of the cramped space, motioning Rain to retake his seat. The two captains dismissed the guards inside the room, then closed the door and stood before it, their stares intense though respectful.

Antara took some time to gather her thoughts. When she spoke to Rain, her tone was softly remonstrative. "You left."

Rain nodded, then slumped his shoulders. "I didn't mean to. I don't know how it happened. I don't want …" he spared a glance for the captains, knowing he couldn't mention the talisman "… I don't want that to ever happen again. I thought I might never get back." The surge of emotion surprised him, but he quelled it. "And then, somehow, I returned. I didn't intend for them to come with me." He nodded toward Hannah and Jared. "Or that … monster to appear."

"That was a griffon," she said calmly, letting her eyes rest briefly on the captains, who scowled but showed no recognition of the word. "They are extremely rare, and quite dangerous, as you witnessed. One of them must have gotten caught up in some magic we do not understand, but I will take this immediately to the Order. Perhaps we can unravel the mystery." Again she looked at the captains, and this time she addressed them. "We must leave immediately so that I can counsel with the Order of the Fallen Moon. You are aware of the Order, I presume?"

Both nodded, and one replied, "Yes, but Chief Magistrate Dynast must assent to it. Murder was committed on the castle grounds, and magic was clearly involved."

She gave a prim, confident nod. "I understand. I will speak with him personally and convey to him the importance of this new discovery. It may portend profound developments for which we must prepare in haste."

Her tone had grown ominous. The two captains glanced at each other with knit brows. One took a step forward, pointing toward the bed. "What about these two? They are foreigners who do not speak our tongue, and we know nothing about them."

Antara gave Hannah and Jared an inquisitive look. They wilted slightly under her regal stare. "I will take charge of them, with the Chief Magistrate's approval, of course. I will vouch for both their safety and their good behavior. Rain here is one of our newest members, and though he is young, I trust him with my life. He is quite remarkable."

Rain blushed, wondering how far she would stretch the truth to help extricate them from the situation. He looked down, not knowing how much Hannah had understood. Jared would be completely lost, especially with everyone speaking so fast.

"Very well," said the captain. "We will take you to the chief magistrate, who has returned for the evening. Just you, Lady Antara. The others must remain here."

Antara tilted her head, like a bird with a sharp beak. Or a griffon. "I would think he would like to lay his own eyes upon our visitors." She let the implication hang in the air, and both captains finally assented.

"Come," the other said gruffly to Rain, who turned to Hannah and Jared.

"It's okay," he said in English, hoping they believed him. They rose after he did, and Hannah put an arm around Jared, who was nearly as tall as she but looked like a desperate child. Rain couldn't blame him; he would have been scared, too.

Rain walked next to Antara, behind the captains, glancing back frequently at his frightened friends as they passed down several hallways. Both tried to put on a brave face, and both failed. Which made him feel even more awful. He knew what they were feeling. A guard had jogged ahead to announce their imminent arrival, so ornate doors stood open to receive them into a spacious hall with tall, stained glass windows at the back. It was indeed dark outside, but a host of candelabras illuminated the room, each polished to a sparkling brilliance. The space had clearly been designed to both intimidate and impress. Yet it still didn't hold a candle to the lighting and architecture of Hannah and Jared's world.

The chief magistrate sat at the head of a long table that extended most of the length of the room. He stood as they entered, revealing a fit frame. His small but gracious smile seemed somehow highlighted by his well-trimmed beard. He looked to be in his forties; Antara hadn't said.

"Welcome, Lady Antara, Council Guardsman Barynd, and honored guests." He gave a slight bow, spreading his hands. "Please be seated. My captains will give us privacy." He looked pointedly at his men, who were obviously uncomfortable with the idea of leaving him alone with strangers, but they saluted, bowed, and withdrew, closing the sculpted doors behind them.

Antara sat on one side, while Rain chose to sit next to Hannah and Jared on the other. Antara quirked an eyebrow at that, but he also detected a smile.

"This has been a dramatic day," said Dynast, having resumed his chair, its tall, intricately carved back reaching a full foot above his crownless head of dark, wavy hair.

"Indeed," agreed Antara, "and many more will come. I have told you something of what we face, but I received an urgent message from the Order just yesterday, and today these events unfolded. I fear they herald trying times, Corvellum."

Rain raised his eyebrows at the use of the magistrate's first name, but the man didn't appear surprised. "And yet you don't seem afraid. Instead, I almost sense … excitement."

She gave a slight frown, and Rain detected a blush as well. "I fear the trials themselves," she replied, "but I recognize the coming fulfillment of great prophecies. Most of the people of our lands—and especially their leaders—have forgotten the God who gives them breath, and he is about to remind them of his existence, *and* of his ability and desire to restore and elevate them … by fire if necessary."

Dynast gave a wry smile. "And you're sure I'm not one of those godless leaders?"

Antara mirrored his smile perfectly. "No, not yet, but I maintain some hope after speaking with you these past few days."

He chuckled. "I could be deceiving you. Anything for a pretty face."

"I am difficult to deceive."

A bold statement, but it clearly made the ruler ponder. "Yes, well, what more do you have to tell me now?"

Antara drew in a long breath. "That these two people do not come from our world." She nodded toward Hannah and Jared, whose eyes widened as they realized the conversation had focused on them.

Dynast squinted, leaning forward and speaking slowly. "What do you mean?"

Antara's gaze intensified. "A few members of the Order recently discovered that the ancients traveled between various worlds by use of paired keys and books, animated by complex, difficult magic that is new to us. For some reason we have not been able to fully determine, the knowledge was lost for several millennia. At least on *this* planet."

Dynast's eyebrows nearly touched. "You speak of other planets, separate worlds. Humans like us live there? And they can visit us through … a portal of some kind?" He glanced at Hannah and Jared, who tried to sink further into their seats.

"Portals, yes. We believed the talismans were quite limited, admitting a few people at once, with time needed to recharge, but there may be more powerful artifacts. That beast your guards killed. It came from a *third* planet—at least originally. I learned recently that many dozens just like it have already been transported here, becoming part of an army preparing to invade Rega, led by General Inzeal of the Tahn Arganda. We do not know yet how that connection was made. Master Ileom has been dispatched to that other world to assess how we may stop this flow of dangerous creatures. The bulk of Inzeal's army is from The Golden Empire on Akris, of course, and he is already powerful enough to inspire great fear without this new weapon."

Dynast's nearly mated eyebrows quivered slightly. "I knew the threats from Akris were building. We all did. Where are the Tahn Arganda gathering?"

She paused, her gaze reproving. "You should know this already. The Order sent messengers. General Inzeal is building forces on the coasts lining the narrow channel between the islands of Chalace and Valkyris."

He grunted, neither admitting nor denying prior knowledge. "How did one of these …?"

"Griffons."

"Griffons. How did one show up *here*, in my castle?"

She took another deep breath. "As I said, I am not sure. Rain here has one of the keys I mentioned, which is bound to him. One possibility is that it is … malfunctioning. At least, it is not behaving as anticipated. It has transported him unexpectedly before, and returned him the same way. How it might have grabbed the griffon and its rider—and from where exactly—is well beyond my understanding. Our best minds will study it, because we cannot afford to underestimate both the benefits and the dangers of these keys. They may be critical in the days ahead."

Dynast's eyes moved to Rain, and he stared at him for long moments. "You cannot control this artifact?"

Rain shook his head, wondering if the mischievous key would be able to ruin his life no matter how deep the hole he dug for it. "I cannot. I have tried, but I am young and inexperienced. I hope Antara and Ileom—and, um, others in the Order—can help me."

Dynast abruptly stood, then pushed back his chair and began pacing slowly around the table, occasionally rubbing chin, jaw, or temple. "Master Ileom is a mystery. One of the most feared men in the world, and yet he pines away as the head of the Council Guard of New Haven? Or pined, rather. We thought perhaps he had retired to play sticks with boys. But clearly that was not true." He flicked his eyes to Rain. "My condolences for the losses among your people."

Rain felt a spike of sorrow.

"And you, Lady Antara. Perhaps you are even more of an enigma. I don't even know who you really are or where you are from, and yet many are familiar with you. The Order clearly values you, even though you, too, are quite young for that august group. How am I to understand your motives?" He stopped, turning to face her from across the table. She didn't flinch, just gave a slight nod.

"You are wise to be cautious," she responded. "You and I do not have much of a personal history, and I cannot point to solid examples of how my work has benefited you or your people. You will have to place some confidence in the Order itself to trust me."

"And what if I find that difficult to do?" he asked, widening his stance and placing his hands behind his back.

"I will not threaten you, if that is what you are thinking."

"Why not?"

"Because you are too valuable."

He chuckled again, then raised his hands and returned to his seat. "Well, you intrigue me, that is for certain. Frighten me a little as well. I do respect the power and influence of the Order, though it has waned of late. Not as many ears lay open to it as in the past."

Antara shrugged. "That may or not be true. I am not many years with the Order. But I believe in what we are doing, and in our ability to see it through."

"And what *are* you doing?" His tone placed a fine point on the question.

"Seeking the knowledge of the ancients to preserve this world from the enslaving evil striving to engulf it."

Dynast furrowed his brow, laying his hands on the table as he stared intently at her. "Hmmm … preserving it? Or transforming it?"

"We certainly need some refining and transforming to unlock our potential. A good refiner purifies and strengthens the metals so that they can be shaped for good, lasting use."

He conceded the point with a quirk of eyebrows and lips. "True. But what if we've already been refined and shaped to our satisfaction, and you are attempting to reverse it? Do we not have a say?"

"You always have a say."

"Do we, truly?"

That was a bold challenge. Rain leaned forward a little in his chair.

"If you are unhappy with the information you are receiving, or with your level of participation in the councils, I am more than happy to present your concerns. In their proper context, of course."

Wow. She had just chided the chief magistrate. Was it nerve, or did she wield that much power? He caught a hard glint in Dynast's eyes.

"Perhaps you forget your place here," he said, his voice carrying more than enough chill for Rain to detect it.

She raised an eyebrow. "I am not perfect, but I never forget my place. Or my purpose."

Dynast squinted, and seconds passed. "I do not fear the Order, and I am beginning to doubt that its purposes align with those of my people."

"Or your own purposes?" she suggested.

Dynast leaned forward, his mien growing menacing. "And what do you mean by *that?*"

Antara remained calm, but her voice became cold steel. "The Dynast I met before would not have turned away so many refugees, nor refused to send military aid northward. I realize there are limits to how much you can do, but you didn't test those limits. What am I to make of that?"

Dynast rose again and placed his fingertips on the table, pressing so hard his knuckles turned white. "I don't care what you make of it, *m'lady*. And I am not alone in my mistrust of the Order."

Rain sensed Antara's magic before he saw it. She placed shields in front of the doors and the stained glass windows. His pulse quickened.

"Well," she said, rising herself, "it appears we have work to do to regain your trust. Would you like a private audience with the senior members of the Order? Or perhaps you can send an advisor, if that is more suitable."

He shook his head. "No. I think I will keep you here until at least two other senior members of the Order come to answer my questions."

Antara shook her head in turn. "That will not be possible."

"You cannot stop me," he huffed. "And you cannot escape. I have mages, too. And more than enough crossbows."

Antara looked at Rain. "Commander Barynd, a brief demonstration, if you will?"

Rain tried to mask the surprise on his face. He knew what she was asking. Something big. And she was clearly harder and more calculating than he had thought.

He swallowed, then sucked in a vast amount of warmth from both inside and outside the castle, forming it into a ballistae-sized missile which hovered above the table, pointed at the chief magistrate and radiating heat in pulses. After an uncertain glance at Antara, he lowered the tip until it just touched the table, a mere two feet from the magistrate's fingers, which he hastily withdrew. The wood sizzled and burned, thick wisps of smoke rising toward the tall ceiling. He righted the missile, then looked at Antara again to see if that sufficed.

She didn't give any indication, instead addressing Dynast. "Whatever you *think* you know about the Order, you do not know nearly enough. We will not force you to cooperate with us, for that is not our way, but you will not hold us prisoner, either. Incredibly powerful forces are at play, and I do not have time to engage in parlor games."

Dynast seemed calmer than Rain expected—obviously still unnerved by the display which hovered before him, but not giving ground. He considered Rain a moment, eyes unreadable, then shifted his gaze back to Antara.

"The Sherayans are training warrior mages again, too. This is not new. How do you know we are not as well?" He crossed his arms.

"I would have seen the evidence of it," she replied, "especially given the events of today. The Sherayans have delved dangerous depths of darkness with their so-called Hearkendoom. Queen Givyren is enamored and obsessed with power. She is also painfully naïve. But she is not my problem. You, it appears, are."

Dynast snorted, then sat back down. At a glance from Antara, Rain released his missile, which dissipated in a fiery, radiating wash of warmth. He noticed Hannah and Jared staring in shock at the place where it had hovered.

"If I let you leave, I will be seen as weak."

"Then have us banished. Escorted out of the city under guard."

Dynast pondered that, then finally nodded. "Very well. One of my captains will accompany you, and he will carry a message for the Order. You can make sure he has safe passage?"

"That is acceptable," Antara responded with pristine diplomatic tact. "And yes, I will. My thanks, Chief Magistrate, for your hospitality and understanding. It does not go unnoticed."

Dynast took on the aspect of a man who has just been snookered, but he changed the subject, nodding toward Hannah and Jared. "You said these two come from a different planet than the griffons?"

After Antara nodded, he added, "What is it called?"

Antara looked at Rain, who turned to Hannah and Jared. He had already asked them about their country. This was bigger—*much* bigger. He wasn't sure he would be able to remember the right word, but suddenly it came.

"Hannah, Jared, um … which … planet?"

Hannah narrowed her eyes, staring at him for several seconds as if he'd grown another head. Jared looked like he wanted to soil himself again. Poor kid. She took a long, slow breath, pure awe filling her eyes.

"We are from Earth. It is the third planet from the sun in our solar system."

Rain repeated the relevant word: Earth. He remembered a picture of it now. She had said that word to him before. He looked at Antara, who directed her gaze at Dynast. "Now we have a name, and you are the first regent on Tenris to know it. Perhaps that means God recognizes you haven't given up on him yet."

Dynast stared at Hannah and Jared, then at Rain.

"Perhaps."

Ileom opened his eyes to darkness, feeling soft pressure all around him, as if he were ... buried. Panic threatened, but he forced himself to assess. Obviously, he could breathe, otherwise he wouldn't have woken up. And the darkness wasn't absolute. He could also move his limbs to press against the boundaries of this confined space. Only a little, but it was something.

What kind of prison was this? The memory of the crossbow bolt rushed back, the sound of the dragons roaring, and then the fading of his consciousness. Suddenly, the weight lessened considerably, and the world brightened. Bitterly cold air invaded the space. He stared, blinking, as he realized he lay underneath a thick latticework of twigs, branches, large feathers, and fur. He almost sneezed as his heart rate spiked. Griffons?

He had been partly on his side, but he shifted to his back and pushed up with his arms. The latticework was thick, but he could move it without straining too much. If he turned over and put his back to the covering, he could probably escape it completely. Then he would deal with whatever he found next. It was a wonder he was still alive. He barely felt his wound ... or any lingering effects of the poison.

He needn't have bothered, because a large section of the barrier heaved up and away, settling to the side in a clatter to reveal ... Meris. And a blast of wintry air. He shivered, then stood, staring in wonder at the dragon.

Lagron sat several paces away on a stony crag, illumined by a sliver of sun peeking above the horizon and revealing a breathtaking view of sharp-spiked mountaintops. Flurries of snow swirled in the air, and he wondered how quickly he could freeze to death in this environment. Had Meris been sitting on top of the latticework to keep him warm? It seemed so. He noted the thinness of the air, too. This was no minor pinnacle.

Meris reached down with her serrated maw and picked up a furry hide from a bundle, swiveling her neck to offer it to him. He stared a moment, took it, and wrapped it around his shoulders, noting he still wore his armor. How long had he been unconscious? He experienced a fierce urge to urinate, and he turned his back on Meris, taking a few steps toward the edge of what appeared to be a sizeable aerie to address the issue. When he turned back, she offered him another hide, which he tried to tuck around his waist. It hung well past his feet. His own thick hair would have to protect his head for now, but already he felt warmer. Where had they gotten the hides? Had they skinned the animals themselves? He wouldn't doubt it. Neither hide was from a griffon, regrettably.

He walked toward Meris, stopping just an arm's length from her before he spoke. "Thank you for saving me, but I don't know why you did. Or how."

Several impressions came to his mind, most of which he couldn't understand. One centered on the talisman he carried, which was Agrancik's. Another concerned Taryn's favorite griffon Charpak, an evil beast if Ileom had ever laid eyes on one. He retrieved the key, staring in wonder that he still possessed it. Of course, he didn't have the matched book. Agrancik did, as they had agreed, not wanting the two artifacts to travel together lest the wrong hands wrest the pair away. Of course, maybe Agrancik was behind this, and the dragons had unwittingly prevented him from holding both key and book again. Ileom didn't want to believe it of the man, but it was a stark possibility.

He held it up, turning his head slightly as the sunlight before his eyes strengthened in intensity. The sun was rising, not setting. Meris arched her neck toward the key, then touched it with the tip of her snout. Ileom's eyes widened as the key warmed in his hand, and he could feel magic flowing both into and out of it. Was she indeed a magical creature? Extraordinary. He focused on the key, closing his eyes. He found that Meris had granted it the same ingredient to travel as the book would, and it awaited Ileom's command.

He opened his eyes, staring at Meris, who had withdrawn her head and gazed back at him proudly.

"This seems impossible, but … do you want to come?" he asked. "You and Lagron?"

She shook her head, just as a human would, and the impression wasn't *no*, but rather, *not yet*.

He got the message. "There is something we must do here first? Perhaps to stop more griffons from being transported to my world?" He was guessing, even hoping.

He sensed affirmation, along with apprehension. "Someone else here has the ability to travel the Crossroads, and they have been busy. Is it far?"

The answer was yes, so he prepared himself as best he could for a long, cold ride, securing the furs and then climbing into the saddle on Meris's back. Lagron still wore his equipage as well.

"Is Jehorim still alive?" he asked. The answer came back as a clear … *maybe*. It appeared the dragons had focused on rescuing him first instead of Jehorim, then fled superior numbers of griffons and humans.

As Meris lifted into the air, he pulled the fur covering his shoulders over his head, holding it tight from the inside. Then he leaned forward, letting her take him where she would.

They remained at a high altitude for scores of scenic miles. He took occasional peeks from under the hide, gauging it to be early afternoon when they finally began to descend. As the air grew warmer, he exposed his face fully, but the improved view didn't give him any better idea where they were. Agrancik had shown him a few simple maps, and nothing looked familiar. They had exited the towering peaks to enter a broad terrain of smaller mountains and rolling hills, cleaved by several meandering watercourses. Towns and villages dotted the landscape, and he noted hundreds of farms and ranches.

Soon they approached a sizeable city, overseen by a sprawling white citadel clamped onto the side of one of the taller hills in the area. Meris and Lagron stopped, hovering on flapping wings as Meris sent him more impressions. The key was inside that citadel, and it was heavily guarded. She seemed to be asking him if he had any ideas how he might get to it, perhaps using his magic. Unfortunately, his abilities were not much aligned with stealth, but if she could pinpoint the area where the key resided, maybe they could drop in from above, surprise the defenders, and escape quickly. It seemed a terrible idea, especially with zero intelligence on what they would face. But did he have a choice?

It turned out he didn't, as a trio of large ballistae bolts streaked up at them from the outer walls of the citadel. Their range was astounding. Fortunately, Meris and Lagron were extremely agile in the air, and the bolts missed. The sight that followed further obliterated any optimism he may have harbored, as a horde of griffons launched into the air from somewhere on the citadel's grounds, at least thirty strong, all with riders. Ileom's head whipped around as he heard the flapping of wings behind him as well. He spotted half a dozen griffons approaching from above, spreading out to prevent their escape.

His chest constricted, and he felt Meris's alarm as well. She wanted to fight their way out, but there was only one good option. He clutched the key, sensing both readiness and a surprising increase in capability. Then he focused, making sure to include Lagron in their travel party, and released the magic.

༺∞༻

The captain Dynast had sent with Rain and Antara looked none too happy once they left Arxhana behind and Antara revealed their destination.

"You have appropriated Mero Vothan lands," he said, scowling. He wasn't a cheery man to begin with. Rain had picked up on that, but he was still elated to be reunited with Sun Tamer, and that made it easier to deal with Captain Palrin.

"Not according to the dwarves," countered Antara. "If you want to contest it with them, be my guest."

"You still passed through our lands to get there."

"Indeed."

"After being expressly forbidden."

"Yes."

She sounded blithely unconcerned, and that made the man even more furious. It seemed she wanted to laugh at him, too, but she didn't. "Captain Palrin, we were chased out of New Haven, and we aided many people. We are no longer on your lands. Please desist."

Surprisingly, he did, though he grumbled a few more times under his breath as their horses trudged along a different route into the foothills, avoiding the Caravan Road.

The bright sun kept them warm throughout the day, and with the reminder that it was *his* sun, not Hannah and Jared's, Rain dropped back again to check on them. Dynast had, somewhat reluctantly, provided them with horses of their own, but it was clear neither knew how to ride. Of course, with those marvelous wheeled beasts on their world, why would they ever need to ride horses? They had them; he remembered spotting some from a distance. Cows, too. Even sheep and goats. And Hannah had shown him pictures.

"Are you okay?" he asked, testing his English. Jared didn't answer, but Hannah nodded. "Yes, we are fine. My butt hurts."

It took a second for the word to register, and he gave an empathetic half-smile. "I am sorry. Soon we … arrive?"

She nodded, and he didn't give her a better explanation of what 'soon' meant. She wouldn't like it.

Hannah switched to Regan Common. "You are … important here? You have, um, power?"

He struggled with how to answer. Was he important? Hardly. And when his vaunted powers intersected with the talisman, he couldn't control it.

"No, not really. I discovered my magic only recently. I'm not very good with it yet. You have magic, too."

Hannah glanced forward, wincing slightly as she shifted in her saddle. "Magic. That is the word. And no, we … do not have magic."

"But your magic window boxes, your wheeled beasts, all the lights, heated water, cooking devices … they are all driven by magic."

She asked him to repeat, more slowly, then smiled at him and laughed. It was the first time he'd seen her smile since they'd arrived. "Those are not magic." She seemed to search for additional words, finally finding them. She pulled her magic talking device from her pocket and held it up, its surface blinking to life. "Technology. We make things, using materials from ... the ground." She stared at the surface of the device, frowned, then held down some buttons to make it go black again.

"Oh." Rain was stunned. How had they learned to make such amazing things? It must have taken a million years. That triggered another question. "How old are you?"

She squinted, looking forward again. He could tell she was trying to remember the numbers they had reviewed. She turned to meet his gaze again. "Twenty-eight years." She said it proudly.

"How long do you live?" Surely, a people who could produce such fantastic objects had incredibly long lifespans, both in order to create the technology and because of the benefits they received from it.

She comprehended the question instantly. "About eighty," she replied, and he gave her a puzzled look.

"Just eighty?"

Her eyes widened. "Why? How long for *you*?"

He understood her misperception. "Oh, less than eighty. I just thought, you know, with all that technology ..."

She shrugged. "We are human. And ... sometimes our technology— our *magic*—hurts us." Her mood became somber again, her smile washed away completely. Rain decided to change the subject.

"The village we're traveling to, it has magic we do not understand. But it is amazing. You will like it there, until I can figure out how to get you back to your home. I *will* figure it out, I promise."

The smile returned, though brief and wan. "Thank you, Rain Barynd. You are a good man." Any hint of suspicion she had harbored was gone.

He wished he could believe her. He knew he had a long way to go.

"How are they?" asked Antara when he had moved back up between her and the captain.

"All right, I guess. They don't ride horses much where they're from, so they're sore."

She nodded. "They'll survive. You know some of their language, which is good, and this, um, Hannah, she knows quite a bit of ours. That will be helpful."

"We need to figure out how to get them home."

"Yes," she agreed. "Do you have any ideas?"

He shook his head, shoulders drooping. "I still don't know how to control it. Are you sure I can't just give the key to you? I would bury it, but … well, I need to help them."

She hummed for a moment after glancing at the captain, making Rain feel stupid for mentioning the talisman. It was done, though, and who knew what Dynast had already told him. "So, if you had traveled back alone, without appearing at Dynast's palace, you might have found a way to get rid of the key already." She flashed him a chiding look. "To me, that says God wants you to hold onto it, and he knows very well you don't want to. Plus, like I said, Hannah and Jared can be useful. We need to know more about their world. The fact we can travel there isn't coincidence. I can promise you that."

He grudgingly agreed in principle, which frustrated him further. He was ready to snap at the captain if he tried to begin an inquisition, but Palrin remained silent—assisted by a pointed glare from Antara. When they stopped to camp for the night, at a small way station on a minor road, Hannah and Jared gazed at Rain questioningly. "We are not there yet?" asked Hannah in Common.

Rain shook his head. "Just two more days. I'm sorry we can't get to our village sooner. We don't have your technology. Though we have some. We can rest now."

"You have … some?"

Rain gave a small shrug. "We have running water there. Indoor plumbing. Plenty of light and heat. The dwarves built it, a long time ago."

"Dwarves?" She wouldn't know that word in Common, and it probably didn't even have a translation into English.

He shrugged again. "Another group of people on our planet. Perhaps we will meet some."

She nodded, her expression a mix of curiosity and apprehension.

Their travel rations didn't constitute much of a meal compared with what Hannah and the man at the orphanage had provided him, but they tasted great to Rain. They signified home. Hannah and Jared didn't complain, though they hesitated when he explained they would have to wait their turn to use one of the public latrines at the way station, which weren't all that private, not like what they were used to. Going off into the trees was actually more private, if also more difficult.

"Camping, great," said Hannah, in English, clapping a still dazed Jared on the back. "My favorite, um, pastime, especially on a different planet with lots of strangers." Rain didn't know that last word, but her sarcasm didn't need translation.

Once they left that road partway through the next day, the going went a little slower than Rain had hoped. Antara called more breaks to help Hannah and Jared endure the long ride, ignoring the captain's occasional complaint. And it got colder. Antara had requested warm clothing from Dynast, including coats, hats, and gloves, for which Hannah and Jared expressed strong appreciation. She herself changed into thick riding pants and a thigh-length, long-sleeved black cloak brocaded in dizzying patterns.

On the morning of the fourth day, they broke camp, ate a light breakfast, and set out again, the hills becoming steeper. Before noon, they crossed over into the hidden valley, and Rain looked back at Hannah and Jared to give them a smiling thumbs up. They gazed around as they removed their hats and gloves, then opened up their coats. They tried to appear relieved, but he saw anxiety plainly etched on their faces. Yes, they were arriving, but to what? He felt for them. At least they would love the indoor plumbing. And the warmth.

Androl greeted them on horseback as they approached the village. Rain noted changes in the landscape, which had become a virtual paradise as the settlers began to cultivate it.

"Lady Antara. Commander Barynd. Captain. We saw you approaching."

"And who might you be?" asked Captain Palrin. Androl no longer wore his uniform.

"Androl Emerin, of the Mero Vothan Border Guard, sir."

"You mean *formerly* of the Border Guard." He didn't sneer, but came close.

Androl nodded, not taken aback. "Yes, it appears that way. Welcome to Thyasendrial. We call it Thysend for short, blessed of the gods."

The man harrumphed, while Antara asked, "You named it?"

Androl gave a nervous smile. "The people wanted to give it a name, and we counseled about it for three full days."

"I like it," said Antara, and Androl seemed relieved.

"A silly name, from a dead language," smirked Palrin.

"Perhaps, little bird," rejoined Antara, and the captain's face reddened. Palrin was a form of an ancient word for a species of bird, and it wasn't a large bird. Even Rain had heard of it. The captain was about to retort when she raised a hand. "Enough." She turned to Androl. "Find Captain Palrin here suitable quarters. Our two guests behind me as well. Mind you, only the woman, named Hannah, speaks a little of our language." That wasn't true. Jared could understand and speak some as well, but Rain didn't correct her.

Androl appeared confused, but he assented without question. Soon, everyone had been settled, and within the hour they were gathered in one of the large rooms of the central building—the new town hall—where bright, warm sunlight filtered through the windows. Chairs had been arranged in a semicircle, enough for Antara, Rain, Hannah, Jared, Androl, Haran, Jerise, and Captain Palrin. Jerise had already attended to Hannah and Jared, leaving them speechless as the pain from their backsides disappeared.

Antara stood and made the introductions. Hannah and Jared gave uncertain smiles, while Palrin folded his arms and glared with enough intensity to roast a pig. It bordered on comical.

"Captain Palrin has a message from Chief Magistrate Dynast for the Order of the Fallen Moon. I have agreed to escort him to one of our councils. The next conclave was to be held in New Haven—in secret, of course—but since that is no longer advisable, it has been moved to Sharai, on the coast of the Crystal Sea. Not a short journey, but doable in the necessary timeframe, especially by taking a ship from Takesul. Rain, you may choose whether you wish to accompany us. I recommend you do, as we can learn more about your key and how to use it properly, thereby allowing us to get Hannah and Jared to their home. They will be well taken care of here, and we will travel back swiftly."

The thought of leaving Hannah and Jared behind troubled him deeply, which prompted something he should have remembered earlier.

"What about taking them to those standing stones near our camp along the New Haven border, where you and I traveled to Earth?" He felt a surge of hope.

Instead of complimenting him on the good idea, her expression grew grim. "The enemy knows we accessed a portal from there. The stones retained a powerful magical signature. They are watching that place now."

He frowned. "How do you know?" He tried—with only partial success—not to sound angry or accusatory.

With a primly arched eyebrow, she responded, "Because the Order has already scouted the area. They detected the use of the magic as well. It was more powerful than even I thought it would be."

This was maddening, but before he could make another protestation, the door to the room swung wide, and in stepped Master Ileom.

Rain nearly fell off his chair. *How?* Ileom surveyed the room, his gleaming armor and red cape making quite an impression. Jared even gave a small yelp. The only people Ileom would recognize were him and Antara, but that didn't seem to faze him. He closed the door behind him, then looked at Antara.

"I have just returned. The situation is more dire than I feared."

ain's mind reeled. *More* dire? And returned from where?

"We are grateful you have found us, Master Ileom," said Antara, rising and smoothing her skirt. "Much has been happening, even since my last report to the Council, and there are many uncertainties. I have also made a promise to Chief Magistrate Dynast. He is wary of the Order, so Captain Palrin here will deliver them ... or rather, us ... a message."

Ileom's eyes scanned the group. He could tell which was the captain, of course, by his dour expression as much as his uniform. The man's eyes showed respect toward Ileom, however. The entire planet seemed to fear Ileom.

"Very well. We are in great need of counseling with each other. And I have a way to get us to the backup location much faster, without the cavern key, which is back at the Keep."

Antara's eyebrows rose, but then she nodded. "Is Agrancik with you?"

"No. I have his key, though. I do not know how it brought me to this particular place, but it involves the dragons I brought." The word "dragons" dropped like a hornets' nest onto the group, and even Palrin lost his composure, jumping to his feet and glancing around in fear, proclaiming such a thing impossible.

Finally, the room quieted, and Antara spoke. "We haven't seen dragons on this world for several millennia. That is ... remarkable."

"Indeed, it is. Rain, you are coming with me. Antara has written about your newfound offensive skills. I have a specific need for them."

Rain dipped his head apologetically. "I'm sorry, Master Ileom. I can't."

Ileom's eyes blinked, then hardened under a scowl. "What do you mean, you *can't?*"

Antara stepped in. "We call him Commander Barynd now. He has performed many heroic feats. And he recently traveled again—to the planet we now know is called Earth—bringing back, quite unexpectedly, these two people." She indicated Hannah and Jared.

"Unexpectedly?" he asked, squinting at Antara, then Rain.

"Oh, and a griffon and its rider came with them," she added, causing Ileom's eyes to widen as he whipped his gaze back to her.

"From the same place?"

She shook her head. "Doubtful, and that is part of the mystery. The griffon is dead, but the rider still lives."

"I must speak to this rider," said Ileom gruffly, eyes piercing Captain Palrin next. The man gamely tried to return a bold stare, but he wilted. Most people would.

"I ... can arrange it," he said after a moment. "But not here, of course."

"And not in Arxhana," said Ileom. "We will work out those arrangements, and quickly. Now," he turned again on Rain, taking a deep breath that ended in a low rumble, "what about you? What are you *proposing* to do?"

Under that familiar glare, Rain's mind stumbled about like a blind man chasing a goat. Finally, he stuttered, "I need ... to get them home."

Ileom glanced at Hannah and Jared, his expression still sharp. "Admirable, but probably not important at this time." He cocked his head, suddenly seeming to soften a little. "But I may have a partial answer. Come. The rest of you, stay."

With that, he ushered Rain from the room, walking briskly as he led him outside, then past the edge of the village and over two small hills until they came to a glade with a pond at its center, fed by a musical rivulet.

Rain nearly tripped when he saw the dragons. They weren't as massive as depicted in the fairy tales, but large enough. And deadly looking. One of them could kill him with a single snap of its jaws.

"Dragons," he whispered.

"Yes," said Ileom. He gestured to the silvery one. "This one is called Meris. The other is Lagron. A female and a male. And I can communicate with them, after a fashion." Rain stared a moment at the coppery scales of Lagron. He noted the saddles, too.

"Yes," confirmed Ileom. "I rode Meris, and we indeed traveled with a key."

Rain nodded dumbly, still transfixed.

"*Without* the book," Ileom added.

It took a couple of seconds for that to register, and Rain's jaw dropped. "The dragons can activate the keys?"

"Yes, apparently. Or the combination of someone like us and one of them. Perhaps the books were created when the dragons went extinct."

Again it took him a few seconds. "And you traveled from a third planet?"

"Yes. It's called Alave. Someone has been sending war griffons here from that world, and I went to investigate, hoping to find a way to stop that flow. I failed … for now."

"But you found *dragons*." Rain heard the wonder in his own voice.

"There aren't many of them, unfortunately. Now, hold out your key."

Rain stared at him, mind suddenly blanking.

"The talisman. Get it out."

Rain did so, proffering it to Ileom.

"No. Hold it up, then approach Lagron. I have a hunch. Don't worry, he won't hurt you."

Rain thought he believed that, but his nervousness belied him. He moved hesitantly toward the beautiful, powerful beast, stretching his arm as far as it would go and holding just the very tip of the key in his fingers.

"He's not going to *eat* it," said Ileom, and Rain felt a wash of embarrassment.

He stopped when he calculated he was close enough, then looked into Lagron's eyes. An image appeared in his mind—high mountain peaks, a clear, blue sky, the freedom of the air currents. It was … exhilarating, almost beyond imagining. Lagron moved his head toward the key, and Rain locked his muscles in place, wondering if the beast could sense him flinching inside. His snout touched it, and Rain felt … control, as if the key had finally decided to open itself up to him now that a dragon was involved. He turned his head toward Ileom, mouth gaping.

"Yes," said Ileom. "I was as surprised as you. You can return those people to their home. Then we can travel to Alave and take care of some business before getting Antara and that idiot captain to Sharai."

Rain nodded, but then he felt another impression from Lagron, this one stronger. *No.*

He blinked, looking into the large, intelligent eyes for several seconds, trying to make sure he understood.

"What?" asked Ileom. "What is it?"

Rain gave him a befuddled look. "Lagron says no. He wants to head … hmmm … northwest? With just you and me and Meris. It is far, maybe beyond the barbarian lands. We can take Hannah and Jared to Earth first, but for some reason the dragons don't wish to return to Alave yet, and they cannot go to Sharai at all."

Ileom studied both Rain and Lagron, obviously confounded. Then he turned to Meris. "Is this true?" He paused, then clenched his jaw and nodded.

"She agrees," he said, "but cannot explain why, at least not in any way I can understand. I don't like it, but I trust them. They saved my life, and they didn't have to. There is a deep, ancient mystery here, critical to the future." His gaze drifted in the direction of the village. "Both my plans and Antara's will have to change, but so be it."

Rain swallowed, then looked again at Lagron, who sat taller, chin lifted. There was no way he was ready for this astounding new twist, though it *was* exciting.

⌒∞⌒

The closer Rain led Hannah and Jared to the clearing with the dragons, the harder he tried to reassure them it would be okay. The beasts were fearsome, but Earth's window boxes sometimes showed terrifying creatures much bigger than dragons, and nobody watching ever seemed threatened by them.

When they entered the glade, Meris and Lagron sat side by side. Antara had accompanied the small group, planting herself at the edge of the clearing to observe while Ileom went to stand next to Meris. She hadn't seemed shocked when Ileom told her the dragons could activate the keys.

Rain joined Ileom, then noted that Hannah and Jared had stopped several yards short, turning pale. He assumed an optimistic smile and repeated what he'd told them back at the village, this time in English. "You go home."

"On *dragons?*" asked Hannah in disbelief, also using English. He hadn't been able to adequately explain that they wouldn't need to get on the creatures' backs, but the saddles—which would hold two people, three in a pinch—were plain for them to see.

"No. No ride. Come. I show you."

Neither moved, but he kept urging until Hannah finally grabbed Jared by the arm and propelled them both forward. Rain took the talisman out of his pocket and showed it to them. Their uncomfortable expressions didn't surprise him; the last time he had held the key in their presence, a traumatic event had followed.

"Let Lagron touch the key again," ordered Ileom, "and then tell me how much control you feel like you have—over place and passengers."

Rain turned and extended the key. Lagron touched it with his snout, and Rain closed his eyes, concentrating. He pictured a destination in his mind; not the middle of the field on Earth, but a small fold in the land near the field's edge which would hide them from the road. Somehow, after just a few seconds, he knew he could travel to that very spot. Then he thought about who he could take with him, and a dome around the glade appeared in his mind. He was about to open his eyes when he sensed other possibilities for place. They flooded his mind so fast he nearly blacked out. He severed the flow, then felt Ileom's strong hands holding him up. His arms hung limply at his sides, and he had nearly dropped the key.

"What happened? What did you find out?"

Rain's vision swam for a few seconds. "It … was a little overwhelming, but I can get us there. I can take anyone or anything in this clearing if I want."

Ileom raised his eyebrows as he gazed around. "We could squeeze a hundred men in here … or twenty griffons and their riders." Worry flecked his face before he set his eyes again on Rain. "I would see this planet, if only briefly. You can bring us back?"

Rain blinked. "I … well, I assume so, with Lagron's help."

"You can control location? And initiate?"

Rain felt less certain by the moment, given Ileom's intense stare and urgent tone. "I think so, yes."

"Well, Meris reassures me it will work, so let's not waste any more time. No need to say anything to our guests. Just do it." He raised his voice. "Antara, you should stay here, just in case. Oh, and delay your departure for Sharai with that captain little bird or whatever his name is until you hear from me."

Antara acknowledged curtly, and Rain resisted the urge to peek at Hannah and Jared. Instead, he lifted the key for Lagron to touch again. He glanced at Ileom, who gave him a stern nod, then closed his eyes and focused. Place, passengers, initiate. *Place … passengers … initiate.* The key obeyed, and he experienced a split second of disorientation before opening his eyes and discovering they were standing just where he had intended. All of them. On Earth.

He turned as Hannah yelped. Her hands covered her mouth as she twisted, eyes darting around in the waning light of an Earth day. Jared appeared frozen in permanent perplexity, as if unsure whether to be happy or not. Or if any of this was real.

Hannah finally looked at Rain, who nodded and said, "Home." He swallowed, knowing firsthand how overjoyed that must make her feel. "I go. Good-bye."

Suddenly heedless of the dragons, she sprang toward him and wrapped him in a hug. Then she backed off a step, tears coursing down her cheeks.

"Thank you, Rain. I'm guessing I won't ever see you again, but … um, have a great life."

He wasn't sure what all of that meant, or even if he'd gotten the correct gist, but he knew how good of a person she was, so she had certainly wished him well.

"Thank you," he replied. "You help. Thank you."

She choked back a sob, then stared at Lagron. "Thank you, too, noble creature," she said. Rain knew the word 'creature,' but not 'noble.' She glanced at Ileom and Meris, giving a slightly nervous nod. "Okay, well, we have to get back." She laughed. "I hope we haven't time traveled, too. That would be awful … and confusing." Rain thought he actually understood that.

Jared suddenly stepped up to her side, addressing Rain. "I want to go back with you."

Rain frowned. He was sure he had understood *that* correctly. He made a sweeping gesture with his arms. "This is home."

Jared shook his head. "I don't have a home here. I'm an orphan. No mother or father. No brothers or sisters. I want to go with *you*." He seemed determined, but also uncertain about showing it.

At first Hannah expressed shock and dismay, but then compassion filled her eyes. She turned and grabbed Jared by the shoulders. "I'll help find you a home here, Jared, I promise. I won't abandon you."

Rain knew *he* had been the reason for Hannah's presence every day at the shelter. Jared surely realized that, too. He shook his head again, then gently removed her hands from his shoulders. He cast a pleading look at Rain.

"Please. Take me with you."

Rain looked at Ileom, who would have no idea what was happening. Well, maybe a hint. His arms were crossed, his expression neutral but still unnerving.

"Jared wants to come back with us. He doesn't have a home here. He is an orphan."

He expected Ileom to deny the request outright, but instead he gave a curt nod to Jared. "He can teach us their language and learn ours. We need to build bridges between our worlds. Find out how we can get in contact with Hannah again, too."

Eyes wide, Rain turned to Hannah, whose gaze had narrowed. She had surely picked up at least some of that exchange. The words 'bridges' and 'worlds' would be enough. "Jared can come. But we return. Speak to you."

She pursed her lips after a deep breath. "Come to the place where you stayed in the city, yes?" She waited to make sure he understood. "Ask for me there. They can find me." She pulled out her magic device again. "They can contact me on this." She looked at Jared. "I will tell them you ran away, and that I tried to find you. It will be okay."

After Jared nodded to her, Rain turned to Ileom. "We can find her. I know who I can talk to here. That is, when I can speak the language better."

Ileom gave Hannah an admiring nod before bowing low, fist over his heart. That was the most respect Rain had ever seen Master Ileom offer to anyone, anywhere, of whatever station.

Hannah did a half-bow, half-curtsy in return, then raised her device again and pressed a thumb into its side for a few seconds. 'Smart phone' was the name he suddenly remembered for it, and he knew Jared didn't have one. An awkward silence followed as everyone stared at her, while she gazed intently at the device.

"What is she doing with that slate?" asked Ileom in a near whisper.

"They can talk to each other with those devices over long distances," answered Rain. "Create lifelike portraits, too. Instantly. It's amazing."

Hannah's eyes suddenly came up. "Can I take a picture?"

Rain translated for Ileom. "She wants to create our portrait, which she can store in that device. Is it okay?"

Ileom shook his head, gazing at Hannah. "No." She nodded in understanding as she pocketed the device. Then she took a lingering look at all of them, including Meris and Lagron, before turning and ascending the gentle bank of the fold. At the top, she pointed and looked back, frowning. "My car is gone, but I expected that. I'll have to get pretty creative with my story. I could claim aliens abducted me and took me to their space-ship." She laughed again, adding a wink, then gave an awkward wave. Rain didn't know the words 'alien' and 'abducted' or what they could possibly have to do with the pictures of spaceships she had shown him. He and Jared waved back, and then she was gone. He felt an odd sadness, which he shook off as he faced Ileom.

"Should we go back now?"

Ileom grunted, a strangely settling sound. "Yes. I started exploring Alave with too little information, and it got me into trouble. Now that we know we can return to Earth, we can plan some things out, take it slowly. If, that is, we have time."

That sounded ominous, not unlike most of the things Ileom said. "How do you feel?" he asked Rain. "Did the traveling drain some of your strength?"

Rain paused, trying to assess that. He felt normal. "No."

"Ask your dragon, too."

Rain blinked. *His* dragon? He turned to Lagron, uncertain.

"Just speak to him," Ileom urged.

"How do you feel, um, Lagron?" he asked, sounding foolish.

A sense of slight fatigue pulsed through Rain, and he answered Ileom. "He feels a little tired, but not much."

Ileom nodded. "That's good. Dragons are stronger than us, and in more ways than one, it seems. Those books must protect us from most of the fatigue of traveling, but they have to recharge after each trip, in a way we haven't been able to decipher yet."

"Oh." Rain noted that Ileom's tone was only slightly gruff, which must mean he was in a good mood. Then he remembered Jared and turned to him.

Jared spoke before Rain could get a word out. "The answer is still yes, right?" He bounced on the balls of his feet.

"Yes," said Rain, grinning with unexpected excitement.

Ileom took charge then, and in a flash Rain was activating the key. Except ... something went wrong. Rain was sure he had focused sufficiently on the destination, intending to return them to the same clearing in the hidden valley.

Instead, they appeared in the central courtyard of a large citadel, tall, colonnaded walls of tan stone surrounding them on three sides. Not more than thirty feet away, a host of griffons with their dismounted riders were assembled in two straight rows, listening to the shouting of a uniformed man pacing along their course, in a foreign language that sounded eerily familiar.

"Into the saddles!" bellowed Ileom, and Rain obeyed, leaping up into the seat as Lagron crouched lower to the ground. He reached out an arm and pulled Jared up behind him, noting the terrified look on his face. He had to be rethinking his decision to come with them.

Without any urging, Meris and Lagron launched themselves into the air, powerful wings propelling them upward much faster than Rain could have imagined, especially with human cargo on their backs. Rain glanced below and witnessed confusion riddling the ranks of men and griffons. The officer who had been yelling stared skyward, his expression hard to determine. He gave another shout, and soon mounted griffons were leaping into the sky.

"Strap in!" Rain could barely hear Ileom over the windstorm caused by the dragons, but he was already trying to figure out the rigging. Several horns sounded below, in repeating patterns, along with an absolutely enormous metal bell. Jared held tight to the straps at the side once Rain had pulled them taut. He could only get his own legs fully secured, but he looped his feet around Jared's ankles. Hopefully they could both stay put if they found themselves upside down in the air.

"Patrol approaching from above!" he heard through the din, then looked up at the wispy clouds. He spied four of the beasts, their riders equipped with long lances, crossbows strapped across their backs. They seemed as surprised as Rain, but also determined as they dove to attack.

Suddenly Ileom was much closer, and Rain could hear him better. "We need your magic! Mine is useless ..." A strange look came over his face, and then he wheeled Meris over, spinning away and diving for a second before arcing back up. Rain watched only a moment, then furiously gathered heat, instantly chilling the surrounding air. As warmer winds rushed into the void, he fashioned three missiles, each as long as an arrow but twice as thick, flinging them at the approaching griffons.

The group scattered, narrowly avoiding his volley, then formed into pairs to attack him from two directions. Ileom they ignored for the moment, probably because help from below was imminent. Rain reached out again, crafting numerous smaller weapons. He wasn't careful with his aim, so while his efforts bought time, they didn't do any real damage. He might have singed one of the griffon's wingtips.

And then a thick rope of—*ice?*—lanced toward one of the griffons, impacting its side and causing it to scream in pain. It broke away at the same instant Rain felt a mental sending from Lagron, who pointed his snout at another griffon and released a bolt of liquid fire from his mouth. It didn't just singe a wing—it put a fist-sized hole through it.

The griffon riders pulled their mounts back with shocked faces, content to await their reinforcements, as Ileom swooped by. "Follow me! Meris says we can outrun them."

Rain wasn't actually in control of Lagron, so Ileom's instructions were superfluous. Lagron understood, and Rain wondered if—and how—the two dragons were communicating with each other. They gained only a little more altitude before leveling off and beginning a slow, deliberate flapping of their wings in a different pattern. As they picked up speed, Rain looked behind to assess their pursuit. The griffons were indeed chasing, but becoming smaller in his sight. He turned his attention to Jared.

"You okay?" he asked.

Jared's eyes were fat plums amid the frozen terror of his face. Finally, he seemed to calm slightly, just as Rain's neck started to hurt from craning back for so long. "I wet myself again," he said, dropping his gaze.

Rain didn't know what to tell him, other than, "It's okay." He looked forward, shielding his eyes with one hand—not just from the midday sun, but from icy particles in the air assaulting them at high speed—and saw Ileom reach forward from his saddle and pat Meris on the base of her neck.

After what seemed like an hour but was probably much less, the dragons dove. As their speed increased, Rain worried they would crash into the dense forests below, but the dragons pulled up, whisking them along the treetops and zig-zagging around small hills.

Suddenly, Meris slowed with several powerful forward sweeps of her wings, and Lagron came to a hover beside her, rocking Rain in the saddle and eliciting a grunt from Jared. The urine smell caught up to Rain's nostrils, though Jared's pants had to be dry by now given all the turbulence.

Ileom looked over, speaking loudly over the slow flapping of wings. "You brought us several hundred miles from where you intended." His tone sounded almost patient.

"Where are we?" Rain hadn't the slightest idea.

"Northeast of Ghent, capital of Ekatowin, on the western edges of the Teeth of Grayshadow, beyond the barbarian lands."

"But ... I've never been here."

"I know, but I have. Maybe the key has, too. I recognized where we were almost instantly. I did *not* expect those griffons, though. That's the second group I've spotted on Tenris, which is a serious problem. I know of a village we can rest in, and perhaps gather some information. Meris seems content with this location, so there might be a reason we're here."

Valid reason or not, Rain would be happy for the surprises from this
infernal key to end. He had been *sure* he was bringing them back
to the valley of Thysend. What had gone wrong? He settled in as Lagron
followed Meris again, and they passed over more foothills until crossing
the first series of the serrated Teeth of Grayshadow. Oddly, the air felt
warmer than it should so far north this time of year, but he was glad for
it. He was exhausted from the recent manic use of his magic and the long
day it had already proven to be. He had nearly fallen asleep when Lagron
gently descended into the middle of a circular plaza carpeted in finely
fit stone, surrounded by clusters of narrow, tall-peaked stone buildings
trimmed with wood. A few people hurried under the eaves—or disappeared completely—as the dragons set down.

"We are just travelers!" Ileom called out in an attempt to calm the
villagers. "We mean no harm!"

A door to one of the buildings burst open, and several men poured
forth, fanning out rapidly. Rain's heart froze at the gray uniforms and
the long wands they all held. At least twenty mages soon surrounded
them. Strangely, almost all looked very old, though they had moved
spritely enough.

Ileom frowned at the man who had emerged first. Perhaps he was the leader? He might have been the oldest, and he stooped slightly. He bore two small six-sided stars on either end of the collar of his tunic.

"I have been here before," Ileom stated flatly.

The man nodded toward the dragons. "Not with those. What are they? They look like, well, dragons, which I understand are extinct."

"Yes, they are dragons, and that will require some explanation, with the right people. I don't remember you possessing wands like that."

"Wands?" The man looked slightly amused for a moment. "Ah, yes … wands. There is much you don't know about us." He grimaced. "We knew the secrets would eventually need to be revealed, though."

"Your people are quite reclusive, occupying a network of villages in this area, is that correct?"

"Yes."

"Is there a central village?"

The man nodded. "This is it."

"Did you send a force through the barbarian lands to attack New Haven recently?" It was a bold question, especially with all those wands still pointed at them. Rain trusted Ileom knew what he was doing.

The man's face darkened, and then he spat to the side. "We did not, as I'm guessing you already knew. Some of our rebellious progeny did, however, after stealing equipment from us."

That seemed like a flimsy claim to Rain, but Ileom nodded as if it made perfect sense. "Who leads you here?"

The man scrunched his brow, studying Ileom, then the dragons, then Rain and Jared. He blinked in what seemed like surprise at Rain and Jared's clothing. Finally, he took another step forward. "I will take you to her. She is the first woman who has led us since … well, you will find out. What do we do about these beasts?"

Ileom thought a moment. "Choose one brave man from among you to lead them to a place of shelter in the trees outside the village. They are tired. They will not harm anyone, but they must not be visible from the air."

The man paused for long moments again, then nodded. "That is wise." He called out a name with a strange guttural sound, and the youngest among them—who was still at least sixty—trotted forward. Ileom ordered Rain and Jared to dismount, and after the soldier had started leading Meris and Lagron away, he turned to the leader.

"My apologies for lack of introductions. I am Ileom Mystrevan, of the Order of the Fallen Moon. Rain Barynd here is one of my aides, and we picked up a straggler, an orphan. We're not sure what to do with him yet."

The wizened mage took that in, then said, "My name is Gunther. I am one of the original founders of these villages. I currently command our defenses."

Ileom squinted. "How many summers have you seen, Master Gunther?"

"Just Gunther. And a hundred and seven."

Ileom's eyebrows crawled upward. "Time has been kind to you."

"By the grace of God," the man replied with a slight nod. "Now come, I'm sure Weldrin is anxious to receive news of what is happening. We moved her to a safer location when we detected you approaching."

Ileom cocked an eyebrow, clearly curious about the detection—and its communication—but said nothing. Gunther led them inside the building from which he and most of the others had issued. They followed him along a hallway, through a door, and down a long set of steps. Their course turned back on itself, and after passing several heavy doors set into smooth rock walls, Gunther opened another door and proceeded down a second flight of stairs.

Rain suddenly noticed how small and bright the lights lining the hallways were. They were also contained somehow, like those on Earth. He didn't have time to study them, as they moved along quickly. After another, longer hallway, Gunther escorted them into a large, high-ceilinged room, decorated like the most opulent of dining halls, replete with two chandeliers and some of the finest furniture Rain had ever seen. He had visited some of the formal areas in the Fortress of the Four Stars, and this room matched the grandeur.

Large maps interrupted the paneled walls, however, and one had been placed in the center of a long rectangular table in the middle of the room. A woman stood opposite them, while several other men and women appeared busy analyzing maps or working with strange … devices. Those also reminded him of his trip to Earth.

All eyes soon settled upon them, and Gunther cleared his throat.

"I made the call, Weldrin," he said, addressing the woman across the table. "I believe they are friends, and I feel they bring important news." He brokered brief introductions, then backed up a step.

The woman, who appeared at least forty years younger than Gunther, which was still old, quirked an eyebrow at him.

"That was a rather sizeable risk."

He cleared his throat again. "Yes, well, they arrived on dragons, not griffons."

Her eyes snapped to Ileom, standing tall in his gleaming armor and long red cape, her expression an odd mixture of hope and nervousness. "Dragons? Where did you come by them?"

Ileom's eyes wandered around the room, taking everything in. Then he focused on Weldrin. "I will tell you, but there are mysteries in this room I need to understand first. I have never seen the like … on this planet."

Weldrin and Gunther shared a look, and then Gunther softly closed the door, gesturing toward some chairs along the wall. "Please, sit, and we will explain."

"We will?" she asked with a note of imperiousness.

Gunther nodded. "I believe it is time, Weldrin. It is ultimately your decision, of course."

When they had taken their chairs, Weldrin moved from the other side of the table to stand in front of Jared, then Rain, and finally Ileom, hands clasped behind her back, nose wrinkling as she glanced back at Jared. Her uniform was also gray, but with dark green trim. And she wore pants, not a skirt.

"Ileom. I have heard your name. You have visited us before, but just once, correct?" Even sitting, he was nearly as tall as her.

"Yes," he replied, "and then only by chance. We foolishly crossed the Teeth late in the year, and we sought refuge."

"Which we gave you."

"Indeed. My thanks again for your kindness and generosity. That was many years ago, but I remembered the location."

"You have a keen sense of direction."

Ileom shrugged. "A small talent."

She seemed on the verge of another question, but then turned slightly and gestured around the room before bringing her hands into a tight ball in front of her. "You wonder about all of this. We brought some of it with us. Some has been replicated and improved, though not greatly. Our reclusiveness is an impediment in that regard, though it is a great boon overall." She paused, then pivoted and moved back to the other side of the table to take a chair. Rain was glad. Having her standing there, so close, had become creepy. Not that he had anything against old people, but she was as intense as Ileom, just in a different sort of way.

She pointed at a contraption sitting on a small desk beneath a wall map. The ancient woman who had been operating it stood at attention beside it, eyes forward. "That is a radio device. It can both receive and transmit sound over long distances. That is how our spotters told us you were coming. They have a similar device, which they can speak into."

Hannah's much smaller gadget from Earth seemed far more impressive, but Rain didn't bring it up, especially since he had no idea how it worked.

Ileom took that in calmly. "You said you brought some of this equipment. From where? The oldest of these villages have existed for, what, about eighty years?"

Weldrin seemed impressed. "You study your history, even the vaguer elements. Yes. You used the word planet earlier, so perhaps this won't surprise you as much as I expected. We came from another planet."

"How?" Indeed, Ileom didn't appear shocked at all. Rain had to click his own maw shut.

She gave a small grunt, higher pitched than Ileom's normal fare. "There are differing accounts, and the memories have faded, but they agree on the basics, which we have written down. It appears to have been a … happy accident, completely unintended, after the discovery of a small metal key, along with a strange book that one of our original founders could partially read, it being written in an ancient language from our world that he had happened to study before the beginning of the war."

"The war?"

Her face melted with sadness. "Yes. I wasn't there, but my grandfather braved the horrors of its recollection to recount some of it to me. It was so pointless. Our nation, so proud, led by a madman, a butcher, a follower of the devil himself. And our pastors, those who should have helped us see it more clearly … five sixths of them—fifteen of eighteen thousand professed men of God—refused to preach openly against him, even though they had clearly been warned by some of the best among them … and by the Spirit of God himself." Her calm intensity was both intimidating and inviting. "Almost all the men in my grandfather's unit—and a few women pressed into service—were God-fearing Christians; that is, ardent followers of the Son of God who came to live on our planet long before our time. They loathed both this evil leader and the gruesome war he had inflicted on our world in his quest for a perfect, and perfectly brutal, society. Perhaps—and many here believe this to be so—God heard their prayers and removed them from the war."

"To come here."

She nodded.

"Which planet?" Rain could feel the answer to Ileom's query before she gave it.

"Earth."

Ileom glanced at Rain, and Weldrin raised her eyebrows. "You have heard of it."

"We have," Ileom responded. "My aide just returned from there. It was a brief trip. We haven't learned much yet."

Her startled gaze rested upon Rain, and silence stilled the air for several seconds. "How did you get there?"

Rain swallowed, glancing at Ileom, who nodded.

"I … er, we … have a talisman. A key. It transported me there."

She took a deep breath. "So there *is* more than one key. We suspect-ed—and feared—as much. We have successfully protected ours, including from our grandchildren and great-grandchildren who have rebelled against us, but such a tool in the wrong hands poses grave dangers."

"Indeed it does," said Ileom. "We know of at least one other key that is being used—to bring war griffons from a third planet, called Alave."

Weldrin's eyes widened. "Those beasts are not from another continent on Tenris?" She glanced at Gunther, who also appeared flummoxed. "We have seen a few, but we had presumed—"

"We encountered some a short distance from here. They attacked, and we escaped."

"How many?"

Ileom considered her question for a few moments, then answered. "At least thirty."

"How did you escape so many?"

"The dragons are faster."

"And they didn't follow you here?"

Ileom shook his head. "No. I made sure of it. We wouldn't have stopped otherwise."

"Of course." She brought one hand up to the table and started tap-ping her fingers in a rhythm, staring at nothing for nearly a full minute.

"These dragons. They are powerful, like the griffons?"

"Yes."

"How many do you have?"

Ileom grimaced. "Only two, from the same world as the griffons. They are natural enemies, and most of the dragons have been killed or forced into hid-ing there … as I understand it, anyway. I have visited that planet only briefly."

"With the same key?"

He gave a slight chuckle. "No, yet another key. So, now we know there are at least four keys in existence, which portends others." His mien returned to normal—intense bordering on angry. "Why didn't you return to Earth later … after the war?"

She gave an uncomfortable shrug. "We started trying after a few years, making many unsuccessful attempts. Unfortunately, the man who had originally read the book died of a heart attack during our first year on Tenris. He had taught a few others a portion of that dead language, but only one ended up being able to make the book work at all. We ended up sending her and one other back. The key deposited them on a small, uninhabited island in one of the oceans … and then promptly returned them in less than a day. We tried to send more people with them, but for some reason the key only allowed two, plus a few supplies and a small motorized boat. They tried using the boat, but the key still brought them back, even if they left it behind on the island. We finally stopped."

"How many people did the key and the book originally bring?" asked Ileom.

She sniffed, rubbing a finger under her nose. "More than a hundred people, plus some very large and heavy items."

Ileom hadn't reacted to the word 'motorized,' but Rain had never heard it before. The experienced master just took it all in with perfect aplomb.

"So, you have no viable escape options."

"Except you, perhaps. Only a handful might be able to escape into the mountains." She resumed her tapping. "The griffons are surrounding us. We suspect our *rebels* are involved with them now. They seek additional technology and equipment we have stored here. Perhaps *you* can read the book?"

Ileom ignored her question for the moment. "So, it doesn't matter if your rebels followed us here or not. The griffon riders already know your location and are intent upon it."

"It matters that they don't know you brought those dragons here today," she retorted, eyes sparkling.

Ileom's lips wrinkled. "Valid point. And either I or someone I know may be able to read your book, though if it originated on Earth, I have my doubts. The talismans are ancient, having lain dormant for several millennia, and we still know very little."

"But you know *something*, at least, and if we decide we can trust you, perhaps there is a chance we can use that key again."

"Perhaps," Ileom agreed, "though I need to know we can trust you as well."

Rain wondered if Meris or Lagron could activate Weldrin's key, but Ileom didn't mention the possibility. Weldrin leaned forward, resting folded arms on the table. Then she took a deep breath. "That is fair. We would be happy to remain here on Tenris, by the way, keeping to ourselves, but our rebels will not leave us in peace. They mean to overpower us and take everything. With enough griffons, they can, and then they can reproduce the firepower of our greatest weapons and turn them on the other peoples of this planet … and perhaps other worlds, too. Such a scenario is dreadful and unacceptable to us. If it comes down to it, we have prepared a final contingency."

Ileom's face softened. "Destroy it all—and yourselves—in a massive conflagration."

Rain had been thinking about the term 'firepower.' He hadn't heard that before, either. But it could apply to the heat he wielded. Then his mind caught up to the dread truth Ileom had just uttered.

"Yes," she replied simply. "We are old. We have lived long, happy, fulfilling lives. And we can hold our heads high as we meet our Maker."

Ileom considered that a moment, his gaze taking on a new, reverent passion. He breathed in and out deeply, then said, "We discovered something else as we escaped the griffons." Rain blinked, guessing what was coming. It made him nervous. Hadn't Ileom just implied he couldn't trust Weldrin yet?

"Young Rain and I both have the use of magic. Somehow, we have also bonded with the dragons. As we fought off the griffon attack, we stumbled upon dragon abilities linked to our magic. Searing fire and piercing ice. We stunned them and made fast our escape."

He still hadn't mentioned anything about enhanced transport, and Rain wasn't going to bring it up. He glanced at Jared, who huddled in his seat trying to go unnoticed. Had he even understood yet that these people originated on his planet? What would he think of that?

Gunther stepped toward the table. "This is the answer to our prayers, Weldrin."

"How so?" she challenged.

"We cannot make good an escape on this planet without air cover, even with our newest weaponry. We waited too long. The griffons have grown numerous, and we know our rebels have aligned with some magic-users as well."

Ileom shifted. "Magic-users? From where?"

Weldrin narrowed her eyes. "I imagine you can guess."

"Sheraya."

She dipped her chin. "Yes. We somewhat accidentally captured one of these 'Hearkendoom,' as they arrogantly call themselves. This one managed to escape, though he was wounded. They are quite powerful as long as they have use of eyes and hands."

"They lack true focus," remarked Ileom. "And truth itself."

She pursed her lips, then redirected her gaze to Gunther, gesturing toward Ileom and Rain. "They are only two."

Gunther nodded, his enthusiasm undampened. "Yes, but we can coordinate with them. And how many does God need?"

She blinked at that, then rubbed her temples. "We must counsel and pray on this. We must be certain. If it is his will that we die, then we die, and we take all our technology with us."

"We must have faith," he countered, "and trust in the promises."

"I'm aware of the promises," she said, her voice rising. She looked at Ileom again. "The heads of the councils and I will discuss these things. We will likely have additional questions for you. In the meantime, one of Gunther's men will guide you back upstairs and make sure your needs are met. Please accept of our hospitality again."

Ileom stood and bowed. "Thank you. That is most gracious."

Gunther led them out of the room, then pointed at one of the guards positioned near the door. "Traeger, please find these men a place to rest and give them anything they need. They will want to make sure their dragons are cared for, too."

That last statement sounded indelibly odd, especially with Rain's mind spinning so fast. How had he gone from the peaceful, hidden valley on Tenris to Earth … and then to this? With dragons.

Traeger showed them to a large, comfortable room on the second floor of the main building, complete with a warming fire in an elaborate stone hearth. While Ileom went to check on Meris and Lagron, Jared, who had to be starving, simply collapsed onto one of the beds, feet still on the floor. Plates, bowls, and pitchers on a table to one side emitted a constant assault of enticing scents.

Rain walked over to Jared. "Eat?"

Jared's eyes were closed, and he kept them that way while he shook his head.

"Scared?" He was surprised he remembered that word.

After a pause, Jared nodded.

"I too." Jared had no reaction to that.

"New people. Earth. Eighty years. Friends." He still wasn't sure about the last part, but Ileom seemed to like them.

Jared finally opened his eyes. They moved back and forth across the ceiling as he scrunched up his face. He finally said, "Their names sounded German. How did they get here?"

Rain didn't know what 'German' meant. "Key." He got out his key. "War. Escape." Another word he surprised himself with.

Jared pondered that a moment. "They have a key, too? Wow. And they escaped a war? Eighty years ago?" He thought for a moment, eyes moving more rapidly. "World War II?" His eyes locked on Rain, and then he sat up, frowning. "They *are* Germans. Hitler was their leader."

Rain hadn't heard the name 'Hitler' from them. But he remembered what they had said about hating the war. "No like ... leader."

Jared blinked. "You mean, they didn't like Hitler and rebelled against him?"

Rain nodded, hoping he had understood the question correctly.

Jared got to his feet, then rubbed his jaw. A new energy seemed to infuse him. "This is totally jacked. Wow. Germans from World War II, and they came here and had kids, and built villages. They have old radios, too, and it looks like they work. Amazing." He shook his head in wonder as he ambled over to the table filled with food and drink and started sampling. Rain followed, his own mouth watering.

"Very old." He cracked a smile.

Jared tried to laugh with his cheeks bulging. His eyes watered. "Ancient."

What did that mean? Jared must have recognized his confusion, and after a few seconds to swallow amended his comment to, "Yes, very, *very* old." Then, "This food is delicious. I love this place."

Rain began partaking of the culinary delights as well, and soon they were both in a food coma, lying on two of the beds. Ileom arrived, took one look at them, glanced at the depleted smorgasbord, and laughed. He actually laughed! That was more miraculous than anything Rain had seen, done, or heard about. Ever.

"I'm glad you two got something to eat. Rain, you especially. Now rest. You'll need energy, because we have some traveling to do. I'll be back in a few hours." With that, he left again, and Rain let sleep take him.

That elegant underground room—what the Germans called their control center now—teemed with people the next morning, most with no place to sit. Rain sat dumbfounded, his incredulous expression mirrored by the Germans. Ileom had just explained that they didn't need to use the dragons' magic to blast their way through a weak point in the collar strangling them … Rain's key could transport dozens of them at a time, and their equipment, with the help of his linked dragon. Meris had apparently confirmed it.

Rain was about to ask about the Germans' key when Ileom added that Meris had assessed their talisman and let him know it was corrupted in some way—neither she nor Lagron would be able to help make it work properly, no matter who held it.

Weldrin and Gunther were astounded and delighted by the notion of using Rain's key, however. Rain still felt tired, his mind fuzzy. He finally spoke up. "But that will only take us back to Earth, in that exposed field. They'll be discovered almost immediately. Unless …"

Ileom shrugged. "Yes. Four trips for you and Lagron each time except the last. To Earth. Back to Tenris—Thysend, preferably. To Earth again. Then back here to pick up the next group. We've never tried something like this. It may take a while, depending on how much energy is expended by you and Lagron, mental and physical."

"And how accurate I am." He shouldn't have said that aloud.

Ileom didn't scowl, surprisingly. "Yes, but you're getting better at it. I have faith in you, *Commander* Barynd, and we have no time to bring their key and book to the right members of the Order, who only *might* be able to understand the impediment. I cannot read it, by the way."

Rain's mouth had started to fall open at Ileom's mention of having faith in him. To cover, he asked, "How many people do we need to move?"

"More than three hundred."

"Plus a great deal of equipment, vehicles, and supplies," added Weldrin. "We did some rough calculations after consulting with Master Ileom. We will likely have twenty groups. The youngest, along with the most sensitive equipment, will go first, in case we run out of time … or energy." Her eyebrows angled in empathy. "We will be grateful for whatever number of us you can save, young Master Rain."

He gulped. Twenty groups. Eighty total trips. Well, minus two. He winced, looking at Ileom. "I … don't think I can do that, um, sir. I'm sorry."

Ileom's face took on its familiar sternness. "You can. I said it might take some time. We've been working on contingencies in case the evacuation is discovered and the rebels try to move in. That will require a full day of preparation. During that time, you can take a few practice runs. If Antara hasn't ignored my instructions and left to escort that Mero Vothan captain to Sharai with his silly message from Dynast, you can bring her back here as well. She can provide you some additional energy."

Rain nodded acquiescence, a lump forming in his throat as his chest constricted. He trusted Ileom … and Antara. But himself, not so much. Not with this big of a task, using skills he barely comprehended.

Weldrin suddenly stood, pinning Ileom with her gaze. "Why *are* you so anxious to help us … at the potential sacrifice of this apparently very promising young man?"

Ileom barely paused before answering, which meant he had expected the question. "Because we can help each other. You are concerned with this continent being subjugated?"

She gave a wary nod.

"Well, it is about to be, and the griffons are only part of the story. An army from the shores of Akris is already building on Chalace. I have seen with my own eyes a gathering of griffons there. I lost several men to them. I didn't know that any of your people—these rebels—would be linked to this imminent invasion. But if we work together, with your technology and our magic, we can buy time for Rega until we can figure out how Earth fits into all of this. We know the involvement of Earth is necessary for ultimate victory, but we don't know how."

"*We* is the Order of the Fallen Moon, I presume," she said. "But how do you know?" Rain had the same question.

"Recent events have made the prophecies very clear." He glanced at Rain. "This young soldier and his talisman are critical. We instructed him to find a prophet or prophetess, without understanding exactly why or who, or what to do. That person, it seems quite evident to me now, is you." He added a small bow as the room went completely silent.

Weldrin stared at Ileom, then at Gunther, standing near the door, for long moments. It was Gunther who responded first.

"She is our spiritual leader as well," he said to Ileom, "and a finer one I have not met."

Ileom studied Gunther's face, then redirected his gaze to Weldrin. "When I traveled to Alave, I was able to determine that my god presided there as well. I've spent just a few moments on Earth, so I cannot answer for—"

"He is the same," she said softly, though her words carried the electricity of a lightning strike.

Ileom took a long breath. "I suspected as much. That is why we are linked. That is why Earth—and Alave—are important to the final outcome here."

"We are important to their final outcomes as well," she said. "This is larger than either of us can possibly imagine. By the way, where is the other boy?"

"The orphan? We left him in the room you provided. He is doing well. Thank you."

"You didn't mention yesterday where he is from. He didn't seem to comprehend much, if anything, of our earlier conversation."

She knew. She must. Ileom glanced at Rain, then answered her. "He is from Earth. He was an orphan there and wanted to return with Rain."

"Hmmm …" She didn't seem perturbed that the knowledge had been kept from her, just intrigued. "What language does he speak? Earth has many."

Ileom turned to Rain to give the answer. "English," he said.

She nodded as Ileom asked, "Do any of you speak English?"

Gunther cleared his throat. "At one point, I spoke it very well. It has been a long time, though I occasionally re-read the one English book I brought with me. A novel. A tragic, somewhat frivolous story about a man who spends his time throwing parties to revel in his wealth while chasing a past he cannot resurrect. It was written just a couple of decades before the war. In America. Our supposed enemy." He blinked as if he had explained far more than was necessary. "Um, I can try."

"You're not confident you can speak with him?" asked Ileom. Gunther shrugged.

"We need information about Earth," said Weldrin, standing. "I gather neither of you speaks English well enough yet." Her gaze took in Rain, and he shook his head.

"Very well," she said. "Gunther, send Traeger to fetch him."

While they waited, Weldrin addressed Ileom again. "Earth will have changed much since we left. Our link to our home is far outdated. If we were to return there, we wouldn't have quick access to avenues of assistance, and acting hastily could prove disastrous. That said, the possibility is intriguing."

Ileom nodded, giving a slight frown. "That is wise, and you are perceptive. I have perhaps been too focused on delaying and defeating the invasion from Akris, ignoring the bigger picture."

Weldrin resumed her seat without comment. She then began requesting reports regarding latest known enemy dispositions from several people in the room, who jolted into action. A few minutes later, a soft knock on the door preceded the entrance of Traeger and Jared. Gunther closed the door behind them, adding in a low voice, "You may stay, Traeger."

Weldrin stood again. "Welcome, Jared," she said in English. Even to Rain, it sounded heavily accented. Jared's eyes went bug-like as he stared at her. "You speak English?"

She gave a slight shake of her head. "I do not speak English well, but … Gunther?"

Gunther maneuvered himself to a position facing Jared, then smiled hesitantly. "I remember some English. It has been … a long time."

"Oh." Jared's elation diminished. He looked at Rain, who gave him an encouraging nod, then returned his gaze to Gunther. "You want to ask me some questions? Like in an alien movie or something?"

Gunther frowned a moment, then nodded. "Yes, we need to ask some questions. About Earth. You speak English. Which country are you from?"

"The U.S."

Gunther cocked his head. "The United States of America? Does everyone there speak English still?"

Jared seemed somewhat confused. "Sure. Well, almost everyone. Why?"

"Do you know about the Second World War?"

Jared gave an embarrassed grimace. "Not very much. I know it happened. I know we won."

Relief washed across Gunther's face. Rain noted it on Weldrin's, too. She seemed to have understood the gist. "Hitler was defeated?"

"Yeah. He ended up killing himself, I think."

Gunther breathed deeply, knees trembling. His eyes began to glisten. "That is good for Earth. Is there peace now?"

Jared shrugged. "Mostly, I guess. I don't pay much attention. There's a lot of crime. Lots of people angry at each other, too. I guess, I dunno, maybe it isn't so peaceful after all."

Gunther gave a commiserating nod. "People are always fighting. It is human nature. Very difficult to … overcome." At that point he stopped and relayed everything he had said and heard to the rest of the group.

Cheers burst out at the first sentence, along with hugs and crying. One man nearly collapsed in joy. Weldrin let the celebration go on for nearly a full minute, then calmed the room, nodding at Gunther to continue.

"Where do you live? Which state?"

"Illinois."

"Illinois … ah, Chicago. Big city."

"Not in Chicago, but near there. Chicago is really dangerous."

"Oh. I am sorry. You are an orphan?"

"Yes." Jared glanced at Rain. "My parents were killed by a drunk driver."

"Drunk?" Gunther looked up for a moment. "Ah, yes, I remember. Drunk. Lots of that in the book I read. Again, I am sorry."

"It wasn't your fault."

"Yes, I know. Ah … is Germany still a country?"

Jared blinked as if the question were strange. "Yeah, sure. Why wouldn't it be? Oh, right."

"Is Germany still an enemy of the United States?"

Jared shook his head. "No. Japan isn't, either. We aren't too friendly with Russia and China, though. Or North Korea."

"North Korea?"

"Oh, yeah, that might be a new one to you."

"We could talk to others on Earth who know more, correct?"

Jared shrugged. "Yeah, I guess so." He looked at Rain and pointed. "He can get you there. I can't."

Gunther smiled warmly. "I know. You have been very helpful. Thank you."

"Oh, you're welcome." He put his hands in his pockets—his clothes had been laundered, fortunately—and then looked around sheepishly at all the eyes focused on him. Luckily, Gunther started into the translation, so the attention shifted.

After he finished, Weldrin nodded to Ileom. "Leave us now, please. And rest. We need to consult with each other regarding all of this new information. We will also begin the preparations already discussed. We can speak again in the morning."

"I understand," Ileom said, bowing. "We will see you in the morning."

Ileom didn't say anything until they arrived at their room, where they discovered that more food and drink had been supplied, and the fire re-stoked. He tore into the food, which meant he had hardly eaten anything since they arrived. The knit of his brow signaled deep concern. Rain didn't ask him his thoughts on the German deliberations.

"We could do a test run while they're discussing things … like you said," Rain finally offered helpfully. Ileom ignored him and kept eating, so Rain looked at Jared and shrugged before beginning to stuff his own mouth. A second food coma later, he opened his eyes and found himself lying on one of the beds. Full dark had fallen at some point. How had he slept so long? A lamp shone from a small writing desk where Ileom sat, scribbling furiously as his armorless but muscular bulk threatened to shatter the chair beneath him.

Rain propped himself up on his elbows, the slight noise causing Ileom to twist his neck and stare at him, hand still poised above paper. "You ready for that test run?"

Rain sat all the way up and swung his legs over the side of the bed, instantly ashamed at his lack of self-control. He stood and saluted. "Yes, sir. Sorry, sir. I ate too much, but … I won't let you down."

Ileom grunted, then returned to his writing. After another minute or so, he pushed the chair away and stood, spinning to face Rain. "We can leave Jared here. He'll be okay. He's fast asleep, and we won't be long."

It was probably Jared's snoring that had awakened Rain. Ileom glanced at Rain's feet. "You should probably take those fancy boots off once in a while. Give your feet some air." Rain couldn't remember if he had or hadn't since arriving at the village, but he thought he had. Either way, his feet felt great. The dark blue pants were the most comfortable he'd ever worn, too. And they had side pockets with something Hannah had called 'zippers.' He *loved* side pockets.

They were about to leave when a knock sounded. Ileom opened the door, and there stood Weldrin, Gunther, and Traeger. Their tight, tired expressions triggered alarm bells in Rain's head.

"The decision, for now, has been taken from us," said Weldrin. "The rebels will attack by dawn. We need to coordinate our defenses with you. Someone will be sent to watch over the boy." Rain blinked at the implication that he himself wasn't considered a boy by the Germans, old and experienced as they were. He looked to Ileom, who nodded, his face a stone.

"No time to waste, then. And they will have Hearkendoom warrior mages with them, I'm sure."

What followed was a whirlwind of activity surpassing those first few minutes after the warning had sounded of the attack on New Haven. The first thing Ileom ordered Rain to do was bring the dragons to the village center, which was bathed in a truly magnificent array of bright lanterns. When they arrived, his feet froze, mouth agape as he witnessed two massive beasts roll into the plaza with roars much throatier than those he'd heard on Earth. Many wheels supported them, not just four, encompassed by thick strips of some kind of interlocking metal plates. They moved slowly and looked extremely heavy. Each had a long tube sticking out from an upper section that could rotate, and on top of the upper section sat a pair of smaller cylinders, kind of like the wands he'd seen used, only larger, with bulbous tips.

He sensed curiosity from Lagron, but neither dragon seemed concerned. They apparently viewed the Germans as allies, and perhaps these contraptions could withstand the griffons and magic-users. An old woman scurried by, and he asked, pointing, "What are those?"

She paused her superannuated scurry and gave him a toothy grin as she threw back her shoulders. "Those are Panzers, young man. Tanks. Big metal boxes that can throw some serious fire with their guns. They're ancient, but we've repaired them recently. And for a long time we've been able to produce the fuel they use. We'll put them on the high ground, with some anti-aircraft batteries. They won't let us down."

Guns. Aircraft. Batteries. Rain didn't know any of those words. But her obvious pride made them seem even more powerful, which gave him some solace. He thanked her, then led the dragons to an open space in one section of the plaza. He stood close to Lagron, absently placing a hand on the dragon's neck as he continued to stare. The tanks moved out of the plaza, belching dark smoke behind them. He watched as men started lifting long, thick spikes onto many of the rooftops with the help of cranes and pulleys far more sophisticated than any he had ever seen. The spikes bore angled crosspieces at their bases to hold them in place on the roof peaks, and the men interlocked many of them. The final effect was to make it extremely difficult to land a griffon on a rooftop, while giving some cover to archers or mages firing upward.

Indeed, as the preparations progressed, he noted several men with their strange wands ascending to take places among the barriers, bearing portable seats designed to balance on the angled surfaces. He marveled again at how old they all were. Though relatively spry, if it came to a physical battle with swords or spears, they would be cut down like grain under a newly sharpened scythe. Those wands were the equalizer.

Some of the lights in the plaza began blinking, along with lights that appeared in nearby trees and some of the closer hills. The patterns varied, and he couldn't make sense of them.

They're communicating. They don't all have talking devices.

Rain turned to see who had spoken to him, but nobody was there. His hand felt unnaturally warm, though.

"Lagron?" he whispered.

Yes. As long as we are in physical contact, we can communicate this way. Meris and I have worked out your language.

"You *have*? And you can *talk*?" He wasn't sure how to use his mind to respond, so his voice would have to do.

In his mind he felt a … chuckle … an odd occurrence from a dragon, nearly indescribable, like a group of boulders crashing into a still lake. *It will take some time to be able to form your sounds with my mouth and tongue, but yes.*

Rain looked around to see if anyone had noticed him talking to a dragon. Everyone was too busy, though.

So many questions sprang to his mind. "Did you talk to humans on your world?"

He sensed both pity and regret. *No.*

"Why not?"

We could not afford to place that much trust in them.

"But ... you can trust *me*? And Ileom?"

Yes.

"How do you know that?"

He sensed wisdom, as if from a great well, in the next words from Lagron. *The same way you* know *things sometimes that you can't logically or physically explain. We are all creatures of the same higher power, and that power reveals itself to us sometimes, in diverse ways. Always for our benefit, in the midst of this our great test, even if we cannot quite perceive that.*

"Oh. Well, I don't think I understand that very well, yet."

Better than you think.

Rain didn't know how to respond. "So, in the air, how can I make contact with you?"

Remove the front strap, lean forward a bit, and hold onto the two small spikes in front of the saddle. You can't wear gloves, but don't worry. I can keep your hands warm.

"Okay. So ... we can coordinate some of our magical attacks?"

And our defenses. You can shape minor shields with your heat, too, and move them around. At how great a distance we will have to test. I know how the griffons fight, but Meris and I understand little of the magic-users we will face. Ileom's knowledge of them also seems sparse. By the way, aided by Ileom, we have been using a scry spell to listen in on your discussions with the Germans. We realize the dire extent of the situation.

Somehow, that part of it didn't shock Rain at all. "Some of the Hearkendoom might be riding griffons."

True. Now try to speak to me without your voice.

It took a couple of tries, but Rain succeeded with less difficulty than expected. Excitement coursed through him as Ileom suddenly appeared in his vision, striding across the plaza in his armor and cape. Rain called out like an over-eager boy who had just discovered a particularly large toad.

"Master Ileom! Come here!"

Ileom halted, quirked a perturbed eyebrow at him, then stalked over, armor gleaming in the artificial lights. "What is it?"

"Our dragons can talk to us."

He nodded. "Yes. I'm glad you know that now."

Rain's chest deflated as his eyes popped. "You knew?"

"Yesterday. It was for Lagron to tell you, not me."

"Oh. All right." He saluted, not knowing what else to do, then felt stupid. He tried to cover with an offer to be useful. "Is there anything else you need me to do?"

"No. Just get your mind right. Lagron will help you. This will be a hellacious battle. You'll need to wrap your ears, both for the cold and loud sounds. Make it thick."

Rain nodded, then patted Lagron's neck as Ileom moved away and entered a building. After a few more minutes of observing the activity in the plaza with Lagron, who didn't seem inclined to offer any immediate advice, he decided to check on Jared. When he entered the room, a man sat at another table, polishing some metallic items arrayed before him. He was applying some sort of oily substance to them as well. He looked up at Rain. "Your friend has been sleeping the whole time."

Rain glanced at Jared's bed, not knowing what to do. He could leave, but the man's work triggered intense curiosity. He was also younger than anyone else Rain had seen in the village, by far.

He slowly approached the table. "What is that?"

The man paused his labor and stared at him. "I'm sure you've never seen anything like this up close, have you?"

Rain shook his head, though something tickled the back of his brain.

"Well, first, my name is Konrad. I know yours is Rain. Rain Barynd, right? From New Haven?"

"Yes."

"Well, I'm sure I'm more than twice your age, but there are only a handful of us so young in the area. The rest went with the rebels, seeking to restore some mythical glory they don't know anything about. Traeger is my father."

"You stayed, while your friends left?"

Sadness filled his eyes. "Yes. My wife, too, and she took our two boys. I still can't comprehend how she fell for the rebels' twisted lies."

"How did you ... um, resist them?" Rain couldn't help but ask.

Konrad's look became distant but determined. "I'd like to say it was my faith, but it was mainly the memory of my late mother. *She* possessed faith and courage that could move mountains. My father, too. God doesn't invite us to seek the glory of the world, but his glory, which far surpasses anything we can do here on our own." He gazed again at Rain, as if judging his reaction.

"You're wondering whether we really do serve the same god," Konrad continued. That was exactly what Rain had been thinking, even though Weldrin's opinion on the matter had sounded quite firm.

"Well, I've never lived on Earth, nor did my parents or even my grandparents, but my great-grandparents did, and according to our family records, they swore, even on their deathbeds, that God was the same in both worlds. I want to visit Earth so I can verify—that is, feel it for myself."

"How will you, um ...?"

"I'll know. It will come." He took a deep breath, then changed the subject. "Now, you wanted to know what this is." He made a small sweeping gesture across the table. "This is a gun. A firearm. It launches a small metal projectile, called a bullet, at incredible speed through the air, so fast you can't even see it. You have to aim it, because the bullet will only travel in a straight line, like an arrow—affected by wind and gravity over long distances, of course. When it hits, it does great damage." His face saddened again. "I wish we didn't need them."

Rain blinked, staring at all the pieces. Some of them definitely looked familiar.

Konrad clapped him on the arm. "Yes, it's a complex mechanism. I've been cleaning and oiling this one so it will function properly. We have a small oil pumping and refining facility nearby, which we also use to make fuel for the vehicles—the tanks and trucks. We've been blessed to find coal, too, and we have a small plant where we burn that, without producing much smoke. It generates electricity, which powers our lights and radios."

"Elec …?"

"I know, this is a lot to take in. Don't worry about understanding it all right now. Here, I'll show you how to put this gun back together, and the bullets it uses."

Rain stood near his shoulder, watching in fascination as he assembled the various pieces, occasionally pausing to test fit or function. In mere minutes he had finished, holding up a perfectly whole, but very heavy wand … or rather, gun. He extended it toward Rain.

"Go ahead, take it. It's not loaded. That is, it doesn't have a bullet in it. It's still a good practice to make sure it isn't pointing at anything you don't want to shoot, though." He chuckled. "You look like you've seen a ghost. It's okay. I know it's your first time seeing one, but—"

"I've seen them before. I've fought men who carried them."

Konrad's smile disappeared, eyes widening. He rose from his chair, holding the gun with one hand, pointing it at the floor. "You fought the rebels?"

Rain nodded. "They were mixed with barbarians. I thought … I thought these were magic devices."

Konrad wrinkled his forehead. "I heard something yesterday about New Haven being attacked? But why?"

Rain shrugged, even though he knew the answer.

Konrad grumbled. "The one thing I agree with the rebels on is that we're too isolated. We don't get enough news here about what's going on in the world. I guess that's about to change."

"Yeah, I guess so," Rain agreed.

Konrad took a deep breath, then looked down at the gun again. "Well, to one unfamiliar, guns would appear to be magic, for sure. But they're very mechanical. Chemical, too, I guess."

"Chemical?" Another unfamiliar word.

"Yes." He reached into a bag on the table and pulled out a small and shiny cylindrical object with a gray point on one end. "This is a bullet.

The gray portion is the actual projectile. I know it seems small, but getting hit with one going so fast is like having a large sword run through you. It fits into the top of the brass shell, which contains a powder that explodes to force the projectile out of the gun at high speed."

"Explode. Like a fireball?"

Konrad chuckled again. "Yes, like a magical fireball. I've never seen one of those, but I've seen lightning strike a tree. It's kind of like that, too." He pointed. "Here's where you put the bullet." He slotted it into an opening, then used a mechanism to push it forward into a hole in the longest piece of the gun. "When you pull the trigger," he tapped lightly on a small piece of metal below the gun, protected by a curved section of steel, "a tiny hammer hits the bottom of the shell, causing the explosion, and the bullet shoots out of the end of the barrel, in the direction the gun is pointing. It spins, by the way, to make it more accurate."

Rain realized even more clearly how lucky he was to still be alive. Konrad did something to re-open the gun, and he extracted the bullet. "It doesn't need to be loaded right now. But soon. I'm not a great warrior like you or your boss. I can use one of these, though, and I'm a pretty good shot. They're excellent for hunting wild game, by the way."

Rain nodded. He could well imagine. He was about to correct Konrad's comment on him being a great warrior when the door to the room swung open. Ileom stepped inside, glancing at the gun. "Konrad, is it? You are wanted downstairs, where you'll receive your assignment." Konrad gathered up his things and left with nod for Rain. Then Ileom approached, laying his hands on Rain's shoulders.

"This is it. I need you sharp, Commander Barynd, and I know you're ready. I almost sent you away to keep you safe, but Lagron won't let me, and he's right. Together, you are an important key to the future, which starts here, today."

Rain dropped his eyes. He didn't deserve such high confidence, but he tingled at Ileom's second use of the title commander. Was he ready for this? Fighting small battles alongside Ileom and Antara on terrain he knew was one thing, but this had spiraled far beyond anything he could have imagined.

The hands grew heavier as they squeezed. "Dawn is almost upon us. We take to the air in fifteen minutes. Wake Jared up, get him some food, and take him down to the command center. He'll be safe there. Then meet us in the plaza."

Rain felt some of his training and discipline kick in. "Yes, sir." Ileom clapped his shoulders hard, then turned and exited the room.

Rain paused only a few seconds in sober contemplation before he approached the log-sawing Jared.

"Strap your legs in tight," admonished Ileom as they prepared to fly. "These griffon riders have trained in the use of formations and tactics in the sky, and we haven't, but we have an advantage over them."

"What is that?" Rain asked.

Ileom grinned. "We can fight easier upside down, as can our dragons, according to Meris."

That thought brought a queasy feeling. How often would he be upside down?

"Not that they can't," Ileom cautioned, "but the dragons and their magic are better suited to it. Meris and Lagron can also communicate with each other mentally—something griffons cannot do—so maintain your contact with Lagron. That will help us coordinate."

Rain nodded as he cinched one of the straps tight. He didn't want to cut off circulation, but falling out of the saddle in mid-air would definitely be worse. Then he checked the thick cloth wrapped around his ears, tied in the back, feeling reasonably certain it wouldn't come off.

Ileom continued his instructions. "They will probably assume we want to stay above them, and we'll start there, but we'll dive through their formation first … a risky move they won't expect. Then we'll attack again from below, letting the German guns have greater effect at altitude. Just follow my lead."

Rain gave him a questioning look as he tugged on another strap—too tightly, so he loosened it a bit.

Ileom grunted from atop Meris. "The Germans have anti-aircraft guns—we'll talk about what aircraft are later—which launch projectiles into the sky that explode at certain heights. Different than bullets, and much larger. After our initial pass, we need to stay either below or above the main body of griffons so they can fire on them without accidentally hurting us. Remember that … above or below."

That sounded simple enough, until he started thinking it through. Once they engaged, the battle would become a chaotic mess. How would he know if he were high or low enough? He wasn't used to fighting in the sky, and … how many times would he puke before this was over? He could feel his stomach prepping for it.

Ileom explained how to alter the upper straps to keep him lower to Lagron's back when they turned over, and so he could maintain physical contact. That would be key, and he was already planning his apology to the noble creature for having to rely so much on him. Rain's very first battle, which now seemed so long ago, flashed in his mind. He hadn't known what he was doing then, either, and without Sun Tamer's help, he would likely be dead. He wondered how she was doing. Was she happy living in paradise, or frustrated to be out of the action? Probably the latter.

"All right, up!" shouted Ileom, and both dragons leaped off the ground, beating the air with mighty wings. Rain lost contact with Lagron for a moment, then reestablished.

We'll stay just behind and to the right of them, came Lagron's soothing voice in his head.

Rain gave a mental nod, which Lagron somehow understood.

The enemy is close. We should hear our allied guns any second. They'll soften the middle just before we dive through. Ground troops are a bit behind the griffons still, so we don't have to worry about them yet. Are you ready?

Yes, I think so. And how did you know about the ground troops? It felt odd to use that term; up until now, *all* troops were ground troops.

Ileom heard it from the Germans.

They climbed sharply, Ileom and Meris staying about thirty yards ahead. Rain tried to spot the griffons in the lightening dawn sky, which was nearly cloudless, though a splotchy, creeping fog covered the ground. After a few seconds, he thought he spied some specks in the distance. As they grew, their number expanded, and he gulped. There must be more than a hundred. Some of the men who rode them would have guns, and others magic. Could a griffon carry two men—a trained rider *and* a Hearkendoom soldier? He asked Lagron.

Yes. They would be much slower, though. If any carry two, we will be able to spot them easily. There was a pause, apparently as he communicated with Meris, and she with Ileom. *They are not a special target. They will not have much training in the air. We are to stay above and below the main group, harassing and destroying whatever we come in contact with, and let the German anti-aircraft guns do their work.*

Nervousness rose over the next couple of minutes, coming to a crescendo as the dragons dove toward the mass of griffons. They rolled as Rain focused on forming weapons and finding targets, ignoring the bile reaching for his throat.

Don't worry about where the ground or the sky are, came Lagron's calming voice, *just focus on your target, his speed and direction, then will your weapons there.*

That was easier said than done, especially because his body *knew* it was nearly upside down. He felt like he could hurtle to the ground at any moment. Lagron's first lance of fire launched toward the griffon horde, jolting Rain out of his miserable reverie, and he picked out a target. It was a slower one, carrying two people. He launched three magical arrows toward it in rapid succession, guiding them in. But then Lagron lurched to the side, and Rain saw several large bolts whiz past them.

Pick new targets and fire as fast as you are able. We won't have time to guide most of them in, or even see if they hit.

Rain gritted his teeth, which had started to chatter in the chill air, as he acknowledged. He picked out a new target, fired two arrows, then found another, casting two more. He did that with three additional targets before they had completed their mad, piercing pass through the griffon ranks. Lagron rolled to level them out, still hawking Meris's tail. Rain looked back and up to see if they had done any damage. There wasn't much he could discern, but puffs of smoke appeared again among the griffons, waves of concussive sound hitting him a moment after each volley. Dozens of griffons had peeled off to pursue Meris and Lagron. The dragons ignored them, climbing swiftly as they carved a gentle arc in the lightening sky. Then they made a pass along the top of the mass of griffons, turning fully upside down.

Lagron increased his attack frequency as he and Meris began a complex weaving pattern. Rain tried to increase his own as well. Griffons soon swarmed them, and if not for Lagron's and Meris's expert maneuvering, they would soon have fallen. Rain saw two of his arrows make significant strikes, along with a fireball, and Lagron took out at least one griffon. Ileom and Meris did slightly better. Ileom was using one of the German guns, since his magic was less effective in the sky—and it was a big one. He had apparently learned quickly.

We're going to take a risk, announced Lagron. *We'll fly through the middle of their formation again and cause as much havoc as we can, but one of the German guns might hit us.* Rain could tell Lagron had been hurt, in at least two places, but he hadn't slowed at all.

Are you sure? asked Rain, remembering Ileom's stern warning.

Meris has already discussed it with Ileom.

Okay. I trust you.

He felt a warm response to that, but what else was he going to do but trust the dragons and Ileom?

The dragons must have used some magic to assist their climb in preparation for the dive, because Rain felt one of his leg straps start to come loose. He worried it might have torn. He shifted his mind from that problem, though, searching for targets as they plunged toward the griffons at incredible speed. Lagron spun, and Rain felt his mind enter another place. Time seemed to slow, and he was able to pick out more targets, launching volleys of fiery arrows at each one. He had another idea, too, based on his solo encounter with the German rebels. He compressed heat into tiny balls, then launched dozens of them as a cluster into a crowd of enemies before releasing his hold. A multitude of small explosions resulted, men and beasts screaming as heated blasts buffeted them. He wasn't sure how much damage he caused, but the way they dodged and then chaotically tried to counter told him they feared his attacks.

Rain and Lagron burst out of the fray and banked away from the village while the sounds of German guns from below intensified.

We need a brief respite, said Lagron. *We'll climb high, then loop around. How are you doing?*

Better than expected, Rain admitted, *but I'm already starting to feel tired. And there are so many of them.*

Yes, but we are thinning their numbers. The German guns have been effective, too. We need to keep harassing the griffons, prevent them from descending and destroying those guns.

All right. Are you or Meris hurt?

Barely. Ileom has taken a more serious wound from a gun. He reports he is still in fighting shape, though.

Rain hoped it wasn't bad, but he didn't have time to dwell on it. Sooner than expected, they made a spinning side swipe of the main formation, then came back around to observe teams of griffons diving toward the German gun emplacements. Gunfire erupted all around the attackers, and several were knocked from the sky, but the danger was serious.

Lagron and Meris descended and split up to launch a flurry of magical fire and ice toward the various groups. Rain joined in with his new fire swarms, noting torrents of snow, dirt, and other debris flying up from the ground. That would be Ileom, now that they were low enough.

They broke up most of the attacks, but a few got through, damaging several German guns. Battles commenced on the ground, too, intensifying as more attackers arrived by foot and horseback through the forest. Rain didn't spy any barbarians this time, just light-green-coated soldiers, all with guns. His eyes widened in amazement as a trio of trees burst apart, followed by a loud boom. Several enemy soldiers lay still in the patchy snow, and he glanced toward one of the defensive positions. A tank moved slowly, its upper piece rotating, massive gun repositioning as smoke wisped from its tip.

He didn't get to see it fire again, as the aerial battle continued anew, intensifying further, the enemy desperate to destroy those anti-aircraft guns. The tanks as well, which were shredding their troops on the ground. Rain could hardly believe all he was witnessing, but Lagron kept him focused on their mission, coordinating with Meris and Ileom.

A German gun almost knocked Rain and Lagron out of the sky. Although Rain blacked out for a moment, the blast likely saved them from a pair of griffons that had closed to within striking distance. Rain's eyes re-opened to see them fluttering helplessly before crashing into the ground. He looked about wildly, seeking targets.

Okay, guide your missiles now, said Lagron, *as much as you can given the distances. Most of the griffons are focused on the German guns. Our risk of getting hit will increase, but we need to take more of them out.*

Rain did as instructed, acquiring a pair of griffons carrying men with guns and bringing both down with larger arrows. Then he found a quad of slower griffons bearing Hearkendoom, downing two of them in similar fashion. He took a magical bolt to the shoulder, though, and another clipped one of Lagron's wings. Lagron finished the other two griffons off, ending that threat.

You were hit, he sent to Rain with obvious concern.

I'm ... he wanted to respond that he was okay, but he couldn't form the thought properly in his mind. The shock was already overpowering him, and he broke contact with Lagron to lean back and put a hand over the wound, which was seeping blood. Lagron rolled away, picking up speed so fast that everything became a blur.

Suddenly, it stopped. Were they on the ground, or was he dead? He couldn't tell. But within moments strong hands had loosened his straps and removed him from the saddle, setting him on the ground between Lagron and Meris, both crouching with necks arched toward the sky. He took in a sharp breath as he experienced a rush of energy, rising from an impossibly deep well. Ileom's magic, which wasn't healing, per se, but at least empowering.

He blinked as his mind started working again. Ileom stared down at him.

"That strike nearly took you. I've given your body some energy, but you need a healer. Lagron could do it, but dragon healing is slower, and the battle is getting hotter. Can you travel?"

Rain thought so, nodding.

"Good. Get to Antara and this Jerise. Then come back as quickly as you can. Meris and I will return to the fray. We're winning, but it's close."

With that, Ileom bounded back into his saddle, barely pausing to strap in before Meris jumped into the air. The sounds of battle had intensified, though they seemed more distant. Rain still had his ears wrapped, thankfully, but his mind remained sluggish.

He took out the key and slowly stood, then approached Lagron's now lowered head. "Okay, we need to get back to that dwarven village, by way of Earth." Lagron touched the key, and in a blink they stood in the clearing near the village. Rain glanced around, relief washing through him, and then he realized they hadn't traveled to Earth first. Or had they? Had that field flashed in his vision? He couldn't remember. All he knew was that he had wanted to come here, and the key responded. With Lagron's help, of course.

He climbed into the saddle, not feeling up to walking, and Lagron lifted them gently into the warm air, laden with scents of every kind of flower, bush, and tree he could imagine. In mere seconds they landed on the edge of Thysend. A young girl screamed when she saw them, and several people came running.

"Get Lady Antara!" Rain shouted, starting to slump in the saddle. Then he passed out.

∞

When he awoke, he felt fully refreshed. How amazing. Antara stood over his bed, situated in a narrow room with windows on either side.

"Jerise has incredible talent," she said. "Your wound was bad, and it was getting worse. I haven't seen anything quite like it."

"I got it from a Hearkendoom."

She pursed her lips. "Curious. And concerning. Where?"

"The ..." he tried to remember. "Grayshadow."

"The mountains?"

"Yes."

"How in the world did you get *there*?"

He shrugged. "Ileom is still there, with Meris. Fighting off griffons and rebels." He sat up suddenly. "How long was I out?"

"Minutes only."

Relief bloomed in his breast. "We have to return and help them."

"And how do we do that?" she asked, folding her arms.

"With Lagron's help, I can take us there ... um, more or less directly."

Her eyes widened. "Directly? Not to Earth first, and without a pause in between?"

"Yes. Well, I think so. And it's colder there."

She stared out one of the windows for a moment. "Of course. I will gather our fighting men, plus Jerise. You're certain you know exactly where to go?"

He nodded, suddenly feeling less sure. What if he messed up again, lost his focus, and dumped them in the ocean? He *wouldn't*, though. He couldn't. Ileom was counting on him. So was Jared. And Konrad and Gunther and the rest.

He was grateful he was still fully dressed ... and that no one had removed his boots. He hopped off the bed, then made his way out of the room, down some stairs, and onto a street in the village. After a quick walk to the plaza he found Lagron, surrounded by a crowd of adults and children. Rain couldn't tell if he was enjoying his celebrity status or not. As Rain approached, he realized he was intensely hungry. That made sense after a serious engagement.

He spotted one of the very first refugees to become part of their group.

"Ingris, can you bring me some food, please?"

The middle-aged woman gave a curtsy, which still made him uncomfortable, and hurried off with a smile.

Rain laid a hand on Lagron's neck, renewing the connection.

I have never seen people overcome their fear of me so quickly, said Lagron. *They have been through some harrowing trials recently.*

And they trust you, Rain.

I guess so.

He felt a … laugh, and then Lagron said, *They do. And you have clearly earned it.*

The discomfort returned.

"What's his name?" asked a young girl in the crowd. She was maybe six. He felt bad he couldn't remember her name, but he smiled at her.

"Lagron. He's a dragon. We don't have them on … I mean, they are very, very rare."

"Can I pet him?"

"Of course."

She stepped closer as Lagron bent his head toward her, making sure to keep his teeth hidden. She tentatively touched his snout, then beamed as she stroked it softly. Other children approached, and Rain felt pure joy through the link. He didn't have long to dwell on that, though, as Antara arrived with Jerise, Haran, Androl, and their other soldiers, including Garrett and Jervin, who glanced nervously at both Lagron and Rain.

"Do you need some armor?" asked Androl.

Rain looked down at his Earth clothes, the shirt singed and half shredded. The armor could be helpful. "Yes, please. A half-helm would be good, too … with a strap to keep it on in the air."

Never had he uttered such a statement. Androl glanced at Lagron, then nodded and turned back. A few seconds later, Ingris returned with a steaming plate of food. Before removing his hand from Lagron, Rain asked, *Do you need something to eat?*

Not right now, but thank you.

I'll feel bad with you watching me eat.

Don't. You need it. I'm fine. Trust me.

I do.

Strips of mutton, warm bread, vegetables, and even apples graced the plate. Rain relished every bit of it, feeling a surprised dismay when the dish was suddenly empty. His stomach didn't feel full yet. He thanked Ingris again, profusely, then turned his head as Androl approached from another direction, carrying mail, plate, greaves, and helm, all of a slightly golden color.

"We found some refined metals here, and the smiths have fashioned some fine equipment. It's strong and light."

"Hold on a moment." Antara stepped up and laid a hand on the plate as she closed her eyes. Rain saw her magic coalesce, then noted a slight sheen enveloping the armor. All of it. About a minute later she announced, "There. Now your armor has some magical protection as well. Against the Hearkendoom, it may be needed."

"Thank you," said Rain. He donned the armor pieces, starting with the mail, all of which was indeed lighter than expected. Then he led their traveling group outside the village a good hundred paces before withdrawing the key and turning to Antara.

"Okay, are you ready?"

She nodded, her mask of confidence cracked in places. Part of that might have been worry for Ileom, and Rain shared that concern. He placed a hand on Lagron as the dragon's snout touched the key, and he focused harder than he ever had. He had to get this right.

After a slightly alarming pause, they traveled, popping out in the middle of the plaza in the German town. Sounds of battle assaulted them, and Rain noted the men stationed on the roofs behind spike barriers firing furiously into the air as griffons swooped low, their riders bringing their own weapons to bear. Several of the old Germans had already succumbed, but most fought on. That gave him some hope.

Antara seemed to assess the situation instantly. An old man tottered out of a building pointing a weapon at her, but a quirk of an eyebrow avoided disaster there. That and seeing Lagron.

"Jerise," she said, "get inside with Haran. Find out who's in charge of the infirmary and begin healing. Androl, set a perimeter around whatever building they end up in, coordinating with the locals here."

After they were gone, Antara looked at Rain. "We will both fit in that saddle, correct?"

Rain glanced at the saddle, mouth slightly ajar. "Um, yes. But are you sure?"

"Yes. I can provide protection while you and Lagron fight. You're not experienced enough to do defense and offense at the same time. The battle has arrived at this town. I assume that is bad."

Rain gulped, then nodded. "Yes, it is."

"All right then, let's go."

Rain mounted first, then helped her up behind him. He worked out how to secure both their legs, but the weakened strap needed attention before he was sure it would hold; he used most of its extra length as reinforcement. Before leaning forward he explained briefly that he and Lagron could communicate if they were in physical contact. She accepted that revelation without comment, the determination in her eyes deepening.

When they were set, Lagron launched them upward into the chaotic battlespace. Antara surveyed the situation and calmly called out observations, but Rain had to settle himself. As her shields went out to block various attacks, he and Lagron responded, guiding their own strikes home. It was beautifully effective, and Rain wished they had brought her here from the start. He and Lagron began shredding the griffons' advance, until so many focused on them they had to retreat, going high. Rain noted that the German guns launching the bursts into the air had largely gone silent. He also realized he no longer had his ear wrap. His ears felt fine, though—another magical gift from Antara, probably.

As he scanned the skies, he reached out to Lagron. *Where are Meris and Ileom?*

I cannot sense Meris's presence here, and I would know if she had died. Perhaps they had to depart, as we did. He didn't seem overly concerned, but Rain was. He turned to Antara, barely able to twist his neck enough in the armor to see her.

"Ileom and Meris have left. Lagron can't find them."

"Nothing we can do about it," she replied after the briefest of pauses. "We must keep fighting. Find a weak spot we can exploit."

It wasn't hard to locate opportunities, and Rain felt their collective resolve grow. Lagron dove, and they launched a brief barrage before breaking away, then suddenly spinning back for a quick strike at a large group in pursuit. Antara's shields shifted in scintillating patterns with impossibly swift precision, and Rain noted the enemy spreading out more, trying to envelope them on all sides. They drifted farther from the town, leaving it to its own defenses, but with Antara's encouragement—and Lagron's—they danced in determined grace through the air, taking out riders, gunners, Hearkendoom, and griffons alike. After several minutes of intense action, Rain knew he couldn't last much longer, and he sensed Lagron's growing exhaustion as well. He turned again to Antara. "We should return to the village. Your shields will help them there."

Antara nodded, creases of exhaustion limning her own eyes. Lagron wheeled toward the village, then made a series of stomach-turning maneuvers to bring them safely to the plaza. Rain was shocked he didn't throw up, but perhaps he would experience a delayed reaction after the adrenaline subsided. Upon landing, he loosened the straps and helped Antara to the ground. Her eyes stayed focused overhead the entire time, shields forming constantly at various spots to blunt griffon attacks. One griffon with a wounded wing landed heavily nearby. Lagron turned on it with a fury of wings, claws, and teeth that nearly sent Rain to his backside. The griffon and its rider died quickly.

Rain focused again on the skies, and with his feet underneath him he felt some renewed strength. He launched a series of attacks at various targets, working around Antara's shields. The remaining men on the rooftops got in some effective shots as well, causing the griffon assault to falter.

Rain jumped as a loud roar sounded from behind him. He spun as one of the tanks rumbled into the plaza at high speed, then skidded to a halt, tearing up the fine cobblestones. The man sticking out of the top turned its smaller guns skyward and began firing at an incredible rate. Since he couldn't see Antara's shields, some of his bullets died in the air. Antara noticed him, though, and Rain watched as she tried to keep her shields out of his line of fire. Several more griffons fell, until one gave a unique, high-pitched scream. The rest turned and retreated, lifting higher into the sky and away from the village.

It wasn't over, though, Rain was certain. Ileom was gone, the defenders few, the battle lines very close. The enemy would regroup.

He looked at Antara. "They'll attack again soon."

"I know," she said. "We have to get out of here using your key. As many of us as possible. It's the only way. We've won a partial victory. We've bloodied them, given them something to think about, slowed them down, bought a little time."

"We can talk to the people in the command center. I know which building."

"You go. I need to stay here to assist the defenders, just in case. Godspeed, Rain. And don't disappear this time." She winked, which seemed so odd in the moment he stumbled as he turned.

He found Jared in the command center, along with Weldrin, Gunther, and just two others, one of them conducting an animated conversation on the radio … in German, apparently.

"I've brought another member of the Order," he said. "Her name is Lady Antara. Ileom and Meris had to leave the battlefield. I don't know why. Antara recommends we leave as well, as many of us as possible, using my talisman, before the enemy regroups and attacks again."

Weldrin studied him a moment, taking in his fine, battle-marked armor. She was clearly listening with one ear to the urgent radio conversation as well. When a pause came, she glanced at the operator. "Can they get here, or do they need to head for the old mountain hideouts?"

The man shook his head. "The mountains."

"Give the order, then. They have suffered enough, and there is a window now."

The man nodded sharply, then talked into the equipment as Weldrin looked at Rain. "We are almost beaten, as you correctly surmised." She rose. "They are too numerous, and many of us have fallen. Help us salvage some of this equipment. We'll destroy what we can't take with us. Gunther, get your men to gather supplies and sensitive gear; documents as well. Bring it all to the plaza." She raised an eyebrow at Rain, and he nodded.

Another storm of activity commenced as the Germans and their Tenrisian friends organized the evacuation. Time was of the essence, with Antara showing up in various places, enjoining people to move faster. At last, after another tank had rumbled into the plaza and the last of the surviving men had come down off the roofs, Rain stood with Antara, Lagron, Haran, Jerise, Androl, Gunther, Weldrin, Jared, Garrett, Jervin, and about forty others amid a multitude of crates, barrels, duffels, and assorted pieces of equipment. The assemblage nearly filled the plaza, which, while not large, wasn't small, either. Konrad was noticeably absent, and that affected Rain more than he would have thought. As he forced back tears, he began to doubt if he and Lagron could transport everyone and everything, but there was no time to debate it. A griffon battle cry sounded. The enemy approached.

He touched Lagron, holding out the key with his other hand.

Okay, he said, *this is a big one. We can do it, right?*

Yes, we can, came the response. *Your fortitude grows. That is good.*

Rain focused, feeling the powers swirling inside the talisman in a way he hadn't achieved before. They seemed sharper and more organized. Lagron touched the key, and Rain triggered the travel, the space around them seeming to expand and then collapse, all in a heartbeat.

He opened his eyes. He had brought them to the field on Earth. And something wet was running down his neck. Then he collapsed.

Ileom had directed Agrancik's key to transport them to the aerie, the safest place he knew on Alave. Meris had somehow healed his gunshot wound over the last two days, just as she had the crossbow injury, but it had taken much of her remaining strength. Her skill at healing was minor, she had explained, though better than Lagron's. He sensed pride in that. She had been hurt, too, in several places. She assured him she would recover. She just needed to rest. And by rest, she meant hibernate. Her impression was vague on the length of time it would take. A few days? A week or two? As for himself, he didn't need to worry about water, but food would become an issue. Before casting off into her hibernation, she had told him where a small village was situated, about two thousand feet below their lofty perch. They could help him, she had been sure. He would have to make that trek today.

Agrancik would know the key had returned to Alave, and with the book he would be able to determine its general location—a recent and useful discovery. Ileom's supposed ally in the Order would surely wish to investigate, but how long would it take him to reach this spot? And would he bring others with him? Worries about betrayal gnawed at Ileom. He had dealt with such things before, but never with so much hanging in the balance and so many moving pieces.

He leaned his head back against Meris's side, sheltered under one of her great wings as a light snow fell. She barely breathed, though her body still generated all the heat he needed to remain there, comfortably. He closed his eyes and began to recite various passages of Jeverian scripture, pondering applications to his present circumstances. He hadn't been doing that as often as he should. He paused often in the recitation to pray, concern for his friends and allies driving his words. His new friends of the German colony occupied a prime place. How had they fared? Had Rain returned with Antara? The enemy forces were much larger than he could have anticipated, which engendered even wider worries.

He also considered anew how different he felt when praying. He was fully aware that he had rough edges, that he could be short with people, as well as highly demanding. But his purpose was to get things done, and he tried to let God use his abilities. If God ever tired of his ways, he would let him know, wouldn't he? Would Ileom recognize it if he did?

He chided himself for such enervating thoughts. He didn't have time for them, even secluded in an aerie with a sleeping dragon for who knew how long. He needed to make plans for when he returned to Tenris. General Inzeal and his Tahn Arganda invasion force were close to launching their assault—that was certain. They had somehow procured *hundreds* of griffons from Alave, and if all of Sheraya wasn't with them, some or all of the Hearkendoom were, which meant Queen Givyren was either all-in with Inzeal or trying to play both sides. Had she secretly convinced any other nations to support her, even conditionally?

The Order had been actively working with all of Rega's leaders to unite the continent, including the tempestuous Sherayan monarch, but they had just lost one of their number—two, really—to assassins. That made the rest more cautious … a clear secondary objective of the strike inside the Keep. Inzeal was a shrewd man. And utterly ruthless. Ileom still didn't even know what he looked like. Soon, hopefully. If Ileom could get close enough to him … well, the world would be a better place without General Inzeal. Emperor Creegan of The Golden Empire as well, who gave Inzeal his financing and manpower.

Who would replace *them*, though? Always a troubling question, but at least the world would get a reprieve. And then … what the people really needed was an Awakening, a return to God, an embrace of accountability and moral behavior, a strong and pure desire for freedom and fair treatment. Many godless tyrants stalked the land, and people turned far too easily toward these supposedly wise leaders to 'save' them—from terrors real or imagined—only to be abused. The cycle never seemed to end, though one day it would. In his lifetime or not, he couldn't say, but the promise was sure.

He dozed off for a while, until his ears caught a voice on the swirling winds. His eyes snapped open, his mind instantly alert. Meris hadn't stirred.

He swung his feet beneath him and got to one knee, listening as he checked his new weapon, courtesy of the Germans. He had little ammunition left—maybe thirty rounds—including only two five-round magazines he could quickly switch out to keep the bolt-action Mauser firing. He had a sword, too, and his magic. Plus the high ground on whoever might be approaching. Unless it was griffons, of course.

He stepped out from under Meris's wing, bracing himself against the biting chill as he moved toward the edge of the aerie. The voices faded, but he could distinguish two people making their way up the narrow, perilous path. Why that path even existed was a mystery. He would have to ask Meris, but he guessed it related to times past when human and dragon cooperation was more common. Or more treacherous: some humans had surely sought to steal dragon eggs. He would have bet all the money in this world on it.

He made sure he had a round chambered, amazed the new terminology came so quickly to his mind, then took a position at the edge of the aerie that gave him a clear view of the final leg of the path.

Within a minute, the two forms came into his vision again, heavily bundled. They had taken several more steps before he got a good glimpse of their faces—Agrancik and Lady Brentia. She didn't seem as elegant in this climate. Nobody would … except maybe Antara. Both labored, their breathing heavy after the long climb.

They paused, and Ileom called down, in Regan Common, "I see you. Why have you come?"

Agrancik looked up, eyes searching until they found Ileom, then widening a little. "I have come because of you and the key, of course." A gust batted him, and he wobbled.

"And Lady Brentia?"

Agrancik turned to her and spoke softly in their language, and she replied, "I seek news of my husband."

"He has not returned?" Ileom asked, switching tongues.

Her eyes hardened. "He has not."

"Proceed up into the aerie. Stay away from Meris."

They continued along the path, following the final winding turn that let them climb the last few feet. They stared a few moments at the rock-still Meris but made no immediate comment, moving to stand near Ileom, who held the rifle loosely, though he could bring it to bear in an instant.

"Lagron, I take it, is missing, too?" asked Lady Brentia.

"I do not know where he is," said Ileom, evading specifics.

"What is that?" asked Agrancik, pointing.

Ileom glanced at the rifle. "An artifact I picked up." He backed up a step and sat on an inner edge of the aerie, motioning for them to do the same.

Lady Brentia's gaze wandered to Meris. "She sleeps deeply. Is she healing?"

Again, Ileom didn't directly answer her question. "If you touch her, you will die." He hadn't expected his voice to sound quite so fierce, but so be it.

Her head snapped to him, eyes filled with offense. "That is *my* dragon."

"She is nobody's dragon. Neither is Lagron."

Her eyes narrowed, but fear edged in from the corners. "Do you know what happened to my husband? I have sent inquiries to Sistrayn but have received no replies."

Ileom nearly growled his response. "We were together when I was betrayed and nearly killed. Meris and Lagron rescued me, brought me here."

"But not my husband?"

"Perhaps they tried but were unsuccessful."

She searched his eyes as if she didn't believe him.

Ileom reverted to Regan Common to address Agrancik again. "Any idea why someone here would want me dead? I presume it must have something to do with the key I bear."

Agrancik frowned deeply. "No, I don't. This is troubling. I thought we could trust Taryn and Juless and their court. I may have been mistaken. And I may have underestimated how widespread this contamination from Tenris has become."

Who was contaminating whom—or if it was mutual—was a question for another time. "General Inzeal. Is his name known here?"

"No, but it is clear his emissaries have visited several leaders."

"Oh? With what message?"

"That invaders are preparing to attack various kingdoms here, and that the invasion might be prevented with a pre-emptive strike."

"What proof do they offer?"

"They have brought back strange weapons, perhaps like the one you hold, demonstrating them to cause great fear, claiming these will be used against the people of Alave."

"When *they* are the ones seeking to start a war with these weapons?" Ileom wasn't surprised, but his anger began boiling again.

Agrancik nodded. "Yes. They have also presented two captured High Priests of New Haven. These men have testified that armies are already consolidating control on Tenris so that they can move on Alave and turn the entire planet into a slave colony."

"Humph. Puppets under duress. And the leaders here believe such histrionic nonsense?"

Agrancik gave a distressed shrug. "Some do. Enough to cause serious problems. You must remember that outside of a handful of us, nobody on Alave knew any other worlds existed besides our own. The leaders who are falling under Inzeal's sway disguise their actions to their people as a response to other nations, both on this continent and across the sea, but eventually the truth will come out … as it will everywhere."

Ileom glared at him for several seconds, hands twitching on the gun. "And how did you address this with *your* queen?" His curiosity burned hot to hear Agrancik's answer.

"I had to confide in her all that I have been doing, explaining the full truth of the matter. She has trusted me in the past, and I believe I made some progress."

Ileom grunted. "Progress? I hope so, since I have been unsuccessful so far in stopping any of the flow of war griffons to Tenris. Meris was wounded in battle with them in the Grayshadow, though she is recovering. My wounds have been healed."

Agrancik's eyes widened, shifting momentarily to Meris. "How many did you face?"

"Over a hundred."

He stared in disbelief, then blinked hard. "How did you even get there? And then back *here*?"

Ileom gave a small shrug. "There is more to the dragons than I could have guessed."

Agrancik angled his eyebrows. Ileom could tell he wanted to explore that topic. "What do we tell Lady Brentia?"

"Do you still trust her?" challenged Ileom.

"Yes, I do."

Ileom pondered that, glaring at her until she looked away. "Tell her the truth, then. The basics, anyway. I don't know if Jehorim was involved in trying to capture or kill me, but I am clearly being hunted here. And tell her I need some food."

"I have a little I can give you. We can bring more from the village."

"You have the book with you as well?"

"Of course."

Ileom nodded in further contemplation. "What more can we do on Alave right now?"

Agrancik shook his head. "Without bringing this to our Council on Tenris, and providing more proof to leaders here, not much. That is one reason I brought Lady Brentia. She may be helpful."

"And you're *certain* you can trust her."

"As much as anyone. Her husband, too … though I know you might not feel that way."

"Very well. Then we travel, to the Keep. And we take Meris with us."

Agrancik raised his eyebrows. "Are you sure that is wise?"

"I'm not sure of anything. And I can't ask Meris's opinion at the moment."

"You can't … *what?*"

"It will wait for the Council." He could tell Lady Brentia was becoming perturbed at not being able to understand the conversation. He also didn't care.

"Very well," said Agrancik. He wriggled out of the straps of his small backpack and brought it around to rummage through it, bringing out the book. Every time Ileom saw it, he marveled at its simplistic beauty. It wasn't large, the cover not overly ornate, but the colors were so vivid, the edges precise and unblemished. Enchantments had kept it in pristine condition over countless centuries. Antara had tried to study them, without much success so far.

"Stay here," said Ileom as he got up. "I will stand next to Meris as you read, with a hand on her side."

"Is that … necessary?"

"Probably not."

"Very well."

Agrancik gave Lady Brentia a quick explanation of what was about to take place as Ileom walked over to Meris. When he laid a hand on her shoulder, he felt a remote sense of peace, but nothing else. After about a minute, he extracted and gripped the key, training his gaze on the pair from Alave. Lady Brentia's eyes were twin white moons, and she trembled a little. Agrancik cleared his throat and began the narration from the book. Ileom followed the words as best he could given his lack of expertise in that particular ancient language, ready to drop the key and seal off his magic if his ally tried to read something that sounded off. Since the person reading the book chose the destination, worry spiked as Agrancik reached the end of the required passages. The only thing left was to pronounce the name of the place.

Relief washed through Ileom as Agrancik spoke the proper words and they were transported into the special room in the Keep dedicated to such travels, Meris included. She didn't stir. He wasn't worried about her; he would have guards posted, and she would remain undisturbed.

"Lead on," he said, motioning to Agrancik and Lady Brentia. The Alavian woman stood marveling at the sudden change of scenery, including wide windows looking out on a completely different set of mountains. Agrancik got her attention and led them from the room, Ileom falling in behind. He was famished, but he could worry about that later. "To the Council chamber," he directed, and Agrancik picked up the pace.

Several floors higher, they arrived at the broad hallway of soaring arches fronting the Council chamber's stately double doors, where a patrolling guard informed them the Council was not in session. Ileom gave the man one of his infamous scowls, causing him to flinch slightly. "Issue the call to order *now*, whoever is present in the Keep, by my authorization. And have a four-man team placed outside the Travel Room. They are not to look inside."

The guard saluted smartly and called for a backup, who emerged from a doorway a short distance away, hustling into place so the first guard could be on his errands.

Ileom took the lead then, drawing their small group inside the Council chamber, with its towering and impossibly thick glass windows overlooking a majestic wintry landscape. Tall curtains draped at the sides, purple trimmed in gold. The sun was midway to its setting amid mostly clear skies, the south-facing apertures capturing its brilliance. Thirty high-backed chairs surrounded a massive oval table made of the finest oak in the center of the room. Gleaming sconces set high in the walls could bathe the room in a warm light, though magical illumination was normally used when the Council met. Ileom himself could barely manage such a thing, and only in a much smaller space. That wasn't his talent.

"Have a seat," he said to Agrancik and Lady Brentia in their native tongue, then felt his hunger again. He peeked outside the door, looking at the new guard. "Have some food brought to the Council chambers, for three people." The man acknowledged, then went through the same procedure to call another backup before fulfilling the task.

Ileom chose a chair almost directly across from the two Alavians, who sat together conversing quietly. Agrancik was explaining the bare minimum about where they were. Ileom tapped fingers on the table as he listened.

Markydis Helstra from Vriesland was the new, rotating head of the Council following Avrenor's untimely death, and he entered the room first, unaccompanied by guards. He closed the door, eyes taking in each of them, pausing the longest on Lady Brentia.

He looked at Ileom. "You have important news to share with the Council?"

Ileom stood respectfully, noting the anxious tone of the question.

"I do," he said carefully, "and some of it is good."

Markydis gave a rueful chuckle. "Which means most of it is bad. I know you too well, Master Ileom."

Blast it, that he did. Ileom liked Markydis. He was more honest than most, and the former cattle rancher wasn't great at hiding things. Apparently, neither was he.

"How many of the Council are here?" asked Ileom.

"Only four of us," Markydis replied with a short sigh. "Thirena, who still recovers slowly despite the best healing we've been able to apply, Nashterikii, and Eliefhim. The rest are visiting various leaders across Rega, furthering the unification work."

"Will Thirena be able to attend?"

"Yes, I believe so."

"And who is calling on Queen Givyren?"

Markydis paused, eyes narrowing in worry. "Oldin and Trinsa."

"You should have sent Santiamen."

"He is Jeverian."

"That shouldn't matter."

"It does to the queen."

"Is it that bad now?"

"I fear so, yes. Where is Antara? We would have sent her with Oldin, instead of Trinsa."

Ileom grunted. "If all is going according to plan, which is a shambles now, she is fighting for her life somewhere. And hopefully winning. I had to leave that fight before she arrived. Members of the Hearkendoom were involved. Some of them have become quite skilled."

Markydis squeezed his eyes shut for a moment, then re-opened them, seeming to notice for the first time the butt and barrel of the German rifle peeking out from behind Ileom's back, secured by the strap across his chest. "You made further contact with our reclusive friends, I see."

"Yes. Their challenge is difficult."

Markydis stepped to the side as a knock came at one of the doors, which opened a second later to admit the three other Council members. Thirena brought up the rear, utilizing a cane to walk. She gave Ileom a long, meaningful look. She clearly feared more traitors in their midst.

Ileom resumed his seat after everyone but Markydis had found a chair. Their leader then sat, folding his hands on the table. "We convene under grave circumstances," he began, "and there is much to consider. But first, we must meet our guest. Agrancik?"

Agrancik nodded. "This is Lady Brentia, from my home world. She has ties to several powerful families there, and things are not as … stable as I believed they were. The arrival of war griffons is only one manifestation of that."

"But only a few have arrived," said Eliefhim with a glance at Ileom.

"Hundreds now," corrected Ileom, causing Eliefhim to blanch slightly. "I have seen them, and killed at least three dozen … with some help."

"Continue," said Markydis, gesturing to Agrancik.

"Yes, well, Lady Brentia can help us make inroads with some of the leaders of Alave. Many regents already know of the existence of this planet … primarily, I am sad to say, through ambassadors sent by Emperor Creegan and General Inzeal. We will need to reveal the nature and purpose of the Order, and how long we've known about the awakening of the Crossroads, along with their prophesied purpose. Most can be persuaded to support us, I believe." He had neglected to mention how much he had already disclosed to his own queen without the Council's concurrence. That was concerning, especially since the highest council of the Order was supposed to be above such petty or calculated dishonesty, whether intra- or inter-planet. Not that Ileom himself was perfect in that regard, of course.

"Does she know our language?" asked Nashterikii.

"No. A few phrases. And she has no magical abilities. Those are rare on my planet, as I've explained. Even mine are limited compared to yours."

"So," said Markydis, "you brought her here so we could meet her, yet none of us can talk to her directly. Maybe Ileom, a little. It will be difficult to approve any proposal involving her." The insinuation was clear. Markydis and Agrancik didn't have the closest of relationships, but such open distrust was destructive—another casualty of the assassination.

Agrancik didn't let on that he noticed, his expression implying he was consumed by worry for his home world. Ileom understood better now why he should be. All three planets hung precariously above a pit of consuming fire. Even Earth, though he couldn't contemplate how. He just knew.

"I understand," acknowledged Agrancik, "but we have little time. I will teach her, and I will translate. We will meet with each of you personally. Master Ileom knows my language quite well, by the way. He even surprised *me*."

Ileom winced a little inside. He hadn't let on how much he had been studying, so now Markydis would suspect him, too. Which made Ileom a hypocrite for wanting more honesty, while creating more issues to fix. "We must open the Vault," he growled, giving each of the other Council members a hard glare in quick succession. A hushed silence fell. Those words hadn't been uttered in more than a hundred years; hadn't been acted upon for nearly two hundred.

After a long, deep silence, Markydis replied, "That will not be easy, as you well know. And the benefits—if any—will take time to develop. There is much inside with which we are wholly unfamiliar."

"Agreed. All the more reason to start now."

"We do not have a quorum to make such a decision. More Council members must agree."

Ileom was familiar with the rules, but surely, given the circumstances, they could agree to act. The others would understand. He took a deep breath. "If we all agree here, today, we can open it. And if a majority of the others disagree with that action, I offer my life as forfeit."

Such a dire proposal was almost unheard of, and it had an impact. Markydis and the others appeared to give it serious thought. After a glance around the table, Markydis replied, "I realize time is of the essence, but we cannot be too hasty. We can discuss it further, then contemplate individually and re-convene tomorrow to make a decision. Is that agreeable?"

Everyone but Ileom—and Lady Brentia, of course—said "Aye."

Ileom finally nodded his assent. "Aye."

"A rebel sniper must have gotten off a shot just before we left," said Gunther as he knelt next to Jerise, who attended with desperate haste to Rain. She wiped tears from her eyes, occasionally letting a sob escape.

Antara studied the boy's—no, the man's—face. Such strength, even if he wasn't always confident in it. They couldn't afford to lose him. "I didn't hear it," she noted.

"The bullet hit before we heard the sound—that's how close the timing was."

Yes, that made sense. If they had traveled just a second sooner!

"It appears to have missed both spine and carotid artery, or perhaps just nicked them," said Gunther. "That is fortunate."

Antara wanted to ask Jerise if that was true, but she let her concentrate. If anyone could save Rain, it was her. Unfortunately, she was extremely fatigued and obviously dismayed. She adored Rain; hopefully that would be more help than hindrance.

Antara removed herself as a distraction, stepping away to check on the rest of the group. She had already retrieved the talisman from the ground where Rain had unexpectedly collapsed, and it felt cold in her hands. Forebodingly so.

Their eccentric ensemble nearly filled the culvert of the Earth field, invisible from any houses or roads as far as she could tell. And now what? She pondered as she made a slow circuit, noting that everyone else seemed whole and hale. When she returned to the small cluster around Rain, she got Lagron's attention and held up the key. He blinked at her, then touched it with his snout. She felt nothing, so she didn't need the shake of his head to know they couldn't travel without Rain. The attunement of this key was more permanent than she had thought—something else the Order must study further.

She turned to Jared, standing with his hands in his pockets as he gazed at Rain. His expression was completely devoid of life. "Jared." He started, then looked at her. "We need to make contact with someone here. Can you find that woman you came with?"

His blank stare reminded her of the density of the language barrier, and she tapped Gunther on the shoulder. He stood and turned, then interpreted her request.

"Yes," Jared said, then added, "Now?"

Gunther interpreted for Antara, and she nodded. It was daytime, but gray clouds blanketed the sky, occasionally sprinkling them, so she wasn't sure what time it was. Jared scrambled out of the culvert and disappeared. When she could no longer hear him, she tested her magic. Yes, she could create shields and use the air as a weapon at close range. Even create some camouflage, which she must assume might be needed. But what if the people of Earth decided to attack them in force? And what would they think of these very old Germans and their machinery? It almost made her laugh. Or scream.

She found a reasonably dry place on the ground to sit and relax. The 'tank' drivers had powered down their machines, and there was little talking. The focus was on Rain and Jerise. Haran hovered over his ward's shoulder, mumbling to himself. Antara put her elbows on her knees and her face in her hands. It felt good to close her eyes. She tried to slow her mind, but it wouldn't cooperate. Their predicament was too complex to measure, and she kept thinking about Rain. She admitted she had grown close—perhaps

CROSSROADS OF AWAKENING MEMORY

too close—to that boy. *Man*, she reminded herself again. He was likeable, and also smarter and more competent than he gave himself credit for. Most people she interacted with paled in comparison. Ileom was different than all of them, of course. He didn't overestimate his own competence … he was just *extremely* competent. And gruff, except toward her. She allowed herself a small smile, hidden as it was by her hands.

She finally lowered her head onto her knees, wrapping arms around shins. Not a projection of strength, but she needed to relax. She didn't sleep, but as the minutes passed, she could hear others trying to make themselves comfortable—mostly soldiers, who knew how to grab whatever sleep they could, whenever they could. Haran continued his mumbling, while Androl assigned his men to take up positions at the edge of the culvert to watch for anyone approaching. Weldrin added some of her people to that mix after getting a brief update from Gunther.

Antara's mind had just started to drift when she felt a tap on her arm. She lifted her head to see Androl filling her vision. The light had waned considerably, and the air carried a chill.

"Yes, Androl?"

"Jerise has finished. Rain is still sleeping."

She straightened her back. "And he will be all right?"

"Jerise thinks so. Also, Jared has returned."

"What? Already?" She scrambled to her feet and cast her eyes about to find him, which was difficult in the growing dimness.

"Yes. He brought the woman who visited, along with a man."

"Did I fall asleep?"

"Yes."

"And you didn't wake me?"

He shrugged, clearly uncomfortable. "Um, I thought you needed rest, m'lady."

She smoothed bodice and skirt and ran fingers through her hair. "Well, I suppose I did. Take me to them."

She followed as Androl weaved his way through dozing German soldiers, most snoring loudly enough to wake a hunting cat twenty miles away.

Perhaps in their younger days they slept lighter and quieter, especially in the field. Few stirred as she passed.

Just below the edge of the fold, Jared stood with Hannah and a man whose stance seemed protective of her. "Get Gunther," she said to Androl.

"Yorel is already retrieving him."

"Good." They stopped within three feet of the trio, and Antara gave a deep curtsy, feeling it appropriate as an extraterrestrial visitor.

"Hannah, it is good to see you again." She didn't know how much of that Hannah would understand, but the woman beamed, her eyes wide with wonder.

"I cannot believe you are here," she said in Regan Common, and while her accent still needed much work, it wasn't as awful as before. Had she continued studying their language? Why? And *how*?

"We intended only to pass through, but Rain has been wounded."

Hannah scrunched her eyebrows, trying to work out the meaning. "Rain is … hurt?"

"Yes." Just then Gunther arrived, bleary eyes taking them all in. He addressed Antara.

"These people are from Earth?"

Antara nodded as Hannah blurted out, "Yes, we are. My name is Hannah. My brother"—she patted the man's arm next to her—"is Gavin."

Gunther gave a welcoming nod, then switched to English. "You are Americans?"

Hannah's eyes widened again, her whole body convulsing slightly. "You speak *English*?"

Gunther gave a small shrug. "It has been a long time, and it is a complicated story. I am from Germany, and my people have been living on Tenris for many years. My name is Gunther."

Hannah looked at Jared, smiling and narrowing her eyes. "You purposely kept this from us."

Jared seemed to fake a sheepish look, and then he laughed, the first time Antara had heard him do so. Of course, he would be happy to see his home, wouldn't he?

Gavin was staring hard into the darkness, and his eyes suddenly popped. "Are those ... *tanks?*"

Gunther turned to follow his gaze. "Yes. We have two Panzer IVs. We used to have many more, and even a pair of Panthers. No Tigers, though. Those were far too heavy, anyway."

Gavin looked at him in slack-jawed perplexity. "From World War II?"

Gunther nodded, then placed his hands behind his back. "Thankfully, we somehow escaped that foolish war started by our mad Führer. Until we met Jared, we did not know who won. We are glad ... ahem ... that it was not us."

Gavin frowned, obviously flummoxed, and then Hannah asked Gunther, "Do you need our help? You said Rain is wounded, and you're stuck out in this field. Can ... can I see him?"

Antara placed a hand on Gunther's shoulder. He jerked, then apologized and translated all that had just been said. She pondered the wisdom of taking them to see Rain, then finally nodded. "Yes. He has been healed, but he is still sleeping."

"I think I understand," said Hannah in Common. "Magic." As Antara turned to lead them, Gavin pulled something from a pocket and a bright, white beam of light shot from its tip, aimed at the ground ahead of him. She sensed no sorcery, so it was ... technology of some kind? As long as he didn't point it in the air, it shouldn't be visible from far. Not to be outdone, she gathered light from a wide area, enough to form a beam of her own, projecting from just below her neck. That elicited the proper impressed response from Gavin and Hannah. Then she led the way to Rain.

She hadn't anticipated that Lagron would now be curled up around him, and she heard twin gasps as they neared. She turned quickly, hands raised, her beam of light winking out. "Don't be alarmed. That is his dragon."

Hannah blinked, not understanding. She looked at Gunther, who said, "I don't remember the word for this creature in English, I'm sorry." He let Antara know what he'd told her, and then Hannah whispered, "Dragon."

"Yes," said Gunther with an exaggerated nod. "Yes, that's it. Dragon."

Gavin's light traveled tentatively along Lagron's body, finally reaching his head. When Lagron snapped an eye open, Gavin dropped his light object, which continued to shine as it lay on the ground.

Gunther took a small step toward them. "This beast is intelligent, and he is an ally. A friend. He is … hmmm … linked somehow with Rain. They brought us here."

"Yes," broke in Jared. "He's friendly. I mean, if he's on your side. I've seen him fight. He's awesome." He gave a boyishly exuberant laugh. Gavin and Hannah glanced at each other, both swallowing, as Gunther translated. So, it seemed there were no dragons on Earth. Or at least not any longer.

Camp stools suddenly appeared, supplied by some of the old German soldiers who had awakened. Gavin picked up his light, hand trembling a little, keeping it aimed at the ground and away from Lagron.

Once they were all sitting, Antara spoke. "Let us discuss further. Gunther, you can translate as necessary, though Hannah seems to understand most of what I say."

Gunther nodded, and Antara studied Hannah. She was pretty, and about her age. Maybe a little older. Her clothes were odd, of course, and her hair was plain, but they were on *her* planet. "We cannot stay here. As soon as Rain is recovered enough, we must return. All is not well on Tenris. War has already begun."

Hannah squinted in intense concentration, obviously trying to work out the full meaning. Antara had tried to speak slowly and clearly.

"War … fighting?"

Antara nodded, and Hannah glanced at Gunther. "These Germans are helping?"

"Yes," Antara answered, "they are valuable allies, but they are few."

Gunther added, in English and then Common, "Many of our children and grandchildren on Tenris have rebelled against us. They are working with an implacable enemy who are much like Adolf Hitler's fanatical followers, trying to subdue everyone to their will and create a 'perfect' society ruled by an elite few. They have summoned allies from a third planet, who ride beasts which are enemies of the dragons."

"A *third* planet?"

Gunther shrugged.

Hannah's expression became a mixture of fright and wonder as Gavin shook his head in disbelief. But determination began to assert itself. She turned to her brother and started speaking rapidly in English. Gunther translated for Antara as best he could.

"This is like a fantasy movie, Gavin, but it's real. You've been telling me something big is coming, but that you couldn't define it. I blew you off. You and your Service buddies. I even made fun of you. I'm sorry. Is this it? Are we supposed to help them? There are three planets involved, and you saw a small example of the magic at least some of them wield. Plus a freaking *dragon*. What if we don't help? Or what if we do?"

Gavin's eyes danced behind his beam of light, taking in the camp again, at least twice. "I was beginning to think maybe I was just going crazy, but yes, this has to be it. Or part of it. Those are real Panzer tanks, with no tracks leading in. I believe the old man's story, at least the little he's told of it so far. And the lady's."

Hannah's head bobbed in excitement. "Our world is linked directly with another world, Gavin, maybe two other worlds. Inhabited by humans. Our parents taught us there were other worlds, that God didn't have just one. I thought maybe I believed that, but it sounded too surreal, right? Now it doesn't. And I've *been* to one of them. Jared has, too. We almost got killed by a griffon. That must be the other type of flying beast Gunther mentioned." She glanced over at Jared, who was listening intently. He gave a terrified nod.

Hannah grabbed Gavin's wrist. "Can you find out who owns this field and talk to them? I don't know how much you'll be able to tell them, but I don't think getting the authorities involved yet is wise. And this part of the field isn't planted, so we aren't damaging the crop."

He gave her a wry grin. "So, you're *against* handing a dragon over to the 'authorities'? Something strange really *is* happening." She gave him a light slap on the arm, but Antara had to wait for Gunther's translation to catch up to understand why. Then she grinned.

Hannah addressed her in Common. "It would be … dangerous … to tell our, um, leaders. For now. But we can bring food, and try to make sure this place is safe for you."

"You are very kind. Thank you."

"Where do you go … next?"

Antara considered how much to tell her, and surprisingly didn't feel any strong restrictions. "We will return to a safe place on our planet to regroup, but then we must make plans to impede our enemy's preparations. We know of one place they are gathering in great numbers, among islands near our shores. If we can disrupt their activities, we can buy ourselves more time."

Gunther gave the English translation to make sure both Hannah and Gavin understood. After a moment, Gavin responded, "Sounds like a SEAL or Ranger operation. Two of my buddies were Rangers, and we know a couple of SEALs."

Gunther blinked. "Rangers I know. But I do not understand seals."

"Special soldiers, like the Rangers," supplied Hannah in Common. "We know some. They can help."

Antara tilted her head. "Special soldiers?"

"Yes," said Gavin after getting the translation. "Expert fighters, with far better weapons than we had eighty years ago. Other technologies, too."

Antara looked at Gunther, who was nodding appreciatively and grinning like a kid with a double fistful of candy. "God is good," he whispered.

32

Markydis expressed surprise when Ileom requested a cot be brought to the Travel Room so he could sleep next to Meris. He seemed less astonished that Meris was an actual dragon. He didn't object to the extra guards, though he couldn't, anyway. That was well within Ileom's purview.

After checking on her, Ileom spent the rest of the evening with Agrancik and Lady Brentia, visiting with the other Council members in the Keep, starting with Thirena and ending with Markydis himself. He went into great detail regarding what they had discovered, and Agrancik elaborated on the evolving political situation on Alave. None but Thirena gave any indication how the information might sway their vote, she being the only one to say she would support Ileom's proposal. Markydis reminded them how serious the decision was, that the powers preserved in the Vault had been locked away for a reason, after being misused to cause untold misery. But he also admitted they faced an unprecedented threat. Ileom couldn't decide if Markydis's behavior was diplomatic, or if he really was torn.

It was late when he returned to the Travel Room, after seeing Agrancik and Lady Brentia to their spacious accommodations. Meris slumbered peacefully, and he almost detected a smile. Did dragons smile as humans did? He hadn't noticed, and he hadn't asked her yet.

Sleep didn't come quickly, and when it did, his dreams were chaotic and confusing. Upon waking, he couldn't remember any of them, which was probably good. He found a place to wash up, and by the time he returned a hot breakfast awaited him outside the doors. After taking it inside and sitting on the hard cot, he felt like he was in heaven. Soldiers appreciated hot meals—enjoyed in peace—more than most. Veteran soldiers especially.

After savoring the meal, his first destination was the library. Antara and a few others sometimes teased that cantankerous war heroes didn't read much, but by hard experience he had learned that one of a soldier's most powerful weapons was knowledge. When combined with experience, humility, and proper motives, it produced astounding wisdom. That was especially true for leaders. And so he vigorously sought knowledge, often in private. He couldn't measure the amount of fruit it had borne.

One of the younger librarians was on duty, but he needed no directions. He knew where to go, and nothing was restricted to him. He made his way to the second floor, to a section not often visited but still benefiting from the light-enhancing, elf-designed steel and glass cupola over the library wing. The elves rarely participated in such projects with humans or dwarves in good times; now it never happened. Pity, that.

It took him several minutes to find the book he sought, one which he had seen referenced elsewhere, some time ago: *Legends of the Lost*. Though just seventy years old, it had been compiled from manuscripts far older, some going back two thousand years. Ileom knew he would have found the work of a historian unbearably tedious, so he was grateful for the husband and wife team who had undertaken the painstaking research to create this tome. Crusty veterans like him now benefitted from it.

He scanned the introduction, noting nothing of major interest. Many ancient civilizations had existed on Tenris. Some had disappeared through natural or man-motivated upheavals, which wasn't surprising. Several had evaporated, melding into other cultures over time until they could no longer be said to exist. A few had vanished mysteriously, and the legends varied. The authors focused mostly on those. Only a handful of people, including Ileom, knew there might be connections with some of the artifacts hidden away in the Vault … and with the interplanetary Crossroads, created millennia ago by the greatest wizards the worlds had ever known. Modern mages thrashed around in cold molasses by comparison—blindfolded, with lead weights on their wrists and ankles.

Midway through Chapter Two, he came across the name of an ancient city he didn't recognize. Kirod. Later peoples had sometimes referred to it as Kirod the Transcendent, its citizens often described as demigods. They possessed magic in abundance, but also technology. Some of the more extravagant tales asserted the people had grown wings, but Ileom—and the historians who had written the book—knew what that really meant. They had developed ways to fly, using contraptions powered by magical or mechanical means. Flying machines. That wasn't what interested him most, however. Legends had arisen claiming the Kirodians could appear anywhere on the planet, almost instantaneously, which was one reason they were often used as advisors and diplomats by many of the world's leaders trying to broker and maintain peace.

Jealousies grew—as they always do among humans—enemies arose, and the Kirodians began to bicker with one another, developing rival factions. Some of their technology was stolen by outsiders, and their leaders reacted harshly. That caused greater divisions, as many Kirodians advocated further sharing. Fighting eventually erupted inside the city, followed by attacks from without. Too late, most of the rich and powerful realized what they had started and where it would lead. They sought to quell the fighting, but, barring that, they intended to *banish* it. What did that mean, exactly?

The authors had investigated several traditions, but one of them intrigued Ileom the most: the creation of a device that could, upon precisely calculated activation using an immense charge of power, transport a small city to a pre-linked location, displacing the same mass and switching places with it. The remaining Kirodians had disappeared shortly thereafter. Then, a hundred and twenty years ago, a round, impossibly heavy object half the size of a man had been found, the runes on its surface studied by the top scholars of Rega. One of the members of the Order had been involved, and she claimed it to be the result of a failed test of this ancient device. The item had eventually been placed—with great magical effort—inside the Vault to gather dust with the other objects. Was the device itself in the Vault? Had it ever worked properly? The Vault's catalog was both incomplete and imprecise.

Before Ileom knew it, five hours had flown by. He had skipped the midday repast, and the time of the meeting drew near. He reluctantly returned the book to its place, wishing he could just take it, then left the library to find Agrancik and Lady Brentia. He also wanted to catch Thirena again.

He didn't find any of them in their suites, so he checked in on Meris. She still slept, but this time she stirred slightly when he entered the room. He guessed that was a good sign. He placed a hand on her side, and he could sense her more strongly—another positive tell—though he couldn't make the link.

He arrived at the Council chambers a few minutes early, finding Agrancik and Lady Brentia already there, huddled in deep conversation. He let them be for the moment, gathering his thoughts as he occupied a chair closer to them this time. When Thirena came in a few minutes later, he rose and approached.

"Welcome, Thirena. You passed a comfortable night, I hope, and it has been a good day?"

"As well as can be, Master Ileom, thank you. Did you visit the training grounds or the library this morning?"

She would rib him over either answer. "The library. I spent considerable time with *Legends of the Lost*."

"Ah, the erudite captain of men," she teased. "I have not read that one. Did you find something useful?"

"Perhaps." He took her cane while she sat, then gave it back to her.

"I do not believe you will be successful today, Master Ileom," she said bluntly. That was one thing he liked about her, which distinguished her from most of the people of Sajin he'd met. "Perhaps later, but not today."

He nodded. "I fear you are right. God is ultimately in charge, though, is he not? I must trust in that."

She gave a shrug. "My faith is not as strong as yours, though I will not discount it. I have seen many unexplainable things in my life, just as you have."

"Indeed. Our collective wisdom often disintegrates as dust in a tornado."

"Are you becoming a scholar?" She put a hand to her chest, the slight mocking tone returning, and he chuckled.

"No. That would be an event for the history books. I'm just a soldier, trying to find the best path."

"Oh, I know you are far more than just a soldier." She winked, and then Markydis entered the room, followed immediately by Nashterikii and Eliefhim, their faces so neutral as to be disguises. That was definitely *not* a good sign. Ileom needed a unanimous decision, and that likelihood appeared bleaker with every passing moment.

Ileom was the last to take his seat, and Markydis began the meeting by calling upon him first. "Master Ileom, the matter before us was presented by you. Do you have any additional information you would like to provide?"

Ileom studied the few faces around the table, ending with Thirena. "Just an opinion. After further study this morning, and speaking with all of you, I believe we do not yet have enough information to make such a decision, quorum or no." He knew that would surprise them, given his hard-charging reputation; indeed, Markydis's eyebrows shook hands with his forelock. It felt right, though. "It is my job to gather that information," Ileom continued. "In the meantime, Agrancik and Lady Brentia can further familiarize you with happenings on Alave. I will leave the key to Alave that I carried, so that you can travel there as well. Time is of great essence, as you know. And I must find Antara, so I will need to requisition the cavern key again. Meris can take us on multiple trips quickly, without the book. She is nearly healed."

"Her magic is that strong?" asked Markydis with a plain look of surprise. "I know some of the accounts ascribe great power to the ancient dragons of Tenris, but most of that is considered myth."

Ileom nodded. "I now doubt it is myth, and I haven't yet begun to plumb the depths of Meris's capabilities. There is much we need to … *re-learn*."

Markydis rubbed his chin. Eliefhim shifted in his seat, and when Ileom glanced at him he sensed some discomfort. Perhaps knowing that so many griffons had already invaded his home country of Ekatowin had set him on edge.

"Regardless," said Markydis, "Trinsa has the cavern key at the moment, in order to bring us swift updates of her and Oldin's efforts with Queen Givyren. You can await her next visit."

That was unfortunate, and he was certain the others needed the Alave key. "Very well. We will fly to Thyasendrial first. Perhaps Antara and Rain have returned."

Markydis leaned forward in his chair. "Thyasendrial?"

"A dwarven village, secreted in a magical valley in the Miracle Mountains near the Mero Vothan border. I do not know if that is the name the dwarves use for it, though."

Markydis leaned back, eyes expressing wonder. "I believe I know the place to which you refer. That village has long been abandoned, though the dwarves jealously guard it. The Dwarven Circle will not speak of it."

Ileom gave a wry smile. "They will now." Before Markydis could delve further, he had a thought, and his eyes shifted to Thirena. "Meris was able to heal me, on two separate occasions. I have a specific connection to her, but perhaps the touch of a dragon could accelerate your healing. Human healing clearly isn't working as hoped." He resisted frowning. What had the assassins done to her that confounded the powerful healers in the Keep? Meris might even be able to provide an answer for that.

Thirena's tired eyes brightened. "It is worth a try. My thanks, Master Ileom."

"We need you," he replied. Then he removed the Alave key from a pocket and placed it on the table, directing his gaze at Markydis again. "I can answer more of your questions, but as soon as Meris awakens and attends to Thirena, we will depart. I suspect that will be no later than the morning."

"Very well," said Markydis, seeming both troubled and relieved. "Now, please tell us more about this young warrior mage named Rain Barynd from the sleepy artisan backwater of New Haven. And Thyasendrial."

Consciousness came suddenly, but Rain had difficulty opening his eyes. They were stuck shut, his commands for them to respond going unheeded for several seconds as his ears picked up the drumming of drizzling rain. Then, slowly, the lids parted, and in the dim light he could tell he was in a large tent, lying on a bed. He blinked a few times, then breathed in deeply, trying to get his brain started. Where was he? Yes, Earth. The field. That was all he could remember. Wait, there had been blood. Had he been shot?

He turned his head and felt no pain. He could move his fingers and toes as well. A sharp intake of breath came from near his feet. He focused, making out Jerise's face. She jumped up and dashed to the tent's opening. "He's awake! He's awake!" Then she returned and knelt near his head. "We were really worried, Rain. I healed you, but your mind … I guess it didn't believe me. There was nothing else I could do."

He shut his eyes again for a moment, then let out the breath he'd been holding. "Thank you. Where are we?"

Antara swept into the tent, moving nearly as fast as Jerise had, but somehow still seeming stately. "We're in the field, on Earth. We're making plans to attack General Inzeal's forces on Chalace, with the help of a few elite soldiers from Earth."

Rain bolted upright, his mind apparently admitting now that he was all right. "We're *what?*"

Antara winked. "I know. It's been happening fast. Amazingly so. This was God's doing, I am sure. Jared found Hannah, whose brother used to be a soldier. They contacted the owner of this land, and he is a former soldier, too. A God-fearing man as well. He is letting us stage here, even providing cover with farm equipment and pretending to repair his fences. We are camouflaged to protect us from eyes above. Some of that farm equipment, by the way, is larger than the German tanks. Using just one person and a massive machine, he can harvest an entire field this size in less than a day."

Rain found all of that hard to believe. "Did someone shoot me?"

Antara frowned. "We think a rebel sniper got you just before we traveled. A quarter inch more on target, and you would have died instantly."

"And we probably wouldn't have traveled," said Jerise. "We would have been trapped there."

"Or trapped here, if the key brought us," said Antara. "It still won't let me use it, though perhaps it will eventually."

Rain took that all in. "When are you planning to attack?"

"I can't say yet," said Antara. "Without knowing where Ileom is, the decision is more difficult. But we can begin the journey to Chalace soon, after returning to a place you are familiar with near Arxhana—perhaps that large way station. Once we make our way to Misery, we can scout and plan further. I have only scant details from Ileom's prior mission there, delivered to me by courier while I was in Arxhana and you were … well, here, where God knew you were supposed to be, preparing the way."

He ignored the implied praise; perhaps he was getting used to her saying things like that. "We should send Androl back to Thysend," he said, wondering why that thought had suddenly popped into his head. "We left Captain Palrin there. That … worries me."

Antara nodded. "Excellent idea. I agree. And he can take Guardsmen Garrett and Jervin with him. Don't worry—they have acquitted themselves well, and I've been speaking with them. We can take care of that assignment right away. Or, well, you can. As I said, the key will not respond to me."

He didn't allow that to upset him again, and he could tell she was only pretending it didn't frustrate her. "How many Earth soldiers will we have?"

"Fifteen. And technically, they're not soldiers anymore."

"You mean they're old, like the Germans?"

She laughed. "No. You'll see. They have powerful weapons, including long-range, um, rifles. Some are bringing equipment that will let them swim underwater for long periods of time, too. That perplexes me, but it will be helpful against the Tahn Arganda ships."

The swimming underwater thing didn't surprise Rain, not after all he'd seen on this planet. "How many people know the enemy is there, building up forces?"

"Most nations are aware now, but none have the courage to act yet. Some are preparing negotiating teams. Others are waiting. Sheraya is likely in full league with them, and Queen Givyren's armies are large, if not the most well trained. If Vriesland and Sajin join her … well, we're in big trouble."

Rain gazed at the peaked tent ceiling, the enormity of the challenge becoming clearer. And to think that less than four months ago his primary goal was to convince Master Ileom to let him into the Council Guard of New Haven, where he would drill and march and posture but not much else. "It's raining," he noted, looking toward the partially open tent flaps. Indeed, it was no longer a mere drizzle.

"Yes," said Antara, turning to glance out, "and it's beautiful. The clouds help hide us. Some of Hannah's friends brought nets to cover the German tanks, too, so they aren't visible from above."

"But there are no griffons here," Rain said, his mind still a bit foggy. "At least, Hannah and Jared acted like they had never seen one. Or … maybe just not in person?"

As if he had called her, Hannah entered the tent, wiping water off her face and shaking a few drops out of her hair. "Rain, it is wonderful to see you. You mentioned griffons? No, we don't have any on Earth. But we have flying machines much more powerful. I showed you a few pictures of them; they always confused you." Her kind smile was a welcome sight, and her Common had gotten much better.

"That could be useful," he said, trying to remember the pictures—wheeled metal beasts with flapping wings? "Some of the griffon riders can use magic now, though."

Her face fell slightly. "Oh. Well, we must always be careful."

"You speak our language well."

She blushed a little. "I've been studying like crazy. I made recordings of all our conversations. I can watch them over and over again. I've run them through an AI, too ... never mind what that is for now. I have also asked Gunther many, *many* questions. He is tired of me, I think."

Rain smiled. "He's just old." He laughed, expecting something to hurt, but it didn't. And then he felt foolish for sitting in a sick bed, so he swung his legs to the side and got up, instantly noting the sheen of chilly water on the floor as he looked down at his bare feet.

"Sorry," said Jerise. "We put this up in a hurry and didn't set the floor well enough for rain."

"That's okay," he said. "Where are my boots?"

"Oh! Here." Jerise pulled them out from under the cot, then twisted to rummage in a large sack on a bench behind her, coming up with a pair of socks. Thick socks, even softer than the ones Hannah had purchased for him. He sat, dried his feet on his pant legs, then donned the socks and laced up the boots. Now he felt somewhat like a soldier again. He stamped his feet a few times after standing—splashing everyone—then nodded.

"Thank you. Can I meet these soldiers?" He looked at Antara.

She smiled. "Of course, Commander Barynd." At which he blushed. "Come, you can meet Gavin, Hannah's brother, first."

She led them out into the rain, throwing up a shield to keep them dry as they crossed a well-ordered camp. Almost everything was under some sort of cover. Impressive. They entered another large tent, well-lit by some sort of lantern hanging from a top post which cast an unusually bright light. Well, not for this world. A small square table of pure white sat in the middle, and three men in metal chairs scribbled on papers as they conversed in English. The one opposite the entrance looked up first, noting each person as they came in. Hannah brought up the rear.

He rose, then addressed Hannah after a glance at Rain. "Is this him? The dragon rider?"

He wasn't as large as Rain, but he looked solidly built. His hair was a deep black, almost shiny. He wore pants and long-sleeved shirt dyed with an incredibly intricate camouflage pattern, as did his two friends, who stared with interest. One of them had skin darker than any Rain had ever seen. The books said some of the people of northern Akris had skin that dark, to protect them from the merciless sun.

Hannah stepped forward, edging past Antara and Jerise. "Yes, this is Rain. The one who mysteriously showed up several weeks ago. Him being from another planet was not on my bingo card."

Rain didn't know what a bingo card was, but Gavin's expression told him it was a joke of some kind.

"Rain," she said, turning to him and still speaking English. "This is my brother, Gavin, and two of his friends, Mike and Hondo. Actually, I don't know Hondo's real name, and nobody will tell me." More smiles, along with some laughter.

"It is good to meet you," said Rain, trying to remember some of the English he had learned. "Thank you for helping us."

"We were getting really bored," said Gavin, "and Hannah believes in your cause. I needed a new job, anyway." His smile seemed friendly and respectful, and Rain couldn't help but grin back. He would ask Hannah later what the word 'bored' meant. And 'job.'

He didn't know what else to say, especially given the language barrier, so he turned and awkwardly exited the tent, Antara, Jerise, and Hannah following. Antara anticipated his next question.

"We should be ready to leave in two days," she said. "Some of Gavin's other friends are gathering more supplies and weapons. They've brought some books, too. The Germans are all practicing their English. I love it.

They're like school children. Centenarian pupils." She giggled—an uncharacteristic sound for her.

When they returned to the first tent, the cot had already been removed, replaced by several collapsible chairs. Gunther and Weldrin occupied two of them.

Rain held both hands up to forestall them from standing. Then he sat, Antara taking the chair next to him.

"We are delighted to see you are well, Commander Barynd," said Weldrin. "We weren't sure we believed Jerise's assurances that you had been fully healed, because you didn't wake up."

Rain gave them an apologetic look. "I'm stubborn, I guess."

Gunther chuckled. "Aren't we all. Well, welcome back. We … um, have a proposal for you and Lady Antara."

Rain would say yes to anything they asked. He deferred to Antara, though.

"What is it?" she asked.

After a shared glance, Weldrin sat straighter in her chair. "We would like to leave two or three of our number here, to learn more about our former home, perhaps even discover what happened to our families back in Germany." She gestured at Hannah, standing near the entrance with Jerise. "Hannah has told us she and her brother know some German speakers nearby, and they have access to genealogical records. Apparently, one can also speak to someone in Germany face-to-face without actually going there. It is astounding, far more advanced than our communications technology."

"We can learn much here," added Gunther. "I know we don't 'exist' on Earth anymore, but Gavin said he could find people for us to stay with. We have some vintage items we might be able to sell, so that we aren't a burden."

They had clearly thought it through, and Rain could only try to imagine how they felt. He had his own experience living on a new planet—only briefly, not for eighty years!—and he had stumbled across some good people. Of course, the Germans had the advantage of speaking at least one Earth language. He looked at Antara, who was tapping her lips with a finger. That pose always made his mouth go dry.

"I like the idea," she finally said, "though we need to do more planning. For instance, how can we check in and get updates? We definitely need to learn more about Earth. Hannah, of course, is part of that. And Jared. I'm curious to see where this goes. Do you agree, Rain?" She turned her gaze upon him, and his mind froze for an instant. He recovered, though.

"Yes, I agree. You will help with the planning?"

She nodded.

"Good. I need to talk with Lagron." He frowned, feeling a little guilty he hadn't done so immediately upon waking. Maybe his mind still wasn't fully functioning yet. "Where is he, by the way?"

Antara laughed. "Oh, I forgot to tell you. Just behind one of the tanks, under the netting. He went hunting last night, I think. Or foraging. I don't know exactly what he eats."

Rain nodded, then excused himself and left the tent. He found Lagron curled up behind a tank, sleeping, but his head rose when Rain ducked under the netting. Rain could have sworn he smiled.

Rain touched his snout, and awareness bloomed. *I guess I'm lucky to be alive.*

We are all lucky you are alive, replied Lagron.

I'm no more important than anyone else.

True, in one sense. But you have specific talents we need. Don't be shy about that.

That marked the first time Lagron had given him such intimate advice. He would be wise to heed it.

I'm sorry you were hurt, Lagron continued. *I might have healed you, given enough time, but I fear we didn't have that time. Jerise's skills are beyond anything I have witnessed in a human. She is remarkable. I needed to see that, and I consider it a blessing.*

Yes, she is … miraculous. And with you, I feel more confident than ever that we can succeed.

Hmmm … there is still great risk, but optimism will serve us well. Shall we find Ileom and Meris?

Rain blinked. *How can we do that? We don't know where they went.*

It should be possible. Meris and I share a special bond among dragons, as permanent mates. Our magic can get us to Tenris, and my bond will guide us to Meris.

You've done this before?

No, but it is in our histories.

Histories?

Yes. Someday I will show you where those are, and how we record them.

I would like that.

As I would enjoy studying your records. You will need to teach me to read them, though. I can speak with you, but I cannot read your language.

Oh. Well, I've never taught anyone how to read.

Lagron chuckled. *Neither have I. We are barren, and therefore have no offspring.* He didn't send it with sadness, but Rain instantly felt for them.

I'm sorry.

Do not be. God's will reigns, and we are content with that; nay, we rejoice in it, for there are none of his creations he doesn't love perfectly. Even the griffons, feral in nature and easily controlled by ambitious men.

Rain felt a warming power in Lagron's words, delivered with such fervent strength directly to his mind, even penetrating his heart. Silence extended for several seconds, and then Lagron said, *Go. Tell Antara what we are doing, and that we will be back soon.*

We need to take Androl and two others with us, to Thysend. Androl's leadership is needed there. He had almost forgotten.

Very well.

Rain broke the link and returned to the tent where he had left Antara. She was still there, speaking with Weldrin, Gunther, and another old German woman.

When they paused their conversation to acknowledge him, he said it straight out. "Lagron believes he can guide us to Meris and Ileom, so we're traveling to Tenris now. We'll take Androl and … the Guardsmen … with us."

Antara's eyes popped, then narrowed. She seemed excited, but wary. "Are you sure?"

"Lagron is."

She blew out a breath, then glanced at Weldrin and Gunther. "If true, and Ileom is well, we can coordinate with him. That is far preferable." They blinked, clearly unsure whether they had anything to add to that statement. She turned back to Rain.

"Very well. Wait until I can write out a message for him."

"About what? He'll tell us where our strike force needs to travel." The juvenile words had barely left his mouth before he felt stupid. Why had he questioned her? About a *note*? He definitely felt anxious to be going, but ... "I'm sorry. Yes, I'll wait for your note." He lowered his head and backed out of the tent, not wanting to see her face. *Idiot.*

He didn't know where to go, but he spotted Jared sitting on a camp stool under a lean-to shelter, listening to a group of Germans discussing a piece of equipment they were working on. They clearly knew he was there, but they couldn't speak English. Jared didn't seem to mind that he could only partially understand Common.

He looked up as Rain approached, then stood. He surprised Rain with an awkward hug. "Welcome back," he said, and his accent wasn't bad.

"Thank you. There is more danger ahead, though."

Jared nodded. "I know. I still want to go with you and Antara."

"You do? I mean, you can, but you won't be able to fight. Not yet, anyway. You need training." Not long ago, he was on the opposite side of that fence. It felt strange.

"I will not fail."

Rain stared at him a moment, brow furrowed. "I believe you won't." He gestured with his chin. "What are they working on?"

Jared glanced over. "A ... uh, radio?"

Just then, Antara tugged on one of Rain's sleeves. He whirled, and she handed him a folded piece of paper. "A short note. Please deliver it to Master Ileom. Oh, and here is the talisman." She didn't appear upset, but she turned and left immediately. He repeated his self-criticism. *Idiot.*

He let Jared know what was going on, then found Androl, Garrett, and Jervin, leading them to Lagron, who stood outside the netting, seeming eager. Rain tucked the note in a pocket, then launched himself up into the saddle. He didn't need to ride, but he wanted to. The others stood next to the dragon as he leaned forward and held the key against Lagron's neck.

As long as we are touching, I don't need to be in contact with the key. In fact ... curious.

What?

You can keep it in your pocket. When we are linked, the key just needs to be nearby, within a few feet of us. It will travel with us, of course.

Oh. He pocketed the key, then re-linked. *Okay, I'm ready. I'm locked onto the clearing near Thyasendrial.*

Proceed.

Rain exerted his focus, then felt them travel. The clearing expanded before them, the humid air of a warm night filling his nostrils. After allowing himself a second to revel in the success, he looked down at the others.

"Give my regards to everyone. Watch Captain Palrin carefully. And thank you."

Androl squared and saluted with a greater measure of respect than Rain had seen before from the capable Mero Vothan. Garrett and Jervin copied him a split second later. After an uncomfortable pause, Rain nodded and linked with Lagron again.

Can you find her?

Yes, I already have.

Good. Here we go. They appeared somewhere else after a flash from another location. They must have passed through Earth again, without stopping. At least he had noticed this time. They were in a large room with stone walls and a high ceiling. Giant glass windows looked out on a twinkling sky. Circular mosaic tiles patterned the floor in pastel colors. And there was Meris, with Ileom sleeping on a cot next to her.

Rain jumped down from the saddle, elated to see his mentor alive. Meris raised her head and turned it toward them, giving that dragon almost-smile. Lagron loped over to her, where they touched snouts and wingtips. When they had re-folded their wings, Ileom awakened, eyes wide at first as his hand went for the knife lying beside him. Then he relaxed, sat up, and shook his head with a grin broader than Rain had thought him capable. It could have been a trick of the darkness, though. The supposed smile disappeared quickly as he rose and straightened his clothes. His armor lay in a nearby alcove.

"How are Antara and the others?" he asked in his usual gruff, down-to-business tone, only a little scratchy from sleep. Rain detected a hint of worry, but saluted before delivering the formal report to his superior.

"She is well, and we took about forty of the Germans with us when we escaped to Earth, along with two tanks and a lot of equipment. The rest was destroyed. A few other Germans escaped into the mountains. I was wounded. After Jerise healed me, I was unconscious for several days. We have made a few friends from Earth, who are helping us, and Antara is working with them on initial planning for an attack on the main enemy base on Chalace. She knows you want to weaken General Inzeal's garrison there. Oh, and she gave me a written message for you."

He retrieved it, and Ileom took it with raised brow. He did something with his fingers that caused a small bubble of light to appear above his shoulder, then rubbed a stubbled jaw as he read, humming low. When he finished, his eyes wandered for a few seconds, revealing nothing. Then his gaze snapped back to Rain. "How did you find me?"

Rain pointed toward Lagron. "He knew how to find Meris, because they're mated. These dragons are beyond amazing."

Ileom nodded agreement. "That they are. Meris woke up just before midnight, and she was able to help another member of the Order. Dragon healing is slightly different in nature than what humans employ, and while it takes longer, it is making a difference. We were going to leave in another few hours for Thysend to begin our search for all of you. We might as well go now, though. I don't need to let anyone know I'm leaving a mite early. In fact, that might be better, and they'll wonder *how* I left, since I don't have a key at the moment." He winked, seeming pleased. "I just need a minute."

Rain saluted again, then turned and walked toward the windows, noting rustling and the clanking of armor as Ileom prepared to travel. The view was spectacular, even at night with only a half-moon and clusters of silver-limned clouds. He thought he spied a large body of water through a gap in the lower mountains, but he couldn't be sure. He didn't have any idea where they were geographically, though he guessed this was the Keep of the Order of the Fallen Moon. He felt a little disappointed it was the only room he would get to see. On this trip, anyway. Antara had called him one of their members now. Had she really meant it, or was it just a cover?

"I'm ready, soldier," came an echoing call. "Let's be on our way."

Rain trotted back, eyes widening as he noticed the massive two-handed sword Ileom had carried the day New Haven fell. It gave off a slight orange glow. Trying hard to rein in boyish excitement, he didn't comment on it, just laid a hand on Lagron's neck without pulling out the key. Ileom raised an eyebrow, and Rain grinned. In another instant, they were standing in the camp on Earth. The rain had lessened to little more than a misting, but the skies were still completely gray.

One of Gavin's friends was returning from the latrine they had set up behind one of the main tents, and he stopped dead in his tracks. Rain could well imagine his shock. Two dragons now, one copper, one silver. And a tall, powerful soldier in exquisite armor carrying what had to be the largest sword in existence on any planet. The man gawked at the beasts for a few seconds, then at Ileom, then hurried off toward the planning tent. Rain guided Ileom in that direction.

Antara gave a great sigh of relief when she saw them enter, eyes flitting between them as she rose from a chair. Gavin stood, too, eyes fixed on Ileom, clearly recognizing him as someone important.

"Master Ileom," said Antara, "we are beyond pleased you have arrived and are well. Meris, too?"

Ileom nodded. "She is fine. We were both wounded but have recovered."

Antara raised an eyebrow, glancing at his legs as a smile tickled the corners of her mouth. She was going to tease him about his fake limp in New Haven *now*? Rain thought he detected the beginnings of a rumble deep in Ileom's throat, but he might have been imagining it.

"I understand you are planning a military operation," Ileom added.

Antara winked at Rain, and the potentially thorny moment passed. She turned to gesture toward Gavin and his two friends at the table, all standing at attention. "Yes, we are. This is Gavin, Hannah's brother, and his friends Mike and Hondo. They are experienced soldiers. They have valuable skills and equipment. Gunther, please introduce Master Ileom to them."

Gunther, standing just behind and to the right of Gavin, did so, and then Ileom addressed Antara again. "The sooner we get to Chalace, the better. I have some men there, and we need updated intelligence."

"Yes," she responded, "that message reached me in Arxhana. If we couldn't find you, we would have gone without you, but we are also awaiting more of Gavin's soldier friends and some additional equipment. I promise you will be impressed."

Ileom glanced at the Earth soldiers, his face nearly expressionless, though Rain detected a hint of admiration. "Very good. Tell me what you have so far."

Rain breathed a sigh of relief that traveling with their large group had succeeded again. Also that they hadn't appeared among the enemy, and that nobody had shot him. They hadn't needed to travel to a place Rain or Lagron—or even the key—had visited before first, because Meris made them aware that through the dragon link Ileom could pass to Rain detailed images of the target area, along with its mapping location. That was new, and amazing. And it had *worked*.

They discovered a group of eight beleaguered Sentinels from the Order's Keep, nearly starving, hiding under trees and a rock ledge in the early morning. Upon sighting the strange ensemble that materialized in their midst, the men didn't make any moves to defend themselves. Instead, they appeared ready to surrender. Until they spotted Ileom. Then they were on their feet and mustering.

Ileom approached the squad leader, designated by a small patch on his right arm. "Status, Keenum."

"Sir, we are pinned down here. The Argandans conduct constant aerial patrols, several griffons strong. We can't even hunt or forage properly. I sent two men to link up with the nearest other group, two weeks ago. We haven't heard anything. The enemy hasn't moved against us in numbers, which they easily could, but they harry us constantly, like it's a game."

Ileom growled. "They won't like the game we're about to play." He scanned the group. "You've lost half your men."

"Yes, sir, and we haven't been able to see much, so I don't have anything new to report."

Ileom frowned as Keenum looked down. "Don't be ashamed, soldier. I shouldn't have sent anyone back here. Not so close, anyway, or not until I could bring an adequate force myself. We have food. Get something to eat." Keenum gave him a blank stare, then glanced around, clearly confused about where to go for that. Ileom motioned Gunther toward him. "Gunther, these men need food, and I want Gavin's flying spy machine in the air. Also, tell him we need two sniper positions set up."

With a spry step and a sharp tongue, Gunther barked out orders for the food as he went to where Gavin and his friends stood near one of the two four-wheeled Earth vehicles they had brought. The 'truck,' as it was called, had arrived at the Earth camp a bright blue, but a hasty re-painting gave it camouflage colors. A large bed in the back carried trunks, crates, and heavy-duty bags, along with incredibly complex backpacks. Rain had studied one of them and counted ten different straps.

After speaking with Gunther, Gavin jumped up onto the back of the vehicle, where he retrieved a medium-sized black crate, then hopped down. Two of his friends grabbed a hefty bag and a pack each before marching off in different directions.

Gavin approached Ileom, Gunther following. He set the crate down, flipped a pair of latches, and opened it up.

What an odd-looking contraption this ... 'drone' was. Rain hadn't seen it before, though he'd heard it described. It was small, no wider than the length of a short sword, and consisted of a body with four arms, each ending in a set of blades within a circle. It was mostly white, but the blades and circles were black. Gavin set it on the ground, then removed a smaller case from the crate and extracted a device. One side of the small artifact featured a window box—called a 'screen,' which word made little sense. Various small objects bulged from its surface.

Gavin looked at Ileom. "Shall I send her up?" Gunther translated, and Ileom nodded. Gavin touched something on the small device, and the drone's blades began to spin, so fast they became invisible. The drone rose into the air about ten feet, making a humming noise, then hovered. Rain noted Meris and Lagron eyeing it speculatively.

"Take it up high to see if we're clear, then begin the grid," said Ileom. After Gunther's translation, Gavin touched the tiny objects on the device again, and the drone climbed quickly, straight up. Rain had no idea how that was possible. He and Ileom moved to stand at either of Gavin's shoulders so they could watch the screen. It would supposedly show them what the drone saw with its … he couldn't remember that word at the moment.

It felt like he was looking through a moving window. Incredible. The image came through crisp and clear amid a beautiful, lightening sky.

The view rotated slowly, giving them a wide panorama of everything around them. They were only a few miles from the channel, and Ileom had said this place was twenty miles from the largest enemy base. Rain thought he spotted it in the distance, but it was tiny. Gavin must have, too. He held the drone's eye on that spot, and it became bigger, then bigger again, then much larger.

"That's as far as I can zoom in, but this gives you an idea," he said. Gunther was staring, too, head squeezed between Rain and Gavin, so there was a pause before he translated.

Ileom gave a satisfied grunt. "Good. Start the grid search." He backed away and turned. "Rain, get Lagron in the air. Don't stray too far. And take these with you. You can see a great distance with them." He pulled a strap from around his neck, attached to a small, oddly shaped contraption made of two cone-like tubes—something Gavin had given him. "Place the narrow ends over your eyes. You can use the wheel in the middle to adjust the focus." Before Rain could ask what that meant, Ileom marched off, turning his attention back to the eight men they had just rescued. He would surely be worried about others in the area suffering similar deprivation.

Rain surveyed the large group he and Lagron had transported, with its panoply of mind-boggling equipment. Antara stood with Jerise and Haran, gazing in the direction of the enemy encampment. Most of the Germans talked softly among themselves, except for the few breaking out food for Ileom's squad, who huddled around them like cats at milking time. The rest of Gavin's friends had split up in two's and three's to make a tight reconnoiter of the area. It seemed automatic; Ileom hadn't asked them to. Their wands, or rather guns, looked far more sophisticated—and deadly—than those the German rebels had used against New Haven. Some had really long barrels—another incongruous word.

Rain returned to Lagron and lifted himself into the saddle, strapping in. He was getting faster at it, and one of the Germans had repaired the damaged strap for him. They launched into the sky, rising higher than the drone had, eyes peeled for both griffons and enemy ground patrols. He asked Lagron to find a current and glide for a bit so he could use the strange scrying device Ileom had given him. When he put it to his eyes and aimed his sight toward the base, the landscape jumped toward him in startling fashion. The image bounced around as he struggled to keep the device steady. After a minute of effort, which included remembering the center wheel and turning it back and forth, he got a good look at the base.

He wasn't an expert, but it appeared quite large. Within his view, he counted hundreds of men tending to various morning duties, including the changing of guards and patrols. He also spotted two of the large barns Ileom had described, along with several griffons in what looked like train-ing yards. He moved the device ever so slowly upward and soon picked out some griffons in the air, keeping watch over the base. Beyond, down a slope, he could make out a portion of the bay, with several masts and hulls visible. One of their goals was to sabotage a great number of those ships. Another was to kill as many griffons as possible, putting fear into the hearts of those soldiers and their commanders. Then, pull back.

The plan they had worked out was bold and multi-pronged, with several diversions. Again, Rain was no expert, but he liked it. They would attack at night. Gavin and his friends had brought several pairs of what they called 'night-vision goggles,' which would give them an advantage in the darkness. At some point, they would also launch 'flares,' both to confuse the enemy and give the others better sightlines and targets. Much of the work on the ground would be what they called 'stand-off.' Essentially, that's what Rain's magic was. He didn't have to grapple or clash weapons with a man. He could launch an attack from a distance. Gavin had described the effective range of their sniper rifles, and even Ileom's jaw had gone slack.

Lagron gave a quick flap of his wings, and Rain lowered the device to lean forward and place a hand on him.

Griffons approaching. I'll point us toward them.

Rain swallowed, glancing down at the camp as Lagron maneuvered in the air. When the dragon had stabilized again, Rain brought the device back to his eyes and focused forward, spying within seconds a foursome of griffons. While still a good distance away, they were flying toward the camp at great speed. He readied some magical arrows, then heard twin cracks from below, accompanied by terrific echoes. Two of the griffons slowed noticeably and started turning away. One of the riders slumped in his saddle.

The other two came on, though they began to weave. Two more cracks sounded, but a slight ruffle of wing feathers was all Rain could discern as the result.

Lead them away from the camp, said Rain after lowering the device again. Lagron turned and dove, then arced back up, accelerating as his wings flapped ferociously. The griffons spotted him and followed, but as they neared the channel it must have become clear to their riders that they had no chance of overtaking him. Rain saw them turn back—not aiming for the area around the camp but on an angle toward the base, probably hoping to intercept their comrades and assess their condition.

Can we take on four? he asked Lagron. *We don't know if they have magic or guns.*

I believe we must, came Lagron's reply, and then he executed a sweeping turn before accelerating back to full speed.

They were upwind of the griffon riders, but Lagron easily outflew the wind. Still, their mounts somehow sensed Lagron's approach. They started turning, both men pulling out crossbows. Rain felt some relief they weren't guns as he focused a volley of missiles on the pair. The riders launched their bolts at the same time, and Lagron veered. Something exploded behind Rain, making his ears ring. Those weren't common bolts. Lagron veered again, then launched his own attack, searing through hide and armor of a griffon and rider, eliciting two screams and a sudden drop in their altitude. The other rider fired again, and Rain instinctively threw a ball of flame toward the bolt, which exploded before it reached them. The rest of his fireball merely singed a griffon wing, but Rain followed it up with another, causing both man and saddle to erupt in flames.

Lagron gained some altitude, then rolled. Certain the burning rider would die, Rain searched for the other griffon, which he found hugging the treetops, its movements erratic. Lagron spun and dove, picking up great speed. This time, the griffon didn't seem to sense them coming, and Lagron signaled his intent to Rain. In an unbelievable maneuver, he dropped hard onto the griffon's flank, grasping it with his hind claws and flipping it haunch over head. The griffon lost all control of its flight, and Rain watched in awe-tinged horror as beast and rider crashed through the canopy and into the ground at terminal velocity.

Lagron flapped mightily again, gaining altitude as they searched for the other two griffons. In less than a minute, they found them, still traveling slowly. One of the riders appeared lifeless, head bobbing with the movement of his mount.

Lagron roared a challenge this time, and the two griffons dove to gain speed. Rain had expected that, and he intercepted them with a hail of fiery arrows. Wounded as they were, and trying to flee, it almost didn't seem fair. But Rain didn't pity them as Lagron finished them off with bolts of fire, knowing that he and the marvelous magical creature had prevented word of their exact location from getting to the enemy base.

Rain took Lagron on a wide circuit around the camp before they landed near the center. Ileom awaited him near the newly erected command tent.

"What happened up there, soldier?"

"Four griffons, sir. All destroyed, with their riders. We had some help from the snipers."

Ileom nodded. "Indeed. Those men are amazing marksmen, as Gavin claimed. You're sure all four are dead?"

"We saw three go down, uncontrolled. I ... burned the other. If anyone survived, they are badly wounded and stranded."

"Good, though they may be running layered patrols. What did you see with those binoculars?"

Ah, yes, that's what they were called. "More than what the, um, drone showed. Hundreds of men, many griffons. I saw a few of the ships, too."

Ileom nodded, then extended his hand. Rain passed over the binoculars. "I'll take Meris up myself a little later. Make sure Lagron is okay, link with him, and show me what you saw through Meris, as best you can. Then speak to Antara. If what Weldrin and Gunther tell me is true, you two make a great fighting pair, and I want you to practice."

"Yes, sir." Rain saluted, then returned to Lagron, feeling even more nervous about the upcoming strike.

∞

"I don't feel good about it," declared Antara to their small planning group that evening in the command tent. "Something isn't right."

The powerful artificial lantern light showcased the stark frown lines on Ileom's face. He waited until Gunther had translated for the others, then responded. "Can you give any specifics? Are you saying we shouldn't attack at all? Or just wait?"

"I ... don't know. Normally, I would defer to you on ... well, all of this. It is your area of expertise. But ... hmmm ... I can tell you that some of the recent information from our spies in Akris doesn't add up for me. And why does Queen Givyren seem to be throwing all her support behind Inzeal? She's a religious zealot. He's a pagan. Still ..."

After a few long seconds, Ileom quirked an eyebrow. "What?"

"The ships," she finally said. "We should still disable as many ships as possible. That was the main goal, anyway. And these, um ... seals? ... they can prepare the attack silently and leave before the actual damage is done, correct?" She looked at Gunther, and he translated for Gavin and his two friends in the planning group, one of which—the man called Hondo—was a former SEAL.

"Yes," said Hondo. "Those ships are all wooden-hulled. We don't have the fancy explosives the U.S. military has, but what we've concocted will do. Ileom took me up on his ... man, I can't believe I'm saying this ... on his dragon, and we scouted the bay from a distance. Fifty-six ships docked or anchored. We can get most of them, but it will take more than one trip to set all the charges. In fact, our inflatable pontoon boat can't carry enough charges for one go. Maybe we can do it all in one night, with the dragons ferrying the pontoon back here to pick up more charges, or to a staging area on the shore. We'll need our backup oxygen tanks, too."

Even after the translation, Rain didn't understand all of it. Nor, it appeared, did Gunther. Ileom, however, seemed to be picking up on their equipment and capabilities fast. He grunted his appreciation, then said to Antara, "Those griffons are still a major threat. They could ravage all of Chalace, and they can easily reach the mainland without the use of a travel key ferrying them through Alave a few at a time. Which means they could hit the Mero Vothan coast en masse, and very soon. The Mero Vothans aren't ready. Nobody is."

Antara fixed him with a level stare. "Many griffons already *have* reached the mainland, as we both know. Far to the north, but they're here. And we haven't stopped the flow. Perhaps this base on Chalace is a diversion, and you stumbled upon the main thrust building in Ekatowin. This could also be a trap, set specifically for *you*. You are feared, and with good reason."

"We have far more capabilities than they expect, even if it is a trap." Ileom directed his glower at a point beyond Antara's shoulder. If it had been aimed at Rain, it would have melted his bones.

"True," she replied calmly. "But do we want to reveal all those capabilities right now?"

Ileom's brow furrowed in deep concentration as he stared down at their map table. Then he looked back up at Antara. "You told me this was my area of expertise, but that is an excellent insight."

Rain blinked. Was Ileom backing down? His eyes hardened, and he added, "But we will give them a brief taste, heavily disguised."

Antara gave a sharp nod. "Good. And then I will speak with the commander of the base, under a flag of parley."

Ileom jumped to his feet, nearly knocking over the table. "*What?* They'll just kill you!"

Antara gave him a patient, though respectful, look. "No, I don't believe they will. I've thought this through, Ileom, and I had a conversation with Gavin while you and Hondo were scouting the bay. That was a long trip, by the way, so we had time. Please, sit, and I will explain."

Ileom slowly resumed his seat, his glower returning in muted form.

"We will converse in the open, within sight of their perimeter. Gavin will place at least one sniper position close enough to provide cover. Rain and Lagron can come with me, so that in an emergency, we can instantly escape to Earth."

Rain had heard little of this. He'd been learning everything he could from the Germans and a pair of the Americans about their various weapons, plus the radios the Americans would be using to communicate with each other—radios a fraction of the size of those the Germans possessed. Like the device Hannah had shown him, they could be carried in a pocket.

He realized Antara was staring at him, as was everyone else. She may have even asked him a question.

"I need to talk with Lagron," Rain said. "I don't like the idea of taking him that close to so many griffons—and Hearkendoom—and I don't think he will, either."

Antara's eyes exuded sympathy. "I understand. And we cannot make Lagron do anything. But we need more information about the big picture, and this will help. I feel strongly about it."

Rain glanced at Ileom, then decided it was best to avoid his superior's simmering scowl. He was grateful for a few seconds to think while Gunther got the Americans caught up on the translation. An idea came, which brought both relief and fear. He almost didn't voice it.

"I could accompany you without Lagron," he said to Antara. "Like you said, we don't want them to know too much about our capabilities. That includes enhanced travel aided by the dragons."

"Another fine point," muttered Ileom. "They would see you touch him and make the logical conclusion."

"I've traveled with the key before," continued Rain, "and without Lagron's help. If I can figure out how to do it again, then we don't have to risk Lagron. And they won't learn about our link."

Antara pursed her lips, then turned the corners down. After a troubled glance at Ileom, she said to Rain, "That is a noble but risky idea. You have the next day to figure it out."

"Provided we all agree this is what needs to happen," said Ileom, seeming even less happy than that fateful day in the practice yard in New Haven's now pillaged Keep.

The group spoke for the next hour. Gavin and his friends had some interesting ideas for Ileom's 'brief taste,' and those seemed to warm him up to the overall outline Antara had proposed. At first, Rain wasn't sure where the conversation would end up, but he found himself unsurprised when Antara's idea prevailed. A knot had already been forming in his gut. He didn't think he was afraid to die. Torture frightened him, but more than that, he didn't want to let Ileom and Antara down. Hannah, Jared, and the others, too. He had a day to learn how to control his dragonless traveling. He would only need to take Antara, which he had done before … but how? He didn't have that strange circle of ancient stones to help him. Could Lagron offer some clues? He latched tightly onto that hope.

The first thing he did after stepping out of the tent into the darkness of the camp was approach the dragons. As he walked, a pair of spotlights snapped on—connected to something Gavin had called portable power—bathing in bright light a pair of griffons which had descended for a closer look. Germans manning machine guns on the tanks immediately opened fire, and after a burst of blood and feathers, the griffons fell, landing only a few yards from the camp perimeter. So much for the secrecy of their location. A mixed squad of Germans and Americans immediately departed the camp to confirm the kills, and the lights were extinguished. Rain paused, blinking as his eyes readjusted and his mind processed how quickly it had all happened. Seconds. Clearly, the camp was well defended, even at night. Incredible.

His thoughts circled back to the talisman, and he tromped on, finding Lagron sniffing the air after the brief but violent interaction. Meris, too, though she seemed less interested. He laid a hand on Lagron's neck.

I need to be able to control the talisman myself.

Why is that?

Antara has a plan, and it might require travel, and ... you can't be with me.

I see. You won't be able to transport nearly as many people as you and I can together.

I can't transport anyone *by myself. Not at will. I would only need to transport me and Antara, but I can't control it.*

We have traveled several times using your talisman. Somewhere, in your mind, you are becoming familiar with it. And it with you.

That sounded strange, and a little disconcerting. *I know. But ... I can't find* any *of that. I've tried. It's like the key ignores me. Maybe it just likes* you.

A chuckle came through the link. *I doubt it has a real personality that drives whimsical preferences, but that would be interesting. I'm afraid Meris and I have not studied much of the ancient lore on traveling. It wasn't around for very long, at least on our world. But I can tell you that if you have traveled with it before, you can do so again. You* can, *young Rain. Perhaps confidence is most of what is needed. Beyond that, I am afraid I cannot help you right now. Meris and I will think on it further, though.*

Thank you.

Feeling even more frustrated, he broke the link and moved on to the tent where he would sleep with several others, including Jared, who had also been splitting his time between the Germans and Americans. Two old German men, off-duty, snored raucously on their bunks, but otherwise Rain was alone. He sat on his cot and closed his eyes, focusing and organizing his thoughts. He didn't need to physically touch the key, just know where it was on his person. He concentrated on finding a way to access its abilities, striving to remember impressions or feelings from the other times he had traveled.

After two solid hours of that, his mind was frazzled. Then Antara came by, suggesting they combine their magic again in another attempt at delving the key. She took him to the tent she shared with Hannah and Jerise, and they began. After three more hours, without any discernible success, he barely remembered his own name. Even Jerise had tried to help, and it was her pleas for them to stop that finally persuaded Antara.

He returned to his tent, took off his boots, and lay down, closing his eyes and relaxing his focus a bit. A few minutes later, he heard Jared and two others enter the tent to sleep. Soon after, the two Germans who had been snoring got up and left. One of them manned a machine gun; he wasn't sure what the other's assignment was. No more gunfire interrupted the night's stillness, though he thought he heard the spotlights snap on twice. By the time he fell fully asleep, it seemed like the edges of the tent's entrance were lightening.

He didn't sleep long but awoke feeling somewhat refreshed. He got up, put on his boots without lacing them, then left quietly so as not to disturb those off-shift who now slumbered.

Mid-morning of a partly cloudy day greeted him, along with smells of warm food. Jared spotted him when he reached the center of the camp, where most of the cooking was done. He was reading a book, but he immediately got up and retrieved a plate heaped with food, which he brought to Rain. After staring at it in surprise for a moment, Rain looked at his friend.

"Breakfast," Jared said in Common. "I saved it for you. Kept it warm. Hannah said you would be hungry. She talked to Antara."

"Oh. Thank you." Rain took the plate, plus a proffered fork, and sat on a camp stool. Eggs and bacon smiled at him. Some potatoes, too. Despite not feeling hungry, he started wolfing it all down.

Jared reverted to English. "We took down two griffons."

Rain nodded, chewing. "I saw."

"They're scared of us."

Rain swallowed. "They should be."

Jared smiled, then suddenly looked glum. "I wish I could help more."

"Be patient." How many times had people told him that, and recently? It sounded strange coming out of his own mouth, especially in English.

"I know. But what if you don't come back from the raids?" Jared wasn't privy to much, but he could certainly deduce the risk wasn't negligible.

Rain shrugged, acting nonchalant. "We have a good plan. It will be okay."

Jared stared at him a moment, then lowered his eyes. "I guess so. At least I can cook eggs now."

That raised a question. "Where did we get eggs?"

Jared shrugged. "I don't know. The Germans brought them, I think. The Americans brought a bunch of dried stuff. Powdered eggs. I've had those before. Yuck."

"Powdered?"

He raised his fingers and rubbed them together. "You know, like dust."

Dust. Eggs like dust. That sounded ridiculous. He kept eating as Jared described various other foodstuffs they had in the camp. He understood most of the words. When he finished, he rose and looked for a place to wash his plate, like any good soldier would. Jared stood and extended a hand.

"Here, I'll take that. I can clean, too." He winked, shrugged again, and said good-bye, claiming Antara had warned him not to pester Rain while he prepared. Rain's shoulders slumped a little as he watched him go, and then he sat back down, thinking about the key again.

He spent the day roving from place to place, talking to a few people, spending the time in between trying to understand and access the key. Ileom went on another patrol with Meris, ordering Rain to stay in the camp. Antara spent most of her time with Hannah and Jerise. By suppertime, he didn't feel like he'd made any real progress, and Lagron said he and Meris hadn't come up with anything new, either. Jared energetically distributed meals to people, and he brought dinner to Rain, who sat near their sleeping tent. A short while later Antara came by. She took a stool next to him and whispered, "How's it going?"

Rain had been dreading that question. "Not good."

"You're getting closer, though."

His chest tightened. "I don't think so."

She didn't frown, just appeared thoughtful. "Well, I have faith in you. Tell Ileom you've figured it out, but it takes a lot of energy."

Rain nearly dropped his fork. "Lie to *Ileom*?" His voice rose to just above a whisper, and she raised a finger to her lips.

"We have to do this, Rain. I can't tell you exactly how I know it, but I do. And it's not just you I have faith in. You need to trust me, trust yourself, and most importantly, trust God."

Rain nodded, but he had no idea how to do *any* of those things. Not in this circumstance. If it were something easier—and less deadly—maybe.

"Good. I'll let Ileom know when he gets back, and I'm sure he'll come talk to you. Wonderful news, too. We rescued two more groups of Ileom's men. They'll be here shortly. Remember, we've got this. Tonight and to-morrow will be amazing." She rose and strode away too quickly to catch his look of bleak disbelief.

He choked down the rest of his dinner, then waited for Ileom, des-perately searching for the key's solution.

A part of Rain was happy to take to the skies with Lagron, Meris, and Master Ileom early in the morning, after another sleep-starved night filled with frustration. The rest of him dreaded it, because it meant the final countdown had started. The Americans had been out all night, with the dragons' help, planting their explosive devices. The SEALs had stayed in radio contact until they made their first dives, and with dawn still more than an hour from breaking, they had reported that all the charges were set, with the timers synchronized. That was yet another amazing techno-logical capability—the people of Earth could precisely coordinate time! The SEALs were on their way back from the shoreline now, to a different forward staging area.

His and Ileom's task would be to monitor the damage to the enemy fleet from a distance, using binoculars, then sweep in for a closer assessment. After that, Lagron would drop Rain off at the staging area where Antara would be waiting, while Ileom went to execute his show of force. Madness. It was all insanity, but he was powerless to stop it. And he had actually lied to Ileom about his ability to travel by himself using the key. He was still stunned he had done it. Ileom would strangle him if he ever found out.

The tanks remained in the camp, partly to protect it, but also because the terrain was too difficult and there weren't any roads for machines so large and heavy. Rain felt reassured that Hannah, Jared, Jerise, and the others staying behind would be safe.

Through the dragon link, Ileom said, *Stay low to the water, but keep an eye out for anything coming at you from above, even though we're swinging wide of their regular patrol patterns.*

Got it, returned Rain. Lagron had heard, too, though Ileom could have directed the communication only to him through the link—another new discovery. They flew fast, and he couldn't deny the exhilarating rush of skimming the waves at high speed, Lagron's wingtips occasionally slicing the water. He spotted a few fish jumping, one of them quite large, and numerous birds protested their swift, turbulent passing. When they reached the right position, they ascended so the dragons could glide and provide a more stable viewing platform.

Rain put the binoculars to his eyes, found the bay, and fiddled with the focus. All seemed calm. A few men walked the decks, but the idle ships were mostly empty. Most of the sailors were probably on shore, still asleep. Several minutes passed, in a pattern of watching through a glide, letting the dragons turn and ascend again, then renewing the surveillance as the light of the coming day grew brighter.

In the middle of a glide, the water in the bay erupted simultaneously in dozens of places. Flames shot up through the decks of several ships, tossing men overboard like tiny bits of kindling. It took several seconds for the muted booming sounds to reach them, and even unlinked for the moment, Rain could sense Lagron reacting in surprise to the remarkable, raw power.

Ships began listing, some heavy at the bow or stern. Several sank within the first minute, and more followed in short order. The dragons had to ascend again, and by the time Rain got eyes back on the bay, he counted only fourteen of the fifty-six ships still above water, three of them heavily damaged. Astonishing beyond words. He lowered the binoculars, letting them hang from his neck, and re-linked with Lagron.

It's time to go, came Ileom's direction. No comment on the massive success they had just witnessed, or the potency of the Earth weapons. Lagron followed Meris's lead, and they dove to hug the surface again, accelerating to full speed. They steered south for a bit, then curled back to make a run near the mouth of the bay. When they breached the boundary, Rain got a detailed look at the devastation. One more ship had sunk, and four of the remaining thirteen listed heavily. Activity along the shore was frantic, with scores of griffons vaulting into the air from the areas behind the barns.

They hadn't planned to slow at all, especially since many griffons and riders would spot them. But a crazy thought entered Rain's head with irresistible force. He asked Lagron to veer slightly, and then he and the dragon raked the remaining ships with bolts of fire, taking out masts, rigging, sails, and superstructure; also punching wide gaps in hulls, some near the water line. Lagron rolled out of the attack pattern, feeling deeply satisfied, which mirrored Rain's own emotions. Then they sped up to catch Meris.

What was that? Ileom didn't sound happy or unhappy, just insistent on a credible answer.

Rain paused only a moment. *An opportunity. No griffons were closing on us yet, so I took it, um, sir.*

A few seconds passed, the screams of griffons fading as Meris and Lagron hugged the shoreline, maintaining top speed.

We'll talk about it later. It seemed effective, though.

Rain took that as high praise, sharing his elation with Lagron—and *only* Lagron. Now, a bare handful of the enemy ships were serviceable to transport troops. A colossal victory.

They banked, rising with the topography, staying hidden behind a line of hills. Then, the dragons came to a shuddering halt, Meris hovering while Lagron landed.

Rain unstrapped and slid from the saddle, then took a few moments to speak with Lagron.

Have you and Meris had any more thoughts on the talisman?

No, brave one. But we are agreed that you will be fine. We have faith in you.

That's what Antara said. He stated it with as much despair as he could emote through the link.

She is wise. Lagron broke the link and rose, raising dust, pebbles, and pine needles in a furious storm. Rain closed his eyes for a few seconds, then gazed upward to watch the dragon pair wheel off in a different direction.

Antara approached him, flanked by a pair of Americans, heavily armed and with sophisticated half helms in camouflage coloring to match the rest of their gear and attire. It was the strangest set of accoutrements he'd ever seen. Their boots were even better than his, though, and he needed a pair of those fantastic gloves.

"How many?" she asked evenly.

"Nearly all of them. Three or four might be able to sail in a couple of weeks. We sank more than forty."

She eased out a breath, almost whistling. "That is excellent news, Rain." She turned her head slightly. "Can you tell them?"

Rain nodded, then looked at the Americans, giving them a thumbs up with a broad smile.

They glanced at each other and grinned.

"In words, Rain," said Antara with a roll of her eyes.

He had been about to do that. "Almost all ships destroyed. Well done."

The men nodded. It was hard to tell how relieved or happy they felt given the dark glasses covering eyes, eyebrows, and the tops of their cheeks. "Thank you," said one. "We will protect you and Lady Antara now. We have two sniper's nests in place, and a backup position."

She was 'Lady' Antara to them already? He almost rolled his own eyes. "How long before Ileom, um, demonstrates?" he asked them.

"About an hour. I don't think he can top the sinking of all those ships, though."

"He doesn't need to."

The soldiers shrugged, and Rain explained the brief conversation to Antara. Then they sat on some boulders, hidden beneath trees, and waited, the two Americans taking positions several yards away in opposite directions. Antara wanted Rain to describe everything he had seen that morning in great detail, which ate up most of the time, especially since she asked so many questions. She never once mentioned the key or displayed any doubt. He couldn't decide if that helped or hurt.

"Whatever happens today, Rain," she finally commented after extracting every bit of information he possessed, "the fight to preserve our freedom will go on. Emperor Creegan is a ruthless, ambitious tyrant. He has subjugated most of Akris, and he will exert great control over the world if he can conquer the major nations of Rega. Perhaps more than one world now. But many people will still valiantly oppose him, led by the Spirit of God, which is the spirit of liberty. I abhor tyranny, whether lauded with noble-sounding reasons or not. Master Ileom and I may disagree on methods and tactics sometimes, but I know he feels the same way, as do all the members of the Order." She held up a finger. "That doesn't mean we are immune from becoming corrupted. We must be careful. That includes you."

Rain nodded dumbly, not vocalizing how low a place on his list of present concerns such a warning occupied. He looked away, and a few seconds later heard a series of soft pops. Antara twisted her neck and rose. "It's starting. We have a good vantage point, just through these trees."

He followed her, barely hearing the Americans moving as well, though he couldn't see them. She stopped near the bole of a large tree, behind some waist-high bushes growing before a scree of boulders that tumbled down the side of a hill. Most of the enemy base was laid out before them, and Rain felt surprise and alarm at how close they actually were. Even without binoculars, he could discern many particulars. Still, he automatically reached for the device before realizing he had tied it to his saddle. As planned. They didn't want the Tahn Arganda getting their hands on it if he and Antara were captured.

The first thing that stood out was the dozen or so red plumes of smoke rising from the ground at even intervals around the base perimeter. Only a light breeze blew in from the shore, so the columns ascended relatively undisturbed for the first fifty feet. He spotted various groups of griffons swirling above the base; several descended to take a closer look but were careful not to get too near.

What followed took him back to a tremendous hailstorm he had experienced as a child. Thousands of tiny ice daggers plummeted from the sky in wave after wave, causing little real damage but great havoc. The griffons on or near the ground went wild, some clearly disobeying their riders as they sought to escape the onslaught, even though it wasn't a significant threat to them. A few of the icicles stuck in the ground on impact, creating a fascinating display of glittering spikes that melted fast. It had to be the work of Meris, and from very high in the air. How much energy had it taken?

More soft pops came, and Rain expected to see additional plumes of red. Instead, blossoms of thick gray smoke appeared in the area before the main base buildings, expanding rapidly while also somehow thickening. Men and beasts scrambled to escape it, heading away from the red-tinged perimeter and beyond the griffon stables.

A few seconds later, a massive boom sounded, and the ground shook. Rain had never felt an earthquake, though Tashiel had described the phenomenon from a book she'd read. It lasted only a few seconds, after which a rumbling sound arose, growing in intensity. Through the billowing smoke, Rain detected large chunks of earth rising into the air, hovering momentarily before hurtling in the direction of the barns. Loud crashes followed, but he couldn't see anything of the actual impacts.

An eerie pause was soon pierced by new shouts of alarm. Meris burst from the smoke, Ileom on her back, climbing swiftly as she executed a complex set of maneuvers to avoid attacks from the griffons. Few came, and those that did seemed confused and hesitant. Ileom had achieved the shock he desired, apparently. Combined with the sinking of the ships, the enemy soldiers might be thinking God himself vented his anger at them. If this Emperor Creegan allowed them to believe in God, that is.

Ileom and Meris disappeared like ghosts when they reached some lower clouds. Rain then pondered the next steps. Most of their force would make its way back to the camp, while the remainder prepared to provide a well-rehearsed path of retreat for Antara and Rain if that became necessary. Lagron would be nearby as well. He had insisted, though that made Rain uncomfortable. Since they hadn't destroyed a large number of the griffons, Lagron was vulnerable to a coordinated, swarming attack from the air until he could reach the relative safety of the camp with its American snipers and heavy-caliber German machine guns. That was another new word he had learned. Caliber. He'd seen the size of those bullets, too.

Of course, the part where he and Antara walked up to the enemy base, exposed under a parley flag, was still the most nerve-wracking. Would the Tahn Arganda commander honor the parley? His troops would be angry as hornets, their nest having just been beaten with a very large club.

"It's showtime for us," said Antara after a couple more minutes. The heavy smoke had begun to dissipate, and Rain caught glimpses of the damage Ileom had done to the griffon barracks. Both structures still stood, though the closer one definitely leaned. Multiple gaping cavities decorated their sides and roofs. A few griffons lay dead or wounded around them, with more probably slain inside, too. *Not nearly enough*, he thought. Why had he trusted Antara and then lied to Ileom?

His nervousness grew as Antara retrieved a long pole she had set against another tree a few feet away, the bright yellow flag of parley attached at the top. She handed it to Rain.

"Here we go. Hold it high and steady. I will lead. I'm ready with shields. Do not worry, but remember the danger word. Marble."

Her smile did little to assuage his fears, especially after reminding him of the word she would utter if they needed to escape using his glaring non-ability to travel at will. But he nodded, doing his best to hide his suffocating insecurity. She turned, seeming completely calm, and instead of picking her way down the hill through the field of strewn stone, she used her magic to create stairs of solidified air wide enough for both of them. When they reached the bottom, she smoothed her bodice and skirt in magnificent scarlet and gold, then strolled at a dignified pace toward the perimeter, marked by dwindling wisps of red smoke. When they arrived, she stopped, motioning Rain to stand next to her.

They waited, still as statues, observing the continued manic activity on the base as men hurried to and fro to occupy defensive positions, help the injured, and assess the damage. The Argandans spoke Common, though Rain could tell it was a different dialect containing several words and phrases he'd never heard. Half the unknowns were probably invectives. Finally, a group of about twenty emerged from the swirling chaos, walking toward them, armed with a combination of long spears, swords, bows, and crossbows. Two men—one on either wing—caught his eye. Hearkendoom, with their grotesquely decorated black armor, highlighted with splashes of crimson and silver. They carried massive two-handed swords on their backs, but that wasn't the weapon Rain most feared. His heart thumped in his ears, and sweat trickled down his back. Antara's shields were powerful, he reminded himself when his knees threatened to shake.

The assemblage stopped twenty feet from them, then parted. Rain felt Antara stiffen as a uniformed, middle-aged man with multiple decorations adorning his broad chest strode confidently through the middle.

"Lady Antara," he said in a welcoming baritone.

"Uncle," she responded, chin lifted, clearly trying to mask surprise. Her voice dropped to a whisper as she turned her head toward Rain.

"Marble."

E N D   O F   B O O K   O N E

ABOUT THE AUTHOR

In late 2020, M.D. House semi-retired from a successful career in Corporate Finance and Business Leadership that allowed him to experience all facets of designing, producing, marketing and selling products to customers across the world. He enjoyed that career, and still consults part-time, but being able to pursue his passion for creative writing has been a tremendous blessing.

During that first career, he published one science fiction novel, called Patriot Star. Since embarking on his new journey with much more time and focus for writing, he's published a sequel (Kindred Star), along with six religious historical fiction novels (which were a surprise) and his first fantasy novel, Crossroads of Awakening Memory, Book 1 of the epic fantasy series called the End Times Convergence.

His docket is filled with new projects, including the sequel to The Servant of Helaman, Book 3 in the Patriot Star series, more Barabbas spin-offs, and additional volumes in the End Times Convergence (plus some side projects, of course).

You can learn more about M.D. House, including interviews with people like Eric Metaxas, Tricia Goyer, Carmen LaBerge, Roger Marsh, Chautona Havig, Jaime Vaughn, and Dr. Paul Reeves, at mdhouselive.com.

Made in the USA
Columbia, SC
03 May 2024

34938480R00213